Sign up for our newsletter to hear
about new and upcoming releases.

www.ylva-publishing.com

Other Books by Rachael Sommers

Never Say Never

Fool for Love

Rachael Sommers

Acknowledgements

First and foremost, I'd like to thank Astrid at Ylva Publishing for giving me the chance to be a published author, and for your patience and help every step of the way. Thanks to C.S. Conrad for everything you did to help me develop and improve this manuscript from its earliest draft. I'm a better writer because of everything you taught me. Thanks to my editors, Alissa McGowan and Sheena Billett for making this story the best it can be. Gane and Yan—I appreciate everything you did for me as beta readers.

Finally, Laura: I know my deadline for this came at the worst possible time, but you did everything you could to support me anyway. I love you more than anything.

Chapter 1

A SEA OF BLACK AND WHITE loomed on the horizon, and Chloe eased her foot off the accelerator, wincing as she failed to skirt around one of the many potholes on the poorly surfaced country road.

In the passenger seat, Naomi jerked away from the window she'd been dozing against for the better part of the last hour. "Are we—"

"—there yet?" Chloe finished the question she'd been asked at least ten times already since they'd driven out of London's city limits. "Nearly. There's a hold up." She nodded toward the herd of animals ambling across the road in front of them and brought her van to a stop a few feet away.

Naomi's face brightened at the sight. "They're so cute!"

"They're bloody dangerous." Chloe had had more than one close encounter with a cow when she was younger.

"But look at those faces." Naomi leaned forward in her seat to get a better look, elbows resting on the dashboard.

The movement disturbed the Labrador sitting at her feet. Bella rested her head on the seat between the two of them, staring at Chloe with big brown eyes.

Chloe reached out to scratch behind her ears. "Not long now," she said. "How are you holding up, gorgeous?"

"Not so bad, thanks," Naomi said, and Chloe smacked her on the side of the arm. "Ow! Is that any way to treat the best friend doing you a massive favour?"

"Please, it didn't hurt."

"It did. Right in my feelings," Naomi said, solemn.

Chloe rolled her eyes.

"How long does it take a herd of cows to cross a road?"

Chloe chuckled. "Has the novelty worn off already?"

"We've been driving for hours, Chloe." Patience had never been one of Naomi's strong suits. "I need to pee."

"I told you to go when we stopped at the service station."

"I didn't need it then."

"Well, there's a bush over there"—Chloe pointed out the window—"if you're desperate." Chloe grinned as Naomi's nose wrinkled. "It's not like there's anyone around."

"Uh, yes, there is. There's someone right there."

She was right. A woman on horseback rode behind the stragglers of the herd. Her jeans were tucked into red wellies, caked in mud, and blonde hair curled around the collar of her black body warmer.

She passed in front of the van, and Chloe sucked in a breath. It had been years—eighteen, to be precise. Her face was older, and there were now laugh lines around the corners of her mouth and her eyes, but she was instantly recognisable.

Amy Edwards.

Chloe had never dreamed she'd lay eyes on her again.

Amy turned, raising a hand as if to thank them for waiting, and Chloe ducked in her seat so she was half-hidden by the wheel.

"Um, what the fuck are you doing?" Naomi looked at her like she'd grown a second head.

"Nothing."

"Nothing?" Naomi's eyebrows twitched. "It sure doesn't look like nothing."

"I had an itch." She scratched the outside of her knee, trying to peer through the windscreen to see if Amy had gone without revealing too much of herself. Thankfully, she had passed into the other field.

"Yeah, right." Naomi's eyes bored into the side of her head as Chloe straightened in her seat and tapped on the accelerator. "Do you know her or something?"

Chloe didn't answer at first. Her throat felt tight, emotion welling in her chest, and she gripped the steering wheel so hard her knuckles flashed white. What was Amy still doing here? She'd sworn once she was out of Corthwaite she'd never come back—but Chloe had, too, and yet, here she was, driving down the single road that wound through the village centre, swallowing against the sudden rush of memories that assaulted her.

"Chloe?"

"Yeah. That's Amy."

"Amy?" Out of the corner of her eye, Chloe watched Naomi's nose wrinkle. "Why do I know the name? Wait." A hand gripped Chloe's elbow, and Chloe kept her gaze trained on the road. "*The* Amy? The one you were still pining over when we first met? The one who broke your heart?"

That's putting it lightly, Chloe thought, clenching her teeth. As far as first loves went, traumatic didn't begin to cover it.

"Did you know she was still going to be around?"

"No." If Chloe had, she might have hesitated to come back—or would have mentally prepared herself for the possibility of seeing her again, at least.

"You okay?"

Chloe blew out a long breath. "Yeah." It didn't change anything, after all. If Chloe had it her way, she wouldn't be seeing much of Amy—or any of the rest of the village—at all. Get in and get out, as fast as physically possible. That was the plan, and Chloe was determined to stick to it.

The village looked the same. A handful of buildings dotted along the main road. The florist where her mum had worked sat beside the newsagents, the only place for four miles if you needed a pint of milk. The hairdresser opposite was new, replacing the butcher, and the King's Head still stood proud on the corner, sign swinging in the wind.

They passed the church, and Chloe turned off the main road and onto a dirt track up a steep hill. In the distance, fields of green dotted with sheep and cows stretched across the horizon, the mountains beyond a dusty brown. In a few months they'd be dotted with snow, the lake winding around the foot of them would ice over, and the view would look like a stock photo for a wintry snow globe.

"Wow." Naomi said, wide eyes taking in the sight. "This is gorgeous."

Despite her misgivings about returning home, Chloe had to agree. As much as she loved the London skyline, it had nothing on a view like this.

The track ended in a gravel driveway, and Chloe's childhood home rose to meet them. It had been nearly three years since it had been occupied, and it showed—the drive was overrun by weeds and the ivy winding up the front wall of the house grew wild, covering the arched windows in places. Through the broken wooden fence leading to the back garden, Chloe spotted grass so high it could probably swallow all five feet eight inches of her.

She dreaded to think what the inside looked like.

Chloe pulled the car to a stop, and Naomi let out a low whistle. "Jesus Christ, Chloe, I knew your family was loaded, but this? This place is massive. Did you…did you have servants?"

A laugh bubbled in Chloe's throat. "No. We had a housekeeper when I was younger. A groundskeeper at one point, too. He'd have a heart attack if he knew I'd let it get this bad."

"Well, it looks like you've got your work cut out for you here, Chlo. You sure you're up for this?"

"You know I like a challenge."

Dust puffed from the hall carpet as Chloe stepped over the threshold, tickling the back of her throat, and she scrunched her nose, fighting back a sneeze.

"Well, I know what our first order of business will be," Naomi said, following her inside and running a finger along the wooden banister of the stairs. She showed Chloe her grey finger. "Scrubbing this place from top to bottom."

"Yup. Aren't you glad you came with me?"

"Oh, delighted." Naomi's voice dripped with sarcasm, but she was smiling, and Chloe hip bumped her as she stepped past to push open the door of the living room. Bella followed along behind.

Small and cosy, it hadn't changed much since Chloe's last visit three years ago, when she'd come to bring her father to a retirement home closer to London. At the time, she'd had the foresight to cover the two leather couches—and much of the other furniture in the house—with large dustsheets, and she was glad for it now.

She reached for the light switch on the wall, breathing out a sigh of relief when the bulb overhead flickered to life. She'd called the electricity company three weeks ago requesting that they turn the supply to the house back on, and she was thankful she wouldn't have to call again to chase them up.

Backing out of the room, she followed the sound of clanging cupboard doors into the kitchen, where she found Naomi standing on her tiptoes.

"Don't take this the wrong way, Chlo, but I think your dad might have been a hoarder."

Chloe groaned at the sight of stacks upon stacks of kitchen utensils and crockery, far more than one man would have ever possibly needed to use. "It's going to take six months to clear everything out."

"Nah." Naomi gave her a comforting pat on the back. "You've got this."

Chloe wasn't so sure, but she hadn't been lying earlier—she *did* love a challenge.

And her first?

Make it so every inhale didn't make her want to cough up a lung.

She locked Bella in the kitchen with some toys to keep her occupied, knowing she'd cower away from the vacuum cleaner anyway. Naomi disappeared upstairs with bleach, a sponge, and some rubber gloves to tackle the bathrooms, and Chloe got to work on reducing the dust level.

Once the ground floor was habitable, she freed Bella and began on the stairs. She started with the picture frames on the wall, gently wiping away the thick layer of grime covering the glass and smiling at the scenes pictured beneath.

The first was her parents on their wedding day, staring at one another like they'd hung the moon and stars in the sky, bathed in the glow of the setting sun. Chloe had grown up wanting to find someone who looked at her like that, who could make her smile so wide it could split her cheeks, but at thirty-six she was still waiting for her perfect woman.

Next was a photograph of the day Chloe was born. She was obscured by blankets but her parents were looking at her like she was their whole world. Then, Chloe and her mother—nothing monumental, Chloe being pushed on a swing, but she knew it was one of the last photos her dad had taken before her mother had turned skinny and pale, succumbing to the disease festering inside her.

Naomi appeared at the top of the staircase as Chloe cleaned the last photo—Chloe at her graduation ceremony in her cap and gown, her dad's arm around her shoulders, a beaming smile on his face.

Chloe ran her fingertip along the face she hadn't seen in half a year, tears stinging at the back of her eyes.

"You okay?" Naomi asked, hand pressing against the small of her back.

"Yeah. Sometimes I forget he's gone, you know?"

"I know." Naomi pulled her into a one-armed hug. "Professional-looking photo, isn't it?"

Chloe cracked a smile—Naomi, the "photographer" in question, always knew exactly what to say to cheer her up. "It's all right."

"Rude."

A plate clattered out of Amy's hands and into the sink, splashing the front of her T-shirt with soapy water.

Gabi, on drying duty, turned to her with a frown. "You okay, Amy? You look like you've seen a ghost."

The ghost of my past, maybe. "I've lived here for well over half my life. I think if it was haunted, I'd know about it." She fished the plate out of the water and scrubbed it clean, trying not to focus on the lights in the distance—lights she hadn't seen on for a long time.

"I don't know," Gabi said, tilting her head to one side as Amy handed her the plate. "Ghosts could be sneaky. Pop up when you least expect them."

"I'm not so sure." With the last of the dishes done, Amy dried her hands on the towel Gabi offered her.

"So?" Gabi asked, turning toward Amy and resting her hip against the counter. "You gonna tell me what's the matter?"

Knowing that if she didn't, Gabi would weasel it out of her anyway, Amy sighed and jerked her head toward the house on the horizon, its bright windows stark against the dark sky of the countryside. "Looks like there's someone in the Roberts house. It took me by surprise, is all."

"Oh yeah." Gabi squinted to see through the kitchen window. "Well, didn't he pass away a few months ago?"

Amy nodded, remembering the sad announcement in the local newspaper. Chris Roberts had kept to himself, for the most part, after his daughter had fled the nest, but Amy had fond memories of the man.

"Maybe they're selling the house. Or maybe someone's moving in. Didn't he have a daughter?"

"Uh, yeah he did. But there's no way she'd move back here."

"Why?"

"She just wouldn't." Amy was sure. Why would Chloe want to come back to a town that had treated her so poorly? Amy knew she'd played her part in it and felt a twinge of guilt settling in her gut like it did when she glanced at the empty Roberts house, sometimes.

"You said that about this place once, too."

"Yeah, before my idiotic brother chopped off half his hand."

Danny strolled into the kitchen at that moment with a squirming three-year-old balanced on his hip. Flipping her off with his good hand behind his son's head, he said, "I think Sam wants his Tía Amy to bathe him tonight."

"Is that right?" Amy asked, peering into a pair of wide green eyes. When Sam nodded, she scooped him out of her brother's arms. "Come on, trouble."

She traipsed up the stairs, glad for her strenuous day job, because the kid was getting *heavy*.

The bathroom door opened, and Adam came barrelling out of it and collided with her knees. "Watch it, kiddo."

"Sorry, Tía Amy." He looked at her with a cheeky grin he knew she found hard to resist.

"You in a hurry to get to bed or something?"

"Abuela said if I was good, I could read comics before bed!"

"Did she now?" Amy smiled as her mum slipped through the bathroom door at a much more reasonable pace than her grandson. "And were you good?"

"I'm always good!"

"I'm not so sure about that." She ruffled his damp hair with her free hand.

"I was, wasn't I, Abuela?"

"You were," Leanne said, eyes fond as she gazed at him. Adam's grin showed off the gap where he'd lost his front tooth a few days ago.

"Go on." Amy stepped aside to let him pass, and he hurtled down the hallway to the bedroom he and Sam shared. Her old room, in fact, but she'd been more than happy to give it up for the privacy of the barn conversion she'd had done when she'd moved back to Corthwaite.

She and Danny had managed eighteen years sharing a roof—any more would be pushing it.

"I left the water in for you. It's still hot."

"Thanks, Mum." Amy stepped into the bathroom and set Sam on the white tiles. The bath was nearly overflowing with bubbles—which Amy suspected had little to do with her mum and everything to do with Adam—and Sam giggled when she scooped some out and put them on her nose.

"You need help with those buttons, kiddo?" she asked, when he struggled with the fastening of his jeans. She waited for him to step toward her before plucking it free, and only tugged his dinosaur shirt over his head when he stuck his hands in the air.

Amy's knees protested when she settled beside the bath to wash his hair. God, she was getting old. She thought of her mum's arthritis, worsening every year, and knew a similar fate awaited her. Such was the life of a farmer, she supposed, carefully tilting Sam's head back when she washed the shampoo out of his hair, knowing he hated getting water in his eyes and wanting to avoid a meltdown at all costs.

He hated the hairdryer, too, so she gently dried his mop of brown curls with a towel once he was out; Sam's gaze remained focused on the water swirling down the drain. His favourite *Paw Patrol* pyjamas sat on the counter, and once he was in them, she let him take her hand and pull her to his bedroom.

Adam sat engrossed in a comic book, and her mum was curled in the armchair situated between the two single beds.

"Do you want me to read your bedtime story, or Abuela?" Amy asked, after Sam had climbed into bed and settled beneath the covers. A tiny hand pointed toward her mum, so Amy leant over to kiss the top of his head. "All right, I'll see you tomorrow, chiquito." She turned to Adam, smiling when he tore himself away from the adventures of Superman to throw his arms around her neck. "Buenas noches, Adam. Don't stay up too late."

"Buenas noches." Despite Gabi teaching the both of them her first language, Adam had the accent perfect, while Amy…well. She couldn't seem to lose her Cumbrian accent no matter how hard she tried. Gabi assured her it was the thought that counted.

Downstairs, the kitchen was dark, but the TV was playing in the living room, where Danny and Gabi sat together on the couch.

"Night, guys."

"You can join us if you want," Gabi said, turning toward her.

"Nah, it's okay." They didn't get enough time alone together as it was—Amy wasn't about to intrude.

She slipped out the front door, and the unmistakable smell of cows and manure hit her nostrils. Above, the sky was unusually clear, the moon and stars illuminating the stone path to her home.

In the distance, the Roberts house caught her attention once more. Who was in there, and why? And did it have anything to do with the unfamiliar white van she'd seen earlier that day with the driver so desperate not to be seen?

Chloe didn't sleep particularly well her first night home.

She was used to a king-sized bed with a memory foam mattress, but her old bed had a lumpy mattress with broken springs that creaked every time she rolled over. And the silence was *deafening*. Chloe didn't have the luxury of affording a flat in London's bustling city centre, but even on the outskirts of Twickenham, nights were never quiet. Loud, drunken voices as people spilled out of bars and pubs usually lulled her to sleep, along with the screech of car tyres or the roaring of motorbike engines, but here?

Nothing but the occasional hoot of an owl.

She gave up on sleep at 5 a.m. and reached blindly for the pair of glasses she'd left on the bedside table last night, not wanting to chance putting her contact lenses in. She'd probably poke herself in the eye. Bella, stretched out across the floor at the foot of the bed, snored away, oblivious to her owner's restlessness.

Weak rays from the rising sun filtered through the thin curtains, glinting off the dusty spines lining the large bookcase leaning against one of the walls of her old room. Deciding reading was as good a way as any to pass the time, she reached for an old favourite and sat on the large wooden windowsill in her bedroom like she'd used to do when she was a kid.

"You'll strain your eyes, reading like that," her dad's voice echoed in her head, and she remembered the wry shake of his head when he'd catch her, out of bed and by the window, wrapped in a blanket, when she was supposed to be sleeping.

Of course, he'd been right. She'd been presented with her first pair of glasses at twelve years old, and her eyesight had been worsening every year since.

A door opened, and Chloe glanced at her watch. Half six, and Naomi was awake and moving? She mustn't have slept well either.

Sure enough, an inhuman grumble greeted her when she found Naomi in the kitchen, bleary-eyed, hair still held in the wrap she'd gone to sleep in, tapping her nails impatiently on the counter as she waited for Chloe's beloved Nespresso coffee machine to brew.

"Good morning to you, too," Chloe said, and Naomi glared.

"How do you sound so awake?"

"Because I have been awake for the last"—she glanced at her watch—"two hours."

"It's too fucking quiet here. Can't cope with it."

"I know. You don't have to stay, you know. You could go back to the city."

"And trust you here alone? I don't think so."

"I'd be fine. It's only a couple weeks." She wasn't ungrateful for Naomi's presence—far from it—but she knew spending two rare weeks away from the office was asking for a lot. "And I'll be alone here soon, anyway. On the weekends, at least."

"Yeah, but at least this way I can help you get a head start. I don't mind, Chlo, honestly."

"Can I have that in writing so in about twelve hours' time when you're grumpy and cursing me I have evidence you agreed to do this of your own volition?"

"It's too early for you and your long words." Naomi sighed happily when the coffee machine beeped. She filled two mugs and pushed one along the counter toward Chloe. "What's the plan for today?"

"First order of business is probably going to be to get more milk," Chloe said, rattling the half-empty carton she'd retrieved from the fridge. "Then I think we should get started with sorting through everything." She'd been hoping that job wouldn't take long, but based on what she'd seen so far, she wasn't optimistic. "Fill the skip I ordered."

"I think you should have ordered six."

"Probably." Chloe sighed, peering into a cupboard overflowing with junk. "I don't know where half this stuff came from."

"I'm going to have a shower before we do anything," Naomi decided, draining the last of her coffee. "We do have hot water, right?"

"I guess you're about to find out."

Chapter 2

AMY SWUNG OPEN THE DOOR to the village shop with her hip, her hands full with a crate of milk and eggs.

"What's this?" She heard a woman say from one of the tiny aisles. The Cockney accent had her doing a double take—tourists in Corthwaite weren't unheard of, but they were rare. It wasn't like the village had much to offer compared to the bigger towns nearby.

"What's what?" Another voice asked, and as Amy approached the counter, she caught a glimpse of one of the speakers, a pretty, black woman lifting a packet from one of the shelves.

"Kendal mint cake," she said, waving the packet in front of her. "It sounds interesting."

"It's basically pure sugar."

"Sold."

"Really, Naomi? The last thing I need is you on a sugar high. Or worse, a sugar crash." The second woman rounded the corner, and Amy nearly dropped the crate.

She'd dyed her hair dark, cut it short so it framed her face, and there was a scar through one eyebrow that hadn't been there last time they'd been face-to-face, but Amy would recognise that wide, crooked smile anywhere.

Chloe Roberts, in the flesh.

The years had been kind to her. She'd grown into limbs once awkward and gangly, her body now lean as she reached over and plucked the mint cake from Naomi's hands.

"I'm vetoing this."

"Need I remind you that neither of us got much sleep last night?" Naomi said, and Amy hastily turned away. She forced a smile as she hefted the crate onto the counter, trying to drown out the conversation happening behind her. "Sugar might be exactly what we need."

"Hey, Amy." Alex climbed to his feet—of the three people who worked in the shop, he was by the far the youngest, and always the happiest to see her. "How—?"

Something crashed to the ground behind her, and Amy turned to see Chloe on her knees, frantically trying to gather the bottles of water she'd knocked off the shelves.

"I'm sorry," she said, cheeks flaming red, arms full of so many bottles it was a wonder she didn't drop them all again.

"It's all right." Alex looked amused as he watched Chloe restock the shelf.

Naomi was staring at Amy, eyes narrowed, and Amy's stomach dropped. *I know what you've done*, her expression seemed to say. Judgement seeped into Amy's skin, and she knew she deserved it.

"I need to go," Chloe muttered, shoving the carton of milk she was holding—not one of her own, Amy noted—into Naomi's hands before charging for the exit.

Amy didn't blame her.

"How much for this?" Naomi asked, gaze flicking over to Alex. "Oh, and this." She paused to grab the packet of mint cake Chloe had taken off her.

"Three pounds thirty."

Naomi dug a hand into her pocket, and Amy used the moment of distraction to take her in. The Doc Martens on her feet looked barely worn, her long red coat seemed expensive, and as she approached Alex to hand over her cash, Amy felt inelegant beside her in her mud-spattered jeans and worn trainers. Naomi and Chloe had spoken with an easy familiarity, the sleepless night comment making Amy wonder if they were together, but she noted the lack of wedding ring on Naomi's left hand as she accepted her change.

"Thanks."

She left with one last contemptuous look thrown Amy's way, and Amy released a long breath once she'd gone.

13

"All right?" Alex asked, eyebrows raised, and Amy gave a jerky nod.

So, her suspicions had been right. Chloe *was* back. Was it for good? Or just for now? And was Amy going to keep bumping into her, sending her hiding behind her steering wheel or hurrying out of doors?

She hoped for both their sakes the answer was no, but something told her she didn't have that kind of luck.

"Christ, Chloe, will you slow down?" Naomi caught her as she breezed past the King's Head, hand catching her elbow. "You're not in London anymore."

"Sorry." She slowed, tugging gently on Bella's lead to bring her to heel. "I know you wanted to have a look around, but I had to get out of there."

"I know. But she's not following you."

Chloe refrained from looking over her shoulder to check. "Right. You still want a tour?"

"Nah, it's okay. I think I've got everything. Shop; vets; florist; pub." Naomi pointed to each of the buildings behind them in turn before pointing in front of them. "Church."

"Do you mind if we cut through here?" Chloe asked, glancing at the gate leading to the attached graveyard. "I want to check something."

"Sure." Naomi followed as Chloe traced a once-familiar path she hadn't walked in a long, long time. She paused before a headstone engraved with the words, *Annie Roberts. Beloved wife, mother and friend*, and was surprised to find a fresh bouquet of flowers. She'd expected it to be overgrown, and was touched to find it in near-perfect condition.

"Your mum?" Naomi asked quietly.

"Yeah. She was cremated, but my dad wanted to have somewhere we could visit to remember her. I was thinking about seeing if I could get one put in beside it for my dad."

"He'd like that."

Chloe stood there for a few minutes, thinking of the brief flashes of memories she had of her mother. She'd been too young to remember much, but her father had kept her alive with his stories, and Chloe could still recall the shape of her smile, the comfort of her arms when Chloe scraped her knee.

"Let's get back," she said, turning away from the headstone and linking her arm through Naomi's. The hill leading to the house was steeper than she remembered, and both of them were out of breath by the time they reached the top.

"Where do you want me?" Naomi asked, stepping inside and kicking off her shoes.

Chloe pursed her lips. "Kitchen? Unless you want to tackle under here." She pulled open the door to the cupboard under the stairs, revealing stacks upon stacks of boxes—all of which needed removing before the plumber came on Tuesday to see if Chloe could stick a downstairs toilet in there.

"And deprive you of discovering what treasures your father left for you? I could never."

Naomi disappeared into the kitchen, and the sound of rattling crockery filled Chloe's ears as she reached for her first box.

"Treasures my ass," she muttered when she found dozens of photo albums within.

In fact, the same could be said for the majority of the boxes—much to Naomi's delight when she appeared to ask Chloe a question sometime later.

"Oh my God, are you in these?" she asked, reaching for one of the albums and flicking through the pages before Chloe could stop her. "You are!" She flipped it around so Chloe could see herself grinning at the camera, missing three of her front teeth. "You were adorable."

She leafed through some more pages, smile widening with every one. Chloe was going to have to make sure she didn't pocket any of them to take back home to show their friends.

"What is this hair?"

"The height of fashion in the late eighties, clearly." She couldn't have been older than four or five in the picture. Her dad's poor attempt at pigtails were lopsided.

She reached for an album of her own, giving in to the distraction. In this one, she was older, around twelve or thirteen. She'd been cast as the lead in the school play, and there were at least twenty photos of the whole sorry production; she remembered her dad sitting in the front row, bursting with pride, smile catching in the stage lights whenever Chloe glanced into the audience.

"Looks like you could've had a career on the stage," Naomi said, holding a photo of her in another play, this time the Christmas nativity. "Were you Joseph?"

"Yup." She remembered her reception teacher, Miss Wolfe, doodling a moustache on her upper lip in eyeliner. "We had one boy in our class that year, and he refused to do it."

"And naturally, you stepped up. Hoping you'd get to kiss a girl?" Naomi asked, eyebrows wiggling.

Chloe snorted. "I think that would've scandalised the village."

"Who was your Mary?"

Chloe didn't have to glance at the photo. "Amy."

"Ah. You, uh, you guys were close, huh?"

Chloe knew Amy was in a lot of the photos. They'd been joined at the hip from the ages of four to seventeen, one never far from the other, and she was willing to bet at least one of these albums was filled with pictures Amy had taken with the camera Chloe's dad had bought her one Christmas.

"Inseparable," Chloe said, eyes on a picture of her and Amy on horseback in one of the nearby fields. There were more: her and Amy in the farmhouse kitchen, in the treehouse in their back garden, playing Monopoly on Chloe's dining room table. Amy's mum's arm around Chloe's shoulder, Amy's dad teaching her how to drive a tractor. "Her family looked after me. I lost my mum, and dad was away on business a lot, so I was always over there. Or she was over here."

"No wonder it's hard being back."

"Yeah." Chloe set the album back in the box—getting lost down memory lane wasn't going to empty out the cupboard, and she was running on a tight schedule. "But at least it's not for long."

Chloe hummed along to the radio as her putty knife scraped along the wall, removing the last stubborn scraps of paper clinging to it.

She'd never liked the decoration in the living room, the white wallpaper covered in a mishmash of brightly coloured garish flowers clashing with the sickly green paint on the ceiling. It was *supposed* to be an ode to her mother's floristry, but to Chloe, it had always felt too...busy.

Hopefully her dad would forgive her for pulling it down.

She knew all the decoration in the house had been done by the two of them when they'd moved in, knew her dad hadn't changed much after her mum died. Keeping the house the way it had been when they'd lived there together, happy, had been part of his coping mechanism after she was gone.

But unfortunately, the styles fashionable in the nineteen-seventies when they'd moved in wouldn't get her a good price for the place. Especially considering her parents' rather questionable taste in décor.

"Um, Chloe?" She turned to find Naomi, wallpaper steamer in hand, looking out the window with a frown. "There is a woman on a horse heading this way."

Chloe moved to stand beside her and watched a magnificent brown shire horse come to a stop beside her van in the drive. Pressing her face closer to the glass, she recognised the woman sitting astride the animal. "It's Amy's mum."

"Want me to go chase her off?" Naomi asked as Leanne dismounted. "Say you've gone out?"

"No, it's okay." She slipped from the room, skirting carefully around the plumber, whose legs were sticking out from the cupboard beneath the stairs, and going out the front door. She met Leanne halfway up the path—where she was immediately enveloped in a warm hug.

"Chloe, it's really you." Leanne sounded like she was fighting back tears, and she smelled like leather and horses and *childhood*. Chloe hugged her back tightly. "Let me look at you." She pulled back and cupped Chloe's cheeks in her hands. "You're too skinny," she said, sounding so much like Naomi's mum that Chloe huffed out a laugh. "But you look well. I'm so sorry about your father. He was a good man."

"Thank you."

"Oh, it's lovely to see you. Are you back for good?"

"Uh, no. I'm here to do some renovations, sell the place on. I'd invite you to come in and have a look, but…" She glanced at the horse resting his head on Leanne's shoulder.

"Yes, I suppose he wouldn't fit through the door. This is Thor."

"He's gorgeous." Chloe held out a hand, letting Thor sniff her before giving his head a gentle stroke.

"Do you still ride?"

"I haven't for years."

"Well, we still have horses. You're welcome to come over any time. It would be lovely to catch up, find out what you've been doing all these years. Or better yet!" Her eyes lit up, and Chloe swallowed. "Come over for dinner."

"Oh, I, uh…" She trailed off, desperately trying to think of a polite way to say *that is literally my idea of hell on earth, no thank you.*

"Your…friend? Girlfriend? Wife?" Leanne's gaze flitted over to the window, and Chloe turned to see the curtain falling back into place. "Is welcome to come, too."

"We wouldn't want to intrude…"

"Nonsense, we'd love to have you."

Who's we? Because it sure as shit isn't Amy or Danny, if he's still around.

"I—"

"We eat at six," Leanne said, seemingly deciding Chloe had accepted the offer. She turned back to Thor and put a foot in the stirrup. "Come over tonight. You don't have any dietary restrictions, do you?"

"I…no, but—"

"Excellent." She climbed onto Thor's back with more grace than a woman of her age should possess. "I'll see you both later." With a click of her tongue, they were off, striding back down the lane and leaving Chloe staring dumbly after them.

What the hell just happened?

"What was that all about?" Naomi asked, when Chloe returned to the living room, feeling as though she was in a waking nightmare. "Chloe? You all right?" Her hands settled on Chloe's shoulders and steered her toward the couch they'd shifted to the centre of the room; the dust sheet crinkled as she sat. "You don't look so good."

"She invited us over for dinner."

"You said no, right?"

"She wouldn't take no for an answer." Chloe dropped her head into her hands, and Naomi squeezed her shoulder.

"Hey, it's okay." She sat beside Chloe, wrapping an arm around her back. "We don't have to go. We can turn off the lights and hide the van in the garage and pretend we're not here. Or we can turn around and go back home."

"I can't do that." Chloe was many things, but a coward wasn't one of them. Eighteen years ago she'd run headlong away from her problems, and she wasn't about to do the same again. "No, we should go. How bad can it be?"

"I dunno. But whatever happens, you're not alone. I got you, okay?"

Chloe shifted to pull Naomi into a hug, throwing her arms around her neck. "I'm so glad you're here."

"Don't go soft on me, now," Naomi said, squeezing. "You know I don't know how to deal with crying women."

Chloe laughed. "I'll try my best," she promised, leaning back. "Okay, these walls aren't going to strip themselves." She nudged Naomi in the side. "Let's get back to it."

"Where was my invite?" Amy asked, when her mum strode into the stable block leading Thor behind her.

"You wouldn't have wanted to come if I told you where I was going."

"And where was that?"

"The Roberts house. I went to see Chloe."

Amy froze, brush hovering a few inches above Regina's back, watching her mum untack Thor with easy efficiency. "You went where?"

"I invited her over for dinner tonight," Leanne continued, and Amy's stomach dropped.

"You did *what*?"

"Have you gone deaf, dear?" She said it pleasantly enough, but her gaze was shrewd, calculating, and Amy took a calming breath. "I thought it would be nice. It's been so long since we were all together."

"Have you forgotten there's a reason for that?" Amy couldn't believe Chloe would accept such an invitation, but her mother could be persuasive when she wanted to be. Had probably strong-armed the poor woman into saying yes.

"Of course I haven't."

Amy had never told her the full story—had barely told her any of the story—but she'd always suspected her mum knew more than she let on, and had blamed her for the loss of the girl she'd considered one of her own. Amy's long stint away at university and travelling had gone a long way to repairing their relationship, but Chloe's re-appearance seemed to be opening more than one old wound.

"But perhaps it's time to make amends."

"Make amends?" Amy echoed. "After eighteen years?"

"Why not? In any case, she's coming, and I expect you to be there, too. It's a family dinner."

"And have you told Gabi and Danny?" She could imagine the sour look on Danny's face when he heard the news. He'd never been Chloe's biggest fan, and after the horrid things he'd said to her, Chloe wasn't his, either.

"Not yet, but I will, and they'll be there too. As will the woman Chloe's with."

"Great." The sarcasm earned her a glare, but Amy didn't care. Her mum let her be, taking Thor to the field and leaving Amy and Regina alone. Sensing her agitation, Regina stamped one of her feet, and Amy gave her a scratch. "Why are you always so grumpy?"

A snort was her answer.

Amy tacked her up, needing the endorphin rush of racing over the fields now more than ever. Riding had always been her escape, her safe space, and she breathed in a lungful of fresh air as she urged Regina toward one of the many dirt tracks winding through the farmland.

Above, the sky was dark grey, rainclouds threatening to drench them, but Amy didn't mind. Wind whipped through her hair as they progressed into a brisk trot, and Regina soon lengthened her stride, raring to go faster. Though her passport said *Irish Sports Horse*, she had the temperament of a thoroughbred, and Amy didn't mind it in the slightest.

But the rush of wind through her hair, cooling her cheeks and sending her eyes streaming, wasn't enough to ward off her churning thoughts. Thanks to the hill it sat upon, Chloe's damn house was visible no matter where she rode, looming on the horizon, and in Amy's mind.

Why had she had to come back? Not that it was fair to blame Chloe. Chloe wasn't to blame for any of it, but God, Amy was—and she owed her one hell of an apology, but didn't have the slightest idea where to start.

Sorry for not standing up for you? Sorry for distancing myself from you when the name calling started? Sorry for making out with you behind closed doors and pretending it never meant anything? Sorry for breaking your heart? For fucking it all up?

She'd known at the time what she was doing was wrong, but looking back on it now...it was reprehensible.

How Chloe could stand to be in the same room as her, Amy didn't know. She didn't think *she'd* be able to, were their positions reversed.

And yet in a few short hours, they were going to be.

Amy sighed, shortened her reins, and turned Regina in a wide circle, pointing her toward home. They were both out of breath, sweat beading on Amy's brow, and she knew there would be marks beneath Regina's saddlecloth, but she still had plenty of energy as she cantered back the way they'd come, ears pricked forward in an unusual show of happiness.

Maybe tonight wouldn't be so awful, Amy thought, slowing Regina to a walk as the farmhouse came into view. Maybe if she could manage to apologise, it would be an opportunity for them to finally put the past behind them and start anew.

But only if Chloe wanted that, too.

Amy wasn't going to force it.

She owed her that much, at least.

Chapter 3

AT HALF PAST FIVE, THE heavens opened, rain sluicing against the windows, and Chloe thought it was apt, considering her stomach had been churning since that morning, mood blackening by the hour.

On the plus side, she'd thrown herself into her work with reckless abandon, and all the downstairs walls were bereft of paper. It left the place looking bleak—not helped by the weather—but she could now assess the walls underneath for damage. As she'd suspected, more than one needed re-plastering, chunks of it missing in places and leaving the underlying brick exposed.

But that would have to be a job for another day. Time was charging onward, each passing minute bringing her closer to her doom.

"There's still time to back out," Naomi said, sticking her head into Chloe's room while she was getting ready. "If you want to."

A tempting offer, to be sure, but Chloe had pulled on her nicest pair of black skinny jeans, and had therefore committed to leaving the house. "No, it's okay. I've got this."

Naomi didn't look convinced but she didn't argue as she followed Chloe downstairs.

Bella stood at the door waiting for them, turning on her best puppy dog eyes when Chloe reached for her boots.

"We won't be long," she promised, kissing the top of Bella's head.

It took five minutes to walk between their houses, but Chloe elected to drive. Rain bounced on the roof of her van as she and Naomi climbed inside. The drive was almost as long, thanks to the lack of a direct road, but Chloe didn't mind.

She could use the time to build herself up.

"We should have a safe word," Naomi said as they walked the path to the farmhouse door. "If you're ever uncomfortable, say…cucumber, and I'll think of an excuse to leave."

"Cucumber?" Chloe asked, lips twitching despite the nausea swirling in her gut. "Seriously?"

"What's wrong with 'cucumber'?"

"How am I supposed to slip that into casual conversation?"

"You're a smart woman. You'll figure it out."

"I—"

The door opened, and Chloe's words died in the back of her throat as they were bathed in light from the hallway.

"I thought I heard voices," Leanne said, looking delighted to see them. "Come in, come in."

She ushered them over the threshold, and Chloe felt like she was stepping back in time. Few changes had occurred in the years since her last visit: the same wooden floors, the cream wallpaper in the hallway unchanged, the large dresser beside the door filled with mismatched trophies, picture frames scattered over the walls.

It still felt like coming home, and Chloe's throat was tight as she shrugged out of her jacket.

"We haven't been introduced," Leanne was saying to Naomi, oblivious to Chloe's inner turmoil. "I'm Leanne."

"Naomi." She offered a hand for Leanne to shake, widening her eyes at Chloe as she was pulled into a hug instead.

"So, you two are…?" Leanne trailed off once Naomi had been released, looking between her and Chloe with her eyebrows raised.

"Friends," Chloe said, and Leanne nodded to herself.

"Food is nearly ready." She retreated down the hall, toward the admittedly fantastic smell of cooking, and Chloe and Naomi followed behind.

"Remember," Naomi said, stepping close and keeping her voice low, hand reaching for Chloe's and squeezing. "'Cucumber' is all you have to say if you want me to put my spectacular acting skills to use."

"Here we are," Leanne said, ushering them inside the largest room in the farmhouse, which Chloe found busier than expected.

Three seats at the round table were occupied: one by Danny—same shaggy blond hair, nose still crooked from the fight he'd gotten into at fifteen with one of the boys at school, eyes as cold as Chloe remembered when they gave her a once-over—and the others by two young boys with the same dark hair. The older of the two was playing cards with Danny, nudging him impatiently to continue the game. The younger one was colouring on a sheet of paper, oversized headphones clamped over his ears.

A slender brunette stood at the counter, a kind smile on her face, but Chloe's gaze skittered away when her eyes landed on Amy, standing beside her, half-empty bottle of beer held in one hand.

Breathe, Chloe reminded herself sternly. *You just have to survive one dinner.*

"This is Gabi," Leanne said, taking it upon herself to do the introductions when no one else spoke up, indicating the brunette with a wave of her hand. "Danny's wife."

"Nice to meet you," Chloe said, fully aware the words sounded hollow— there was nothing nice about this. She felt Gabi's eyes appraising her, and wondered what, if anything, she'd been told.

"Snap!" the older boy cried, hand lying flat over the pile of cards on the table, his eyes bright.

"That's Adam," Leanne said, "and his brother Sam."

Sam didn't look away from his colouring, and Chloe didn't blame him. She wished she could bury her head in a book and not take part in this charade.

"And this is Chloe's friend, Naomi," Leanne finished. "Please, take a seat."

Chloe glanced at the table, weighing up the best place to sit. She settled on the chair beside Adam. Naomi sat next to her, the chairs crammed so close together their shoulders brushed.

"Can I get you anything to drink?" Gabi asked, her words lightly accented. "We have wine, beer, soda."

"Water for me, please," Chloe said. Mixing alcohol and stress with the dark, winding road home probably wasn't a good idea.

"I'll take a beer."

"I hope you're both okay with cottage pie," Leanne said, pulling a dish out of the oven. "Chloe, I know it used to be your favourite."

In truth, most of Amy's mum's cooking had been her favourite. Chloe had inherited her limited skills in the kitchen from her dad, who, while he'd tried his best, had never managed to live up to Leanne's home-cooked meals.

"Though there are some chicken nuggets available if not," Gabi said, pulling out a baking tray once Leanne had moved aside and tipping them onto a plastic *Paw Patrol* plate along with some vegetables. "Sam might spare you a few if you ask nicely."

"Cottage pie is more than okay with me," Naomi said. "It smells amazing."

"Thank you, dear."

"Shall we put the cards away, mijo?" Danny asked, the endearment only a little clunky in his accent, and Chloe tried not to do a double take when he reached for the pack. Two fingers and half of his thumb were missing on his right hand.

"Can you give this to Sam?" Gabi handed the *Paw Patrol* plate to Amy, already turning back to help Leanne dish out the food for the rest of them.

Amy leaned over Adam's shoulder to get his brother's attention, rapping her knuckles gently on the table. Sam glanced up, lifting one of the headphones away from his ears. "Dinner time, chiquito. You can finish your colouring later."

He dropped his crayon in favour of a fork, letting his headphones fall back into place as Amy pushed the plate in front of him.

"Here we are." Leanne and Gabi set full plates in front of everyone, the table filling up as they took their seats. "Enjoy."

It was as good as Chloe remembered—the meat perfectly cooked, flavour exploding on her tongue—and when she told Leanne as much, she beamed.

"So, Chloe, tell us what you've been doing all this time. What do you do?"

Chloe finished her mouthful of food before she answered, feeling a few curious pairs of eyes on her. "I run a property development company in London."

"Like your father?"

"Similar. He asked me if I wanted to take over his company when he retired, but...it was too big for me to want to take on by the time I was ready for it. More business and planning high-rises, less of the hands-on stuff." Getting her hands dirty was the best part of the job. "So he helped me start my own. We focus on smaller buildings. A lot of renovations, but we've been getting some bigger contracts lately."

"Wow. And do you two work together?"

"Yeah, but not at the same company."

"I have my own," Naomi said. "An architectural firm. And I'm the only architect Chloe knows, so naturally she comes crawling to me whenever she needs my expertise."

"Both business owners," Leanne said. "Impressive."

"I'd like it to be known that she copied me," Naomi said, taking a sip of her beer. "I branched out first."

"By like a month."

"Hey, it still counts."

Chloe relaxed into the familiar banter despite her surroundings. "As you keep reminding me."

"And how did you meet?"

"At university. Naomi was president of one of the clubs I joined my first week there. Took me under her wing."

"I couldn't not. She walked into our first meeting, this country girl lost in the big city, scared of her own shadow."

"I was not," Chloe muttered, but it was a lie. It had been a month after she'd left Corthwaite, her heartbreak fresh, and the sign for the LGBT club had caught her eye. She'd barely been able to say her own sexuality aloud when she'd joined, but Naomi had coaxed her out her shell, and Chloe had found comfort in her own skin, surrounded by others like her.

"You were. And you kept getting lost."

"London is a big place!"

"I can sympathise with you there, Chloe," Leanne said, watching her and Naomi with a fond smile. "When Stephen and I went to visit Amy there, we got lost all the time."

Chloe's eyes snapped to Amy. "You were in London?"

"I…yeah. I had an apprenticeship there at a photography studio."

"When?" Chloe had been so fixated on the two of them being in the same place again, but had it happened before? Could their paths have crossed without either of them realising it?

"Eleven, twelve years ago. I lived there for a couple of years before I came back here."

Two years. Two years they'd been in the same city, and Chloe had had no idea.

"Did you not like it?" Naomi asked, and Chloe wondered if she could sense her distress. "Is that why you moved back?"

"No, I loved it. But after Dad passed away…" Amy trailed off, the pain of it evident in her eyes.

"I was sorry to hear about that," Chloe said. Stephen had always been kind to her when she was a kid, and when her dad had told her he'd died, Chloe had mourned the loss of a good man, taken too soon.

"We still miss him." Leanne twirled the wedding ring hanging on a chain around her neck. "But I'm sure you know that better than most."

Chloe's throat tightened at the reminder her own loss. "Yeah, I do."

"I went back to London after the funeral," Amy continued, inspecting the label on her beer bottle. "But then Danny got into an accident, and I was needed here more than I was there."

Chloe had been wondering what would draw Amy back to this place, to the job she'd sworn she never wanted, and now she had her answer, rooted in tragedy and misfortune.

"And now she thinks she owns this place," Danny said.

Amy gave him the finger.

"Mami, Amy hizo algo malo!" Adam said.

"Traitor," Amy said, but she was smiling, and Adam stuck his tongue out at her.

"English when we have guests Adam, remember?" Gabi touched his shoulder gently. "Sorry," she said, turning toward Chloe and Naomi. "It's hard to keep them connected to their Mexican roots all the way out here, so we try and use the language as much as possible."

"Oh, please, don't stop on our account." Naomi leant back in her chair, plate clean. "I speak some Spanish. And after being subjected to my family on the regular, Chloe's good at getting the gist even if she has no idea what's being said."

"True. Although I know some Patois now."

"You've had enough years to learn." Naomi turned back to Gabi. "Where in Mexico are you from?"

"Guadalajara."

"We spent a week in Cancun when I took Chloe to see some of my family back in Jamaica one year, but I always wish we could've stayed longer, explored some more. We did get to see Chichén-Itzá, though. It was beautiful."

"You're not the only one to think so," Gabi said, glancing at Amy. "Amy and I met when she was backpacking through Mexico, in search of the perfect photograph."

"I was wondering why you traded Guadalajara for here." Chloe tried not to obsess over each piece of information about Amy, tried not to put them together, solve the puzzle of what she'd been doing with her life for the last eighteen years.

"All Amy's fault. We travelled together, for a while, across South America. At the end, she asked if I wanted to visit England, see where she grew up. I got here, and I met this one"—Gabi reached for one of Danny's hands—"and I fell in love."

Chloe bit her tongue to refrain from asking *how*. Maybe Danny's personality had improved since she'd left town. It certainly couldn't have gotten much worse.

"Do you work on the farm, too?" she asked instead.

Gabi shook her head. "No, I teach over at the high school. Spanish, with some History and Geography thrown in when they need it. I love it. The variety's nice, and because the classes are so small you really get to know all the kids."

And the kids really get to know each other, Chloe thought. *Which isn't always a good thing.*

She was relieved when the plates were cleared and Danny began shooing both his sons upstairs for baths. Chloe sensed an opportunity to make her escape. She was halfway out of her seat, mouth opening to bid everyone goodbye, when Amy paused by the side of her chair.

"Can we talk?" she asked, tugging at her sleeves again, teeth worrying at her bottom lip.

And say what? Chloe wondered. Hadn't they already dredged up enough of the past tonight?

But curiosity raged within her, an itching desire to see what Amy had to say for herself, after all these years.

"Okay."

Chloe followed Amy onto the deck outside, away from prying eyes, her stomach twisting as the door clicked shut behind them. The rain had eased, though the scent of it hung thick in the air, and the wood of the deck was slick beneath the soles of Chloe's shoes.

One of the few things she'd missed about living in the depths of the countryside was the night sky and how clear it was without the pollution of thousands of lights. But now, with the moon and the stars obscured by clouds, the darkness felt oppressive.

Amy's face was cast in shadow, and she wrung her hands, her mouth opening and closing like she was struggling to find the words she wanted to say.

Chloe wasn't going to help her.

She wasn't even sure any words would come out if she tried.

Allowing herself to look in a way she hadn't dared in the kitchen, Chloe catalogued all the differences in the woman standing in front of her. The woman who had once meant everything to her, but was now a stranger.

Her hair was shorter than Chloe remembered, lightened by years of working outside, and her skin was tanned by the rays of the spring sun. Her arms held more muscle, her hands were calloused and no longer perfectly manicured, and there was dirt under her nails.

The eyes were the same, brilliantly blue, even in the dark. Eyes that had always been bright and sparkling, until they'd turned hard and cruel. Now, they shimmered with so many words left unsaid.

"I'm sorry about your dad," Amy said eventually. "He was a good guy."

"Yeah. He was." Somehow, Chloe doubted that was what Amy had brought her out here to say. She waited, trying to ignore the adrenaline flowing through her veins, screaming for her to run.

"And I'm so sorry about everything else, Chloe." Amy's eyes burned into her own. "If I could go back and change it…"

There were a lot of things Chloe would change if she could go back, too. Like not fall in love with her best friend.

"If I could go back and change it, I'd do everything differently. But I can't, so an apology is the best I can do. I know it's long overdue. Eighteen years overdue. I know I hurt you. I was downright cruel to you, did so many unforgivable things. And you don't have to accept it. God knows I probably wouldn't, if I were in your shoes, but I…I wanted—needed—you to know. What I put you through wasn't fair."

Chloe's throat tightened under the weight of Amy's gaze, the only sound the hoot of a nearby owl. Eighteen years, she'd waited for this. Eighteen years, and it felt like an anti-climax.

"You're right," Chloe said, her voice hoarse. "It wasn't fair."

Amy winced, but what did she expect? For Chloe to smile and say "Okay, no problem." like it erased everything between them?

"I'm sorry. I know that doesn't come close to making up for it. And it's not an excuse, but back then I…I was so confused. I didn't understand what I was feeling. I didn't think it was normal. You thought I was just messing you around, using you for practice, but it…it wasn't one-sided. I had feelings for you, too, but I didn't know how to deal with them, so I pushed you away."

Chloe blinked, letting the words sink in. All this time, she'd never once thought her feelings were reciprocated. How could Amy have discarded her so easily, if Chloe had meant so much to her?

Eighteen years, and she was finally getting the truth. Proof she hadn't been crazy, when she'd sworn she'd seen something in Amy's eyes. But it didn't feel like vindication.

It felt like regret. Felt like: what were you *thinking*? Felt like: we could have had it all, you and I, if you'd *talked* to me.

"Why are you telling me this?" Chloe asked, because what was Amy hoping to get from this? Why was she dredging up old wounds? Chloe hadn't asked for closure; she'd put this behind her years ago, and if Amy had just let her go on her way—ignored her the way she had in the months before Chloe had left Corthwaite behind—they'd both be better for it.

"Because you deserve to know." Amy ran a hand through her hair, her fingers trembling. "I just wish I'd been brave enough to tell you earlier."

So do I. "So you're…" Chloe trailed off, needing Amy to say it.

"Gay? Yeah." Amy tucked her hands into the back pocket of her jeans and rocked back on her heels. "And like I said—insecurity and fear was no excuse for hurting you the way I did, but…hopefully it explains some of the things I did."

"I don't know if I can forgive you," Chloe said, teeth worrying at her bottom lip. "I know it's been a long time, and we're both different people now, but…"

"One conversation doesn't magically make all the pain and the hurt go away," Amy said, her smile sad. "I get it. I...I'd like the chance to try and make it up to you. I know I don't deserve your forgiveness or your time, and certainly not your friendship, but it's been nice, having you here tonight. Learning about your life. So if you ever get lonely while you're here, I know my mum would like to see you. And...I'd like that, too."

"I...I don't know." Years ago, Chloe would have jumped at the offer. But older and wiser—not the same girl she'd been when she'd left Corthwaite— she hesitated. Tonight had been too much, in every way, and her head was a scrambled mess.

"I think I need some time to think about things." Time, and distance, to see if she could set her head straight. To decide if she wanted to bother repairing bridges that had long ago been burned, especially since she was only going to be in the village for a few months.

"Okay." Amy ducked her head, and for a moment, Chloe was reminded of the girl she used to know. "I—"

Amy was cut off by the back door banging open, and Chloe tried not to flinch when she saw Danny looming in the doorway.

Had he come to check up on them? *Just like old times.*

"Are you going to stand out here all night?" he asked, voice gruff, eyes on Amy's face and ignoring Chloe entirely. "Or are you going to do your job? It's your turn to do the night milking."

"I'm aware of what day it is, thank you," Amy said, teeth gritted, and she glanced at her watch. "It's not time yet."

"Near enough." He let the door slam behind him, and Amy rolled her eyes.

Chloe blinked at where Danny had disappeared, feeling like she could breathe a little easier now he'd gone. "I see he's still a ray of sunshine."

"Oh, he's delightful. I should probably..." She jerked a thumb over her shoulder in the direction of the milking shed.

"Right, of course."

"It was nice to see you again," Amy said, and Chloe paused with her hand wrapped around the door handle. "I'm glad you came."

Chloe couldn't quite return the sentiment.

She slipped back inside to where Naomi was waiting, eager to say her goodbyes and get back to the safety of their own house.

Chapter 4

AMY CLOSED THE OVEN DOOR carefully, not wanting to disturb the rise of the red velvet cupcakes she and Gabi had spent the last forty-five minutes making.

Baking nights were a highlight of her week: she and Gabi carved out some precious time together away from the rest of the family to watch trashy reality TV while Gabi filled her in on the latest school news.

Amy wondered if her own teachers had been like this—some of the conversations Gabi relayed were *not* things she could imagine sweet old Mrs. Peterson or Mr. Murphy discussing over a coffee break.

"I'm telling you, Amy, they're sleeping together." Gabi licked the spoon clean, and Amy regarded her sceptically as she set a timer for the cakes.

"I find it hard to believe the headteacher is sleeping with the receptionist."

"You haven't seen the way they look at each other."

"Isn't he old enough to be her grandfather? He was the head when I went there."

"Father, but some people are into that. Aren't you into older women?"

"Okay, you have a point there. But still. You're worse than the kids."

"I am not. And anyway—don't pretend you don't like being kept up to date with all the goings on."

Amy hummed under her breath, turning to start the dishes. She didn't mind harmless gossip between friends, but the nosy, insidious nature of townspeople in everyone else's business was where she drew the line.

"So, tell me what's going on in your life," Gabi said, wiping traces of flour and cake batter from the counter.

"Gabi, you see me every day. You know what's going on in my life: nothing."

"Untrue." Gabi leant against the sink, arms folded across her chest, gaze heavy on the side of Amy's face, and Amy knew what she was going to say before she opened her mouth. "What's the deal with you and this Chloe girl?"

Amy managed to keep her face neutral, frowning at the glass bowl she was scrubbing clean. After the excruciatingly awkward dinner, she was surprised it had taken Gabi so long to ask.

"What do you mean?"

"Your mum is acting like she's her long-lost daughter, and yet you and Danny barely said a word to her when she came over last night. It's weird. And Danny won't tell me anything about it. Spill."

"It's complicated."

"Well, we've got ten minutes until the cakes come out and another hour to wait for them to cool, so come on." Gabi crossed over to Amy's couch and patted the cushion beside her. "Tell me everything. Start at the beginning."

"I think it's easier to start at the end." Amy joined her on the couch and pulled a pillow into her lap, fingers playing with the fringe lining the edges. "I've told you before it took me a while to get to grips with my sexuality."

"And that my sometimes pig-headed husband didn't help."

"Yeah. Well, when I was younger Chloe was my best friend. We met on our first day of primary school and were inseparable from then on. People used to joke you couldn't have one of us without the other. And as we got older, I...I started to have feelings for her, but at the time I didn't understand them. Didn't want them. Didn't know what to do with them."

"Did she hurt you?" Gabi's eyebrows creased into a frown, a glint of fire in her eyes, and Amy shook her head.

"God, no. She never did anything to me. I, on the other hand..." She trailed off with a sigh, knowing she didn't come off well in this story. There was a reason she'd never told Gabi before. "Anyway, it turned out she had feelings for me, too. We kissed, once, at a party. Once turned into twice, twice turned into a dozen more over the summer, but we didn't tell anyone about it. And we didn't ever talk about it."

Sometimes, Amy wondered what might have happened if they had. If they'd managed to be honest, would things have still turned out the way they did?

"When we went back for our final year at school, the rumours started. I don't know where they came from. But people started whispering about us. I don't know how they knew." She still didn't, all these years later. "We were called names, we lost friends, and it was…it was horrible. I was already struggling, and now people were calling me disgusting and wrong, and I…I panicked. The only way I could see out of it was to stop seeing her, so I distanced myself. Put up a wall. Told her all those kisses were just for practice, and I got a boyfriend. And I could see it was killing her—and it killed me too—but I was too much of a coward to do anything to fix it."

"Jesus, Amy."

Amy didn't look at her, instead focused on her hands, plaiting the fringe. She didn't want to see Gabi looking at her with disdain.

"She tried to reach out to me a few times, but I shut her down, and eventually she gave up. She swapped Corthwaite for London, and I never saw or heard from her again."

"Until the other night. That's why you looked so weird when you first saw lights in the house. You had seen a ghost."

The timer beeped, and Amy got up to pull the muffin tray out of the oven. The cupcakes were perfectly risen—if she did say so herself.

"What are you going to do now she's back in town?" Gabi asked once Amy was back on the couch.

"I apologised to her the other night, after dinner. And I said I'd like to get to know her again, if she wanted." Which might have been asking for too much. "She said she'd think about it."

"Good."

Hoping the conversation was finished, Amy reached for the TV remote, the episode of *Married at First Sight* they were on already queued to play.

"Did you love her?" Gabi asked, casual as anything, and Amy nearly dropped the remote.

"I…yeah. I did." It had taken her a long time to admit it. By then, Chloe was long gone, and it was much too late for her to do anything about it.

"And she never knew?"

34

"No. And she's never going to, either." What would be the point in telling her now? In opening old wounds and leaving them to fester? "Can we stop talking about this now? We have four episodes to watch."

"All right," Gabi said, but the look in her eyes made Amy think this wouldn't be the last time they had this conversation. "Let's see who's arguing this week, shall we?"

Chloe eased the edge of her trowel over the wall, smoothing the plaster beneath into a flat layer.

She knew a lot of people hated plastering—Naomi included—but Chloe didn't mind it. The movements were second nature to her by now, the process streamlined by years and years of practice. She liked how methodical it was, making something old and cracked become new, the repetitive actions soothing, leaving her mind free to wander.

And wander it did, flashing back to the other night. The bombshell of Amy's sexuality and the apology she'd never dreamed of getting. It didn't make it any easier to be back here, and she didn't know if they could be friends again, but at least she no longer dreaded running into Amy in the village shop.

With one final sweep of the trowel, Chloe stepped back to admire her handiwork, looking for any imperfections. Finding none, she dropped the trowel into a bucket of water and swiped her sleeve across her brow, wiping away beads of sweat. It was an uncharacteristically warm spring day, the sun beaming through the living room windows turning it into more of a greenhouse.

She hoped it kept up—the plaster would dry quicker.

Upstairs was next on her list of things to tackle, including the rooms she'd thus far been avoiding. The door to her father's bedroom and study had remained staunchly closed since she'd come back, but it was time to take the plunge.

Bella, stretched out in a patch of sunlight, didn't so much as lift her head when Chloe stepped over her. She took the radio upstairs with her, indie rock propelling her into her father's study.

Dust sheets were draped over the furniture, and Chloe pulled them up. Beneath were the large mahogany desk he'd spent so much time behind, the leather sofa by the window where Chloe used to do her homework, and the large bookcases around the edge of the room, filled to the brim.

The desk chair creaked when she sat in it and pulled open one of the desk drawers at random. It was filled with dozens of notebooks, her dad's messy scrawl within the pages, notes from meetings with clients and a few hasty sketches of building designs.

In the bottom drawer she found an unmarked shoebox. Setting it carefully on her knee, Chloe lifted the lid; her breath caught when she was confronted with some of her mother's belongings.

A bottle of perfume, almost empty, the label long-faded, but it still had a scent. Chloe closed her eyes and pressed the lid to her nose, hoping it would spark a memory of the woman who had worn it. A scarf was nestled beneath it, thin and silken, and Chloe recognised the floral pattern from countless photos her dad had shown her over the years.

Her fingers brushed a velvet box—the wedding and engagement rings Chloe knew her dad had planned to give to her, but she'd never come close to a proposal. She found a note, too, its edges crinkled and worn, the letters barely visible, and Chloe wondered how many times he'd pulled out this piece of paper and traced his fingers over the words like she was doing now.

Tears sprang to her eyes, and she carefully put the note away, not wanting to ruin it.

She was leafing through another photo album tucked in one of the drawers when she heard the front door open and Naomi's voice call from below.

"Chloe?"

"I'm here," Chloe called, wiping furiously at her eyes as Naomi's footsteps sounded on the stairs.

"You should have seen the manager's face when I pulled up with all those boxes, Chlo. I think we made his—" She appeared in the doorway, frowning when she got a look at Chloe's face. "Hey, what's wrong?"

"I'm okay." She managed a watery smile, and Naomi was by her side in an instant. "I just… I miss them, you know?" She showed Naomi the photo in her lap, her parents standing in front of the Eiffel Tower and looking besotted.

"I know. They look happy."

"So happy he never moved on. I can't ever imagine feeling that way about someone."

"Me either." Naomi watched her trace a finger across her mother's face. "You gonna be okay sorting through the rest of this stuff? If it's going to be too painful, I can help. Do it for you."

"No, I think I need to do it," Chloe said, setting the album down. "Need to see what's in here, you know? Some help would be nice, though. There's a lot."

"Let me know what you want me to do."

How she'd gotten so lucky in the best friend department, Chloe would never know. She'd have to buy Naomi a nice bottle of Merlot when this was all over.

She more than deserved it.

Amy watched in horror as a football thudded off the side of Adam's boot—and straight into the head of one of his teammates, knocking the poor girl off her feet.

Shit.

Amy was by Jenna's side quicker than her mother, Adam racing toward them with his hand covering his mouth.

"I'm sorry! I didn't mean to!" He looked stricken as he skidded to a stop beside Amy and peered at his fallen friend.

"Take it easy," Amy said, halting Jenna's progress as she tried to clamber back to her feet. "You okay? You seeing stars?"

"No, it's daytime."

Amy chuckled, gently turning Jenna's head to one side and inspecting her cheek where the ball had struck. Luckily, kiddie footballs were light, and she doubted there would be a bruise there in the morning.

"Are you okay, baby?" Jenna's mum fretted on Amy's other side.

Jenna nodded. "Can I go now?"

Amy let go, and she scampered off to join the rest of her friends, happy as anything. Amy wished all kids were as easy going when they took a tumble. Usually there was more screaming.

"She's okay, Adam," Amy said, ruffling his hair. "Accidents happen."

Especially when you coached a bunch of six-year-olds how to play football. Not a role Amy had ever imagined herself filling, but now that she did, she couldn't imagine *not* doing it. She loved seeing them all chasing after the ball, and hearing their cheers when they did something to make her proud.

Glancing at the time, Amy decided to call it a day. A blow of the whistle around her neck called all ten of them to attention. "I think that's enough for today, team. Who can collect the most cones?"

One thing she'd learned early on—turning things into a competition usually got them done faster.

Jenna, the winner, trotted off with her mother once she'd handed the cones to Amy, knock on the head long forgotten.

"Come on, Adam." Amy gathered the rest of their training supplies and began the long trudge back to the car park. "You ready for a drink?"

"Yeah!"

Amy loved their Sunday mornings together, a precious few hours away from the farm, making their own traditions. Adam spent the five-minute drive to the King's Head chattering away about the training session, practically vibrating with excitement over having scored all five of his penalty kicks.

The pub was quiet, the sound of the news on the TV drowning out any chatter from the handful of patrons inside. Amy did a double take when she saw Chloe and Naomi huddled together over a tablet screen, a black Labrador lying at Chloe's feet. Chloe was laughing at something Naomi said, free and uninhibited in a way Amy hadn't seen in years, and she swallowed a stab of unexpected jealousy.

They hadn't noticed her, so she forged on toward the bar.

Mark smiled as she laid her arms on the counter. "Let me guess," he said, setting down the glass he'd been polishing. "A pint of Diet Coke and a strawberry milkshake?"

"It's like you're saying we come here too often."

"You do," he said, grinning as he began filling the blender for Adam's milkshake. Amy noted with amusement that he'd already had all the ingredients on the side, ready to go. When the blender finished, he added, "But I'm not complaining. You watch the match last night?"

"Unfortunately."

"We were terrible," Adam said, and Amy ruffled his hair.

"There's always next season, eh?" Mark said, setting their drinks in front of them with a flourish. "Gotta win something one of these days."

"I wouldn't hold your breath."

Adam tugged at the sleeve of her hoodie. "Tía Amy, isn't that your friend?"

She turned her head and found him looking at Chloe. She was alone, and Amy spotted Naomi through the pub window, pacing outside with her phone pressed to her ear. "Yeah."

"Can I go pet her dog?"

"I don't know, Adam…" If Chloe wanted space, Amy was going to give it to her.

"Please?"

"You can ask," she decided, and he nearly fell off the barstool in his haste. "Politely!"

She watched him approach, watched Chloe smile as he bent to stroke the Lab's ears. When a tongue licked his cheek, his giggles carried across the room.

"I didn't realise she was back," Mark said, following the path of Amy's gaze. "Told me she works in construction now, like her dad. He'd be proud of her."

"Yeah, he would."

Chloe glanced up, and her eyes found Amy's. She nodded toward the empty seat across from her, and Amy took the invitation, grabbing her drink and leaving a fiver on the bar as she bade Mark goodbye.

"Adam was telling me all about football practice," Chloe said when Amy sat. "You're a coach?"

"I am." If Chloe was surprised, it didn't show on her face. "Two years and counting. They're old enough for proper matches now. Got our first one in a few weeks." Amy smiled down at Adam, who knelt on the floor with the dog's head in his lap.

"We're gonna win," he said, always full of confidence.

"Where do you play, Adam?"

"Striker."

"Oh yeah? You know, that's where your auntie used to play when we were in school."

"Was she good?"

"She was all right," Chloe said, and Amy's jaw dropped.

"I was better than you!"

"A matter of opinion." Chloe's lips were curved into a teasing smile, and Amy could barely believe her luck. Could it be this easy? Could they repair all the damage between them? "So, if Adam's following in your footsteps does that mean you've turned him into a Tottenham supporter, too?"

"Of course."

"Disgusting."

Amy snorted, enjoying herself, enjoying the two of them existing in the same space again. Through the window, she caught Naomi watching them with quiet contemplation, and wondered what she thought of all this.

From the look in her eye, Amy suspected Chloe wasn't the only person she'd have to win over.

"How's the house going?" she asked, turning back to Chloe, away from Naomi's piercing stare. "I never asked the other day."

"Good. I've done all the re-plastering, and I've had all the pipework done to put in a new toilet downstairs. That was what we were looking at." She unlocked the tablet sitting on the table. "You don't happen to know anywhere local, do you? I prefer giving money to smaller business, but I don't know where's good around here."

"I do know somewhere fitting that description. May I?"

Chloe handed her the tablet.

Amy opened up the map app and zoomed in on one of the nearby villages. "Here. It's family-run, and I've worked with them before. They're also one of my regular deliveries, so I can probably get you a good deal. If you're interested, I could take you there one day to have a look?"

Chloe hesitated, and Amy cursed herself for being so eager to offer a helping hand. Chloe had said she needed time, and here Amy was, pushing at her boundaries.

She was searching for a way to take it back when Chloe opened her mouth.

"That...would be really kind."

"I drive out there every other day, so let me know when you'd like to tag along."

"We're heading back to the city tonight," Chloe said, and Amy tried not to be disappointed—she hadn't realised Chloe's stint in Corthwaite would be so short. "But maybe next weekend?"

"You're driving between here and London every weekend?" Amy asked, eyebrows raising. "Isn't it, like, a five-hour journey?"

"Yep." Chloe grimaced, and Amy didn't blame her. "Up on Fridays, back on Sundays. It's not ideal, but I can't take too much time off. And it shouldn't be for too long. Few months at most."

Amy's stomach dropped. She had known Chloe's time in the village was limited, but hearing her say it hit different. "Still. I dread to see your petrol bill."

"It's not going to be pretty," Chloe agreed. "I should probably get back to the house. There's a few more things I want to do before we leave. But I'll see you next weekend?"

"Sure."

"Come on, Bella." The Lab rose to her feet and stretched, and Adam gave her one last stroke. "Let's go find Naomi. It was nice to see you again."

"Yeah, you too."

Amy watched her go. Outside, Chloe slotted her arm through Naomi's and tugged her back toward the house with Bella leading the way.

Amy was already looking forward to next weekend.

Chapter 5

A DOUBLE SHOT OF ESPRESSO FROM Chloe's favourite coffee shop wasn't enough to stop her yawning as she and Bella walked up the stairs to her office on Monday morning. She'd given herself a late start and was strolling in at noon rather than her usual 8 a.m., but she was still bone tired.

She didn't want to think about how she was going to feel in a few weeks' time.

Maria smiled at her from behind the reception desk, and Chloe unclipped Bella's lead, freeing her to say hello to Maria's spaniel, Dash.

"Hey, boss. Jin will be glad to see you."

"Has he been fretting?"

"Nah, he's not been too bad. We have had to confiscate his phone a few times, though. I think if he'd had it his way, he would have been calling you non-stop."

Chloe chuckled and glanced at her second-in-command across the office. He had yet to notice her, frowning at his computer screen, glasses falling down his nose as he bobbed his head along to the music playing through his headphones.

"Well, the place is still standing, so I'd say he's done a good job."

"He's a worthy replacement, but it's good to have you back."

"It's good to be back." Back to normality, where no ghosts of her past were lying in wait.

Here she knew exactly what to expect, which was the way she liked it, although her mind couldn't help but wander over the events of the past two weeks. Had she made a mistake, agreeing to spend more time with Amy?

She'd wanted time, needed space, but it had been so easy to be friendly with her in the King's Head.

That didn't mean Chloe was ready to forgive, though. One conversation didn't erase it all. Only time would tell if their former friendship could be salvaged.

Chloe still wasn't sure if she wanted it to be.

She shook her head and crossed over to her desk, waving at Devon, who was on the phone. The office was otherwise empty, her contractors all out on jobs. Jin was still oblivious to her presence, and Chloe decided to wait and see how long it took him to notice her.

Long enough for her to boot up her computer and get halfway through replying to her long list of unread e-mails.

"You're back!" he said at last, eyes wide, halfway out of his chair, mug clutched close to his chest.

"Been back for about half an hour. Didn't want to disturb you while you were in the zone."

"Sorry, I was going over the presentation for tomorrow. Can I run through it with you later? Bring you up to speed?"

"Sure, but I want you to deliver it."

"Really?"

"Yeah. You're the one who made it," Chloe said. "You're the one who knows the project inside and out." They'd landed the lecture hall remodel two months ago, and Chloe had been more than happy to let Jin handle the majority of the project. "You've earned it."

"I'll say thank you after it's over," he said, looking a shade paler than usual.

"You'll be fine." She leaned over to give his shoulder a pat. "And I'll be there for moral support. How's the Harrison Street property looking?"

"Good. I've got the floorplans here, along with the reports from the inspection, and some ideas Chris and I had for what we can do with it." He handed her a folder. "We've got the keys if you want to go and have a look at."

"Not today," Chloe said, not planning on leaving the office before the day was done. The prospect of hopping on the Tube to travel deeper into the city was unappealing. "But maybe later in the week."

"Want to do the presentation before or after lunch? Devon and I made too much food last night, so we brought you leftovers."

"You did?"

"Uh-huh. Chicken donburi."

"I knew I hired you for a reason."

"There'll be enough for you too, Maria," Devon said, hanging up the phone and stretching their arms above their head. "If you want."

"Oh, go on. You know I can never turn down your cooking."

The four of them filed into the office kitchen. Chloe's mouth watered when she caught a glimpse of the Tupperware container Jin put into the microwave. Between him and Devon and Naomi's family, Chloe would never starve, despite her limited culinary skills.

"So, Chloe," Devon said, settling at their usual seat at the table. "How was going back home?"

"Not as bad as I thought." She accepted a steaming plate from Jin with a grateful smile. "And the house is coming along nicely."

"Is it in a bad way?"

She shook her head, mouth full of rice. "Better than some of the projects we've taken on. It's old, but my dad did a good job with it before he got sick. Things just need a refresh. Lick of paint, new wallpaper. Kitchen and bathrooms are bigger jobs, but nothing too major."

"We could send some teams there if you wanted," Jin said. "Give you a hand. Ease the load. It's got to get difficult, going back and forth."

"I know, but I…I need to do this." The thought of someone else in the house, ripping out and replacing things her dad had put there didn't sit right with her. It was her house—had been *their* house—and it felt right for Chloe to do it herself, leave some mark of her family long after they'd left it behind.

"Are you sure?" Jin didn't look convinced, and Chloe knew that while he'd support her decision either way, he didn't understand.

"Yeah. It's only a few months. And you've proved you're more than capable of holding down the fort while I'm gone."

"Mum texted," Naomi said, shoulder leaning against one of the carriage's handrails as she glanced at her phone. "Mind if we stop at the market on the way? She's given me a shopping list."

"Not at all." They slipped through the doors when they opened at Brixton Station and wove their way through the people lining the platform and heading for the exit.

Even outside, the streets were heaving, a sharp contrast to the sleepy village they'd left behind, but Chloe didn't mind. The city was always on the go, and she loved the anonymity of it, the ability to melt seamlessly into the crowd.

"What does she need?" Chloe asked, following Naomi into the bustling indoor market where various flags hung from the ceiling.

"Ackee, plantains, and allspice."

The greengrocers was one Chloe had been to dozens of times over the years, and the two women behind the counter smiled as they stepped inside.

"Is your sister coming tonight?" Chloe asked, holding out her arms for Naomi to load them up.

"Nope, she's working."

"I could never do nights. Especially as a surgeon. I'd be asleep on the operating table."

Shopping completed, they walked the short distance to the Alleyene residence, where both of them were swept into a hug as soon as they were through the door.

"I've missed you."

"We were gone two weeks, Mum."

"Exactly. Two family dinners missed." Jada tutted, releasing them and ushering them into the kitchen, where Naomi's father sat at the table reading the newspaper. "So, how was your trip north? Did you miss us?"

"Missed your cooking. Chloe nearly poisoned me several times."

"I did not. You cooked every night."

Naomi grinned, bending to press a kiss to her father's cheek. "But it was good. Different. And so quiet! I don't think I managed a decent night's sleep."

"Don't I know it," Chloe said, folding herself into her usual seat. "My poor coffee machine could barely keep up with demand."

"Well, I'm glad you're both back. And I hope you're hungry."

Chloe certainly was. Her stomach rumbled as Jada lifted one of the pan lids on the hob and the smell of spices filled the air.

"How's work been?" Naomi asked, helping herself to a bottle of beer from the fridge.

"Busy," Leroy said, turning his paper to the puzzle pages. "Want to help with the crossword?"

"I feel like 'help' is a loose term," Naomi said, sitting beside Chloe and sliding a beer toward her. "But go on."

"Young cow. Six letters."

Naomi quirked an eyebrow at Chloe. "You should get that."

"Why?"

"You were practically raised on a farm."

"I didn't exactly take an interest in the farming process."

"I'll bet," Naomi said, eyebrows wiggling, and Chloe punched her in the shoulder. "Ow! Uncalled for."

"Try heifer," Jada suggested, adding large spoonfuls of rice to four plates at the counter. Chloe itched with the desire to help her, but knew if she tried she'd be batted out of the way.

"See, Dad, you don't need us. We're slowing you down."

"Hatred," he said, ignoring Naomi. "Nine letters."

"Revulsion?" Chloe suggested. "Or animosity?"

"Antipathy," Naomi said. "That's been a crossword clue before."

"Perhaps we'll come back it," Leroy said, shifting the paper to one side to make room for the plate set in front of him. "Thank you, dear."

Chloe echoed the sentiment as she accepted her own plate of curried chicken, digging in once Jada had taken her place at the table. Wednesday dinners with the Alleyenes were always the best part of her week. She liked her space, liked living alone, but there was a comfort in good food and even better company that Chloe craved.

"How has work been for you two this week?" Leroy asked, crossword temporarily forgotten. "Caught up on everything you missed?"

"Not much to catch up on—Emil sent me daily e-mails summarising what he'd done, bless him. The Foster building is coming along nicely. I'm hoping the plans will get approved next week, and I can finally start focusing on other things."

"Like converting a three-storey townhouse into separate flats?" Chloe asked hopefully.

"I guess," Naomi said, and Chloe stuck out her tongue. "I'll come and have a look at it next week, and we can brainstorm."

After they'd finished eating, Chloe and Naomi cleared the plates, Chloe washing and Naomi drying while her parents read out the crossword clues. Then it was time for a film, and the four of them piled into the living room while Leroy assumed control of the remote. It was his turn to pick the title.

"What are we in the mood for tonight, ladies?" he asked, opening Netflix.

"Horror," Chloe suggested, and Naomi socked her in the side with a couch cushion. "Better keep hold of that," she said, grinning. "You'll need it to hide behind."

"We watched horror last time," Naomi protested.

"No, we didn't." Leroy's voice was genial as he scrolled to the horror section. "We had a musical."

"I think you're mistaken," Naomi said. "Do we need to get your memory checked?"

"I'm a doctor, Naomi," he said, voice deadpan. "I think I know the signs. Here we are. This looks lovely."

The still was a bloody handprint on a window, and Naomi sighed, accepting defeat and clutching the pillow close to her chest.

"Fine. But when I can't sleep tonight, it's you I'm going to be calling, Chloe."

"I'll be sure my phone is on silent."

Naomi grumbled under her breath, and Chloe stretched out on the couch, already knowing she'd be spending more time watching Naomi's reactions than the film itself. Jada was usually as bad, but she seemed to have come prepared tonight, armed with knitting needles.

The film was terrible, but Chloe didn't mind. Naomi was entertaining enough all by herself, and Chloe revelled in the feeling of being home.

Chapter 6

AMY'S MALLET THUDDED ONTO THE wooden fence post, driving it deeper into the ground. Stepping back, she gave it an experimental tug and smiled when it didn't budge. Good thing she'd noticed it was loose before letting her bull free in his new pasture—he'd gotten out once before, and trying to catch him had been a nightmare she didn't plan on repeating.

She was turning back toward home when she noticed a figure walking along the path beside the field, a familiar black Labrador leading the way. Chloe was back, it seemed, and she raised a hand to wave when she noticed Amy looking her way.

She lingered, testing the other posts in the fence line—despite having done it once already—and waited for Chloe to reach her.

"Hey," Chloe called when she was a few feet away and Bella paused to sniff at the base of a tree. "Having fun?" She nodded at the mallet in Amy's hand, and Amy swung it onto her shoulder.

"Oh yeah. Good way to get my anger out."

"You got a lot of it?"

"I work with Danny—what do you think?"

Chloe chuckled, tugging gently on Bella's lead to stop her from wandering too far ahead. "Your offer to take me to the bathroom place still stand?"

"Yeah, of course. I'll be—" She cut herself off, hearing hooves on concrete and frowning, because the herd were on the other side of the farm. "It's not just me hearing that, is it?"

"No. It sounds like—"

A horse, careening toward them from the direction of the farmhouse. Stirrups slapped against Regina's sides, her ears pricked forward, and Chloe seemed frozen, her and Bella standing directly in the horse's path.

Amy reacted quickly, diving through the gap in the electric fence and knocking both Chloe and Bella out of the way. Regina sped past them without a care in the world. In Amy's haste, she pushed Chloe back into the fence behind, her arm catching on the razor-wire lining the top of it.

"Shit, I'm sorry," Amy said, watching beads of blood well on Chloe's arm. "Are you okay?"

"Yeah, it's not too deep." Chloe pressed her palm to the wound with a wince. "Better than being flattened."

"Let me see." She pried Chloe's hand away and bent her head over her arm. "Looks nasty. Come on. I've got a first aid kit back at the house."

"That's not necessary," Chloe said, but Amy was already turning toward the farm. "Shouldn't you be going after the horse?"

"She won't go far. She'll be stuffing her face full of grass, happy as anything."

"Where did she even come from?"

"Amy!" Danny called, and he stomped into a view a moment later, face like thunder and his clothes spattered with mud. "I'm going to kill that fucking horse of yours."

"There's your answer," Amy said to Chloe, keeping her voice low. To her brother, she said, "It serves you right. You know she doesn't like you. I don't know why you keep trying to take her out. Oh wait, I do. It's stubbornness."

He glared, and Amy was surprised steam wasn't coming off the top of his head.

"And seeing as you were the one who let her go, you can go and find her. She went that way." Amy pointed behind her and took hold of Chloe's elbow, not giving Danny a chance to protest. "Come on. Let's get your arm seen to."

Chloe expected Amy to lead her to the farmhouse, but she was steered into one of the barns instead.

Last time Chloe had been inside, it was derelict, used for storage, but it had since been converted into an open-plan living space, bright and airy. Exposed beams were visible along the walls and roof, and a wooden ladder led to an alcove that must be where Amy slept. The edge of a double bed was visible from where Chloe stood.

"Wow." Chloe looked around with wide-eyed wonder. "This place is beautiful. You live here?"

"Uh-huh." Amy kicked off her wellies by the door and crossed over the plush grey rug stretched across the centre of the space, past fabric sofas and to the kitchen lining the back wall, where wide windows looked out at the fields beyond. "I got it done when I moved back here. After six years living on my own, I couldn't cope in the farmhouse with Danny and my mum. I like having my own space."

She retrieved a first aid kit from one of the kitchen cupboards and set it on her wooden dining table, then pulled out a chair with her foot and nodded toward it.

"You got a towel?" Chloe asked, glancing at Bella, pressed close to her legs. "Her paws are muddy."

"It's all right. I can mop the floors afterward if I need to. It's not like they've never seen mud before."

Chloe unclipped Bella's lead, keeping one eye on her as she sniffed around the unfamiliar space.

"Did you do any of the work in here yourself?" Chloe asked, dropping into the proffered chair.

"God, no. I had some input on the plans, but that was about it. It's how I know the bathroom guys. They put mine in." She nodded toward the walled-off section of the barn. "I kind of need to see your arm if I'm going to patch you up," she said, and Chloe realised she was still holding it close to her chest.

"I can do it myself. I'm no stranger to injury." The thought of Amy's hands on her skin made Chloe's stomach flip, and her heartbeat quickened when Amy levelled her with a cool stare.

"Maybe so, but it's my fault you're hurt, so please let me help."

Reluctantly, Chloe extended her arm across the table, sucking in a sharp breath when Amy swiped the wound with an antiseptic wipe, the sting making her jaw clench.

"Sorry." Amy bent her head, and Chloe tried to keep her breathing level beneath Amy's feather light touches. "It's not too deep, but it's long. Too long for a plaster." She measured out a bandage instead, cutting it to size and wrapping it securely around Chloe's forearm. "There you go. When's the last time you had a tetanus shot?"

"I'm up to date with it. Necessity of the job. I've jabbed myself with many a nail over the years."

"You always were clumsy. Remember when you sprained your ankle?"

"That was stubbornness, not clumsiness. And your fault, if I recall."

"Just because I dared you to do something didn't mean you had to do it," Amy said, a smile playing on the edges of her lips—it dropped when Chloe tensed, realising what she'd said.

Chloe's mind flashed back to being seventeen years old at a party she hadn't wanted to go to, Amy finding her hiding from a game of truth or dare in another room. *I dare you to kiss me*, she'd said, eyes dark, alcohol on her tongue. *I want to know what it feels like.* And Chloe...

Chloe hadn't been able to move away.

She sighed. They'd been doing so well, their first time alone together. The first real test of whether this would work, or if there was too much heavy history weighing them down, putting a stop to new beginnings.

Awkwardness settled heavy and stifling in the air.

"I, um." Chloe cleared her throat, her voice hoarse. "I should be getting back. Got a bathroom to paint and tile."

"Right, of course." Amy stepped backwards until she couldn't go any further, back pressed against her kitchen counter, cheeks tinged pink, and Chloe wondered if she was thinking of the same memory. Wondered if she remembered it differently. Wondered what on earth she'd been *thinking*, most of all.

But she wasn't going to ask.

Things were awkward enough.

"Do you...do you still want me to take you to the shop? I'm going there on Sunday."

Chloe hesitated, and Amy's face fell.

"I'll give you the address. Let them know to give you the family and friends discount." Amy reached for a piece of paper from the pad clipped to the fridge, lips downturned.

That would be easier, Chloe thought. Less complicated. Less likely to dredge up the past. And yet, she hesitated. Until five minutes ago, she'd been enjoying herself—the easy banter they'd fallen back into, the glimpse into the life Amy had been living in Chloe's absence. She might not be ready to forgive Amy yet, but she wasn't sure she wanted to slam the door shut.

Wanted to keep it slightly ajar, just to see what might happen.

"No, it's okay. I'll go with you."

Amy's face brightened, hope blooming in her eyes. "Is nine okay with you? I'll pick you up from the house."

"Sure." Chloe got to her feet, glancing over her shoulder to find Bella stretched out on the rug in front of Amy's fireplace. "Thanks for the first aid."

"Anytime."

"Come on, trouble." She clipped Bella back onto her lead, hoping the walk back to the house would be less eventful.

When she passed Danny, pulling along the black horse that had nearly flattened her, face red from exertion and dirt all over his face, she turned away so he wouldn't see her smile.

The knock came at quarter past nine, and Chloe opened the door to find a flustered Amy on the other side.

"I'm running late, sorry. I've got a few stops to make on the way. Is that okay?"

"That's fine." Chloe bent to give Bella a quick pat goodbye, ignoring the puppy dog eyes as she closed the front door behind her and followed Amy over to her van. "Is everything all right?"

"Yeah." Amy waited for Chloe to buckle her seatbelt before starting the ignition. "Had a stuck calf this morning, but we got him out eventually." She held the steering wheel tightly, some tension still in her body.

"I don't envy you. It must be stressful."

"It's no cake walk," Amy said, her smile wry. "But it's rewarding." She pulled onto the curb in the village centre, her seatbelt off and door half-open before she'd yanked the handbrake all the way up. "Be right back."

"You need any help?"

"No, it's okay. You can stay there."

Chloe watched her disappear into the village shop with a crate tucked under her arm. It was two weeks since she'd run into Amy in there and nearly had a meltdown, and look at her now. Strapped into Amy's van, and with no means of escape if things got awkward between them again.

Which was not a helpful thought.

Amy returned to grab another crate, which she passed off to Mark, who hovered in the doorway of the King's Head. When she turned back to the van, she was laughing, eyes bright and the shining sun in her hair.

It wasn't fair, Chloe decided, that the years had been so kind to her. She'd been pretty at eighteen, but at thirty-six she was beautiful, and Chloe wished it wasn't something she noticed.

"Two more stops," Amy said, a touch out of breath as she slid back behind the wheel. "And then we'll be on our way."

The stops were at houses on the outskirts of the village. Amy left the engine running while she dashed out to swap the empty glass milk bottles on their doorsteps for full ones.

"So, you do this every day?" Chloe asked once Amy was back in the van, trying to fill the silence with a topic assured to be safe. "The deliveries?"

"Yep, I head out once the morning chores are done. Danny does everything to do with the land, and we have a farmhand, Jack, who handles sterilizing and washing the bottles, and taking the tanker to the ice cream parlour."

Chloe listened with rapt attention, fascinated by what Amy did on a day-to-day basis, this woman who had never planned on taking the reins of the family business. "Wait, you have an ice cream parlour?"

"Not ours, specifically. We supply their milk. To be honest, it's what kept us afloat. When I inherited the place, it wasn't doing great. Danny had been in charge for two years, but he only knew what Dad had taught him, and things have changed a lot in the past fifteen years or so. Land and food are more expensive, but milk is selling for less."

She kept her gaze on the winding road as she spoke, her fingers tapping along to the rhythm of the song playing on the radio. "They were struggling, and then Danny had his accident. Gabi didn't know the first thing about farming, and Mum couldn't do it on her own, so…I came back. Made a few changes. We got an organic label, and got involved in artisan ice cream. Did enough to keep us from going under."

"Well, from what I can see, you've done a great job. And I want the address of this ice cream place."

Amy chuckled. "I'll take you one weekend, if you want. Give you the tour."

"I'd like that."

She glanced away from the road to meet Chloe's gaze, her smile soft and open. Maybe being friends again *was* possible, after all.

"You go inside," Amy said, pulling into the car park of Smith's Bathrooms. "I'll drop the stuff off at the house next door."

A bell jingled above the door when Chloe pushed it open. Inside was small but pleasant, and there was a wide variety of different styles of sinks, toilets, and baths scattered across the space.

A man stood behind the counter, a book open in his hands. "Let me know if you need any help," he said, rather than rushing over to her and bombarding her with questions. Chloe liked the place already.

She had some idea of what she wanted, styles she'd come to gravitate toward on her previous renovation projects. Sleek and modern was her modus operandi, and she was pleased to find more than one sink and toilet fitting the bill.

Amy joined her as she was measuring one of the sinks, and Chloe watched the guy behind the counter brighten at the sight of her.

Amy didn't appear to notice.

"Find anything you like?" Amy asked, leaning her hip against the sink beside the one holding Chloe's interest.

"Uh-huh. And luckily, it's a perfect fit." She turned to glance at the employee over her shoulder. "You got any of these in stock? And any of these toilets?"

"Let me check for you." He put down his book and moved to the desktop beside him, and Chloe crossed over to the counter with Amy trailing a few steps behind. "You're not replacing your bathroom already are you, Amy?"

"Not at all, Brendan. Chloe asked me for recommendations, and you guys are the best bathroom people I know."

"Aren't we the only bathroom people you know?"

"Semantics," Amy said, and he grinned. "If she could get the same ten percent discount your dad gave me last time…"

"I'll see what I can do. Looks like we've got both in stock."

"Can I take them away now?" If Chloe could get the bathroom finished before she left today, she'd be ahead of schedule.

"Uh, yeah. But if you want a fitting, we can't arrange one of those until next weekend."

"That won't be necessary."

He nodded, scribbling something on a piece of paper. "I can do both for…two hundred and seventy-five."

It was a better price than Chloe had expected, and she tried not to look too pleased as she paid.

"If you bring your van around the back, I'll load it up for you," Brendan said, handing Chloe her receipt.

Amy knocked her shoulder against Chloe's as they walked back outside. "See, I told you I'd get you a good deal."

"You did. Didn't expect it to be because the guy behind the counter has a crush on you, but…"

"What?" Amy looked at her askance as she climbed behind the wheel, and Chloe snorted.

"Oh, come on. He lit up like a Christmas tree when you walked in the door."

"He did not."

"He did! Have you never noticed?"

"No." Amy frowned in concentration as she backed the van against the warehouse door at the rear of the shop. "But then, he's not really my type." Amy grinned at the joke, and Chloe bit her lip at the reminder. Seeing Amy—who had only ever kissed her behind closed doors, who had insisted it was only so her first kiss with a boy wasn't a disaster—be so sure of herself was startling.

She was glad Amy had the confidence to be herself now, though. It couldn't be easy in Corthwaite. "Can I ask you something?"

Amy nodded.

"When…when did you know? That you were gay." It had been bothering her since Amy had told her; she wanted to know the story behind it. See how different it was from her own.

"I think deep down I always knew, but it took me a while to figure it out. To know it wasn't just you."

Chloe swallowed, still not used to the idea Amy had used to have feelings for her.

"It wasn't until after you'd gone—after we'd both gone—that I properly came to terms with it."

"And do people know?"

"I mean I didn't have a coming out party in the village green," Amy said, grinning when Chloe rolled her eyes. "But yeah. I've dated women before. Haven't hid it. Things have gotten better around here since we were kids."

Well, they can't have gotten much worse.

She wondered what kind of women Amy had dated, and decided she didn't want to know.

It was weird, how easily things were falling back into place. She hadn't expected it, and she was still wary, no matter how much it seemed like Amy had changed. Could she trust her again? Chloe still wasn't sure.

Brendan knocked on the back of the van, and Amy hopped out to open it for him. Chloe helped them load everything into the back, fitting it around Amy's crates and making sure everything was secure before they started the journey home.

"How long will it take you to put everything together?" Amy asked.

"I'm hoping I can get it done before I head back to London."

Amy's eyes widened. "That quick?"

"Once you've done it a few times, yeah. And all the pipework's already been laid, so it should just be a matter of connecting everything."

"How many times have you done it?"

"God, I don't know. Less now I'm the one in charge."

"Got other people to do it for you?"

"Yeah, but I miss it, sometimes. As much as I like the planning and the researching of a project, the most rewarding thing is getting stuck in. My hands dirty. I jump at any chance I get, now, but…there's often something else I should be doing instead."

"That why you're handling this house yourself?"

"Partly. But it's also because it's my house, you know? I might not have been in it for a while, but I grew up there. I've got so many memories of it. It's been nice to sort through everything, even if it's sad at the same time."

Amy nodded. "It's hard. I remember having to do it after dad died. His office and all his records were a mess. Not to him, of course—he'd always say he knew exactly where everything was—but he didn't leave us with a guide. It took weeks to get it in order."

It was an unfortunate thing to have in common. Chloe had no idea how she'd have coped with it when she was still in her twenties. "My dad said it was sudden."

"A stroke," Amy said, her hands tight on the wheel. "One day he was fine, and the next..."

"I'm sorry." While her own father's slow decline hadn't been pleasant to watch, at least she'd had time to prepare herself for the end. "I can't imagine how hard that was."

"Alzheimer's couldn't have been fun, either."

Chloe threw Amy a sharp look—she wasn't aware the details of her dad's illness had been widely-known.

"Mum guessed. They didn't talk much, after everything, but a couple of times he ran into her in the village and started talking like your mum was still alive. She kept an eye on him after that. Though it was only a few months later he moved out."

"He never mentioned it." Her dad had barely mentioned Amy or her family at all. "I moved him closer to me. There's a retirement home with an Alzheimer's ward not too far from my flat. I think he liked it there. Better than him being cooped up in that big house all alone."

"And you could see him more often."

"Every day after I finished at the office."

"You must miss him."

"Yeah." Chloe lowered her gaze to her hands and tugged at a loose thread in the ripped knees of her jeans. "When...when does it get easier?" She asked, her throat tight. "Knowing that they're gone?"

With her mum, she'd been too young to truly mourn, and even her memories were fuzzy. She'd missed her—of course she had—but it was almost like missing the imprint of something she'd never fully been able to grasp. But after a lifetime of being able to pick up the phone and speak to her dad, or pop down the road to curl up in an armchair and listen to him tell tales, she was still struggling. Amy was the only other person she knew who had been through it.

"It took me a long time. Even now, there are still days where I walk through the barn and I can almost still see him standing there, and it's been eleven years. But I know he wouldn't want me to sit around getting sad about it. Especially if it affected the running of his beloved farm." Amy's lips curved into a wry smile.

"He'd be proud of you," Chloe said, her voice soft, and she heard Amy draw a sharp breath.

"I hope so. Sometimes I wonder...I've had to change so much, you know? I don't know what he'd think about it."

"He'd be happy you did what you could to keep the place afloat."

Amy's gaze darted toward her, a faint sheen of tears shining in her eyes. "How are you doing this?"

"Doing what?"

"Being so nice to me."

Chloe blinked, taken aback by the change in Amy's tone. "I...I thought this was what you wanted."

"It is." Amy took in a ragged breath, a hand twisting through her hair. "It is, but I don't know how you do it. How you don't hate me."

"I did," Chloe said, and Amy sucked in a sharp breath. "For a long time, I did. But I realise I can't change the past, no matter how much I want to. And everything that happened made me into who I am today, and I'm happy with who that is. There's no point dwelling on the mistakes we made when we were too young to know better. No point torturing yourself any more than you already have."

Amy reached out a hand, curling trembling fingers around Chloe's forearm and squeezing gently. "Thank you."

Chloe realised with a start they were back at the house, and Amy had eased the van to a stop in her driveway. They'd survived a morning together, and though it hadn't been an easy conversation, she felt better about Amy than she had in a long, long time.

"Do you want to come in?" she asked, noticing the way Amy's gaze lingered on the front door. "See what I'm doing with the place?"

"I'd like that."

Chapter 7

"It's a bit of a mess," Chloe said, propping her new toilet against the side of the staircase just before Bella pounced on her. The Lab's tail thudded against Amy's legs as she followed Chloe inside.

"I feel like you'd be doing the renovation wrong if it wasn't." Amy looked around her, the space familiar and unfamiliar at the same time, the walls stripped of paper and pictures. Through the open living room door, she spotted a large leather couch and a television, the cabinets and bookcases long gone. "It's very empty."

"Yeah. But I don't need any extra furniture in my flat, and it's easier to sell an empty house. The charity shops will get more use out of it than I will."

It made sense, but thinking about Chloe out here in this empty house made Amy's heart clench.

"It'll look better when the walls aren't bare."

"When will that be?"

"Not for a while," Chloe said, smile wry. "Kitchen is next on my list." She pushed the door open, beckoning Amy inside. "As you can see, this room is nowhere near empty."

"God, it's like stepping back in time." The same pine cabinets and shiny wooden countertops, the old gas cooker Chloe's dad had attempted to make food on, his specialties being scrambled eggs and beans on toast. A small table was tucked in the corner, three chairs around it, and Amy wondered if hers and Chloe's initials were still visible, carved into the wood where they used to sit.

"Not for long. It'll be ripped out soon."

Amy wondered if, by the time Chloe was done, all tangible traces of her life here—*their* life here—would be gone. Did it bring her some sense of catharsis, stripping away the memories of a place so haunted for her? Would she think about this place at all, once it was out of her hands?

Would Amy ever stop thinking about it as the Roberts house, even when someone else moved in? Would she ever glance at the lights across the fields and not think of Chloe?

"Have you already picked out a replacement?" Amy asked, because Chloe was looking at her strangely, and Amy didn't want her to read the turmoil on her face. "Or do you need some kitchen guys, too?"

Chloe chuckled, tapping her fingers against a folder sitting on the table. "Already got one picked out."

"Can I see?"

"Sure." Chloe flicked through the pages—Amy caught glimpses of carpet swatches and wallpaper samples, paint splotches and bathroom tiles, examples of showers and bathtubs cut from catalogues—and paused on a page of different kitchen styles, one of them circled in red pen. "Here."

"Wow." Sleek grey cabinets and a black quartz counter with an integrated hob stared back at her. "That's beautiful."

"Thanks. Come on, I'll show you the new toilet."

Under the stairs, what had once been merely storage had been transformed, crisp white paint and blue tiles on the walls, grey linoleum spread across the floor. Chloe carried the new toilet in and positioned it near the wall.

"This is amazing. I didn't know it was this spacious under here."

"Honestly? Neither did I, it was piled so high with boxes. It turned out better than I thought."

"Do you, um, want any help finishing it off? Seeing as you're on a tight schedule."

Chloe paused where she'd begun the process of unboxing the toilet, turning to Amy with a raised eyebrow. "You got a lot of experience assembling bathroom furniture?"

"Well, no." Her cheeks heated under Chloe's gaze. "But…I guess I'm kind of curious how it all goes together. I can pass you tools. Make you tea."

"More of a coffee kinda girl," Chloe said, tucking her hands in the back pockets of her jeans. "But are you not needed back on the farm? Last thing I need is your brother racing over here to yell at me for stealing you away."

"Let me worry about Danny. They won't need me back over there for a couple of hours anyway."

Chloe shrugged. "All right. You're going to be bored, though. Fitting a toilet isn't exactly the most thrilling of activities."

Maybe so, but Amy didn't see how she could be bored watching Chloe roll up her sleeves and kneel on the floor, laying out tools on a dust sheet beside the cistern and the toilet pan. Amy wondered if her hovering would be an unwelcome distraction, but then she recognised the look in Chloe's eyes, one she'd seen a thousand times before when Chloe had a puzzle or a problem to solve: laser-focused, her attention impossible to pull away.

Amy should know—she'd used to try all the time whenever they'd had maths homework.

Chloe moved with an easy grace, at home with a screwdriver in her hand, attaching the cistern to the base with ease. Amy tried not to stare when Chloe moved the finished product into position against the wall, the muscles of her forearms flexing with the exertion, a not altogether unwelcome reminder that Chloe wasn't the same scrawny teenager Amy had known so well.

No, she'd grown in more ways than one: physically, into the physique Amy knew she used to loathe, and mentally, her confidence grown with time spent away from the place where people had tried so hard to tear her down.

But despite those changes, some things remained the same, giving Amy rare glimpses of the girl beneath, the one she used to know.

Like the way Chloe fidgeted when she felt Amy's gaze on her back, the tips of her ears turning red.

"You're staring."

"Sorry," Amy said, though she wasn't sorry at all. It was fascinating, this insight into Chloe's life, a precious gift she didn't want to squander. She'd never looked more at home, more *relaxed*, with a spirit level in her hand and a pencil tucked behind her ear. "You're really good at that."

"At checking things are level?" she asked, one eyebrow arched.

Amy shook her head. "No. All of it. Not so long ago this was full of boxes, and now it's something new."

"It's what I do," Chloe said, trying to hide her smile by turning her back, marking on the wall with the pencil where she needed to drill holes to secure the toilet in place.

"I know, but seeing it is different. I'm trying to put Chloe the construction expert together with Chloe the teenager I knew, and...I'm coming up empty. I know it's similar to what your dad did, but I don't know. I guess it's not what I expected for you."

"And running the family farm was what you expected for you?"

"Touché. Goes to show, doesn't it—you have all these grand ideas at eighteen of what the future holds and...none of them come true." At eighteen, Amy had been naïve, hard-headed, and determined she was going to be the next great photographer, going to make something of herself in the world and have her pictures hung on gallery walls.

"Because when you're a kid you have no idea what curveballs life is going to throw your way." Chloe sounded sad, lips downturned as she sketched a quick outline on the linoleum around the base of the toilet. Amy thought of the mother she'd lost when she was so young, of stolen kisses behind closed doors, of the look in Chloe's eye when Amy had breezed by her in the halls of their high school like she didn't know her name. The whispers, the slurs, the jibes Amy had been terrified would turn on her too. A girl, young and heartbroken, running away from her home town and into the bright lights of a city far enough away to drown out the litany of hatred she'd left behind.

Amy wondered if Chloe would have befriended her, all those years ago, if she'd known exactly what curveballs were heading her way.

Amy swallowed around the lump in her throat, around the unexpected weight sitting heavy on her shoulders. Chloe had told her to stop torturing herself, wanted them to move on, which she couldn't do if she kept dwelling on the past, seized by the guilt she'd never truly been able to let go of, even after all this time.

"You okay?" Chloe asked, glancing at Amy, brows creased.

"Yeah." She forced a smile, hoped it was convincing. "So, how *did* you end up doing this, anyway? Didn't you go to uni for engineering?"

"I did. But I didn't enjoy it. Not as much as I thought I would." She hopped to her feet and skirted around Amy—careful not to touch her—to reach for a drill, which she wielded with an easy kind of familiarity. "I was always building stuff as a kid, Legos and models," she said, around bursts of the drill whirring as it bored into wall and then floor, and Amy remembered dozens of them, scattered all around this house and her own, remembered having no patience for them, not understanding Chloe's unwavering focus as she slotted piece after piece into place. "Figured engineering, building bigger things, would be right up my street. But…I don't know. Turned out I liked the hands-on stuff more than anything. I did an internship with a big construction company for my year in industry and I loved it. They offered me a job there after I finished so I took it, much to my dad's disgust."

"He didn't approve?"

"I think he was offended I didn't want a role in his company. He wasn't bitter about it or anything. Supported me even if he didn't necessarily agree. He was good like that."

"Yeah, he was."

"And what about you?"

"What about me? You know how I ended up back here."

"Pieces, sure. I know you went to Manchester Uni for photography, and there was a stopgap in Mexico along the way; that somehow you ended up in London, and came back when you lost your dad, but that doesn't feel like the full story."

"It's the most interesting parts of it," Amy said, leaning against the doorframe as Chloe set the drill down, tongue poking out of the corner of her mouth as she put the toilet back into place, a victorious smile spreading across her face when the holes she'd drilled lined up perfectly.

"What if I think all of it is interesting?" Chloe said, the words soft, distracted, and Amy's heart beat faster in her chest at the thought of Chloe wanting to know everything about her. "You've travelled the world."

"I've travelled parts of the world."

"Still. Tell me about it. Why Mexico?"

"The ruins, mostly. And its beauty. Photographer's dream, really. But I also went through a lot of South America. Saw Angel Falls, Machu Pichu. Almost didn't come back, but then I got the internship in London. And I fell in love."

"It can do that to people," Chloe said, and Amy nodded, knowing a part of her heart would always reside there. How *lucky* Chloe was, to call it home. "Do you ever regret it? Coming back here?"

The question sounded heavy on Chloe's tongue, but Amy didn't hesitate to shake her head. "Don't get me wrong—some days I wish I was picking my way through Mayan ruins with a camera around my neck, but...I've built something here, you know? Something that's mine."

Chloe nodded, and Amy wondered if she felt the same way about her own company, a piece of herself carefully cultivated, growing into something wonderful.

"You still take pictures?"

"Not for a while. I built a darkroom into the barn, but I sort of...lost my motivation when I came back here. Not as much time for it."

"Well, if you ever pick it up again, I'd like to see the pictures. You were good."

"Thanks." Amy's cheeks burned, and she was grateful Chloe's attention was fixed elsewhere, tightening the last of the screws and giving the toilet an experimental tug to check it was secure.

"There you go." Chloe climbed to her feet. "One toilet, fully assembled. Not so difficult, was it?"

"For you maybe. I won't be rushing to install my own if mine breaks."

"Don't need to," Chloe said, voice light. "You can call me."

"I'd need your number for that."

"Oh yeah." Chloe looked like the idea hadn't occurred to her. She dug a hand into her pocket and pulled out her phone. "What's your number?"

"Are you sure?"

Chloe shrugged. "Why not? We're trying to be friends, right?"

Amy tried not to smile too wide as she rattled off her number. Her phone buzzed with an incoming text a few minutes later. Things between them grew easier, more familiar, every moment they spent together, and Amy felt lighter, felt hope in her own heart as she clung to this precious second chance with both hands, not wanting to let it go.

"Sorry I'm late," Chloe whispered, sliding into the empty seat next to Naomi in the school hall, her jacket dripping onto the wooden floor. "Trains were delayed because of the storm."

Even now, surrounded by the low chatter of the friends and families of the children at St. Stephen's Primary, Chloe could hear the wind howling outside. She'd nearly been blown over on exiting the station.

"I had to fight off an old lady to keep that seat for you."

Beside her, Jada rolled her eyes. "Take no notice of her. Are you all right, dear? You look drenched."

"I'm fine." She shrugged out of her jacket and waved further down the line of seats to Kiara and Tristan. "How are the kids?"

"Tessa is nervous, and Zara is raring to go," Naomi said, and Chloe nodded—of Naomi's two nieces, Zara was the most confident. "I'll be glad when this is over. I've heard the same bloody song every day for the past two months."

"Please. You love it."

Naomi grunted, but she smiled as the lights dimmed and the curtain rose, revealing a cluster of kids on the stage, Tessa and Zara among them.

As far as school plays went, the musical rendition of *Hansel and Gretel* wasn't the worst Chloe had seen. The kids were adorable, stumbling over their lines in their rush to get all the words out. Naomi mouthed along to both Tessa and Zara's lines the whole way through the play—a fact Chloe would tease her endlessly about later.

After the final bow, the kids spilled out into the audience, Tessa making a beeline for her family.

"Chloe!" Tessa leapt into her arms, not as easy to catch at eight as she had been when she was four, but Chloe could still manage. Though not for much longer, she suspected—Tessa seemed to grow an inch every time Chloe saw her. "I didn't know if you'd come."

"And miss your big performance? Not a chance."

"Did you like it?"

"I loved it, munchkin. You were amazing."

Tessa hid her head in Chloe's shoulder, and Chloe chuckled. Even after Chloe dropped her to the floor, Tessa seemed determined to stick nearby, pressing close to Chloe's side. Chloe slung an arm around her shoulders.

"I've missed you," Tessa said. "Missed our Saturdays with you and Auntie Naomi."

Chloe felt a stab of guilt that time with Tessa and Zara was one of the sacrifices she'd had to make. "Yeah? I've missed them, too."

"Is the house nearly done?"

"Not yet," she said, watching Tessa's face fall. "But it will be soon."

"Can we come visit?"

"Uh, not right now." The place was full of hazards, and Chloe dreaded to think what mischief the pair of them would get up to when her back was turned. "Maybe when I've cleaned it up a little. Tell you what," she said, when Tessa continued to look miserable. "How about I ask your mum if I can come by one afternoon after school? I'll take you out."

"Can I come, too?"

Chloe turned and found Zara peering at her, back from talking to her friends. "Course you can."

"Did you like my song?"

"I did. You had fun?"

"Yeah! And Mum said we can go for ice cream now."

"Ice cream, huh? In this weather?" Chloe turned to Kiara, who shrugged.

"In my defence, I promised before I saw the forecast. Is everyone ready?" She cast a glance at the door as it was pushed open, grimacing at the rain sluicing down. "We're probably going to have to run so we don't get too wet."

They did, racing through the streets to the dessert place nearby, Chloe with Zara's hand in one of hers and Tessa's in the other, splashing through puddles and soaking her socks and her jeans. It was hard to care when she had the girls' laughter ringing in her ears.

"All right, what do you want?" Chloe asked, steering them toward the counter while they waited for the rest of the family to catch up, their longer legs no match for the girls' enthusiasm.

Zara pressed her face against the glass, eyes scanning over the day's offerings. "Chocolate brownie."

"Cookie dough, please," Tessa said, not needing to look at the flavours—she was a creature of habit, whereas Zara's tastes changed so often it was difficult for Chloe to keep up.

"You two go and find a table while I order."

She added a scoop of salted caramel for herself and, leaving Naomi to handle everyone else's orders, joined the rest of the Alleyenes at a table next to the window, where Jada was playing videos she'd taken of the performance.

Chloe suspected she'd be able to quote the whole damn play soon enough, but she didn't mind. It reminded her of her own dad, camped out in the front row of her school productions, a massive camcorder in his hands.

The rain continued to pour, thundering against the glass with no sign of slowing. It didn't bode well for a smooth trip north in the morning, a fact Jada was keen to point out when they parted ways a while later, with full stomachs and aching cheeks.

"You be careful driving all that way tomorrow," she said, drawing Chloe into a hug in the doorway of the dessert place. "All those country roads…"

"I'll be fine. Got the van, remember? And I'll take it slow." She turned to Zara and Tessa, whose arms quickly wrapped around her waist. "I'll see you two soon, okay? Behave yourselves."

"We will!"

After another round of hugs, she and Naomi jogged out the door and were soon wet through despite the station only being a few minutes away. Chloe offered the sky a baleful look, wondering if it would ease by morning.

She hoped the weather in Corthwaite was better.

Rain pattered against the window, wind sending the panes rattling in their frames, and Sam pressed closer against Amy's side beneath the blanket they were sharing. He was trembling, and Amy wrapped an arm around his back, pulled him close, and smoothed his hair.

"It's okay."

"It'll pass," Adam said around a mouthful of popcorn, the bowl on his lap emptying at an alarming rate. Maybe giving him sweet had been a bad idea—the sugar high might keep him awake all night.

"You want your headphones?" Amy asked, but Sam shook his head. "Shall we turn it up? Drown out the storm?" She reached for the remote and pressed the volume button until Adam was giggling and the film echoed through the speakers. "That better?"

67

Sam nodded, thumb tucked into his mouth and gaze firmly fixed on the TV screen. His shaking subsided, and Amy breathed out a sigh of relief. Her mum was always the best with him, but Amy was loathe to disturb her on her night off. Amy's movie nights with her nephews gave the rest of the family a break—not that Danny and Gabi were probably grateful for it right now.

They'd chosen a bad night to go out for dinner.

A flash of lightning illuminated the room, and Amy spared a thought for her poor animals, glad she'd gotten them inside before the worst of the rain had begun. She hoped none of the daft buggers knocked over the buckets she'd strategically placed around the barn to catch the drips from the newly leaking roof.

Hopefully tomorrow would be a brighter day, giving her a chance to assess the damage, but based on the colour of the sky, she wasn't too confident. Early July evenings were supposed to be bright, but Amy hadn't caught a glimpse of the sun for hours.

She dreaded to think what the damage would be, come sunrise.

Hopefully her flood defences held up.

Her phone buzzed on the coffee table, and Amy reached for it, not worried about missing any of the film—*Coco* was their favourite, and Amy had long ago lost count of how many times she'd been forced to watch it. Her eyes widened when she saw Chloe's name on the screen.

They were yet to utilise one another's numbers—hadn't spoken since Amy had left Chloe's house with her phone burning a hole in her pocket— though she'd been tempted on more than one occasion in the days since.

Please tell me the weather there is better than it is here.

Depends on your definition of better, Amy replied, smile playing around the edges of her lips. *It's been raining for seven straight hours. I might not be here when you next come up. Might have been washed away.*

Are you flooded?

That would involve me venturing outside to check, which isn't going to happen. I have got a few leaks, though. Know anyone who could help?

Danny?

Amy snorted, and Adam nudged her with his elbow for daring to interrupt the closing song. *Please. He'd make it worse.*

If I manage to make it there, I'll come and have a look.

Amy smiled and swiped away the message as the credits rolled, needing to corral the boys into bed—her own, for the night.

Once she was squished in next to them, Sam tucked close like her arms alone could ward off the sound of the thunder, she found herself opening the message chain again. Texts from Chloe when they were kids had been few and sparse, thanks to the relative newness of mobile phones and the truly terrible signal in the village, leaving her with no easy way to keep in touch after they'd both moved to new pastures. No messages to read back through when she was sad, no conversations to relive when she was missing her, when she was wishing she could go back to an easier time.

But now things were different—*so* many things were different—and at least if they lost touch again once Chloe was gone back to the city she loved, Amy would have something.

Some trace of Chloe, a tangible reminder she was *here*, for Amy to keep close and remember her by.

Chapter 8

"Why," Chloe said, staring at Bella with disdain as she pounced into a deep puddle, spraying the side of Chloe's wellies, "do you always have to jump in the puddles?"

Bella's response was a wagging tail, tugging at the lead, and pulling Chloe on toward the village centre. Despite the main road resembling a river more than tarmac, there didn't appear to be too much flood damage, and sandbags were carefully wedged against doorways to ward off the worst of the water.

Mark, who was standing outside of the King's Head with his hands on his hips, waved when he saw Chloe and Bella approaching.

"You survive the storm all right?"

"Not much to survive—I got here a couple hours ago. How about you?"

"All good apart from this damn sign." Mark tapped his foot against the metal sign proclaiming the pub's name, which usually hung on the wall but was now resting on the floor. "The wind blew it off, and my back's too bad for me to fix it."

"Oh. Well, I, uh, I could do it for you if you want?" Chloe offered, scratching at the back of her neck.

"Really?"

"Sure," Chloe said, shrugging. She didn't mind Mark—he'd always been kind to her when she was younger, and he'd welcomed her back to the village with a warm smile and a free pint on her first trip to the pub. "You got a ladder?"

He hurried away to find one, and Chloe looped Bella's lead around a nearby lamppost to keep her out of the way.

"Here you go." Mark re-appeared with a small wooden step-ladder tucked under his arm. "Thanks for doing this, Chloe."

"It's not a problem." Chloe set the ladder underneath where the sign used to hang, then climbed it to inspect the wall and the holes in the brick from where the bracket had been ripped out. "I might have to drill some new holes," Chloe called. "I don't think these will hold it anymore."

"I'll get you a drill."

"Is here all right?" Chloe asked when he returned, pointing to a spot with the drill bit. "It shouldn't look too different."

"As long as it's up there hanging, you put it where you want," Mark replied, keeping the ladder steady as Chloe carefully drilled into the wall. The bracket was soon secured and the King's Head sign swinging gently in the breeze.

"Careful, Chloe," a voice called as she hopped back to the ground, and she turned to see Amy standing a few feet away, a sparkle in her eye and a crate propped against her hip. "If people see you, they're going to treat you like the village handywoman."

"Like you intend to, you mean?" Chloe wiped her dusty hands on her jeans, aware they were already spattered with mud and needed a wash anyway.

"Oh, absolutely."

"What time d'you want me to come over?"

"I'll be free around two, if that works for you?"

"I'm not sure, let me check my busy schedule…" Chloe reached for her phone, and Amy stuck her tongue out at her. "I'll see you then."

"Delivery in the usual place, Mark?"

"Please."

Amy disappeared into the pub with a nod, and Chloe tried not to watch her go. She was pleased by how things were going, by having a familiar face around town, but she couldn't stop the flicker of apprehension, the feeling like she was waiting for the other shoe to drop.

"She's a good egg," Mark said, fond smile on his face when Amy emerged from the pub and waved at the two of them on her way back to her van. "Does a cracking job on that farm. And then there's you." He turned to her, smile never faltering. "Mending things. Construction business. You've done well."

Chloe felt her cheeks warm and focused her gaze on her feet, scuffing her wellie across the pavement. "Thanks."

"Thank you for doing this." He glanced at the sign. "I appreciate it."

"Any time," Chloe said. She dug a hand into her pocket and pulled a business card from her wallet. "My number's on here. Call me if you ever need anything."

Mark grinned. "I might hold you to that."

He did, as it turned out—though not for his own benefit. Chloe was clearing out the last of the bookshelves in her father's study when her phone rang, an unfamiliar number on the screen.

Her voice was breathless when she answered. "Hello?"

"Hello?" The voice on the other end was unfamiliar, though they sounded older, and Chloe wondered if they'd dialled the wrong number. "Is that Chloe? Chloe Roberts?"

So, not a mistake, after all. "Uh, yes, it is. Who is this?"

"This is Mrs. Peterson."

Peterson… Chloe cast her mind back. The name was familiar, and she wondered if she was on the phone to her old maths teacher. The age was probably right—she'd been one of the older members of staff, and one of the nicest, never growing frustrated despite Chloe's utter hopelessness at simple equations.

"How can I help you, Mrs. Peterson?"

"I hope you don't mind me calling you like this, dear, but I was on my daily walk through the village—got to keep myself active, you know—and I ran into Mark. Lovely man, Mark. He always takes the time to talk to me."

One other thing Chloe was remembering about Mrs. Peterson?

She had a tendency to ramble.

"Anyway, I was talking to Mark, and he told me you fixed that sign of his."

"I did."

"Well, I lost a few fence panels in the storm, and now I can't let my dogs out in the garden. I don't want them to go missing, you see. I was wondering if perhaps you could come and have a look for me. I've asked my son, but he can't come until Sunday at the earliest, and I don't think we can wait that long. It's okay if you can't."

"Oh." Chloe blinked, surprised by the request, but she figured with the amount of effort Mrs. Peterson had put into her education, it was the least she could do. "Uh, yeah, sure, I can try and fix it for you. Do you still live in the row of houses behind the vets?"

"That's right. Number three. Thank you, dear."

"No worries, Mrs. Peterson. I'll be there soon." Hanging up the phone, she reached for her trusty toolbox and slipped on a pair of trainers. "I'm afraid I'm leaving you again," she said to Bella, placating her with a few treats as she shut her in the kitchen, out of trouble. "I'll be back soon."

Maybe Amy had been right, before—it seemed she *was* becoming the village handywoman.

But she didn't mind. It was good to feel useful, even if it took precious time away from her own project.

The front curtains of Mrs. Peterson's house twitched when Chloe pulled up outside, and the door opened as she killed the engine.

"Hi, Mrs. Peterson." Chloe heard the sound of yapping dogs as she approached the house, and found the elderly woman trying to keep three bichon frises at bay.

"Chloe, it's nice to see you again."

"You're not having flashbacks to spending an hour trying to get me to understand algebra?" Chloe asked, bending to slip out of her trainers before walking into the house, where she was immediately swarmed by all three dogs.

"You weren't that bad, dear." Mrs. Peterson gave Chloe a pat on the shoulder when she straightened up. "Thank you for coming here."

"It's no trouble."

"I didn't realise you were back in town. Mark said you're here to sell your old house."

"That's the plan." Chloe glimpsed the three downed fence panels through the kitchen window before Mrs. Peterson pointed them out. "That shouldn't take too long."

"Can I get you a drink or anything? I made fresh lemonade this morning."

"Lemonade would be lovely." Chloe waited to be handed the glass before slipping out the back door.

Luckily, none of the fence panels appeared to be damaged, only blown out of the posts, so it was a case of hammering them back in and making sure they were straight. It didn't take her long, and Mrs Peterson looked so appreciative when Chloe ducked back inside that it made the trip worth it.

"I think the storm has weakened your posts, so they might need re-enforcing before we next have heavy wind or it's likely to fall again. I have some concrete at home that should do the trick. Next time we have a couple of dry days, I'll come and do it for you."

"Thank you, Chloe. My husband used to take care of everything like that." Her eyes turned sad, and she played with the wedding ring on her finger. "There's so many things he did that I always took for granted."

"How long ago did he pass?"

"It's been about a year now. My son lives a few towns over, but he has a family of his own, so he doesn't manage to make the trip back here too often. At least I have the dogs to keep me company." They were huddled around her slippered feet, and from their immaculate coats and rounded bellies, Chloe had no doubt they were spoilt rotten. "Would you like to stay for lunch?"

She looked so hopeful, sounded so lonely, that Chloe was powerless to do anything other than agree. "I'd love to."

Mrs. Peterson's face brightened, and she ushered Chloe into one of the chairs at the small table in the corner of the kitchen, waving off offers to help as she bustled around, heating a pan of homemade soup on the stove.

"Tell me what you've been doing these past few years," she said, placing a steaming bowl in front of Chloe and refilling her glass of lemonade unprompted. "Am I right in thinking your father told me you stayed in London after university? I'm sorry for your loss, by the way. I should've said that sooner."

"Thank you." Chloe knew her dad had left a lasting mark here. "And yes, that's right."

"You like it there?"

"I do."

"It's a change of pace from here, but I imagine for a youngster like you, that's not a bad thing."

Chloe hadn't been called a youngster in about ten years, and certainly didn't feel like one, most days, when her back was killing her. "No, I don't mind it. There's always something to do, and there's enough people around that business is always booming."

"You have a business?"

"Property development. Makes me handy at repairing fence panels."

"I wouldn't have guessed that's what you'd have ended up doing."

"Oh yeah?" Chloe hadn't considered that teachers formed opinions about their students in the same way students did about their teachers. "What did you see me as?"

"I'm not sure." Mrs. Peterson pursed her lips, observing Chloe over the rim of her mug of tea, clasped in both hands. "You were always quiet and reserved, so I wouldn't have necessarily put you as someone who would like being in charge. Doing something hands-on sounds right, though. You were always restless whenever we had double lessons."

"I hated those. No offence."

She laughed. "None taken. I hated those, too."

"Do you still teach?"

"Oh, no, I retired a few years ago. I lend a hand if they ever need a substitute, and I do some private tutoring, too, to keep the mind active, you know. Not much else has changed over there since you left, though."

"It feels like nothing's changed around here, either."

"Well, you're right about that. Small things, but that's all. It does make them easier to keep up with."

Chloe tried to help Mrs. Peterson clear up the plates, and was promptly waved away, levelled with a steely stare she recognised from when kids in class hadn't known when to shut up.

When it was time to leave, she lingered on the front doorstep, finding she didn't like the thought of Mrs. Peterson feeling alone and isolated, out here on her own. "I'll be back with the concrete as soon as I can," Chloe promised. "You take care."

"You too, dear. Do you like scones?"

Chloe paused, halfway down the path when she heard the question, and turned back to Mrs. Peterson with a frown of confusion on her face. "Uh, what?"

"Scones. I'll make you some, for when you next come. As a thank you."

"Oh. You don't have to, Mrs Peterson."

"I know, but I'd like to."

"Well, in that case, yes, I do."

"I'll have a batch waiting for you." She waited in the doorway until Chloe had started her van, and waved goodbye as she drove off. Chloe found herself smiling as she turned onto the main road, and decided that maybe being back here wasn't so bad, after all.

Hands covered in grime, Amy leaned forward, trying to spot any obvious sign of why the tractor engine had merely spluttered when Danny had attempted to start it earlier. Before she had the chance, she heard the crunch of footsteps on gravel and turned to see Chloe approaching, armed with a tool belt, her bare arms showing corded muscle.

Amy tried not to stare. Much as she'd tried to deny it in the past, she'd always found Chloe attractive—but it wouldn't do to be caught admiring the view.

Not when they were trying to be friends.

She wasn't going to mess it up this time, no matter how good Chloe looked in the afternoon sun. Yesterday's storm was well and truly washed away.

"Hey. Your mum said you'd be out here. Although I did think she was lying."

"How come?" Amy asked, wiping her hands on the towel tucked into her back pocket.

"Because the Amy I used to know would never get her hands dirty."

"You have no idea where my hands have been," Amy said, and she *meant* it in the context of stuck calves and colicky cows, sick nephews and injured horses, but from the twitch of Chloe's eyebrows and the faint stain of a blush on her cheeks, that wasn't how she took it. "Not like that!"

"I didn't say anything!"

"Maybe not, but your face did." Amy bit her tongue so she didn't tease like she would have done, once upon a time.

"So, you fix tractors now?"

Amy shrugged and closed the bonnet, leaving that job for another day—Danny could use their old one, for now. "I dabble with the basics. Saves having to call out a mechanic if it's a small problem."

"Well, colour me impressed. I know how to change a tyre, and that's about it."

"More than some people know. Come on, I'll show you the roof." She led Chloe over to the cow shed and showed her the buckets. "As you can see, there seem to be a few holes."

"I'll go and check it out. You got a ladder?"

"Already put one against the wall."

Amy rested a foot on the lowest rung while Chloe climbed.

She'd barely stepped onto the roof before she leaned her head over the side. "I see your problem. The felt's come loose."

"Probably should've checked it myself," Amy said as Chloe disappeared and the sound of hammering filtered through from above. "Could've saved you a trip." She felt guilty for dragging Chloe out when she had other things to do, but Chloe looked unbothered when she climbed back down.

"It's all right. Though it is my third job today—maybe I should start charging. Although Mrs. Peterson did say she'd make me some scones, so I guess that's a form of payment."

"Mrs. Peterson?" Amy saw their old maths teacher around the village sometimes. The woman was always happy to talk her ear off, but Amy didn't mind.

"Uh-huh. Fixed her fence."

"Well, I can't offer you scones, but I think we do have some tiramisu left over from last night. Or I could pay you in pony rides."

"On the horse that nearly killed me and your brother on the same day?"

"Nah, she's mine. We do have two others, though, who are far less dangerous."

"Maybe another weekend," Chloe said, a flicker of interest in her eyes. "I wouldn't say no to tiramisu, though."

"I thought you wouldn't." The key to her heart had always been good food. "Come on."

The kitchen in the main house was empty, and Amy basked in the quiet as she crossed over to the fridge and pulled out the promised dessert.

"Where is everyone?" Chloe asked, taking a seat at the table when Amy waved her toward it.

"Gabi and Adam are at school, and Danny took Sam out to a petting zoo. Mum will be around somewhere. Probably having a nap. God knows she's earned it."

"Does she still work?"

"Not as a vet, barring the occasional emergency. She retired a few years ago. But she's Sam's full-time carer right now. He's autistic and struggles with processing sounds, among other things, so as you can imagine, he hated going to nursey. Mum watches him during the days."

"I bet she's amazing at it," Chloe said, and Amy wondered if she was thinking of how she'd been welcomed into the family—both then and now—with open arms.

"Yeah, she is. Dunno what she's going to do when he starts school."

"How old is he?"

"He's four next month, but we're holding him back a year. Figure it might be easier for him to adapt if he's older." Amy set a bowl in front of Chloe, and another in front of her usual seat. Having Chloe at her kitchen table felt as surreal as it had the last time, though at least now she wasn't desperately trying to avoid her gaze.

"At least it's a small school. We had what, thirty people total in our primary? City schools have that in a single class."

"Small mercies. And he'll have Adam there, too."

"Do they get on well?"

"A lot better than Danny and I did when we were their age," Amy said, her smile wry. "Though maybe that's because Sam doesn't speak. There's no backchat or arguments. Just the occasional tantrum or meltdown."

"You know, I never imagined Danny as a parent."

"Me neither. But mostly because I couldn't imagine anyone ever wanting to procreate with him." She scrunched her nose, and Chloe nearly choked on a mouthful of tiramisu. "Little did I know it would be with one of my friends. It worked out, though. I got to keep her around, and it made moving back here easier."

Chloe nodded, spoon scraping across her bowl as she chased the last of her dessert. "This is amazing," she said, once she was done. "Did you make it?"

"Me and Gabi."

"You did always make the best cakes in food tech."

"No offence, Chloe, but next to your attempts, anyone would look like a potential winner of a bake-off." Chloe's jaw dropped, and Amy grinned, relaxing against the back of her chair when her own bowl was empty. "Tell me you're not still hopeless in the kitchen."

"I could, but it would be a lie. I am a beans-on-toast aficionado, like my father."

"How do you survive living on your own?" Amy realised as soon as the question was out that it might not be true—Chloe had never mentioned a girlfriend or a partner, but that didn't mean she didn't have one.

"On the kindness of others. Naomi's mum keeps me fed, and so do some of the people at work. They are all aware I'm a disaster."

No mention of someone else sharing her space, but that didn't necessarily mean she had no one waiting for her at home. Why would she tell Amy if there was, after how she'd treated her in the past? The thought made her stomach twist.

"Well, I'm glad you don't starve. If you ever feel like a home-cooked meal when you're up here, you can come over anytime you want. Tonight, even."

"I should probably do some work on the house for the rest of the day," Chloe said, and Amy nearly smacked herself on the forehead—Chloe wasn't here for fun, she was here for a job. A job Amy kept pulling her attention away from.

"Right, of course."

"But maybe I could come tomorrow?" Chloe suggested, and Amy tried not to look too hopeful. "I could take you up on that riding offer beforehand, maybe."

"I'd like that."

Amy gathered up their bowls, not wanting to keep Chloe any longer, but happy she'd be seeing her again tomorrow. Chloe's presence in Corthwaite at the weekend was fast becoming the highlight of her week. As Amy saw Chloe to her van, she tried not to think too hard about why that might be. Now was not the time for old feelings to resurface.

Friends, she told herself, sternly. *You're supposed to be friends.*

Chapter 9

"Pick your poison," Amy said the next evening, when Chloe found her in the stables between the familiar black mare and a smaller dapple grey, both munching happily on hay nets. "You've already met Regina." She gave the mare a pat. "And this is Storm."

"I'm going to go with the non-murderous one," Chloe decided, approaching Storm and letting him sniff her outstretched hand.

"A solid choice. Wanna brush him?" Amy offered the one in her hand. "I promise he's harmless."

Chloe took the brush and ran it over Storm's back, flanks, and legs, the movement familiar despite her rustiness. It was as relaxing as she remembered. As a kid, she'd loved nothing more than rushing to the stable block with Amy after school, eager to wash away a day of learning with a ride through the farm's fields.

"Now for the true test," Amy said, handing Chloe a bridle when Storm's coat was clean. "Remember how this goes on?"

"I think so." She held it out in front of her. Amy's mouth twitched at Chloe's concentration as she tried to recall which part went where. Reins over the head, bit in the mouth—obviously—and hope everything else fell into place once it was over his head.

Luckily, Storm was mild-mannered, opening his mouth obediently when she slid the bit in front of his nose and the top of the bridle over his ears, unmoving when she fiddled with the straps to secure it in place.

"I'm impressed," Amy said when Chloe was done. "Saddle next. This one's easier." She handed it over and left Chloe to it while she tacked Regina up. She came back to check the girth and nodded in approval. "Sure you haven't been practicing?"

"Do you have any idea how expensive lessons are in London?"

"I'm guessing a lot?"

"I'd be paying thirty quid an hour for the privilege. At least."

Amy's eyebrows twitched. "Pony up. I'll only charge you fifteen." She held out a hand, eyes glinting, looking more relaxed than Chloe had seen her in years.

"I thought this was supposed to be a thank you for fixing your roof?"

"Nah, that was the tiramisu. I'll waive the charge this time, seeing as it's your first session."

"How kind."

Amy grinned and passed Chloe a helmet before taking hold of Storm's reins and leading him out of the stables. "There are some steps to help you on board."

Chloe needed them—not, apparently, as flexible as she had once been. She swung one leg over Storm's back, already thinking she was going to be sore in the morning. It was higher than she remembered, and a flicker of apprehension settled in her stomach, but Amy's smile was reassuring, her grip on Storm's reins firm, and she didn't let go until Chloe had both feet in the stirrups.

"Don't put him in a death grip," Amy said, her hand closing on Chloe's where they gripped the reins and gently loosening her fingers. "He doesn't need to be kept on a short lead."

Chloe nodded, trying to force herself to stay calm, to remember everything Amy's mum had taught her about riding all those years ago. As a kid she'd been fearless, not a care in the world as she'd hurtled at a gallop over wide open fields, and she wondered where that confidence had come from.

"Okay?" Amy asked, hand still covering hers, and Chloe nodded. She left to fetch Regina, who, unlike Storm, refused to stand still while Amy climbed on board, but she didn't let it phase her. She looked at home on Regina's back, holding the reins loosely in one hand as she fiddled with the girth. "Ready to go?"

"Lead the way."

Storm seemed content to follow along beside Regina, which suited Chloe. She soon got used to the rocking movement of his walk, relaxing as every stride took them further away from the stable block.

The path was one they'd taken together a lifetime ago, winding around the edge of the fields and through woodland, ending in a small clearing where the grass grew high, a stream running through the centre.

Of course, they'd used to race, flying over fallen trees and open ditches as they went, making it there in less than ten minutes. At the glacial pace they were currently going, Chloe thought it might take closer to half an hour.

"I'm holding you back," she said, noticing Regina pulling at the reins and shaking her head whenever Amy squeezed them to slow her down.

"It's fine."

"Regina doesn't seem to think so."

"Regina doesn't think much of anything."

"How long have you had her?"

"Ten years. I got her not long after I moved back. It was difficult, to go from somewhere like London where there's a million things to do, to here, where there's not much of anything. I wanted a project, something I could do when I wasn't working. Went to an auction and bought myself a scrawny six-month-old filly with an attitude problem."

"Do you still compete?" Show days had been a fun part of their youth— loading the horses early on a Sunday morning and driving to the nearest competition, one of them usually coming back with a new rosette to add to the collection.

"Sometimes, but not regularly. It's less fun as an adult. You have to do everything yourself."

"Do the kids ride?"

"Adam learned, but he didn't like it. Sam loves it, though. He's got his own Shetland pony. He's called Rubble."

"He's a big fan of *Paw Patrol*," Chloe said, remembering the plate from that first awkward dinner, and Amy nodded.

"The biggest. I have seen more episodes than I care to admit—though I am curious how you know a thing about it."

"It's my favourite TV show." Chloe grinned when Amy twisted to shoot her a disbelieving look over her shoulder. "Okay, it's not, but Naomi's nieces were fans when they were younger. I, too, have seen many episodes. *Peppa Pig* was a big one, too. Sometimes I still hear the theme tune at night, haunting me."

Amy snorted. "You're close with them?"

"I'm close with her whole family. They practically adopted me the first time Naomi took me home."

"That's good."

Is it? Chloe wanted to ask, because Amy's smile seemed forced, but they weren't *there* yet. Once upon a time, Chloe could have read Amy easily, wouldn't need to ask what was wrong because she'd already know the answer, but now she was a closed book Chloe desperately wanted to open.

Silence fell between them, but it wasn't an uncomfortable one. Chloe took in the landscape around them: the rise and fall of the hills in the distance, green fields dotted with sheep, the herd of cows grazing in a pasture nearby.

She could still smell the rain of the storm, the ground beneath Storm's hooves was soft and squelching, and birdsong rang in her ears—it was this kind of thing she'd never get back home.

"You look like you're thinking too hard," Amy said as she steered Regina through the first trees of the forest, their leaves green and glinting in the sunlight. Chloe ducked to avoid a low-hanging branch as Storm followed. "This is supposed to be relaxing."

"It is. I'm just thinking about how nice it is to be here. I dreaded coming back for months—built it up to be this awful, terrible place in my mind—but it's not as bad as I thought it would be. Really, it's…home. Memories. Familiarity."

"Well, I'm glad. Both that it's not so bad and that you're here. Wish it was under better circumstances, of course, but it's been nice. Getting to know you again."

"Yeah, it has." Chloe wondered if her return to Corthwaite would have felt so warm if Amy—or her mother—had no longer been around, and she didn't think so. It certainly wouldn't hold the same appeal, wouldn't be as bright, if she knew all that awaited her at the end of her drive was an empty, half-decorated house.

A house she knew she'd be further along with, if she didn't have the distraction of Amy and her family a stone's throw away.

This weekend alone she'd barely done half of the jobs on her list. The kitchen was supposed to be gutted and freshly painted, and the wall between it and the dining room ready to be knocked through, but all she'd managed to do so far was to tear out a few cabinets.

Jin would kill her if he saw her slacking, but he wasn't here, and Chloe wasn't planning on telling him.

The sound of trickling water hit her ears as the pair of them reached the clearing at last, and Chloe let the reins slip through her fingers. Storm lowered his head to snatch mouthfuls of the grass brushing his fetlocks while Chloe basked in the rays of sunlight filtering through the tree canopy, trying not to think about all the things she was supposed to be doing instead.

She wondered if Amy was shirking her responsibilities, too, if she felt the same calling toward Chloe as Chloe did toward her, if she looked at the lights flickering to life in her dad's house and tried to think of an excuse to see her.

They do say old habits die hard, and their former friendship had been a hard habit for Chloe to break in those months they'd hardly spoken before she'd moved away. Falling back into it had been easy—far easier than she could have ever imagined, considering their history—and Chloe hoped they kept in touch once the house was sold.

"I haven't been here for ages," Amy said, looking at home, reins held in one hand, fingers of the other playing with Regina's mane.

"I thought the path seemed overgrown." Luckily, Storm was sure-footed, and Chloe felt safe on his back. "How come?"

"I dunno. I guess it was always sorta our place. Felt weird coming here on my own." She didn't look at Chloe when she said it, choosing instead to examine the bark of a nearby tree, worn and rotted away by the elements.

Chloe remembered them stumbling upon this place, Amy daring Chloe to follow her into the woods, which had seemed far scarier and denser at thirteen than they did now. She'd forged ahead despite her fears, sending her pony after Amy's; the two of them found the stream and followed it, stumbling upon the clearing by accident.

It had taken them another five attempts to find it again, but once the path was worn and familiar, it had become their hideout, the place where they'd tell one another secrets, shrouded by the trees, hidden away from the outside world.

"Remember when you fell in the stream?" Chloe asked, lips twitching. Amy had urged her pony to jump from one bank to the other, but instead, he had lowered his head and tossed her into the water, and Chloe had laughed so hard she'd nearly fallen off her own pony.

"Remember when you didn't notice that branch and got knocked clean on your ass?" Amy fired back, and Chloe winced, hand reflexively going toward the small of her back.

"That bruise didn't fade for weeks."

"Serves you right for not paying attention."

"I think you'll find it was your fault for distracting me."

"Lies."

Chloe grinned, enjoying herself far more than she'd thought she would. When Amy suggested they should get back for dinner, pulling Regina's head up with some resistance, Chloe agreed.

"Want to try a trot?" Amy asked once they'd broken through the treeline. Fields stretched out before them, the farmhouse barely visible over the hills.

"Sure."

Chloe didn't need to do anything to urge Storm along—he followed Regina's brisk pace, the movement jerky, but Chloe soon settled into it, muscle memory flooding back and taking over.

Wind rushed through her hair, turning her cheeks pink. Amy's breathless laughter rang in her ears, and Chloe felt freer than she'd felt in a long, long time.

"Did you guys have a good ride?" Gabi asked when Amy and Chloe stepped into the kitchen, windswept and flushed from exertion. The smell of the food sent Amy's stomach rumbling.

"Yeah, it was great." Chloe looked brighter than Amy had seen her in an age, an easy smile on her mouth as she met Gabi's gaze. "That smells amazing."

"Thank you. I hope you like tacos."

"I love tacos."

"Where's everyone else?" Amy asked, sitting at the table and grabbing a tortilla chip from the bowl in the centre.

Gabi's eyes narrowed when she took a bite.

"Do not spoil your appetite," she said in her best teacher voice, and Amy grinned. "They're playing dominoes in the living room. You can go and join them, if you want."

"Nah, we're good in here." She had a feeling Chloe wouldn't appreciate being subjected to Danny for any longer than necessary. "You need any help?"

"You can make the salad. Oh, not you, Chloe," Gabi added when Chloe made to follow Amy to the fridge. "You're the guest. Sit, please."

"I don't mind."

"There's no use arguing with her," Amy said, tucking a lettuce under her arm. "She's more stubborn than I am."

"Please," Gabi scoffed. "Simply not possible."

Amy bumped her with her hip, feeling Chloe's eyes weighing on them. She wondered what she thought about their relationship—Gabi in the position Chloe herself used to occupy. Wondered if watching the two of them together had Chloe feeling the same way Amy did when she was around Chloe and Naomi.

Not jealousy, necessarily, but maybe envy. Maybe a longing for that same kind of familiarity once shared.

"How's the house, Chloe?" Gabi asked, stirring a pan full of sizzling peppers and onions. "It must be coming along."

"I'm behind where I hoped I'd be by now," Chloe said, and Amy felt a flash of guilt, wondering if it was because of her. "But yeah, it's going okay. I'd ask how school is, but you're on summer holidays now, right?"

"I am, thankfully. Not that it's all fun and games—I still have lessons to plan for the start of term—but the break is always welcome."

"Have you got anything exciting planned?"

"Danny and I are taking the boys to see my family in Mexico next week, so it'll be quieter around here for a while."

It was Amy's least favourite time of year—her workload nearly doubled, and she missed Gabi and the kids like crazy when they weren't around. Not to mention the insane jealousy she felt whenever she saw their photos.

"Yeah, so if you want to swing by at any point to keep me company, feel free." The house always felt so empty without them, and she knew her mum hated those days, too.

"Please do," Gabi said, taking a sip from a glass of wine. "Because all she'll be doing is moping about the place."

"That"—Amy wielded the knife she'd been using to cut the lettuce—"is untrue."

"No, it's not. You miss us."

"I guess." She grinned when Gabi kicked her in the calf.

"Do you not go, too?" Chloe asked, and Amy shook her head.

"Nah. Couldn't leave this place alone for that long."

"She's too much of a control freak."

"Will you shut up?" Amy rounded on Gabi, who was enjoying teasing her far too much. "It's not that. It's finding someone to watch it while we're gone."

"Exactly—you don't trust anyone. Because you're a control freak."

Amy grumbled under her breath.

"I get it," Chloe said, seeming to take pity on her. "It was hard for me to leave my company my first couple of weeks here. And if you ask Naomi, she would call me a control freak, so." Chloe shrugged. "Take that as you will. What about your mum? Is she staying here with you?"

"Yeah, so I won't be alone. She's gone with them a couple of times, but she's not the biggest fan of flying."

"Plus, it gives her a nice break from watching Sam. Not that she thinks of it as work."

"Nah, she loves it." Amy could hear them in the other room, Sam letting out a rare giggle as they played.

"Does your family ever visit here, Gabi?"

"Twice a year," she said, and those were some of Amy's craziest weeks, when the farmhouse was bustling with activity and rapid-fire Spanish. "Easter and Christmas, usually."

"Do they like it here?"

"Oh yeah. Papi loves following Amy and Danny around the farm, and Mami spends her time doting on the kids. Sometimes my sisters and their families come, too, and that's when it gets really chaotic."

The timer on the countertop chimed, and Gabi reached to turn it off. "Want to go and rally the troops?" she asked, and Amy nodded, setting the salad on the table and flashing Chloe a smile on her way to the living room.

Dominoes seemed to be in full swing. Sam was perched on her mum's lap, and Adam sat in Danny's, both of them frowning at the game in deep concentration.

"Dinner's ready," Amy said, tearing their attention away. "You can finish afterwards."

"Okay." Adam, permanently hungry, scrambled to his feet immediately and scampered off to the kitchen. Sam was slower, accepting the headphones Amy's mum handed him before following in his brother's wake.

It was a squeeze around the table. Amy chose her usual seat—the one beside Chloe—and cursed her choice as soon as she sat. Chloe's arm brushed against hers when she reached for a glass of water.

They'd been so careful not to touch one another that it sent a jolt through her, and Amy tried to be subtle as she leaned further into Gabi on her other side. She didn't think she could handle the feeling of Chloe's bare skin pressed to her own, not when she could remember the feeling of those arms around her waist, those hands twisted in her hair, the heat coiling low in her stomach.

Which she should *not* be thinking about at all—let alone around the dinner table. She hoped her cheeks weren't as hot as they felt.

Luckily, everyone else seemed to be too invested in their tacos to notice her inner turmoil.

Chloe was much more at ease at this dinner than the last, chatting away to Gabi and Amy's mum, even drawing Adam into the conversation—once he'd finished stuffing his face and could actually reply.

"Are you looking forward to your trip, Adam?"

"Yeah!"

"What's your favourite thing to do there?"

"When we drive to the beach. I get to build sandcastles and go in the sea."

"I think that's Sam's favourite, too," Gabi said, resting a hand on the back of his chair. "The city's too busy for him."

Amy knew the feeling. The bustling streets of Guadalajara were a world away from the quiet of Corthwaite, but she'd go back in a heartbeat.

After dinner, the boys returned to their dominoes and Amy helped clear the table. It was time for the nightly milking before she knew it, and Chloe walked out with her.

"Had a good night?" Amy asked, lingering outside the front door, hands tucked into the pockets of her jeans.

"Yeah." Chloe's smile was soft, and she shivered in the summer breeze. "Thanks for having me."

"Any time. If you want to come keep me company next weekend..."

"Well, if all goes to plan, I won't have a working kitchen, so I might take you up on that offer."

"All right."

Chloe left with a wave, and Amy watched her walk the path home before making her way to the milking shed. Chloe slotted back into place like she'd never left, like the years of distance between them had melted away, and Amy...

Amy couldn't stop thinking about the shape of her smile, about her laughter caught on the wind as they raced across the fields, about how having Chloe back felt *right* in a way nothing else ever had.

Chapter 10

"This is...not good." Chloe stared at the rotted floorboards, hands settled on her hips, thinking it was a miracle no one had fallen through them yet. "How was this missed on the survey?"

"I don't know." Chris wrung his hands together nervously. Not that it was his fault—he was a contractor, not a surveyor, and Chloe was going to be making a strongly-worded phone call later that afternoon. "It's fixable. It's just..."

"A lot more work," Chloe finished, her sigh heavy. The Harrison Street property was supposed to be a quick project, the turnaround a few months, and any setback was an unwelcome one. Let alone one that meant replacing the floorboards across most of the ground floor.

"And money," Chris said, tucking his hands into the pockets of his high-vis vest. "Not to mention finding someone on such short notice. I know a few guys, but whether or not they're free is another matter entirely."

Chloe's teeth worried at her bottom lip, mind mulling over her options, and she made a snap decision.

"I'll do it myself." She was more than capable, and while it would mean sacrificing a weekend in Corthwaite, if it meant the delay to this project would be minimal, it was more than worth it. "Think you can get me all the supplies I need?"

"Yes, boss."

He hurried off, phone already in his hand, and Chloe bent to pull up more of the dusty old carpet to survey the extent of the damage. Some of the joists needed replacing, too, but she was relieved to see some were fine—it shouldn't take longer than the weekend to fix, at least.

A weekend she'd been looking forward to spending in Corthwaite.

With a pang in her chest, she reached for her phone, knowing Amy would worry if she didn't let her know.

Something's come up at work, so I won't be at the house this weekend. Raincheck on dinner?

She pressed send and slipped the phone back into her pocket. Deciding to take a look at what work was going on in the rest of the house—and hoping not to find any more issues—she headed for the stairs. They creaked underfoot, the sound not quite masked by the hammering going on two floors up.

Naomi stood at the top of the staircase tapping a pencil against her lips.

"You've wearing your 'I have a plan' face," Chloe said when she reached her. "Are you going to add more work for me to do?"

"You could stick a wall in the bathroom to split it in two. Make separate toilet and shower rooms. There's also space for a walk-in wardrobe in the master bedroom. And have you seen the size of the cellar downstairs? Easily space for another flat."

"So, in short: yes."

"Hey, you were the one who wanted my opinion on the place," Naomi said. "And don't tell me you haven't already thought of all of those things. How's the floor looking?"

Chloe grimaced. "Not great. But I'm going to come and fix it tomorrow."

"What about your dad's house?"

"One weekend won't hurt."

"Aren't you already behind? Because you keep spending all your time with Amy?"

"I do not spend all my time with her."

"But you do spend a lot." Naomi's eyes weighed heavy on Chloe's face, regarding her with scrutiny.

"I go over there sometimes," Chloe said, turning away from Naomi to wander down the hall, fingers brushing against the frankly hideous yellow wallpaper she couldn't wait to get rid of. "I didn't realise that was a crime."

"It's not. But it's surprising, considering what she put you through."

Chloe shrugged. "She apologised. And she's different now. We both are."

"Maybe not that different."

"What's that supposed to mean?"

Naomi's lips pursed, and she folded her arms across her chest as she leant against the wall. "Do you like her?"

"What?" Chloe huffed out a laugh. "Of course I don't. I made that mistake once—I'm not going to make it again."

Naomi hummed, and didn't look like she believed her in the slightest. But she chose not to argue, trailing after Chloe as she continued through the house. They were in the cellar, discussing potential floorplans for if they *did* convert it into a living space, when Chloe's phone buzzed.

That sucks. I guess I'll have to entertain myself...might have died of boredom by the time you make it back here.

Chloe chuckled at the message, but the smile slipped off her face when she glanced away and found Naomi watching her.

"That's her, isn't it?" she asked, and Chloe chose not to answer. "What was it you were saying?"

"I don't like her."

"Uh-huh." Naomi eyed her.

"We're friends."

"U-huh. You've never once made that face when I've texted you before, but sure. Keep being in denial."

"I am not in denial, and"—she saw Naomi's mouth opening—"if you say 'uh-huh' one more time—"

"All right, all right. I'll stop. For now."

Chloe rolled her eyes. "So, bathroom here?" she asked, eager to change the subject, pointing toward the back corner of the cellar. "Or over here?"

"I'm more than capable of cooking for myself, you know," Amy's mum said, upon finding Amy in her kitchen, stirring a pot of pasta on the hob. "You should sit. Rest."

"I'm okay, Mum."

Leanne tutted in disapproval. "You're not. You're working yourself to the bone. Sit." Her mother took her shoulders in a firm grip and steered her toward the kitchen table. "We don't want you burning out."

"It's only a couple of weeks."

"Still. You've been restless all weekend—what's gotten into you?"

Amy bit her lip in lieu of a reply, because she knew exactly what had gotten into her, but she wasn't going to say it aloud. *Chloe* had gotten into her—or rather, the lack of.

Which was stupid, because it was *one* weekend, and to miss her when Amy had seen her a few days ago was ridiculous. But she'd gotten used to the prospect of hanging out with Chloe when Fridays rolled around, a bright spot to look forward to at the end of the week, and until Chloe's text, she'd thought this weekend would be no different.

Maybe it was because they'd had solid plans, instead of the chance of an encounter that might draw Chloe over. Maybe that was why Amy's stomach had dropped when she'd found out Chloe wasn't coming. Maybe that was why she'd been trying to keep herself busy ever since—so she didn't dwell on what the depth of her disappointment might mean.

Or why she was already impatient for next Friday to roll around.

"Why don't you invite Chloe over for dinner?" her mum asked, unwittingly driving Amy's thoughts back toward the one thing she didn't want to think about.

"She's not here, Mum. I told you that yesterday."

"Oh, of course. I forgot."

Amy wished she could forget so easily. God, what was wrong with her?

You know what's wrong with you, a voice whispered in the back of her head. *You know why you can't stop thinking about her.*

"It's been nice having her back around, though. I'm glad you two are getting along again."

Amy shuffled in her chair, not sure she liked where this conversation was headed.

"Such a shame you fell out in the first place."

A shame, a regret, a mistake she was trying to fix.

She could feel the weight of her mum's eyes on her and prayed she wasn't about to push for the real reason they'd stopped talking. It had been bad enough telling Gabi—she didn't want to see the weight of her mum's disappointment if she knew the whole truth.

"I'm glad the two of you managed to make amends."

"Yeah." Amy reached for the bottle of beer she'd left on the table, nails scratching at the label. "Me too."

"It's been nice having her around," her mum said again.

Amy made a non-committal sound around a sip of beer.

"How's the house coming along?"

"I don't know." And she didn't want to ask. An expiry date was stamped on Chloe's presence in Corthwaite, and thinking about weekends where she wouldn't be able to pop over was something Amy tried her best to avoid. "I think she's working on the kitchen right now."

"Maybe I'll go and have a look one day."

"I'm sure she'd like that." Amy's phone buzzed on the table, and she hated, as she reached for it, that her first hope was for it to be another message from Chloe.

It wasn't.

It was Gabi sending a grinning photo of the boys, their skin sun-kissed, hair shining in the sun, looking like they were having their time of their lives.

Well, at least they were having fun.

And she and her mum could too, she decided. They could eat dinner, stick on a movie, and have a spa night like they used to when she was a kid and her mum's hands needed pampering after a long day at work.

She could steal some of Gabi's face masks, and a few bottles of nail polish, and they'd make a night of it.

And maybe, if she tried hard enough, she could stop wishing Chloe was there to share it with them.

Chloe's first order of business when she returned to Corthwaite wasn't anything in her own house: it was packing concrete, a shovel, and a wheelbarrow into the back of her van and driving over to Mrs. Peterson's place.

"Sorry I couldn't make it over sooner," she said when Mrs. Peterson opened her door.

"It's all right, dear. I'll unlock the back gate for you." She bustled past in her fuzzy slippers, ushering Chloe into the garden once she'd taken off the padlock. "Can I get you anything to drink? Or eat? I've got some scones ready for you to take away. I made clotted cream, too."

"You didn't have to, Mrs. P."

"Oh, it was no trouble at all. It's nice to have someone to bake for. I'll go and get you one." She hurried off before Chloe could protest, disappearing into the kitchen, the yapping of the dogs audible through the open door.

Chloe got to work mixing the cement in the wheelbarrow. Once it was ready, she widened the existing holes around the fence posts and shovelled it in.

Mrs. Peterson returned with a plate and a glass. "I brought you a lemonade, too." She set them down on the table on the nearby patio and gestured for Chloe to take a seat.

She did, taking a grateful sip of lemonade. Sweat beaded on her forehead—the day was warmer than she'd anticipated, but at least the cement would set quicker.

"Do you mind if I join you?" Mrs. Peterson asked, pointing toward the chair opposite Chloe.

"Not at all."

Mrs. Peterson beamed, cupping her hands around a mug of steaming tea when she sat.

"This scone is amazing," Chloe said around a mouthful, jam and clotted cream exploding on her tongue. "Thank you."

"You're very welcome dear."

Chloe demolished the scone in record time before getting to her feet and returning to the job at hand.

"Lovely day today, isn't it?" Mrs. Peterson said. "Don't get too many of these out here. It makes the grass grow too quickly, though." She glanced at the lawn, at the grass tickling Chloe's bare ankles. "I'm going to lose the dogs in it soon."

"Have you got a mower?"

"Yes, in the garage, but it's much too heavy for me."

"Do you want me to do it for you before I leave?"

"Oh, no. I couldn't ask you to do that, Chloe. You've done so much already."

"I don't mind. It won't take me long."

"Are you sure?"

"Absolutely." Chloe knew all too well how lonely a big house in this village could feel when there was no one to share it with, and Mrs. Peterson looked so grateful it made a couple more hours away from her own project worth it.

After the fence was fixed and the lawn mown, Chloe cleared the gutters, too. It earned her a warm hug and an armful of scones. Chloe was still smiling when she drove back through the village and spotted Amy chatting to Mark outside the King's Head.

She pulled over to the curb and waved, rolling down her window when Amy approached.

"Work emergency sorted?" Amy asked.

"Uh-huh." It had been a long weekend, but she'd managed to finish the floor before her contractors had returned to work on the house on Monday, and things were firmly back on schedule. "I see you didn't die of boredom."

"It was a close call."

"Well, I'm glad you didn't."

"How goes the kitchen?"

Chloe grimaced. "It doesn't, yet. I don't suppose you feel like helping me rip out the rest of it, do you?"

"Fun as that sounds, I have a few jobs of my own to do this afternoon. Double the workload, and all."

"Of course." Chloe should have thought about that.

"I could come over when I'm done, though? I can bring you dinner, if your oven is going to be out of action."

"Gee, I don't know, I was looking forward to my microwave lasagne…"

Amy chuckled, eyes bright. "I think I can whip up something more exciting than that. I can come over around six?"

"See you then."

The skip outside Chloe's house was close to overflowing when Amy knocked on the door, stacked high with the pine cabinets, linoleum floor, and bits of plaster. The oven sat beside it.

"It's open!" Chloe called, and Amy stepped inside, chuckling when she was greeted by Bella skidding across the hardwood floor and thudding into her legs, tail wagging fiercely.

"Sorry about her," Chloe said, appearing in the kitchen doorway wearing overalls speckled with dust and paint. "We don't get a lot of visitors, and she's used to getting all of the attention in the office."

"You take her to work with you?"

"Yup. Perk of being the boss—every day can be bring your dog to work day. She loves it."

"I'll bet. You look like you've had a productive day."

"I have. You don't want to see the carnage in here, though."

"Now I kinda do."

Chloe's eyes twinkled, and she stepped back through the doorway, imploring Amy to follow. The kitchen was stripped bare, pipes and cables sticking out of the walls, the concrete of the floor hidden beneath sheets.

The wall between the kitchen and the dining room was half-gone, plaster and brick exposed, the weight of the ceiling held by supports bolted into the floor.

"Wow. Now I feel like I've spent the afternoon slacking."

"To be fair, I am working on a schedule. I've got a few of my guys coming out to help me finish off that wall tomorrow."

"How much are you paying them to drive all the way out here?"

"A lot."

"I could've helped you find someone closer, you know."

"I know, but I'd prefer it to be them. I know they'll listen to me when I'm telling them what to do."

"I'm guessing not everybody does."

"There are a lot of people who write me off after a single look, yeah." Chloe fiddled with the straps of her overalls as she talked, tugging them so they hung around her waist and revealing a fitted band T-shirt beneath. "Don't think a woman knows her way around a construction site."

"I'm guessing you love to prove them wrong?"

"Oh yeah. Doesn't happen so much these days, though. Think I've gotten myself a reputation. Do you get that, too? Not many female farmers around here when we were kids."

"Sometimes. But less so now everybody knows me."

"Is that dinner?" Chloe's eyes fell to the bag in Amy's hand that Bella was trying to surreptitiously sniff.

"It is." She pulled out one of the Tupperware containers of stir fry and passed it over. "I'm hoping it lives up to your expectations."

"Well, it smells delicious. We can sit in the living room—I think it's the least dusty."

It hadn't changed since the last time Amy had been in there, but lit by the rays of the setting sun, it didn't look quite so bleak.

"When does everyone get back from Mexico?" Chloe asked, once they were settled on the couch and Bella had curled up on the armchair.

"Wednesday. They keep sending me pictures, as if I wasn't jealous enough. Want to see so you can share in my misery?"

When Chloe nodded, Amy grabbed her phone and shuffled closer on the couch. She was careful to stop before they touched, keeping a few inches of space between them as she scrolled through her gallery.

She got at least five photos a day, usually of the kids. She had dozens of them at the beach, beaming in front of their respective sandcastle creations, or paddling in the waves lapping at the shore. Her favourite was one of Sam, on the couch, fast asleep with all three of the Martinez's cats piled on top of him.

"What's that building?"

"The cathedral." Amy paused on the picture of a grinning Adam on Danny's shoulders, posing in front of the fountain in its foreground. The gothic spires behind them extended into a cloudless sky.

"It's beautiful."

"Yeah. A lot of the buildings over there are. I've got stacks of photos in the farmhouse somewhere." She couldn't keep the wistful note out of her voice. "Next time I'll tell Danny he has to stay here and I'll go with Gabi and the kids."

"Does he get along well with the in-laws?"

"He won them over with his broken Spanish. Although I like to say I had a hand in it, too—they already loved me before he and Gabi met. Also because of my broken Spanish."

"You speak it better than I ever could. I was awful at French."

"Me too. Although I do find languages easier to learn when Mrs. Forrester isn't yelling at me." She'd been their scariest teacher by far—and they'd had her for science, too. "Remember when Carly got the words for jam and condom mixed up?"

"And she asked her if she could have some strawberry-flavoured condoms?"

"I've never seen a teacher's face go so red."

"I thought she was going to explode." Amy chuckled at the memory—and how the differences between the two words had been drilled into the whole class for weeks afterward. "God, I miss those days."

"Do you?" Chloe turned to her, cheek pressed against the back of the couch, empty Tupperware container balanced on her knee.

"Being a kid? Yeah. You had no responsibilities to speak of, and your biggest problem was worrying about getting all your homework done in time to go out for a ride before it got dark. Do you not?"

"No. The no-responsibilities part, maybe a little, but…I don't know. It took me a long time to feel comfortable in my skin." It wasn't said with any blame, and Amy tried not to react to it. "I like where I'm at now. I don't think I'd change it."

"You wouldn't change anything?"

"I mean, I wouldn't say no to a lottery win," Chloe said, her smile wry. "And obviously, it'd be nice to have my mum and dad still around, but other than that… No, I don't think so. Would you?"

I'd go back eighteen years and I wouldn't be such a coward. I wouldn't listen to what anyone said. I wouldn't let you go.

But she couldn't say any of that. Not without the mood turning heavy, not without potentially ruining things.

"I guess not," she said instead, and if Chloe thought she was lying, she had the grace not to mention it.

Chapter 11

"MORNING, BOSS." CHRIS GREETED HER bright and early on Sunday morning, and Chloe dreaded to think what time he'd left the city. "Gorgeous place you've got out here."

"You find it all right?"

"Some of the roads were dicey with the trailer, but everything made it in one piece. Show me what we're working with."

Chloe stepped aside to admit him and his two sons—both part of their father's business and neither of them looking fully awake as they followed her into the kitchen. "It shouldn't take too long."

She'd spent a few hours last night after Amy had gone back to the farm demolishing as much of the wall as she could manage on her own. All that was left now was the heavier of the concrete blocks she hadn't been able to lift, and then they could get to work inserting the joist Chris had brought along to support the ceiling.

Lifting it into place was the hardest part, Chloe on one side and Chris on the other, the boys in the middle, making sure everything was in the right place. Sweat was running down Chloe's forehead by the time it was done and she stepped from her ladder to survey their handiwork.

The place was a mess—dust, plaster, and bits of broken brick and concrete everywhere, rafters exposed on either side of the joist—but already it looked bigger, brighter, and in her mind's eye, she could imagine how it was going to look when it was done.

There was something therapeutic about clearing a room, readying it to be replaced with something new. It was part of the job that Chloe had always loved, seeing what she could do with an empty space, how she could make improvements to what had been there before.

"Looking good," Chris said, taking a swig from a bottle of water. "Have you got much work left to do here?"

"The list keeps on growing. This place hasn't been re-decorated since my parents moved here in the late seventies."

"Yeah, I can tell," Chris said with a grin. "The oven outside? I haven't seen that style in a long, long time."

"It probably counts as an antique in some circles."

"I'm surprised your dad didn't update the place."

"I think it's because he and my mum decorated it together. After she died, he couldn't bear to change a thing. It was like he'd be losing another piece of her."

"You feel that way about it?" Chris asked, curiosity in his gaze. "About changing so much?"

"Part of me feels guilty," Chloe admitted. "But more because I'm selling the place than anything else."

"Makes sense. It's always hard to let go of something near and dear. And your childhood home? Can't get much dearer than that."

Chloe supposed he had a point. She felt more of a pull to the house every time she visited, every time she opened a drawer she hadn't noticed before and found another old photo that triggered a memory of happier times.

"Right, let's get this place looking a bit more presentable before we leave, shall we, boss? Where d'you want us?"

Chloe set them the task of plastering over the joist and the ceiling while she busied herself with clearing the floor and painting the walls. By the time she shooed the three of them out of the door, Chloe was pleased with how much they'd managed to do in a day.

The walls and ceiling were now covered in a fresh coat of paint, and all the debris was stacked into the skip outside, ready for the new kitchen to come next week. Four hands worked much quicker than one, and she wasn't as far behind schedule as she had been at the start of the day.

Glancing at her watch, she decided she should probably be getting back on the road soon, too. Her stomach rumbled, reminding her she hadn't eaten in hours. She wouldn't make it back home without something to tide her over.

She had to drive past the King's Head to leave the village, so she loaded Bella into the car and stopped there on the way.

"Hey, Chloe." Mark waved at her as she stepped through the door. "Sign's still looking good."

"Glad to hear it." The inside of the pub was quiet, only two other tables occupied. Chloe vaguely recognised one of the patrons as the pastor from the local church, but the other face was an unfamiliar one. She grabbed one of the seats at the bar and glanced over the menu. Bella was happy to lie at her feet. "Slow night?"

"Most nights are slow," Mark admitted, resting his hands on the top of the bar. "But we still manage to make ends meet. What can I get for you?"

"I'll have the steak and ale pie and a pint of Diet Coke, please."

"Coming right up." He disappeared into the kitchen, and Chloe got a glimpse of the bored-looking chef within, lounging on a stool and playing around on his phone, before Mark returned. "So, what brings you here?"

"My kitchen's currently out of order, and I needed something to eat before I head back home."

"I'll bet, with that drive. You still an Arsenal fan like your father?"

Chloe's lips twitched, remembering her dad bantering with Mark whenever he'd taken her to the pub for a drink. "I am. Though I don't follow it as religiously as he did."

"Then you'll be glad to hear that Tottenham are kicking off in a few minutes." He nodded to the TV on the wall.

Chloe turned her head, saw the build-up, and wrinkled her nose.

The door opened as the referee blew his whistle, and Amy walked in with a flush high on her cheeks, trying to catch her breath.

"Just in time," Mark said, reaching for a pint glass as Amy approached the bar. She slipped onto the stool next to Chloe with a smile.

"Cheers," she said, accepting the beer Mark handed her before turning to Chloe. "This is a pleasant surprise. What are you doing here? Come to watch us win?"

"You? Win?" Chloe raised an eyebrow, and Amy's eyes narrowed. "Seems unlikely." Amy shoved at her shoulder, and Chloe grinned. "Nah, came for something to eat."

"What about your microwaveable lasagne?"

"I think it can wait until next week."

"How long 'til you get a new kitchen?"

"Depends how long it takes me to install it. But a couple more weeks before I have a working oven, I think. So plenty of opportunities for lasagne."

"If you need feeding next weekend," Mark said, sliding Chloe's pie across the bar toward her. "Come by the village fair. I'm on catering duty."

Chloe had seen the flyers when walking Bella and debated whether or not to check it out.

"Oh yeah, you should come. I'll save you some ice cream."

"You have a stall?"

"Yeah. Dad never used to, but it seemed like a good opportunity to sell a few things."

"Has it changed since we were kids?" It had been a summer staple during their childhood, somewhat tinged with sadness because it meant the end of their precious summer holiday was approaching.

"Not in the slightest."

"Maybe I'll swing by."

"You should. Mum'd love to see you."

"Why isn't she with you tonight?"

"She hates football, unless Adam is playing."

"Haven't you got a match coming up, Amy?" Mark asked, and she nodded.

"Last Saturday of August."

"If I can get someone to watch this place for a few hours, I'll come and cheer you on."

"Adam will like that. What about you, Chloe? Want to come see the chaos?"

"Sure." It would be fun to see Amy in action, because she couldn't imagine her as a coach.

Then again, maybe it wouldn't be so different from how she watched the match now, eyebrows drawn into a scowl, muttering under her breath whenever a decision went against her beloved team.

"For fuck's sake, that's clearly a free-kick!"

"Do referees in the kiddie leagues tolerate this level of abuse?" Chloe asked, pie finished, fiddling with her straw.

"Not if they hear me." Amy's smile was wry, her eyes twinkling in the pub's dim lighting. "But they're usually old, so their hearing isn't the greatest. Or their eyesight. Luckily there aren't many fouls when six-year-olds are playing."

"I dunno, you were savage when we used to play in primary school. I've still got a scar from when you tripped me on sport's day."

"Please, you fell."

"Yeah, over your foot."

"Nope. Over thin air."

"You and I remember things differently." Chloe leaned her arm on the bar, settling her chin in the palm of her hand. Every hour she spent with Amy she grew more comfortable, falling back into the friendship they'd used to have much more easily than she'd ever dreamed they could.

Amy's attention had turned away from the match, her body angled toward Chloe's. "Yeah, because I remember them the right way, and you"— she reached out and prodded Chloe in the thigh—"remember them the wrong way."

Amy's touch was fleeting, but it was enough to make Chloe's breath catch, and it shouldn't. It shouldn't incite any feeling at all, shouldn't make her feel like she was a teenager all over again, and yet...

It did.

Which was *not* good. Where the hell had that come from?

"I think you'll find it's the other way around." Much to her relief, her voice was level, betraying none of the feelings churning around her stomach. "I should probably be heading back," she said, because it was getting late, and otherwise she wasn't going to be able to function tomorrow.

The fact that it would buy her some time and distance away from Amy so she could figure out whatever the hell was happening inside her idiotic brain was an added bonus.

"Of course. I'll hopefully see you at the fair."

Chloe settled the bill with Mark before waking a snoozing Bella and heading back to her van. She set off on the long drive home with her mind still reeling. Had she grown so comfortable around Amy that she was slipping back into old habits? Or had it just been so long since she'd been involved with a woman that a simple touch could stoke a fire?

Either way, she wasn't going there, wasn't making that mistake again. It had taken her years to get over Amy the first time, and she'd do well to remember that.

She didn't ever want to feel like that again.

Amy welcomed Danny back from Mexico with a trip to an auction with a handful of their calves.

She drove, Danny suffering the lingering effects of jetlag even after a long night's sleep, but she didn't mind. It was a half-hour journey to the auction house, her van winding along the roads pulling a trailer full of six wobbly calves.

"You have Chloe over while we were away?" Danny's question was innocent enough, his gaze fixed out the windscreen, but Amy tensed, her hands tightening on the wheel.

"I don't see how that's any of your business."

Chloe had been a sore subject between them for a long time, and Amy knew she couldn't blame him for the distance between her and Chloe when they were younger—knew that was all on her—but he hadn't exactly helped the situation, either.

"Jeez, I was only asking. No need to bite my head off."

"And why, exactly, are you asking?"

"I'm trying to take an interest in your life." Which wasn't something he did often. "You guys seem like you're getting along well, that's all."

No thanks to you, Amy thought, but she bit her tongue. "And?"

"And, uh, I'm glad you worked everything out after…"

"After you bullied her in high school?" Amy suggested, and Danny sighed. She glanced at him out of the corner of her eye and found him chewing on his bottom lip.

"You know, I saw you kissing, once," he said, after a long silence, and Amy felt ice slip down her spine. "In your room. The door wasn't shut properly, and I…I saw you."

Realisation dawned. Amy had never known where the rumours had come from, how anyone could have possibly known, because Chloe had sworn she'd never told anyone, and the panic in her eyes when she said it had made Amy believe her.

"Is that why you were so horrible to her? Why you tried to warn me away from her? Why you told me to stop hanging out with her, or I'd turn into a dyke too?" She injected it with the same poison that had been in Danny's voice when he'd spat the words at her, cornering her in her bedroom at seventeen years old.

Danny slumped in his seat, hiding his eyes beneath his mop of hair. "I was a stupid kid—"

"You ruined our friendship!" *Ruined the chance for anything more, too.*

"I didn't know any better! And I...I'm sorry."

"Are you? Why are you telling me this now?" She ran a hand through her hair and breathed out a sigh of relief when she spotted the first of the signs for the auction house—she needed to get out of this van before she reached over and throttled him.

"I don't know. I thought you deserved to know. Deserved an apology."

"You know who else deserves an apology?"

"Chloe. I know. I should've done it when she first came back, but I...I didn't know how to find the words."

"You start with 'I'm' and 'sorry' and go from there."

"I will. I promise." Danny at least looked contrite, and Amy pulled into their usual space in the car park, already bustling with activity. "I'll go and register."

He slunk off inside, leaving Amy to seethe.

Would things have been different, if he'd never caught them? If those rumours had never started? If he hadn't started whispering in her ear?

She ground her teeth, knowing she shouldn't dwell on the past, but unable to stop thinking about it. If Danny survived the rest of the day—if Amy didn't "accidentally" leave him behind at the auction house when she drove home—it would be a goddamn miracle.

Chapter 12

BELLA'S EARS PRICKED AS THEY neared the village green, the sound of chatter and laughter audible long before the fair came into sight.

When it did, Chloe saw that Amy was right. It was exactly as she remembered it, craft tables ringing the edge of the field, filled with various creations people were selling or games for the kids to play, the smell of food grilling on a large barbeque lingering in the air.

The only change was some of the faces, a few younger ones that Chloe didn't recognise, and those she did looking older. Mark was flipping burgers on the barbeque, and Mrs. Peterson sat behind the raffle table. Chloe waved when she noticed her looking.

She didn't see Amy, but she did spot Danny, Gabi, and the boys standing beside a table lined with cartons of eggs, milk, and ice cream chilling in large coolers.

Chloe planned to keep her distance, but Adam spotted them and came barrelling toward Bella as fast as his little legs could carry him.

"Hi Chloe! Hi Bella! Can I stroke her again?"

"Of course you can."

Adam wrapped his arms around her neck, burying his face in her fur. Bella's tail thumped against Chloe's legs.

"She's cute."

"Yes, she is."

Sam followed after his brother, curiosity drawing him close, and Chloe tightened her hold on Bella's lead.

"Do you want to stroke her, too, Sam?"

Sam, headphones safely clamped around his ears, looked at her with wide eyes as his hand closed around the back of Adam's shirt and tugged.

"He doesn't talk," Adam said, leaning away from Bella so he could turn toward his brother. "But he likes dogs. C'mere." Taking Sam's hand, he set it on Bella's fur, letting him cord his fingers through her coat.

Bella lifted her chin, and Sam's lips curved into a smile as he scratched under her chin.

A shadow fell over them, and Chloe glanced up, swallowing when she saw Danny standing in front of her.

"You enjoying yourselves, mijos?"

Chloe felt trepidation settle in the pit of her stomach. She half-expected him to wrench the boys away from her, to accuse her of corrupting them like he thought she had his sister.

She's not like *you*, Chloe heard, and she resisted the urge to take a step back, to flee, to get away from the weight of Danny's gaze. His eyes were the same shade as Amy's, but with none of the warmth.

"Can I have a word?" he asked, and Chloe swallowed hard around the lump in her throat.

"Um…" She glanced at Bella, who looked like she was having the time of her life with an Edwards boy on either side.

"Adam can take her," Danny suggested. "Gabi will keep an eye on them." His eyes sought out his wife, who stood chatting to someone a few feet away.

"Okay."

Adam's eyes lit up when Chloe handed him Bella's lead, and Chloe followed Danny to a spot on the edge of the green, away from prying ears.

"Look, I…I was a jerk to you when we were younger," he said, staring at his wellies. "I said a lot of shit to you that you didn't deserve. What you do deserve is an apology, so: I'm sorry, Chloe." At that, he looked up, eyes meeting hers, teeth biting his bottom lip. "For all of it."

Stunned, all Chloe could do was blink at him—this was *not* what she'd expected. She'd never expected any kind of apology from him, in fact, especially considering he'd barely looked her way once when she'd been over at the farmhouse.

"You don't have to say anything, I just…wanted you to know. Eighteen years is a long time, and I like to think I'm a better person now, but the best way to prove that is to show it. And I can't do that by ignoring you every time I see you, so"—he held out his good hand, a truce Chloe had never dreamed of being offered—"can we start fresh?"

"I...yeah. Okay." She shook his calloused hand in one of her own, and he gave her a gruff nod before slouching back over to the boys and Bella, who was still preening over the attention she was getting. Chloe followed.

"So, property development, huh?" Danny asked. "You like it?"

"I do." Was this where they were at now? Awkward small talk?

"What're you working on at the minute?"

Talking about work, she could do, and she relaxed, digging her hands into the pockets of her jeans. "We've got a few things in the works. One conversion and three renovations on the go. We're re-doing a lecture hall at SOAS. And we're in the middle of planning a new building for a homeless charity."

"Sounds busy."

"It's never boring," Chloe agreed, feeling a flicker of relief when she spotted Amy and her mum over Danny's shoulder.

Surprise flashed over Amy's face when she saw them standing together. Her gaze settled on Chloe's face, the concern in her eyes ebbing away when Chloe smiled.

"We're here to relieve you and Gabi," Amy said when she reached them, bending to sweep both nephews into a hug. "Have you sold much?"

"About half."

"Half? You'd never make it on *The Apprentice*."

"Well, let's see if you do much better this afternoon."

"Oh, I will." Amy glanced at the boys. "Are you two troublemakers staying here with me and Abuela, or do you want to go home?"

"Stay, please," Adam said, returning to Bella's side, and Sam pressed close to her, too.

"You like Bella, huh, chiquito?" Amy asked, her eyes fond, and Sam nodded, hands back in Bella's fur.

"All right, I'll see you both later." Danny kissed the top of each their heads before slinking off toward Gabi, who was talking to Amy's mum at their stall. Chloe stared after him, still not able to believe what had happened. Warm fingers wrapped around her wrist, and Chloe blinked, tearing her attention away from Danny to find Amy watching her with a frown.

"You okay?"

"Yeah, I am. Don't take this the wrong way, but has he had a personality transplant in the past few days?"

"Not that I'm aware of. Why?"

"He apologised to me."

"He did, huh?" Amy glanced toward him, a smile tugging at her lips. "Good."

"Did you have something to do with that?"

"Only to give him a little push." Amy turned back to Chloe. "So, was I right? Is it exactly as you remember it?" Amy indicated the fair with a sweep of her arm, and Chloe laughed.

"Like walking back in time. I think the games are the same, too."

There were the classics: hook a duck, apple bobbing, and Chloe's personal favourite, the coconut shy. Her dad had used to joke that she should take up shot-put because of her accuracy in knocking them off, and Chloe swallowed around the lump in her throat, surprised by the rush of emotion.

"You okay?"

"Yeah. Thinking about all the times my dad brought me here. His expression if he could see me here now would be priceless."

"He'd love it."

"Yeah, he would."

"You still got good aim?" Amy asked, gaze flitting over to the coconut shy.

Chloe shrugged and handed Bella's lead over to Amy. "Dunno, but I'm happy to find out."

There were six coconuts and three balls, and when Chloe managed to topple five of them, the kid manning the stall looked amazed.

"For that, you can take your pick of the prizes," he told her, waving toward the table beside him, which was covered in all manner of assorted items.

"What do you think, boys?" she asked Adam and Sam, who were watching her with wide eyes.

"Big teddy bear!"

She wasn't remotely surprised by their answer. "Big teddy bear it is."

The kid handed it over, and Chloe knelt on the grass so that she was the same height as the boys.

"You know, I think you two would give this guy a better home than I would. Can you share him nicely?"

"Yeah!"

"How about you, Sam?"

He gave a small nod, and when Chloe handed him the bear, he nearly toppled over because it was practically the same size as him. He hugged it close to his chest and toddled off to show Amy's mum, Adam trailing behind him.

"I'm gonna go buy a raffle ticket," Chloe decided, because Mrs. Peterson looked lonely. "You coming?"

"Sure."

"Hi, girls." Mrs Peterson greeted them with a smile. "It's nice to see you together again."

"How's that fence of yours?"

"Better than ever, dear, thank you. She's a good one, you know." Mrs. Peterson directed the comment at Amy, for no clear reason whatsoever. "Mended my fence, free of charge."

"I did accept payment in the form of scones."

"If I'd known you were coming to this, I would've made you some more."

"That's not necessary, Mrs P. How much for a ticket?"

"One pound per strip."

"I'll take five." Chloe fished a fiver out of her wallet, replacing it with the tickets that Mrs. Peterson handed her.

"We'll be drawing it at about five. If you're not still going to be here then, you can leave your number."

"I'll leave it just in case."

"You're fixing fences now?" Amy asked, when they turned back toward her family's stall. "You really are becoming the village handywoman."

"Hardly."

"You are. Soon you'll be—"

A ball flew toward them. Chloe tightened her hold on Bella's lead, and Amy stopped it dead under her foot with impressive skill, eyes narrowing as they landed on the culprit, a young boy with sandy hair and a sheepish smile.

"Sorry, coach."

"You'd better pass more accurately than that next weekend, Carter." Amy kicked the ball back toward him and his friends. "Get some practice in, all of you."

"We will," they promised, and Amy smiled fondly. It slipped from her face when one of the kids toppled over the ball and sprawled face-first into the grass. "Be careful, Dylan!"

He bounced back to his feet with pink cheeks, and Amy knelt beside him, dusting dirt off the front of his shirt with gentle hands. "Pick your feet up, little man. Are you all right?"

"Yeah."

"You sure? Can't have one of my star players out injured."

He beamed brightly enough to rival the rays of the summer sun, and Amy ruffled his hair before letting him skip away back to the others.

"Star player, huh?" Chloe asked when Amy joined her, watching her wince as Dylan nearly stumbled again.

"He's six. You've gotta pump up their egos."

"You're good with them."

Amy turned to her, smile playing around the edges of her lips. "What, did you think I'd yell at them?"

"Well, you are super competitive..." Amy bumped Chloe with her shoulder. "I guess I found it hard to imagine you as a coach. But it makes sense."

"God, I can't watch this anymore." Amy groaned when Dylan and Carter ran into one another, neither looking where they were going. "We're doomed."

Chloe was still laughing when they reached the stall, where Amy's mum greeted them with a smile and patted the chair beside her. Chloe sat, while Amy chose to sprawl on the grass beside the boys, who had matching colouring books spread open in front of them. Bella curled up in the shade beneath the table.

"Glad you made it, Chloe."

"She only came because I promised her ice cream." Amy peered into one of the coolers, dug around, and produced a small tub. "Salted caramel good with you?"

"Sounds amazing." And it was. Chloe sighed happily as it melted on her tongue. "Can I buy one of these?"

"I think we're all out of caramel," Leanne said, chuckling at Chloe's distress. "But you could get some at the parlour. I'm surprised Amy hasn't taken you there yet."

"It's been long promised," Chloe said, turning an accusing gaze Amy's way. "But she's yet to follow through."

"It's not my fault you're a busy woman, Roberts." Amy looked relaxed, leaning her weight on her elbows, tilting her head to meet Chloe's gaze, squinting against the sun. "Pick a day and I'll take you. How about next weekend?"

"Isn't that when your match is?"

"We could go Friday. Ice cream will help my stress levels."

"Friday it is." She'd have to remember to bring a cooler with her—Naomi would kill her if she didn't bring her back something.

"Have you enjoyed the fair, Chloe?" Leanne asked. "I bet it brings back a lot of memories."

"Yeah, it's been nice."

"I see you're still good at the games." Amy's mum nodded toward the stuffed bear, sitting between her two grandsons.

"Has he got a name yet?"

"Miguel," Adam answered, and Amy chuckled.

"Shoulda guessed. *Coco* is their favourite film."

"I've never seen it," Chloe said, and several pairs of horrified eyes turned toward her. "What?"

"Outrageous," Amy said, shaking her head.

"You have to watch it, Chloe!" Adam was so disappointed it tore his attention away from his colouring. "Next film night you can come over."

"Film night?"

"Once a week we go to Tía Amy's barn for films and popcorn and a sleepover. You can sleep over too!"

Sleepovers at Amy's had been commonplace, once upon a time. She'd often spent the weekends her dad was working at the farmhouse, lying in Amy's single bed, chatting until they could no longer keep their eyes open.

As a teenager, those sleepovers had turned into a form of torture, Chloe pressing her back against the wall, desperately trying to avoid touching Amy, barely able to sleep at all while she listened to the sound of Amy's soft breathing, terrified she'd wake with her arms around Amy and give the game away.

It had gotten so bad that eventually she'd claimed the bed was getting too small for their growing bodies—not a lie, after Chloe's furious growth spurt—and she slept on a mattress on the floor instead.

Until things changed, until Amy dared Chloe to kiss her, and then sleepovers were spent lying in the same bed, lips grazing lips and hands grazing skin, Chloe's heartbeat loud in her ears.

Adam was looking at her expectantly, and Chloe cleared her throat, praying Amy couldn't tell what she was thinking. Chloe risked a glance over and found her staring at a strand of grass she was winding around her fingers, cheeks stained pink. It seemed Chloe wasn't the only one lost in the past.

"I, uh, I don't think I'll be staying over, but I'll come for the film."

"Why not? The sleepover's the best bit!"

"She won't fit in the bed with you two little gremlins taking up all the space." Leanne took pity on them—and oh, God, did *she* know why Chloe and Amy were suddenly unable to look one another in the eye? At the time, Chloe had thought they were subtle—had *needed* to feel like they were subtle—but she wondered if Leanne had picked up on more than she thought.

How utterly *mortifying*.

Adam, unwilling to give up, said, "We can squeeze!" and Chloe couldn't imagine anything more awkward. "Can we do it tonight?"

"I don't know, chiquito. Chloe might be busy."

Adam turned to Chloe, eyes wide and pleading. "Are you?"

"Uh…" She *did* have a kitchen floor to lay, but how could she say no to that face? "I think I can spare an hour or two."

Adam squealed, clapping his hands together in delight.

114

Amy's eyes met hers over the top of his head, her smile soft, and Chloe's heart skipped a beat.

This was not good.

A knock sounded through the barn, and Amy—on popcorn duty—kept a careful eye on Adam as he hurried to answer it.

"Hi, Chloe! You brought Bella!" Adam looked overjoyed when he was greeted by the sight of Chloe and her faithful companion.

"I was told her presence had been requested." Chloe kicked off her trainers and unclipped Bella's lead, letting the Labrador follow Adam back over to the couch, where she settled her head on the cushions between him and Sam. "I feel like I've been replaced as her favourite," Chloe said, joining Amy in the kitchen. "She won't want to come home with me later."

You could stay, Amy nearly said, before her brain thought better of it. She blamed Adam for putting the thought into her head, for making her think of sleepovers gone by—the heat of Chloe's body close to her own, the feeling of Chloe's breath on her lips.

Which was not what she needed to be thinking about with Chloe so close.

"I feel overdressed." Chloe tugged at the hem of her T-shirt, revealing a splash of ink below her collarbone. It was only visible for a moment—a line of stars, black against pale skin—and Amy tried not to stare at the spot once it was covered, wondering what it meant. Wondering how many other tattoos Chloe was hiding.

"Hm?" she asked, distracted, as Chloe's eyes flickered over her figure. She glanced at her own attire: worn flannel pants and thin white tank. "I figured you wouldn't want to traipse across the fields in your pjs."

"Would've made quite a sight, considering I don't own any."

"You don't own a single pair of pyjamas?"

Chloe shrugged. "I live and sleep alone. Never saw the point in buying any."

"You can borrow some," Amy said, trying not to think about the fact Chloe slept naked, trying not to *imagine* Chloe sleeping naked.

"I think I can survive in jeans. Aren't Disney movies like an hour long?"

"This one is nearly two."

"They can concentrate for that long?" Chloe's eyes flickered over to the kids, both curled on the couch—along with Miguel the teddy bear, who Sam had yet to go anywhere without. "Naomi's nieces get bored after half an hour, and they're eight and nine."

"They both love it. They could watch it on repeat for the rest of their lives." The microwave dinged, and Amy retrieved the bag from inside and tipped the popped kernels into a large bowl. "If you want any of this," she said, balancing the bowl against her hip, "you're going to have to fight Adam for it."

He peered over the back of the couch at the mention of his name, impatience in his gaze and the remote in his hand. "Hurry up, Tía Amy."

"We're coming."

Her couch was large, but between the bear, Sam, and Adam, the remaining space didn't look big enough for both Chloe and Amy to fit into.

Chloe seemed to come to the same conclusion, leaving the couch to Amy and making a beeline for the armchair.

"No, Chloe, you have to sit with us." Adam patted the couch cushion beside him. "It's a rule."

"A rule, huh?" Chloe looked amused, hands settling on her hips. "I don't think there's enough space."

"Yeah, there is. We can squeeze." He shuffled closer to his brother, earning him a glare that eased when Bella shifted her head into Sam's lap and blinked her big brown eyes at him. "Come on."

Amy sat beside him, close as physically possible, wanting to give Chloe as much room as she could. Which still wasn't enough, it turned out. Chloe's thigh pressed against Amy's and their arms brushed when she sat.

Adam pressed play, but Amy couldn't concentrate on the screen—not that she needed to, since she could probably recite the whole damn thing from memory at this point—too hyper focused on Chloe beside her.

They'd done so well with barely touching that this felt overwhelming. Amy's mind buzzed as she tried to keep her breathing even, tried not to react to the sensory overload she was currently experiencing. The roughness of Chloe's jeans against Amy's flannel, the heat of her body like a goddamn furnace, the timbre of her laugh. Every tiny shift of Chloe's body sent shockwaves through Amy's, where their bare skin touched, the hairs on her arm standing to attention.

She remembered other film nights, on hers or Chloe's sofa or beneath a pillow fort, pressing close, her heart beating faster whenever they touched. Remembered watching romantic comedies, and how Chloe always looked away whenever the two leads kissed, but Amy never did. Remembered wondering what it was like, what kissing *Chloe* would be like, and why it was never two women locking lips on screen.

Amy's throat felt dry, and she reached for the bottle of water she'd left on the table. It did nothing to quench her thirst, to calm her racing heart. She was surprised Chloe couldn't hear it, and grateful Adam and Sam liked the TV to be so loud, and that Adam was singing along at the top of his lungs.

It felt like torture, and Amy wondered if Chloe felt the same, or if she was unaffected. Amy tried to glance at her out the corner of her eye. Chloe's attention was focused forward, locked on the TV, but then Amy noticed her right hand, fingers digging into the arm of the couch so hard all the muscles in her arms were tensed.

Which didn't help Amy in the slightest, because those arms were used to doing work, to hauling around wood and concrete, tearing down walls and building them back up again, all hard lines and pure strength...

Amy tore her gaze away.

Chloe as a teenager had been meek, hiding herself in baggy, oversized clothing and desperately trying to blend in, for no one to notice her as *other*. Now she strolled around in sleeveless shirts clinging to her in all the right places, and it was driving Amy insane.

She'd found Chloe attractive when they were younger, but now, she was something else entirely. The same but different. Different in all the ways that mattered. Different enough to traverse all the years of time and distance between them like they'd never happened at all. Like she was eighteen all over again, heart thudding in her chest whenever Chloe looked at her, utterly terrified in an entirely new way.

Back then she'd been too scared of what other people would think to admit to herself how she felt, and now...she was too scared to admit to *herself* why it was the film was nearly over and she hadn't heard a single word. Why her life had been brighter ever since the lights had come back on in the Roberts house. Why she counted the days to the weekend with a fervour unlike her, because she knew it meant a chance of seeing Chloe again.

Amy was falling, and she couldn't do a damn thing about it. She certainly couldn't *tell* Chloe, not after all the history between them. And not when Chloe had a life to get back to, a home and a job and friends and her new-found family back in London, too many miles away from Corthwaite for her to consider coming back with any degree of regularity.

What Amy *could* do was enjoy the time they had together before she left, and not do anything to mess it up. Chloe had borne the brunt of the torture, last time around—now, it was Amy's turn to grin and bear it.

"Did you like it?" Adam asked, once the end credits rolled, leaning around Amy to peer at Chloe's face. "What was your favourite part?"

"Um..." Chloe paused, blinking, and Amy wondered if maybe she hadn't been the only one distracted. "The ending."

"The ending?"

"Yeah. I like a happy ending."

Amy left Chloe to fend for herself, needing the space. She snatched the empty popcorn bowl and took it to the sink as Adam chattered away, happy to have someone new to share his obsession with.

He and Sam were yawning before long, which Chloe took as her cue to leave. Amy walked her and Bella—who went with little resistance, despite Chloe's earlier fears—to the door.

"I'll see you next weekend?" Chloe asked, bending to slip on her trainers, revealing another glimpse of that goddamn tattoo, and Amy traced it with her eyes. Was it a constellation? A star sign? A random collection of stars?

"Yeah. I'll text you."

Amy watched her go, then wrangled both boys into the bathroom to brush their teeth before they scampered up the ladder to her bed.

When she joined them, it took her a while to fall asleep, her mind still reeling, remembering the feeling of Chloe against her, the smell of her perfume and the softness of her skin.

It was going to be a long few months.

Chapter 13

CHLOE TOOK THE STEPS LEADING to Naomi's office three at a time.

The queue at the Chinese place Naomi had requested lunch from had been huge, and she'd already been running late, having lost track of time when she'd gone to check the progress of the house on Harrison Street.

She was out of breath by the time she shouldered open the glass door of Alleyene and Associates. Barbara shot her a smile from behind the reception desk.

"Hi, Chloe. She's in a meeting."

"She is?" Chloe turned toward Naomi's conference room and spotted her through the frosted glass walls, laughing at something the woman she was with said. "I thought she was free now. She told me to come over."

"She's supposed to be free. That meeting was supposed to finish"— Barbara paused to glance at her watch—"oh, an hour or so ago."

"Really." Chloe focused in on Naomi's face, eyes crinkled at the corners, bright with a spark Chloe hadn't seen in a long, long time. "Interesting."

"It is, isn't it?"

Chloe leant her arms on the top of the desk, taking the chance to catch her breath. "Who is she?"

"Melissa Thornton," Barbara said, without having to look at Naomi's schedule. "From the local library. They've got a grant, want a new building, and want us to design it for them."

"And do their meetings often overrun?"

"Every week, like clockwork."

"And is she pretty?" Chloe couldn't tell. Melissa was sitting with her back to the door. All she could see was her hair, box braids falling to the hem of her white blouse.

"She's beautiful. And, between you and me," Barbara said, lowering her voice, forcing Chloe to lean in close so she could hear. "I'm not the only one who thinks so."

Chloe was delighted. Naomi had been giving her shit about Amy for weeks—now it seemed it was time for her to return the favour.

The conference room door opened, and Chloe turned her head. Naomi's smile faltered when she saw the grin on Chloe's face, the way she and Barbara had their heads close together.

"Same time next week?" Melissa asked, with the hint of a Jamaican accent. Barbara was right—she *was* beautiful. Tall and curvy, with a smile that warmed when her eyes met Naomi's. Chloe didn't know if she'd ever seen someone who would be more Naomi's type.

"Looking forward to it," Naomi said.

Chloe was going to have a field day with this.

Naomi watched her go, waiting until the door had swung shut behind her before she turned to Chloe. "Why," she said, eyes narrowed, "are you looking at me like that?"

"Who's your friend, Naomi?"

"Client," she corrected, eyes narrowing further. "A professional client."

"Right, yeah—do your meetings with all of your professional clients last an hour longer than they're supposed to? Aren't you a stickler for keeping to time? Don't you proudly tell me about kicking people out once their allotted time is done, so it doesn't set a precedent, that your time is valuable?"

Naomi ground her teeth, shooting Barbara a glare when she chuckled. "This is your fault."

"I'm not the one who invited Chloe over here so close to your meeting with Melissa," Barbara said, hands raised.

"Although it wasn't supposed to be close, was it?" Chloe's grin was so wide her cheeks ached. "You thought she'd be long gone by the time I got here. No crossover."

"Are you implying I'm trying to hide her from you?"

"Yes, because you *like* her."

"I do not." But Naomi looked away as she said it, thumb fiddling with the button of her cardigan, both tell-tale signs she was lying. "Is that food? I'm famished."

"Don't think you're getting away with it that easy." Chloe followed Naomi into the conference room. "The amount of shit you gave me about Amy the other week? It's your turn."

Naomi rolled her eyes. "It's nothing, all right? And even if it was something, it doesn't matter. She's a client. And I don't go there."

"She won't be a client forever. How long does it take to build a library?"

"How do you know about the lib—wait. Barbara. She is such a gossip."

"You knew this when you hired her. And don't pretend you don't like it. She keeps you up to date with everything going on around here."

"It's less useful when she's spying on *me*." Naomi stabbed at a dumpling with a chopstick. "And the library will take a while. So nothing is going to happen. Just like nothing is going to happen between you and Amy."

Chloe thought about the weekend, about spending two torturous hours with Amy flush against her, heart beating like a jackhammer, breath hitching whenever their arms brushed, and decided to let it go.

Naomi would only ramp up the teasing in retaliation, and Chloe was quickly losing a leg to stand on in the not-liking-Amy department.

Best not to give Naomi more ammunition.

"Don't you have a presentation to show me?" Chloe asked, and Naomi nodded.

"Uh-huh. For the Lennox Building bid. This is a big one, so it needs to be perfect." She reached for her laptop, starting the presentation on the large screen at one end of the room. "Okay, so…"

"Want to do something Friday afternoon?" Gabi asked once their chocolate chip cookies were nicely browning in the oven. "Celebrate my last day of freedom?"

"It's a bank holiday on Monday—isn't that technically your last day of freedom?"

"Technically, but seeing as I have done hardly anything over the summer, I have a week's worth of lessons to plan."

"Are all teachers as disorganised as you?"

"Most. I can guarantee none of them had their shit together like you thought they did when you were a kid." Gabi topped up her glass of red wine, and Amy pushed her own across the counter for a refill. "So, Friday?"

"I can't. I already have plans."

"What do you mean you already have plans?"

Amy tried not to be offended by the note of disbelief in her voice. "I do have a life outside of this place, you know."

"Since when?" Gabi grinned when Amy narrowed her eyes. "What're you doing? Got a hot date?"

"Hardly." She could barely remember the last one of those she'd had. "I'm taking Chloe to the ice cream parlour."

"So you do have a hot date," Gabi said, voice even, assessing Amy over the rim of her wine glass as she sputtered.

"What? No. Not a date. Just ice cream." She protested too much, she knew. Gabi's eyes were shrewd, seeing far more than Amy wanted to show, and she took a gulp of her own wine, hoping to blame the alcohol for the heat on her cheeks.

"Then why haven't you invited me?" Gabi asked, one brow arched. "Chloe and I get on all right. Why can't the three of us go for a nice afternoon there together?"

Amy blinked, the thought honestly having not occurred to her. *Had* she been thinking of it subconsciously as a date? Did she *want* it to be? Certainly, her immediate reaction to Gabi's suggestion was a flicker of disappointment that she wouldn't get Chloe to herself for the afternoon— but she couldn't tell Gabi that.

Maybe it was best for her to come. Act as a buffer, prevent Amy from doing something stupid.

"Yeah, you're right. You should come."

"And be a third wheel?" Gabi scoffed. "No, thank you. I just wanted to see the look of panic on your face. It is so a date."

"It is not!"

"You want it to be," Gabi said, and Amy forced herself to hold Gabi's gaze, to not look away when she said:

"I don't."

"You shouldn't lie, Amy. You're terrible at it."

Amy's teeth clacked together when she clenched her jaw, and she breathed out a sigh of relief when the timer beeped, but it seemed Gabi wasn't done.

"It's okay, you know," she said to Amy's back as she pulled out the tray of gooey cookies. "To like her. You fell for her for a reason when you were kids—it makes sense for that to come flooding back now."

"Except it's not okay." The tray clattered against the counter, and she shoved the oven door closed more viciously than it deserved. "I already had my chance, and I fucked it up. How could she ever trust me like that again? Why would she want to?"

"Amy..." Gentle fingers brushed against the small of her back, and she bit her bottom lip, annoyed at the tears in her eyes. "C'mere." Gabi wrapped a hand around her waist and steered her over to the couch, not letting go when they were sat. "I'm sorry for pushing. I didn't mean to upset you."

"It's okay. You didn't know it would."

"You really do like her, huh?"

Amy let out a long breath. "Yeah, I do." Saying it aloud didn't feel like relief. Only telling Chloe would do that, and...Amy didn't have the balls for that.

Not then, not now.

Not ever.

"I tried not to, but I...I guess I can't ignore it anymore. How did you know?"

Gabi chuckled, palm of her hand rubbing along Amy's arm. "You're not as subtle as you think. You've been happier since she came back. Not that you were unhappy before, but... I don't know, it's different. Lighter, maybe? Especially at the weekends. And never more so than right after you've seen her. To be honest, we thought you might already be together and not telling anyone."

"We?" Amy asked, arching an eyebrow, and Gabi's cheeks darkened. "Who have you been discussing my love life with, Gabi? Please tell me it's not my brother. Although that leaves my mother, which might be worse."

"Um..."

"It's both, isn't it?" She groaned. "What, do you all wait for me to leave the room and start gossiping about me like I'm one of your students?" She jerked away from Gabi's touch, rose to her feet, snatched her wine glass off the kitchen counter, and poured the last of the bottle into it with shaking hands.

"No! It's not like that, Amy. We just want you to be happy. And she seems to make you happy."

"We're friends," Amy said, repeating it like a mantra inside her head. "Okay?"

"But don't you want more than that?"

"No," she said, and this time, Gabi couldn't accuse her of lying. She *didn't* want more, didn't want to complicate things, didn't want to *ruin* things, not when they were going so well. Gabi was right—having Chloe in her life did make her happier, and she'd endure the torture of being close to her if it meant she'd stick around. "I don't."

Gabi pressed her lips together, and Amy knew she disapproved, but she was done with this conversation, done with Chloe haunting her even when she wasn't in the damn village.

"Want a cookie before they go cold?"

Chloe gazed at the large board scrawled with more varieties of ice cream than she'd ever dreamed could exist, with wide eyes.

"How am I possibly supposed to choose a flavour from this list, Amy?"

Beside her, Amy chuckled, seeming to enjoy Chloe's crisis. "You wanted ice cream."

"Yeah, but this is something else."

From the outside, the parlour looked nondescript, an old farm building made of worn brick tucked away on a country road. Inside was a different story. Tables and booths dotted the modernised barn conversion, and large windows offered a view of the endless fields beyond.

Behind the counter were more tubs of ice cream than Chloe had ever seen in one place before, and she was grateful for the queue, giving her a chance to decide what to order.

"Be careful what you wish for, and all that."

"Do you have any recommendations?"

"Depends what you like. I'm partial to bonfire toffee and Eton mess myself, but they're all good."

"That's not helpful," Chloe said, a whine to her voice that made Amy chuckle. "Help."

"Well—"

She was interrupted by a kindly older man. "That you, Amy? Haven't seen you out here in a while."

Amy's face broke into a smile when she saw him, and Chloe watched her get drawn into a fierce hug. "Been busy."

"And now you've got a lackey to bring the milk here for you."

"Also that."

The man chuckled, his eyes brightening with interest when they landed on Chloe. "And who is this? Is this your—"

"Friend," Amy said quickly, something like panic flashing across her face and piquing Chloe's interest. "Chloe, this is Roger, the owner of this place."

"Nice to meet you, Chloe." He held out a hand, his fingers calloused where they gripped hers.

"It's Chloe's first time here."

"It is? Oh, well, we'll have to give you the full red-carpet experience. Any friend of Amy's is family to us. Would you like a tour?"

"Sure." It would buy her more time to choose a flavour, at least.

"Come on." He took her by the elbow and steered her toward a door behind the counter. "I'll show you where the magic happens."

The door led into the kitchen, where a flurry of activity made Chloe think she'd be getting in the way. But Roger forged forward, manoeuvring them past people wearing hairnets and white coats with the parlour's name emblazoned on the pocket.

"I'd show you how we turn the milk into cream, but that's the boring bit," Roger said, pulling open a fridge.

"Hey." Amy feigned outrage. "You wouldn't have a parlour without that milk."

"And what wonderful milk it is, dear." Roger patted Amy on the shoulder. "But the factory is boring to the uninitiated."

"There's a factory as well?"

"A small one. We used to have a farm on-site, too, until the costs got too high. Which is where Amy swooped in to save the day. Now, let me

125

show you how we make it. I've got some new flavours I'm thinking of trying out, you see—you can be my guinea pigs."

"As long as it's not rhubarb and custard," Amy said, looking faintly nauseous.

"That wasn't my best work," Roger admitted, grabbing a container from the fridge and leading them over to what looked like a large, stainless-steel table, but the thermostat attached to the base suggested otherwise. Shelves on the wall behind it were covered with jars and bottles of ingredients, from golden syrup to chocolate bars to meringue pieces. "But I think you'll find this more palatable. How does Oreo brownie sound?"

"Amazing," Amy said, and Chloe nodded in agreement, her mouth already watering at the thought.

"Excellent." He reached for a box of Oreo brownie pieces and tipped them onto the table as Chloe watched with fascination. "These were homemade by the wife," Roger said, chopping them into smaller pieces with two metal spatulas as he talked. "And this ice cream mix was made in our factory." He poured some of the mixture he'd taken from the fridge onto the table, mixing it with the brownie. "Anything else you want to add?"

"What do you want?" Amy glanced toward Chloe, already reaching for a bottle of chocolate syrup. "More Oreos? Or chocolate?"

Chloe hesitated, and Roger paused his process to pat her on the arm. "It's all right, dear, choose whatever you like."

"More Oreos sound good."

Amy reached for a packet of them, tossing a couple into the ice cream for Roger to slice. It was already beginning to freeze, Chloe saw with delight, and Roger was handing her and Amy a small tub a few minutes later.

"How is it?"

"Amazing," Chloe said around a mouthful of creamy deliciousness, and Roger beamed. "I'd buy a batch right now."

"So much better than rhubarb and custard," Amy agreed.

"Well, don't eat too much," Roger said, clearing the remainder of the ice cream from the table. "I've got some other flavours for you to try."

Some other flavours turned out to be a dozen—Chloe lost track somewhere between cinnamon bun and peanut butter—and she felt like she was in a food coma by the time Roger let them leave, pressing her hands to her stomach as Amy led her back out of the kitchen and into the parlour beyond.

"So, what do you want?" Amy asked, eyes sparkling as she gestured toward the board.

Chloe groaned. "God, don't. If I eat any more, you're going to have to roll me back to your van."

"But you haven't tried anything!"

"I've tried plenty. But I won't say no to taking some tubs home." A giant freezer stood at the rear of the parlour, and Chloe made a beeline for it, trying to decide what flavour Naomi would like the most. "Does he always feed you that much?"

"I think he was showing off for you. He likes it when I bring new people around."

"You bring new people around often?" Chloe asked, and Amy scratched at the back of her neck.

"Uh. Sometimes." She shifted her weight from one foot to the other, and Chloe arched an eyebrow, waiting for an explanation. "It's not a bad date spot."

"Oh."

Well, Chloe supposed there weren't a lot of other choices nearby, and getting tailor-made ice cream just for you would certainly have won Chloe over. She wondered how many people Amy had brought here, and decided she didn't want to know.

She thought about Roger's eyes widening when he'd seen Chloe, and Amy's interjection before he could finish his sentence. Had he thought *they* were here on a date?

Amy had brought *Chloe* to a place where she occasionally brought dates, and Chloe felt like her head might be about to explode, because what the hell did that mean?

"What flavour are you thinking?" Amy asked, when Chloe did nothing but blink at her, too busy drowning in her own thoughts to be able to answer. "I've been told I have to get a rum and raisin for Mum."

"Rum and raisin is an abomination," Chloe managed to say eventually, and Amy breathed out a small sigh of what might have been relief.

"I have told her that on many occasions, believe me."

Chloe forced herself to read the labels of the cartons.

127

She settled on a tub of salted caramel for herself, and a chocolate brownie and a raspberry cheesecake for Naomi and her parents.

"Did it live up to your expectations?" Amy asked when they were back in her van, their purchases wedged between them on the seat.

"Better. Although I have no idea how I'm supposed to manage doing work for the rest of the day when I can barely move."

"What've you got to do?"

"I have a kitchen to build. You any good at cabinet assembly?"

"Oh, I'm excellent—if you want them to be extremely wonky."

"Better not make you help, then."

"I think that's for the best."

By the time Amy pulled into Chloe's driveway, Chloe no longer felt quite so full, and was ready for an afternoon of work.

"See you at the match tomorrow?" Amy asked, before Chloe got out of the van.

"Yes, Bella and I will be there to cheer you on."

"Adam will be over the moon. We're also doing a barbeque thing back at the farm afterwards if you wanna come. Sort of an end of summer thing for the team and their parents."

"I'll see how much work I get done today."

"I'll let you get to it."

Chloe grabbed her ice cream and retreated into the house, where she shoved it in her freezer—temporarily located in the living room—before getting to work. Her kitchen currently resembled an Ikea factory, her beautiful new hardwood floor covered by an array of boxes, wooden cabinet parts, and instruction sheets.

"It's gonna be a fun afternoon, isn't it, girl?" Chloe said to Bella, who sat next to her on the floor, tail thumping when Chloe rested a hand on the top of her head.

Chapter 14

CHLOE PULLED INTO A PARKING space at her old high school and felt a flutter of trepidation settle in her gut.

It looked innocuous enough in the sun, the grey and brown buildings bathed in golden hues, hiding the insidious nature beneath.

"Don't be ridiculous," she muttered as she climbed out of her van with Bella in tow. "It's just a school."

At least none of the people who had made her last year here a living hell would be around today, and she drew strength from that fact as she followed the once-familiar path around the science building to the football pitches, following the sound of children's voices, snatched away by the breeze.

Two different clusters of kids warmed up on the AstroTurf, the edge of the pitch ringed by groups of parents. Overall, it was busier than she'd expected, and Chloe was relieved when she spotted a waving hand, Gabi beckoning her over to where she stood with Danny.

"Hey, Chloe. Amy said we should look out for you."

"Thanks. There's a lot of people."

"Well, as you know, not much exciting happens here," Danny said, one arm around Gabi's shoulders. "So when something's on, everyone rallies around."

"Is Sam not here?"

"He's back at the house with Mum. It's too much noise for him. He hates the cheering."

Chloe nodded and cast her eyes around, searching for Amy in the crowd. She was hard to spot, and Chloe realised it was because she was crouching, surrounded by her tiny charges, apparently giving them some kind of team talk.

"Are they likely to win?" Chloe asked, looking toward the opposition, but it was hard to tell who was good or not considering the age of the players.

"Who can say?" Danny said, waving at Adam when he looked their way. "It's anyone's game. They mostly chase after the ball."

"How long does it last?"

"They play two ten-minute halves. Any longer and they'd get too tired."

Based on the boundless energy exuding from all the kids, Chloe couldn't see tiredness being a problem.

"Is Adam excited?"

"He hasn't talked about anything else all week," Gabi said, with the faintly exasperated air of someone who was tired of having the same conversation over and over again. "He thinks he's going to score a hat-trick."

Chloe chuckled, watching Amy rise to her feet and give the kids her final instructions. She had a patient look on her face as she listened to one of them say something, and warmth flooded through Chloe's chest, happy that Amy had found something she loved in a place she'd been reluctant to return to.

Amy turned her head, eyes meeting Chloe's across the pitch, and her face split into a smile that made Chloe's stomach swoop.

"She won't come over until the end," Gabi said, noticing the path of Chloe's gaze. "Likes to stay in the zone."

"She takes it far too seriously." Danny shook his head, his hair falling into his eyes.

Gabi nudged him in the side. "Like you wouldn't if you were in her place."

"Not a job I'd want," he said, gesturing at the kids screeching as they arranged themselves on the pitch. "I dunno how she keeps track of them all." He waved when Adam looked their way. "Having two is bad enough."

Amy took her place on the side lines, on the opposite side of the pitch to them, affording Chloe a perfect view as the referee lifted his whistle to his mouth. She spent more time watching Amy than the match itself, noting the way she reacted to every pass, every tackle, and every save, celebrating goals like she'd scored a world cup winner herself.

Chaos had been the right way to describe the game. Ten kids swarmed around the ball, but the giggles were infectious, and Amy was smiling the widest when the final whistle blew, her team the victor.

Adam didn't get a hat-trick, but he did score a goal, and he raced over to his parents once the match had finished. "Did you see it?"

"Of course we saw it, mijo." Danny scooped him into his arms. "Got it on video, too, so we can show Abuela when we get back."

He beamed, then wriggled free of Danny's arms so he could return to his teammates, who were swarming around Amy's legs, all of them looking at her like she'd placed the stars in the sky with her own hands.

The high for any of them wasn't going to wear off for a long time. Chloe would have to tease Amy about not letting her ego get too big later. But for now, she let Amy bask in the joy of victory and enjoyed the feeling of the sun on her skin, because soon the weather would turn, autumn bringing with it wind and rain and grey skies.

When Amy did eventually make her way over to them with Adam in tow, her cheeks were flushed and her eyes bright, and she looked happier than Chloe thought she'd ever seen her before.

"Well done, you." Gabi pulled her into a hug, and Danny mussed her hair, earning himself a glare. "I told you you'd win."

Chloe imagined her up late last night, stressing like she'd used to do before a big test, and smiled.

"Did you have fun, Chloe?" Adam asked, stroking Bella's fur and looking at her with hopeful eyes.

"I loved it, buddy." She crouched so they were same height. "You were great. My man of the match for sure."

He beamed and threw his arms around her neck, and Chloe swallowed her surprise to hug him back.

"Why would you say that?" Amy asked, once Chloe had been released, but her smile was soft. "You're going to feed his ego."

"And what about your ego?" Chloe asked, climbing to her feet and bumping Amy's hip with her own. "I recognise that look on your face. It's the same one you had when you beat me at high jump in PE after four years of trying. You're going to be insufferable, aren't you?"

"Maybe. And beating you was an achievement. You've got about four inches on me."

"It was a fluke. I had a bad back that day."

Amy's mouth opened to argue, but her outrage was halted by Gabi's interjection.

"Um, guys? Pleasant as this is, Amy, have you forgotten you invited the whole team over to the farm to celebrate? They're going to beat us there."

"Oh, shoot."

Chloe glanced around and realised that the pitch was starting to empty out, a steady stream of people making their way back to the car park.

"Best get going, hadn't we?"

Adam raced off, Gabi and Danny hurried after him, and Amy fell into a slower step beside Chloe. "Are you coming?"

"I have a couple of things I need to do back at the house," she said, because she'd had to abandon cabinet assembly at a rather delicate point so she didn't miss kick-off, and the longer she left it, the more likely it was to collapse. "But I can come by later?"

Amy's face, which had fallen, broke into a smile. "Yes, please. Save me from the boredom of supervising kids while their parents get drunk and gossip."

"You make it sound so fun."

She shrugged. "It's not so bad. But it would be better if you were there."

Amy tossed the words out carelessly, like they weren't supposed to have any effect, but Chloe's heart skipped a beat. How could she say no after that?

Amy nursed a bottle of beer, one shoulder leaning back against the trunk of the large oak tree in her garden, trying her best not to listen to whatever scandal Jenna's mum was trying to drum up at the table of parents beside her.

In truth, nothing truly scandalous ever happened in Corthwaite or its surrounding villages, but that didn't stop everyone from being all up in everyone else's business. Amy had used to thrive on it, on the desire to be in the know, the desire to be popular, but her appetite for gossip had dwindled when Chloe had been thrust into the spotlight of it all, and she despised it even more now. Gabi regaling her with the latest South Lake High tales was different, without any of the malice of Jenna's mum insisting her neighbour was having an affair.

"I'm telling you, he disappears for hours at night. Hours! What else could he possibly be doing?"

Getting away from your annoying voice for a few hours? Amy thought, biting her lip so she didn't say the words aloud.

She knew she didn't fit in with the crowd scattered around her garden. She'd never wanted to be a country girl, had rebelled against it when she'd been in school and escaped the confines of Corthwaite as soon as she'd had the means, soon losing touch with the friends she'd left behind.

When she'd returned, all of the people she'd known had either left or settled down with families, and Amy hadn't fit the mould. Didn't fit this one, either. Wasn't made for idle chit-chat about who was sleeping with who, or gushing that Thomas read a *whole* book unaided last week.

She probably fit better with the kids darting over the grass, adding more stains to football kits that had been pristine earlier in the day, chasing one another with glee and not a single care who saw.

The kids knew it, too. Knew she could be counted on to join in their games where some of the adults wouldn't. She drew the line at pin the tail on the donkey, though—because more often than not, she *was* the donkey—and retreated into the safety of the kitchen. Her mum sat at the kitchen table with her knitting, Sam colouring beside her.

"Not having fun?" Her mum asked when she got a look at Amy's face.

"They're so loud. And the parents are annoying."

"You're the one who invited them," she said, lips twitching, and Amy grimaced, well aware it was her own fault.

But Adam had requested it, and she couldn't say no to her nephew's pleading eyes when he really wanted something.

"I don't know what I was thinking."

"Please. You love them."

Amy glanced out the window, at the infectious joy on their little faces as they raced around. They'd located a tail from somewhere—or made one, it seemed, out of a branch that wasn't going to stay wherever they were going to stick it, but no one had told them that.

"Yeah, I do." She swapped her empty beer bottle for a fresh one out of the fridge, where the good stuff was hidden, and leant against the kitchen counter, watching Sam doing his colouring. "If you want to go outside, I can watch him."

"Oh, no thank you. I did all my time at children's parties when you and Danny were little. I've more than earned myself a break. You brought this on yourself."

"Not like anyone will miss me." Adam was happy with his friends, and Gabi and Danny were wrapped around one another at the barbeque. Her brother never missed an opportunity for grilling duty.

"Did you not invite Chloe?" Her mum asked the question casually enough, but after Gabi's slip the other day, Amy was immediately on edge, fingers tensing around the bottle in her hand.

"She had some stuff to do back at the house, but she said she'd come by later."

"Good." Leanne paused her knitting, dropping the needles onto the table and stretching out her fingers. "You two seem to be getting along well."

Too well, according to you. God, was she going to ask about it? Amy hoped not. She couldn't tell her *mother* how she felt about Chloe.

There wasn't enough beer in the world for her to be able to have that conversation.

Maybe coming into the kitchen hadn't been such a good idea after all.

"Yeah. It's been nice." Amy knew the best way to avoid her mum's probing glare was to avoid the woman entirely. The mob of parents outside would be preferable to being grilled. "I'm gonna head back out. Let me know if you wanna swap."

She was pounced upon as soon as she stepped outside, by Adam asking if she wanted to play duck, duck, goose.

She hoped Chloe would get there soon.

Chloe heard the party before she saw it, the sounds and the smell of smoke carrying over the fields as she walked the familiar path to the farmhouse with Bella trotting along beside her.

The garden was full, parents gathered around two large picnic tables, kids playing football on the grass, Danny flipping burgers on the grill Chloe recognised from her youth, when Amy's dad used to warn anyone else away from touching it with a wave of his tongs.

She spotted Amy by the side of the house talking to Gabi, but was intercepted by Adam before she could get to them.

"Chloe!"

"Hi, kiddo."

"Does Bella like footballs?"

"Bella likes chewing footballs," she said, tightening her hold of the lead when said football was kicked in front of her. "So unless you want it to burst, I'd keep it well away."

He looked disappointed, but was soon distracted by one of his friends yelling, "C'mon, we're doing penalties."

Adam was dragged away, leaving Chloe free to join Amy and Gabi.

"Having fun?" she asked, because Amy looked like she'd rather be anywhere else.

"Oh, she's loving life," Gabi said, patting Amy on the shoulder. "Such a social butterfly. I'm going to go and check Danny hasn't incinerated anything."

She slipped away, and Chloe leaned against the wall beside Amy. Bella sat at her feet, eyes still locked on Adam's football.

"You never used to hate parties. In fact, I distinctly remember you dragging me to many of them." Chloe never would have gone without her, had never wanted to go to any of them in the first place, but Amy had a persuasive smile that Chloe had never been able to deny.

"That was a long time ago. I'm old and boring now. Prefer my own company."

"Ouch. I'll see myself out, shall I?" Chloe half-turned away, and warm fingers wrapped around her wrist, stopping her in her tracks.

"I didn't mean you," Amy said, her voice soft, her grip firm, and she squeezed once before letting go and leaving Chloe's breath stuttering. "But them..." Amy trailed off, gaze flickering over to the table of parents. "They're exhausting."

Chloe turned her head and found more than one of them looking their way, faces interested, whispers starting. Her chest felt tight for an entirely different reason. "And they're staring. At me." *At us* was probably more accurate; gazes flickered from Chloe to Amy and back again. "Why?"

"Because they're nosy gits," Amy said, a bite to her voice. "They haven't seen you around before, that's all. They'll be wondering who you are."

And who *did* they think she was? A friend? Or something more?

"Ignore them," Amy said, glaring toward the few people still looking their way. "They'll get bored soon enough."

Easier said than done, but Chloe vowed to try, turning her back away from the picnic tables and ignoring the prickling feeling at the back of her neck, the sense of being watched from afar.

"Why did you invite them over if you don't like them?"

"Not the kids' fault I don't like their parents," Amy said. "They like spending time together. Team bonding. And it's not that I don't like stuff like this, it's just... Everyone has someone, you know? Danny has Gabi, Adam's got all his friends, my mum hangs out with Sam. Usually the parents all come together, and it's lonely, sometimes. No way to feel it more than being surrounded by people when you're the only one without someone by your side." The words were heavy, and her eyes focused on the bottle in her hand, thumbnail scratching at the label. "Sorry," she said, meeting Chloe's gaze. "That was a lot to drop on you all at once. Blame the beer."

"No, it's okay." It was the first time Amy had really opened up to her, laid herself bare, in as long as Chloe could remember. "I get it. And you're not alone right now. You've got me to keep you company."

"Yeah, you're right. Thanks for coming."

Chloe shrugged. "Beats sitting at home on my own."

"Don't you have stuff to do?"

"Are you trying to get rid of me again?" she asked, narrowing her eyes, and Amy smiled, though it didn't reach her eyes.

"No. But I know I'm taking up a lot of your time. Time you're supposed to be spending somewhere else."

"Hey." Chloe reached out before she could think better of it, curling her fingers around Amy's shoulder and squeezing. And they'd touched before, of course—hell, they'd spent the whole of *Coco* pressed so close together Chloe could hardly stand it—but this was deliberate, the first time Chloe had initiated any meaningful contact between them. She tried to ignore the hitch of Amy's breath when her fingertips brushed against bare skin. "I'm right where I want to be. Okay?"

Amy's eyes locked on hers, blue and dizzying, trapping Chloe in her gaze. Chloe's heart thudded hard in her chest, more affected than it should be by Amy's proximity, by the softness of her skin, by the smell of the perfume she must've put on when she changed out of her football jersey and into this T-shirt.

"Okay," Amy said, and Chloe pretended not to hear the tremble in her voice as she let her arm drop to her side.

"Now, where can I get me one of those?" she said, nodding toward the beer held loosely in Amy's hand.

"The crappy stuff is in that cooler over there." She pointed to a makeshift bar of cans and bottles stacked into coolers.

"And the non-crappy stuff?"

Amy grinned, spinning Chloe around with a gentle hand on her shoulder. "Kitchen. Come on."

She followed Amy inside, away from prying eyes, and flashed a grateful smile when a cold Peroni was placed in her hand. "Thanks. Party too much for Sam?" she asked, nodding at the colouring book left open on the table.

"Yeah. I dunno where they've gone. To see the horses, maybe." A pack of cards also sat in the middle of the table, and Amy twirled it around in her hand, seemingly reluctant to go back outside. "Want a game?"

"Sure."

Chapter 15

THE PARTY WOUND DOWN AT eight, kids dropping like flies as sugar rushes and the high of winning wore off.

"You don't have to," Amy said, when Chloe started to help her clean up. "It's not like you made any of this mess."

She'd made none of it, in fact, had spent most of the afternoon with Amy and various card games, with Sam and her mum joining in when they'd returned from their ride. All in all, Amy had had a much better afternoon than expected, and she knew it was entirely due to Chloe.

"I don't mind. Besides, I think you could use an extra set of hands."

Well, she wasn't wrong about that—Danny was dealing with the cows, and her mum and Gabi were getting the boys into bed—so Amy didn't argue. A stack of dishes sat piled high by the sink, and Chloe washed while Amy dried, the two of them falling into the roles they used to have when they were younger, after a family dinner.

"I'm going to do a sweep of the garden," Amy said when they were done. "Check no one's left any rubbish out there. Last thing we need is foxes roaming the place."

"I'll help." Chloe left Bella beneath the kitchen table to follow Amy out the back door. "It's getting dark already."

"Don't remind me." Amy used the torch on her phone to light up the grass, the new moon offering no source of illumination as she checked around the picnic tables. "I hate winter nights. Do you have any idea how hard it is to check you've got your whole herd of mostly black cows in when it's pitch-black outside?"

"I'm guessing very?"

"It's not fun."

"Oh my God, you still have the treehouse?"

She found Chloe standing at the base of the oak tree, fingers running over the notches of the ladder etched into its trunk. "Uh-huh. The boys use it now, but it's still standing. We can go up, if you want."

"Will we fit?" Chloe asked, frowning at the platform their dads had built for them so many years ago.

"One way to find out."

She let Chloe go first before joining her. It was a squeeze. The treehouse wasn't built for someone of Chloe's stature, and she had to duck her head to she didn't hit it on the roof.

"Looks different in here," Chloe said, eyes tracing the walls, slathered with Adam and Sam's drawings. "And it's a lot smaller than I remember."

"Because we're bigger."

"I don't think I've grown much since I was seventeen. And you've definitely not."

"Rude," Amy said, trying not to think about the last time she and Chloe had been in this treehouse. That the reason it had felt bigger then was because they hadn't been trying to keep a careful few inches of space between them—had been doing the opposite, in fact, their legs tangled together and their kisses frantic.

One of their last kisses, Amy realised, at the end of the summer before everything had changed.

Maybe coming up hadn't been such a good idea. The heat was stifling, humid in a way that made it hard for her to draw breath.

"You all right?" Chloe asked, frowning.

Amy nodded. "Yeah. Warm." She plucked at the neckline of her shirt, peeling it away from sticky skin.

"This window still open?" Chloe asked, already fiddling with the catch. It did, but the slight breeze it afforded did little to cool the heat on Amy's cheeks. "One of the downsides of living in the city is you don't get a view like this."

Amy followed her gaze, the cloudless sky affording them a gorgeous view of the stars above. "We used to lie here and make up constellations," she said, glad her voice was steady. "You remember any?"

"Not sure." Chloe shifted to lie on her back, propping her head on her hands as she stared at the sky, and Amy couldn't stop staring at Chloe. Shadows played across her face, her eyes bright in the muted darkness. Amy had never ached to have a camera in her hand more.

"There was a dragon, wasn't there?" Chloe looked over at her when Amy didn't answer, seemingly unperturbed to find Amy's gaze on her face. "You can't see them from there."

Amy swallowed, moving to lie beside her, their arms pressing together. "We had a pan. And a square." She could vaguely see the shapes if she squinted, her eyes starting to adjust to the dark.

"And the tennis racquet."

"That looked nothing like a tennis racquet."

"Sure it did." Chloe turned her head, and Amy made the mistake of facing her, Chloe's breath hot on her lips. "You're just blind."

"Says the woman wearing contact lenses."

"Exactly. I have perfect vision right now." She was smiling, and Amy's gaze flickered to her mouth, wondering what that smile would feel like against her lips.

She felt intoxicated, knew it had nothing to do with the three beers she'd put away earlier and everything to do with Chloe a scant few inches away, and with the hazy memory of kisses shared within these walls.

Want curled in her gut, had her reaching out to trace a finger along the length of Chloe's collarbone, over the mark hidden beneath her shirt. Chloe's breath rushed out when Amy made contact.

"You have a tattoo," she said, her voice a whisper, afraid if she spoke too loud the moment would shatter. "Of the stars."

"It...it's my mum's star sign," Chloe said, whispering too, eyes locked on Amy's.

"Can I see it?"

"O-okay."

Amy tugged at the collar of her shirt, and Chloe sucked in a harsh breath when Amy retraced her path, this time brushing her fingertip over soft skin. "It's beautiful." *You're beautiful*, she wanted to say, and bit her bottom lip to fight the temptation. When Chloe's gaze dropped to her mouth, she nearly whimpered.

She could curl her fingers in Chloe's shirt and drag her in, could press close and kiss her senseless, could give in to the desire pulsing through her veins that wanted to draw Chloe to her and never let her go.

But she hesitated, because she wasn't supposed to be doing this, was supposed to be keeping her distance, supposed to be Chloe's *friend*, supposed to not be messing this up.

Chloe was frozen beside her, eyes wide and dark and staring into Amy's, her breathing laboured and her cheeks flushed, and Amy could feel Chloe's heart pounding beneath the palm of her hand.

Did she feel it, too? The pull, the want, the draw? Did it drive her crazy, too?

Or had Amy read this all wrong?

"I—"

She didn't get a chance to decide what she was going to do, as Gabi's voice suddenly boomed across the garden.

"Amy, are you out here? You haven't seen my phone, have you?"

It shattered the moment like a hammer hitting glass. Chloe jerked away from her so hard and so fast she banged her head on the treehouse roof.

"Haven't seen it!" Amy yelled, hands reaching for a cursing Chloe. "Are you okay?"

"I'm fine." But her voice shook, and she wouldn't turn around, kept her back to Amy as she shuffled toward the ladder. "I should go."

"Chloe, wait—"

She was already gone.

Amy swore and took off after her. Chloe was halfway to the house by the time Amy's feet touched solid ground.

"Chloe, slow down, Jesus Christ."

Amy caught up with her before she reached the back door, fingers wrapping around her wrist and tugging her to a halt. "I…I'm sorry, I didn't mean to—oh, shit, Chloe, your head."

"What about my head?"

"It's bleeding." Not much, a thin line beading beneath her hairline, but enough to raise Amy's concern. She reached out a hand, and Chloe flinched away like she'd been burned. "Let me clean you up."

"I'm fine," she said again, not sounding remotely like it, and Amy blinked away the hot sting of tears because this was what she'd wanted to avoid. She'd gone and ruined things again, all because she couldn't control herself.

"Please," she said, voice edged with desperation. "You could have a concussion. Let me get you home safe."

Chloe's jaw clenched, and Amy didn't know if the pain in her eyes was from the head wound or Amy's betrayal. "I don't need your help."

"I'm not letting you walk home in the dark like this."

Chloe stared at her, and Amy stared right back, each as stubborn as the other. She couldn't leave things like this, not with so much left unsaid, not with so much pain and anger between them. She didn't know if she could fix it, but she could *try*. What she couldn't do was let Chloe walk away now, because what if she didn't come back?

"Fine," Chloe finally said, her teeth gritted.

Amy breathed out a sigh of relief. She still had a chance to salvage things.

She just hoped there was something left *to* salvage.

Chloe's head throbbed with every step she took.

The walk was five minutes, but it felt like an eternity with pain lancing through her skull. The silence between them was oppressive and suffocating, but Chloe wasn't going to be the one to break it.

Didn't have the faintest idea what she would say.

Her head would be a mess even if she hadn't nearly knocked herself out, thanks to Amy's hands on her skin, Amy's fingers bunched in her shirt, Amy's gaze on her lips.

Stupid, stupid, stupid, she thought, anger propelling her toward the house, toward the safety it offered, and the promise of distance from the woman hurrying to keep up with her long strides. What had she been thinking, crawling with Amy into a place packed so densely with memories that it was hard for her to breathe?

She certainly hadn't been expecting to make *more* memories, for Amy to press close in the dark, like they were teenagers all over again. She was *falling* over all over again, for a woman she knew she could never have, and that wasn't supposed to be what she was here for.

She was here for the house, didn't need any distractions—had already *let* herself get distracted, Amy drawing her in with magnetic force. She'd been an idiot to think they could ever be friends.

It didn't *work*, not then and not now. Not if they couldn't be trusted to be alone together. It had been building, Chloe realised, casting her mind back over the last few months.

The time spent together, the walls falling, the casual touches lingering a beat longer than they should. Building to this, to a near-kiss in the dark—a kiss Chloe could almost feel, the ghost of Amy's breath on her lips. A kiss Chloe still *wanted*, and wasn't that the most pathetic part of it all? Still feeling this way for the girl who had shattered her heart all those years ago?

The house loomed on the horizon, and she breathed out a sigh, practically sprinting those final few steps to the door, dragging a bewildered Bella along behind her.

"There," she said, out of breath and unable to look Amy in the eye. "I'm home. Happy?"

The twist of Amy's mouth suggested she was anything but. "Will you at least let me patch you up?" she asked again. Standing on the step below Chloe, hunched in on herself, she looked small and frail, and like the girl Chloe had left behind. "Please. And then I'll go, and you won't ever have to see me again if you don't want to. I just...I need to know you're okay."

How could I be okay after that? Chloe wanted to ask, wanted to scream. *Where was this concern when you tossed me aside? Why are you* doing *this to me?*

But her head was pounding, exhaustion settling deep into her bones, and she didn't have the strength to argue. "Five minutes," she said, watching the relief watch over Amy's face. "And then I want you gone."

Relief turned to a wince, and Chloe turned her back, slipping into the house and grabbing the first aid kit she kept in case of emergencies. She set it on the dining room table she was going to chop up next weekend, and perched herself on one of the chairs, staring resolutely at a spot on the wall as Amy stood in front of her.

"Things have come along since I was last here," Amy said, her touch gentle as she gripped Chloe's chin and tilted her head toward the light. "It's looking good."

It did. The new floor was laid, the walls brightened with a fresh coat of paint, and most of the cabinets had been secured to the walls, awaiting the worktops to be placed on top of them. But Chloe wasn't interested in small talk, wasn't interested in anything other than getting Amy *out*, because she was finding it hard to breathe, trapped by the fingers around her jaw, by ocean-blue eyes.

"It's not deep," Amy said, apparently needing to fill the silence, and Chloe hissed as she pressed an antiseptic wipe against the cut. "Won't need stitches." She covered it with a plaster, and Chloe winced as she ran her fingertip around the edge. "You're going to have a wicked bruise tomorrow. Probably a wicked headache, too."

"I'll be fine," she said—aware she was repeating it like a mantra, aware she didn't mean it at all—craning her neck and leaning away from Amy's touch.

Amy's hands fell to her sides, and she bit at the inside of her cheek, looking like she wanted to cry. "Chloe, I'm so sorry. I didn't mean to...to mess things up between us."

Chloe scoffed. "Again, you mean?" She couldn't hide the bite to her voice, and Amy flinched. "I don't understand you. Why did you do that?"

"Because I wanted to," Amy said, her voice soft. "I don't want you to think I was messing with your head again. I know how it looks, especially when I was telling you I was lonely earlier, but I...that's not what I was doing. I got caught up in the moment, in the past, and I'm sorry."

She closed her eyes, pressing the heels of her palms into them like she could push it all away. "God, I'm sorry for all of it. You are my biggest regret, and now I've gone and fucked it all up again when I promised myself I wouldn't."

"You wanted to kiss me," Chloe repeated, the words coming out slowly.

"Yes. I've wanted to kiss you for a long time. But I know I don't deserve that. Don't deserve you."

"I don't...what am I supposed to do with this?"

Amy's hands wrapped around one of her own, warm and gentle. "You don't have to do anything with it. But you deserve the truth. And I meant what I said before—you don't ever have to see me again if you don't want to."

And she *did* mean it, Chloe could see it in her eyes. Could see the pain it would cause her, but knew she'd do it anyway, if that was what Chloe wanted. And maybe that would be the easiest thing for them both.

A clean break, mutually decided.

A stark contrast to the last time, to Amy stripping away Chloe's choice and deciding for her. This time, she was leaving it in Chloe's hands, and in the end, that was why she hesitated.

Because Amy had changed, in all of the ways that mattered, and it was no clearer to Chloe than now, after she'd laid it all on the line, with her hands still shaking around Chloe's, waiting to see what she wanted.

"I don't think we work as friends," she said, and Amy jerked away like she'd been slapped, the small noise of surprise she made like a knife through Chloe's heart.

"I understand," Amy said, reeling away, and this time, it was Chloe who had to reach out and stop her, climbing to her feet and grabbing Amy's arm.

"Hey, come here." She stood too quickly, head spinning, body swaying, and she had to steady herself by settling her other hand on Amy's shoulder.

Amy manoeuvred her carefully backwards and propped her against the table, but Chloe didn't loosen her grip, didn't want Amy slipping away before she could stop her.

Amy frowned, concern in her eyes, and a tear slipped down her cheek. Chloe brushed it away.

"Let me go, Chloe."

But Chloe curled her fingers in the collar of Amy's shirt, swiping at another tear as it fell. "That came out wrong. I just bashed my head, remember. My brain is a little scrambled right now."

"Then what did you mean?" Amy asked, voice low, her breath on Chloe's lips, skin soft where the backs of Chloe's fingers pressed against it.

"We don't work as friends, do we? Not just friends. Not then and not now." Chloe couldn't pretend this night never happened, knew she wouldn't be able to see Amy again without wanting to kiss her, wanting to give in to the tension thrumming beneath the surface of her skin, craving Amy's touch. "I try not to make a habit of kissing my friends." A hand settled at her waist, and Amy's fingers slid beneath the hem of her shirt. Chloe sucked in her breath. "But kissing you is a habit I wouldn't mind starting."

"Oh yeah?"

"Yeah." She cupped a hand around Amy's jaw, heart beating like a jackhammer—she was surprised Amy couldn't see it, tattooing against her ribcage. "If that's something you want, too."

Amy made an undignified noise in the back of her throat and leaned on her toes to brush her lips against Chloe's before she had the chance to tease her about it. Amy's skin was soft, but her lips were softer, and Chloe sighed at the feeling, parting her own lips for Amy's searching tongue.

There were no fireworks. She didn't feel her world shattering and rebuilding, didn't feel herself splitting apart at the seams. It wasn't an endless, perfect, moment, but God, none of that mattered, because Amy's mouth was on hers, and it felt like coming home.

Chloe could hear her heart thundering loud in her ears, taste the beer on Amy's tongue, sliding against hers, feel the electricity buzzing through her fingertips wherever they touched. Amy's fingers curled into her the skin of her waist, tugging her closer, their hips slotting together, and Chloe groaned at the feeling.

"What are we doing?" Amy asked when they parted, breaths coming quick and fast against Chloe's cheek.

"I don't know. But I want to do it again." She slid her fingers into Amy's hair, kissed her until she was breathless, until her head wasn't the only thing making her dizzy.

Would she regret this in the morning? Would she regret re-learning the way Amy's mouth moved against hers, the taste of her, the heat of her, pressed so close no space existed between them?

Probably.

But when Amy's teeth nibbled her bottom lip, all rational thought flew from her mind.

"I mean it, Chloe." Amy flattened one hand against Chloe's sternum, and if she noticed the frantic beat of her heart, she didn't say a word.

"So did I." Chloe tucked a strand of hair behind Amy's ear, fingers brushing against the slope of her cheek. "I don't want to stop seeing you. But I also don't know how I'm going to keep seeing you without kissing you senseless, so…"

"So…friends with benefits?" Amy suggested, and Chloe swallowed.

"Sure. If you want that. It's not like I can offer you more." She kept her voice light, though the words cut deep. Her time in Corthwaite was running out, the sand in the timer already more than halfway gone, and she knew after tonight leaving would be much harder.

"N-no, that's…okay. Casual. I can do casual."

Could Chloe, though? With Amy? Without falling head over heels?

Probably not.

Was she going to anyway?

Yes.

"Okay." Chloe pulled Amy to her again, slotting a thigh between her legs, revelling in the taste of Amy's moan on her tongue.

"I should go," Amy said, when they next paused for breath, hand splayed across the small of Chloe's back.

"Or you could stay," Chloe suggested, lips brushing the shell of Amy's ear.

"I shouldn't."

"Why not?"

"Because you told me your brain is scrambled, and I don't want to do anything you might regret in the morning."

A fair point, Chloe knew. She was no stranger to the light of morning bringing with it a sense of clarity, a sense of *what the hell were you thinking*? But time and space away from her would have Chloe overthinking and second-guessing, when she could have Amy in her arms instead.

"What if I am concussed?"

Amy's eyes twinkled as she shook her head. "Funny, you seemed fine before."

"That was then. You know, I'm feeling hot under the collar now. Maybe I'm getting a fever. You want to risk leaving me alone?"

"You are impossible." But she let Chloe pull her into another kiss, sighing into her mouth. "Fine, I'll stay."

Chapter 16

AMY BRUSHED HER TEETH IN a bathroom that hadn't changed since the last time she'd slept over in the Roberts house. The same purple paint covered the walls, the same white tiles with little yellow ducks on them were set around the bath.

The only thing that was different was her—the hum of anticipation beneath her skin, the disbelief that she'd somehow managed to turn this night around.

She still couldn't believe her luck, was half-convinced if she blinked one time too many, she'd wake in her own bed with Chloe refusing to talk to her and their relationship fractured beyond repair.

Casual, Amy thought, slipping into the clothes Chloe had offered her: soft, worn sweatpants and a T-shirt that fell to mid-thigh on her. *Casual* in a way wearing Chloe's clothes didn't feel. There was something exceedingly intimate about being surrounded by the scent of someone else's laundry detergent.

Spending the night together didn't scream casual either, but Amy didn't have the heart to deny either Chloe, with her pleading eyes and persuasive kisses, or the pull in her own stomach telling her to keep Chloe close and not let her go.

Which was the exact opposite of what they should be doing, and Amy scolded herself as she padded down the hall to Chloe's bedroom. Chloe was right—she couldn't offer Amy more, and Amy wasn't greedy enough to ask.

If this was all Chloe could give, then she would take it with open arms, knowing it was more than she deserved, more than she'd ever dreamed of having.

She'd take these snippets of Chloe's time, stolen moments between her life in London and her time on the renovation, and she'd deal with the fallout when she was gone.

Chloe was perched on the end of the bed when Amy pushed open the door, clad in a thin shirt and a pair of boxers, and Amy tried not to stare at the expanse of skin on display.

"Thanks for the clothes," she said, draping her own over the back of Chloe's desk chair and patting Bella, who was lying on a fluffy blanket in the middle of the floor, on her way to Chloe's bed. "You were lying when you said you didn't have any pyjamas."

"I don't." Chloe reached for Amy's hips, pulling her in until she had a knee on either side of Chloe's thighs, sinking into the mattress. "They're comfy pants."

"Otherwise known as pyjamas."

The neckline of Chloe's shirt was low, and Amy rubbed a thumb against her collarbone, against the smattering of stars that made up the sign she and Chloe's mum shared.

"I'm starting to think," Chloe said, smirking, her hands settling on Amy's back, burning through her shirt, "you have a thing for tattoos."

Amy felt her cheeks warm, Chloe's low chuckle making her heart race.

"It's okay," Chloe said, wrapping her fingers around Amy's wrist, lifting it back toward her chest. "I have more, you know."

"Where?"

Chloe's smirk pressed against Amy's skin, lips dragging over the column of Amy's throat. "I think it would be more fun if I left you to find them." She nipped at Amy's pulse point, and Amy fisted her hands in Chloe's hair. Breath rushed out of her, and she tugged Chloe to meet her lips in an open-mouthed kiss.

All the times they'd kissed before, Chloe had been timid, hesitant, like she was terrified of Amy wrenching herself away at a moment's notice, but this new-found confidence was going to be the death of her.

A hand slipped beneath Amy's shirt, blazing heat up her ribcage as Chloe's tongue flickered against her own, and Amy's hips shifted in Chloe's lap, a desperate need to be *closer* making her clutch at the back of Chloe's neck.

"We should…we should stop," Amy said, trying not to arch into Chloe's hand as questing fingers brushed against the side of her breast.

"Why?" Chloe's breath warmed the shell of her ear, and Amy swallowed a curse.

Definitely going to be the death of her.

"I'm not going to regret this," Chloe said, pulling back, eyes dark and hazy with the same desire Amy felt swirling in her gut.

"But what if you do?" Amy couldn't handle it, if she woke beside Chloe and got kicked to the curb with the memory of lips still lingering on her skin. "And your head." She brushed her fingers against the mark, already purpling around the edges of the plaster. "You might not be thinking clearly. What if I'm taking advantage of you right now?"

"You can take advantage of me however you please," Chloe said, and Amy smacked her on the shoulder. "Fine." Her hands slid to Amy's hips, lifting her off her lap and pressing her onto the bed.

Amy swallowed around the lump in her throat, the display of raw strength making her want to take back everything she'd said. She slid under the sheets, back pressed to the wall, and faced Chloe in the dark, one arm slung low over her waist.

She yawned, the excitement of the day catching up with her.

Chloe chuckled and cupped her cheek. "Tired?"

"Sorry. Long day." Long, emotionally-charged day, though Amy didn't know if she was ready for it to end, didn't know if things would look different in the morning.

"Go to sleep," Chloe said, before kissing her, soft and slow like she was trying to memorise the feeling. When she rolled over, Amy pressed against her back, keeping her arm wrapped around her waist.

Casual, Amy thought, trying to drill it into her head. *Casual*, because in a few months, she'd be gone, and Amy knew if she let herself get too attached, Chloe would be taking a piece of her heart along with her.

You're fooling yourself if you think you're getting out of this unscathed, a voice whispered in the back of her head, a voice Amy tried to push deep, tried to drown out with the sound of Chloe's deepening breaths.

Fooling herself, maybe. Walking a path of destruction, maybe. But if it meant a night of this, of Chloe's shampoo in her nose, of Chloe's body warm beside her, Amy would gladly take the consequences.

They'd be worth it all.

"Chloe."

Chloe frowned, caught in the state between sleeping and waking. A hand was on her shoulder, warm and firm, a soft voice in her ear.

"Chloe, wake up."

She blinked open her eyes, and found Amy crouched beside the bed, sleep rumpled and wearing yesterday's clothes. The previous night came rushing back, leaving her breathless, and she rubbed sleep out of her eyes.

"What time is it?"

"Six," Amy said. No wonder no light was coming through the curtains. "Sorry, I know it's early, but I didn't want you to wake up alone."

"Where're you going?"

"I need to get back. Before anyone notices I'm gone. Not that I'm trying to hide this," she added hastily, biting at her bottom lip. "But my family is nosy, and I figure you probably don't want them all up in your business. Our business, I guess."

"Makes sense."

"You could come by, later. If you wanted. We could take the horses out, or something. It'd be nice to see you before you go."

"Yeah. Okay."

Amy's smile was bright in the darkness, and she leaned forward to press a soft kiss to Chloe's lips. "I'll see you later."

Chloe watched her go, and knew she wouldn't be getting back to sleep, not with the smell of Amy lingering on the pillow, on her sheets. Not with the memory of her kiss and the feeling of her hands on Chloe's skin so fresh in her memory.

She rolled onto her back to stare at the ceiling and groaned when Bella took that as an invitation to join her, a bony elbow jabbing into her ribs as the dog lay flat on top of her, cold nose touching her chin.

She ran her fingers over Bella's fur, wondering if last night had been a dream. If she didn't talk about it, she was going to go insane. She reached blindly for her phone and lifted it to her ear, forgetting all about the time.

"You'd better be fucking dying," Naomi groaned.

"What?"

"Chloe, it's half six. On a Sunday. So, I repeat: you'd better be fucking dying, because what other possible reason would you have for disturbing my beauty sleep at such an ungodly hour?"

"Amy and I kissed."

Silence.

Chloe lifted the phone away from her ear, wondering if she'd accidentally hung up the phone. "Naomi? You there?"

"You…kissed Amy? At half six in the morning?" She spoke slowly, and Chloe could imagine the frown of confusion on her face, half-asleep brain not fully functioning.

"No, we kissed last night, but she stayed over so I couldn't call—"

"She stayed over? Christ, Chloe, you don't waste much time, do you? Did you at least buy her dinner first?"

"Nothing happened. Not that it's any of your business—"

"Um, you made it my business when you called me at the ass crack of dawn—"

"Do you want to know what did happen or not?" Chloe heard sheets ruffling on the other end of the line, Naomi getting herself situated more comfortably.

"I'm listening."

Chloe told her everything, starting with the treehouse and ending with the morning after, knowing Naomi was hooked because she didn't interrupt once.

"Remember when you told me you didn't like her?" Naomi asked, and Chloe imagined the arched brow, the "I told you so." smug smirk. "Remember that? Your absolute insistence that you were just friends, and nothing more? You big fat liar."

"But we are just friends—"

"Oh, please. You are falling in love with her."

"I am not," Chloe said, but the sputtering gave her away. "That's not… that's not what this is."

"What is it, then?"

"You know. Casual fun."

"Casual," Naomi said, the word dripping with scepticism. "You."

"I can do casual," she protested. "I have before."

"Not with women you're in love with."

152

"I am not—"

"Okay, fine, if you're going to be so insistent about it—not with women you *have been* in love with."

Chloe couldn't argue with that one.

"Look, I just…I don't want her to break your heart again, Chloe. That's all."

"I know. I don't want that, either." Chloe scratched beneath Bella's chin, scrunching her nose when Bella decided to thank her by licking her cheek. "Do you think it's a bad idea?"

"Sleeping with her?"

"Yeah."

"I think it's an exceptionally bad idea," Naomi said, and Chloe winced. "But I'm also not stupid enough to think you're going to listen to me if I tell you not to. Be careful, yeah? Try not to fall in love with her."

"I thought you already think I am?"

"Oh, I do. But seeing as you keep insisting you aren't…" She trailed off, sheets rustling again, and Chloe imagined a shrug. "What're you doing on the house today?"

"Finishing the kitchen." It'd be the first room she'd properly finished, and one step closer to the end—an end she was no longer looking forward to. "How was your meeting on Friday? You get the bid?"

"Of course I got the bid. My presentation was flawless."

"Yeah, I know. You made me watch it three thousand times."

"That is an exaggeration. I reckon it was only two thousand." Naomi yawned, and Chloe took pity on her.

"I'll let you get back to sleep."

"And if I can't, you'll get to deal with my grumpy, sleep-deprived ass at the zoo tomorrow."

"I'll bring you coffee," Chloe promised. "Are the girls looking forward to it?"

"They haven't talked about anything else since I told them. 'Chloe this' and 'Chloe that'. Anyone would think you were their favourite auntie."

"The novelty will wear off once I'm around every weekend again."

"It'd better," Naomi grumbled, but Chloe knew she didn't mean it.

They hung up with the promise of seeing each other bright and early in the morning, and Chloe dragged herself into the shower, hoping the rush of hot water would re-energise her.

She felt less sluggish afterwards, munching on a piece of toast as she examined the quartz laminate countertops on her agenda for today. They weren't the fanciest option she could have gone for, but she liked the shiny, black finish, and the price and ease of installation were an added bonus.

After breakfast, she propped the first of the worktops onto the cabinets, marking out where she needed to cut with a pencil on the wooden underside and then transferring it to her work bench.

Bella scarpered when she grabbed the saw—she hated the noise. Chloe slipped on her safety glasses and gloves before shearing the worktop to size. She never felt more at home than when she had a tool in her hand.

Cutting the holes out for the sink and the oven hob required more finesse, and Chloe made sure she'd finished a cup of coffee before tackling it. She measured the dimensions carefully, double- and triple-checking them before she carved them out with her jigsaw, breathing a sigh of relief when both sink and hob slotted perfectly into the gaps.

Once the last of the counters was safely drilled and screwed into place, Chloe stood back and admired her handiwork. Some of the paint had been chipped—a hazard of doing the walls first—but that was an easy fix, one she knew she could have done before she went to meet Amy later.

Her first room, almost done. The bathrooms were her only major projects left. A handful of weekends, if she stretched it—certainly not enough to last into the New Year. Four months, at most, to get the place ready to sell.

Four months, to spend as much time with Amy as she dared.

Chapter 17

"I can't believe you left me." A pout was on Chloe's lips, an accusation in her voice as she followed Amy to her door. "What if I fell?"

"I had faith in you." She wouldn't have told Chloe—aboard Storm, and looking much more at ease than her first time out—to race her and Regina back to the stables if she didn't think she could handle it.

Chloe didn't seem to share the sentiment.

"What if I'd died?"

"I think that's a bit dramatic." Amy pushed her door open, steering Chloe inside ahead of her with her hands on her hips, pressing her back against it to shut it behind them. "You were fine."

"I might not have been," Chloe said, grumbling as Amy leaned close, breath ghosting over her lips.

"How about I make it up to you, hm?" Amy asked, and Chloe answered her with a kiss.

She'd feared that, once back at the farm and away from the warm presence of Chloe pressed close to her side, doubts would start to set in. That things would be awkward when they met up again—that Chloe might have changed her mind.

She was pleasantly surprised to find that wasn't the case. Chloe's tongue licked into her mouth, and Amy melted into her as Chloe's fingers threaded through her hair.

"Forgive me yet?" Amy asked, lips pressed to the hollow of Chloe's throat, Chloe's fingers tugging when she nipped her skin.

"I'm not sure. I think I could use more persuasion."

Amy laughed, using her grip on Chloe's hips to pull her backwards, situating her on the couch and straddling her hips. Chloe's hands slid into the back pockets of her jeans, dragging her closer, mouth a hot slide against Amy's throat, too much and not enough contact at the same time.

She was debating wrapping a fist in Chloe's shirt and dragging her up the ladder and into her bed when she heard the faint sound of voices filtering in through her open kitchen window, and both of them froze in place.

"Come on, Bella," Adam said, the jingling of the lead sounding alarmingly close to Amy's front door. "I think they're in here."

Amy had the presence of mind to scramble off of Chloe's lap, because she hadn't thought to latch the door—never did, in truth, never had any need to. She righted herself just in time for it to crash open. Bella led Adam inside.

"Tía Amy! There you are. Can we go to the King's Head to watch the football game? Please?"

"I, uh…" She ran a hand through her hair, her heart pounding, and when Gabi joined Adam at the door, she wanted the floor to swallow her whole.

Adam might be oblivious to what he'd walked in on, but Gabi, judging from the look on her face as her eyes flickered from Amy to Chloe and back again, was not.

So much for keeping her family out of it.

"I don't know, buddy. What did your mum say?"

"That he had to ask you," Gabi said, curling a hand around Adam's shoulder and pressing her lips together to hide her obvious amusement.

"So can we?" Adam asked, hopeful eyes peering at her.

"O-okay. Kick-off's at half four, right? Wanna go and put your shirt on?"

"Okay! Can I take Bella with me?" He turned to Chloe, seeming to take his role of Bella's guardian for the afternoon very seriously indeed.

"Sure, buddy."

He scampered off, but Gabi lingered, no longer trying to hide her grin.

"Can I help you?" Amy asked, mortification and annoyance blending together as Gabi's grin widened.

156

"No. But you, uh, might want to check your own shirt before you go. It's a little…rumpled."

Amy groaned, passing a hand over her face. "Please leave."

Thankfully, Gabi did, cackling as she went.

Amy dropped onto the couch beside Chloe, her cheeks blazing. "I am so sorry."

"So much for no one knowing, huh?" Chloe didn't sound mad, but Amy didn't want to look her in the eye, to see her expression, didn't want Chloe to decide this wasn't for her, after all, other people knowing about them. "Hey." She ran a hand over Amy's arm. "It's okay. But maybe we should lock the door next time."

Next time. So she hadn't changed her mind. Relief snatched at Amy's breath, and oh, she was so screwed.

"You're probably right." She turned her head and found Chloe watching her, lips quirked, showing none of the embarrassment Amy knew was splashed across her own face. "You can come to the pub with us, if you want."

"Won't Adam mind?"

"Are you kidding? He loves you. He'll be delighted."

"Who are you playing?"

"Liverpool."

Chloe grinned. "Oh, I'll come. See the first half, at least. Watch you get your ass handed to you."

"Oh, Jesus Christ." Amy's head thudded onto the table as the second goal flew into the net.

Chloe chuckled and gave her a pat on the back. "There, there. You've still got"—she squinted at the time on the clock—"sixty minutes to turn it around."

"Oh, hush, you!" Amy turned to her with a glare. "You're enjoying this."

"Consider this payback, for abandoning me earlier."

"Am I ever going to hear the last of this?"

"Hmm, I'm not sure. I don't think you've suitably made up for it."

A hand slid onto her thigh under the table, and Chloe jumped, throwing a hasty glance over at Adam, but his attention was fixed on the screen.

"Not my fault you have to leave early," Amy said, leaning close to murmur the words into her ear. "I had plans."

"Oh yeah?" Chloe's heart beat faster, fingers trembling as they wrapped around her glass of coke. "What plans were those?"

"None suitable for this setting." Amy's breath was hot against Chloe's neck, hand teasing along the seam of her jeans.

Chloe squeezed her legs together, skin feeling like it was on fire. She could still remember the solid weight of Amy in her lap, the rock of her hips as Chloe's fingers had dug into her ass, the heat of her mouth, sliding against Chloe's own.

It was going to be a long week.

"Do you think we'll win, Tía Amy?" Adam asked, turning to them, teeth worrying at his bottom lip.

Amy leant away, hand falling from Chloe's thigh. "I dunno, buddy. I hope so."

Another shot thudded against the Tottenham goal, and Amy swore under her breath. "I need another drink."

"I'll go and get you one," Chloe said, because she could use the space. Her shirt felt tight against her neck, Amy's hand still imprinted on her skin. "Peroni?"

"Yes, please."

"Is Adam allowed another milkshake?"

"Why not? We're not the ones who will have to deal with his sugar crash."

Adam beamed, and Chloe chuckled, crossing over to the bar and leaving Bella in Adam's more than capable hands.

"Refills?" Mark asked when she approached.

"Except for the coke." The more she drank, the more likely she was to need to stop to pee at a service station on the drive home, and she liked to limit those as much as possible.

Mark was mixing the milkshake when a woman leant on the bar next to her. "Chloe, right?" she asked, and Chloe blinked. She didn't recognise the woman, a brunette maybe a couple of years younger than her and Amy.

"Uh, yeah."

"Louise." She held out a hand, and Chloe shook it warily. "I hope you don't mind me coming over here. My mum lives opposite Eleanor Peterson, and she mentioned that a couple of weeks ago you did a few odd jobs for her?"

"Oh. Yeah, I did." Chloe flashed Mark a grateful smile as he set the drinks in front of her, fishing a note out of her wallet and handing it over. "Keep the change."

"Thanks, Chloe."

"Well, my mum's gutters were overflowing the last time we had rain," Louise continued. "And with autumn coming up it's going to get worse, so I was wondering if you'd be able to take a look at them for her? She's too old to go up there, and I wouldn't have the faintest idea what I'm doing. We'd pay you, of course, for your time."

"Uh, yeah, sure, I can take a look." Amy was going to love this. Chloe could see her watching the two of them over Louise's shoulder, brows knit. "I won't be back around until next weekend, but I can come over then if you like?"

"That would be wonderful."

"Here." Chloe fished a business card out of her wallet. "Give me a call, and we can set up a time."

"Oh, thank you so much."

She tucked the card into her pocket, and Chloe grabbed the drinks and made her way back to their table.

"What was that about?" Amy asked, once Chloe had squeezed into the booth beside her.

"She wanted my assistance with her mother's overflowing gutters."

"Oh, wow." Glee flashed across Amy's face. "Word is getting around. I told you you'd soon become the village handywoman."

In truth, Chloe didn't mind lending a hand. Not when it wouldn't take long, and not if it made someone's life easier.

"You have to go?" Amy asked, when the half-time whistle blew.

"Probably should. Otherwise it'll be late by the time I get back."

"I don't know how you do it. How are you not exhausted all of the time?"

"Who says I'm not?" Chloe asked, her smile tired. "It's not so bad. I'm used to it by now."

159

Amy didn't look convinced. "I'll walk you out," she said, following Chloe out of the booth. "You all right here for a sec, Adam?"

"Can I go see Mark?"

"Of course you can."

He bent to say goodbye to Bella. Amy waited for him to cross to the bar, scramble onto one of the bar stools, and start chattering away at high speed before she took Chloe's hand and pulled her toward the door.

Outside, in the quiet of the car park, she pressed Chloe against the door of her van, one hand in her hair and the other on the curve of her hip, and kissed her until she was breathless and dizzy, knees weak as Amy's tongue slid against her own.

"Fuck."

Amy chuckled, low and dark, and Chloe's stomach swooped. "I'll see you next weekend. Get home safe." She kissed Chloe one last time before waltzing back into the pub like she didn't have a care in the world.

It took Chloe a moment to remember how her limbs functioned, shaking her head to clear it before opening the van door and letting Bella hop inside.

It was the first time she didn't want to leave, feeling the pull back to Corthwaite as soon as she'd driven out of the village centre.

Gabi's gaze burned a hole into the side of Amy's face throughout dinner—later than normal, thanks to her and Adam's impromptu journey to the King's Head—and she resolutely kept her own eyes focused on her plate, as though her Yorkshire pudding contained the meaning of life itself.

She knew she wouldn't get away with it forever. Gabi was relentless when she wanted to know something, and this? Walking in on Amy and Chloe?

Oh, she'd think that was the juiciest thing she'd ever seen.

Sure enough, Gabi cornered her as soon as dinner was over.

"I'll help you with the milking, Amy," she said, blinking innocently from across the table. "Seeing as it's late and all. An extra pair of hands won't hurt."

If anyone else thought it was suspicious, they didn't say, and Amy dragged her feet on the way to the front door, prompting Gabi to grip her elbow and propel her through it.

"Spill."

"Spill what?" Amy asked, because Gabi wasn't the only one who could play innocent.

"You. Chloe. Couch. Go."

"I don't know what you're talking about." She pushed open the barn door, where the cows were already separated into groups of twelve. "Come on, girls." She whistled, opening the gate on the first pen, and the cows trotted along the familiar route to the milking parlour.

"Amy."

"Gabi."

"I need details."

"You don't need anything."

She could ignore Gabi for a while as they closed each cow into a single pen in the parlour. The animals happily chewed hay as Amy and Gabi split up to attach the pumps to each of their teats.

But once they were all hooked up, milk pumping into the tank, there was no escape.

"What happened to just friends?" Gabi asked, pushing Amy in the chest with each word.

She sighed. "Things got…complicated."

"Didn't look complicated. Looked simple to me."

Simple didn't come close to describing the feelings swirling through Amy whenever she thought of Chloe, from the memory of trapping her against the door of her van, to the scent of her perfume clinging to Amy's clothes.

"So, what changed?"

"Nothing, really." Nothing in the sense that mattered. "Couldn't keep my distance anymore."

"You know, I wondered why you were so happy this morning. Now it makes perfect sense. Oh! We can go on double dates. You two and me and Danny."

"I can think of nothing worse," Amy said, nose wrinkling. "And that's not what we're doing."

"Dating?"

"Yeah. Or anything…emotional. Just physical."

"Hm." Gabi's eyes narrowed, arms folding across her chest, and Amy raised her eyebrows.

"What?"

"Aren't things already emotional? You like her."

Amy lowered her gaze to her wellie, scuffing it along the stone floor. "She doesn't need to know that."

"You're an idiot."

"Gee, thanks."

"She likes you, too. I've seen the way she looks at you."

"Doesn't matter," Amy said, lifting one of her shoulders in a shrug. "Because she's not got much longer here, and then she's back in London full-time. There's no point in getting invested. Not when it's temporary."

Not when that's all she's willing to give.

"She said that?"

"Not in those exact words, but yeah."

"And you're okay with that? With letting her go?"

"Kinda have to be." She ran a hand through her hair, mussing it much like Chloe had earlier that day. "I can't ask her to stay. Won't. Not for me."

"You *really* like her."

"Yeah. Always have." *Always will*, she didn't say, but Gabi seemed to read it on her face and wrapped an arm around her waist, squeezing tight. "Can you, uh, keep this between us, please? Mum will be insufferable if she finds out. And Danny… I know he and Chloe have made amends, but…"

"It's still a sore spot," Gabi finished. "I won't say a word."

"Thank you." She leaned her head against Gabi's, knowing she couldn't have asked for a better sister-in-law.

"So, is she a good kisser?" she asked, and Amy huffed out a laugh. "She looks like she'd be a good kisser."

"What do you mean, she looks like she'd be a good kisser?"

"I dunno. She has a vibe."

"A vibe?"

"Yeah. Self-assured. Confident."

Amy turned her head, squinting at her. "Are you sure you don't have a crush on her?"

"I mean, if I wasn't with Danny…" She laughed when Amy smacked her on the top of the head. "You haven't answered my question. Is she?"

"Yes. And that's all the detail you're getting," she said when Gabi opened her mouth. "Okay?"

Gabi pouted, but Amy kept her expression stern—she'd already learned too much, and some cards Amy would like to keep close to her chest.

"Fine."

Chapter 18

"CHLOE!"

Two sets of arms wrapped around her when Chloe stepped outside of Camden Town station, Tessa and Zara having spotted her through the steady stream of traffic. Naomi leaned against a nearby lamppost, tapping away on her phone.

"Hey, troublemakers. How you doing?"

"Good," Zara said, taking Chloe's hand in her own.

"Excited for the zoo?"

"Yeah!" Tessa took her other hand in one of hers, and Naomi's in the other, and the four of them headed toward Regent's Park. "I want to see the penguins."

"Lions are better than penguins," Zara said, puffing out her chest to show the rainbow-coloured pride of lions on her shirt.

"No, they're not. All they do is sleep. They're boring."

"They are not."

"They are. At least the penguins swim around. They're fun to watch."

"Are not."

"Are so."

"Girls," Naomi said, and Chloe wondered if she had heard this argument already today. "Enough about the penguins and the lions. We'll spend time by both."

"You had a good summer holiday?" Chloe asked, eager to change the subject. "What've you been up to?"

"Spent time with my friends. And my boyfriend."

"Boyfriend?" Chloe echoed, staring at Zara with wide eyes. She was nine, too young to turn boy-crazy—Chloe had thought they had another few years before they lost her to that. "Why did I not know about this? Is this not family dinner conversation?"

"Uh, no, because my mum would have a heart attack if she knew," Naomi said. "So it's our little secret."

"You're too young to have a boyfriend."

"Am not."

"Are so." Chloe could remember clearly the day she'd been born, a squalling pile of blankets thrust into her arms. "Way too young."

"That's what I said, too." Naomi shook her head. "I'm still waiting to meet him. Give him the talk."

"No way," Zara said, as Naomi cracked her knuckles. "You'll scare him away."

"Maybe he needs to be scared away."

"You don't have a boyfriend, do you, Tessa?" Chloe asked, turning to Zara's sister with a vague sense of panic settling in her chest. She was relieved when Tessa scrunched her nose.

"Ew. No."

"Thank God."

"She spends all her time drawing," Zara said, turning to Tessa with a roll of her eyes. "She's boring."

Tessa's face fell.

"Hey." Naomi's voice was sharp. "Enough."

"You got your sketchbook with you?" Chloe asked, knowing sweet, sweet Tessa had serious talent that needed nurturing. "You'll have to show me later," she said when Tessa nodded, and her smile lit up her whole face.

The zoo was busy, screaming kids wherever they looked, tourists and locals alike taking advantage of a rare, sunny bank holiday Monday, the last day of the summer holidays, but Chloe didn't mind.

She liked seeing their infectious joy, their endless enthusiasm, was glad it hadn't yet faded from either Tessa or Zara, no matter how grown-up the latter tried to appear. Their eyes sparkled brightly as they pressed their faces to the glass of the gorilla exhibit.

"Can we go get ice cream?" Zara asked, spotting a stand with a queue so long it nearly wrapped around the block.

"I guess," Naomi said, turning toward Chloe. "Want to go find somewhere to sit? Not you." She stopped Zara by grabbing a handful of her shirt. "You want ice cream, you gotta queue for it. Keep me company."

Zara pouted, but didn't argue, and Chloe and Tessa found a quiet spot on a wall, shaded beneath some trees.

"Can I see your drawings?" Chloe asked, and Tessa opened her rucksack and carefully pulled out the sketchbook Chloe had gotten her for her birthday.

"They're not that good," she said, handing it over and chewing on her thumbnail when Chloe opened the first page.

Dozens of still-life drawings greeted her, of bowls of fruit and random objects from her bedroom. "Are you kidding? These are amazing."

Tessa's head ducked at the praise.

"You've come along so much already. You still having your lessons?" Also part of her present. Tessa nodded. "Like them?"

"Yeah. My teacher's nice. She thinks I should enter a competition, but I don't know if I want to."

"Why not?"

She shrugged. "I dunno. What if I don't win?"

"You definitely won't win if you don't try," Chloe said, wrapping an arm around Tessa's back and pulling her close, hoping the day would never come where she shied away from hugs.

Chloe felt like she'd missed so much these past few months—Zara's boyfriend, Tessa's progress, and both of them had grown an inch since she'd last seen them. She hated feeling out of the loop with Naomi's nieces, hated it being her own fault.

Time in Corthwaite was precious—now more than ever—but so was her time here, with the girls, with Naomi and her family, long weekends spent relaxing in the summer sun.

She'd missed a whole summer of Tessa and Zara's lives, a whole summer she'd never get back, and it was a stark reminder of what she was giving up, stretching herself so thin.

"You all right?" Naomi asked when she and Zara re-joined them, passing Chloe a cone with vanilla ice cream dripping over the side and making her fingers sticky.

"Yeah. Just thinking."

"Never a good thing." Naomi sat close to Chloe on the wall, knocking her shoulder with her own. "About Amy?"

"No." For once, Amy wasn't at the forefront of her mind. "About how much I've been missing."

"You know how quick kids change. One week they like *Peppa Pig*, the next week they're too old for it. I wouldn't worry about it. And you'll be back full-time soon, won't you?"

"Yeah." It lacked enthusiasm, and Naomi shot her a knowing look. "Don't look at me like that."

"Like what? Like I think you're dragging out your time there because you're falling in love with a certain farmer you're now making out with on the weekends?"

"You have a girlfriend?" Zara gasped, her eyes wide.

"I do not have a girlfriend."

"But Auntie Naomi said—"

"Auntie Naomi has no idea what she's talking about," Chloe said, eyes narrowed in her direction.

She at least had the grace to look sheepish.

"You were telling me off for having a boyfriend when you have a secret girlfriend!"

"I do not have a secret girlfriend." Chloe groaned, because this was going to get back to Jada, and she'd never hear the end of it. "But if I did, it would be fine, because I am old enough to date."

"I'm old enough to date," Zara said, tossing braided hair over her shoulder.

"Not until you're eighteen, you're not."

Zara rolled her eyes. "Chloe has a secret girlfriend," she sang, and Chloe rubbed her non-sticky hand over her face.

"I am going to kill you," she hissed at Naomi, brightening when she realised a way out of this. "Do you girls know that your Auntie Naomi has a girlfriend, too?"

"What?"

Twin pairs of brown eyes turned toward Naomi, who reached for Chloe, trying to clamp a hand over her mouth, but she dodged easily out of the way by scrambling to her feet.

"Uh-huh. She's called Melissa."

"Chloe!"

"Is she pretty?" Zara asked.

Naomi caught Chloe, tickling her sides so she couldn't answer.

"Now I'm going to kill you! I told you about those drinks in confidence!"

"Your date, you mean," Chloe said, gasping for breath. "And you deserve it. You brought this on yourself."

Naomi ground her teeth together, an endless torrent of questions coming from both Zara and Tessa now.

At least she wouldn't be the only one getting the Spanish Inquisition about her love life at dinner on Wednesday.

Chloe thought she and Naomi had managed to escape an interrogation. She had expected to be cross-examined on the doorstep, but instead they were waved inside after the usual round of hugs and ushered to the dinner table, where Kiara, Tristan, and the kids were already seated.

"Twice in one week," Chloe said, hugging the girls. "This is a pleasant surprise."

"They've moved me onto day shifts," Kiara said, drawing Chloe into a hug. "So we'll be around more often."

"Glad to hear it. How is work?"

If she managed to keep everyone else talking, maybe conversation would never stray to her. Naomi seemed to feel the same, as she was currently drawing Tristan into a discussion of his latest cases.

They were both naïve, as it turned out.

Jada eyed the pair of them across the table with her lips pursed. "So," she said, reaching for her glass of wine. "I hear the two of you have been keeping secrets from me."

"Secrets?" Chloe said, playing dumb.

"Us?" Naomi shook her head. "Doesn't sound right. Must be mistaken."

"So there's no farmer? No Melissa?" She arched an eyebrow, and Naomi turned a glare toward Zara.

"Traitor."

Zara smiled serenely back at her, munching on a piece of broccoli.

"Have you heard about Zara's boyfriend?" Naomi asked, trying to take the heat off herself, but her mum didn't even blink.

"Yes, we had a nice discussion about him before you came over."

"And you're okay with that." Naomi's brows creased. "But angry at us?"

"Yes." Jada steepled her fingers in front of her mouth. "Because she didn't hide it from me."

"There's nothing to hide!"

"Then who is Melissa?"

"A client. Who I had drinks with one time. That's all."

Jada stared her down, searching for any hint of a lie. Apparently satisfied, she turned her head toward Chloe. "And you. The farmer."

Chloe sighed. "Amy. Her name is Amy."

"And she's your...?"

"Friend," she said, kicking Naomi hard in the shin when she scoffed.

"Ow!"

"You deserve it," Chloe whispered. "This is all your fault."

"I think you'll find it's your fault, for getting involved with her in the first—"

"Involved?" Jada asked. "I thought you were just friends?"

"Not...involved. Not romantically." Chloe's face felt hot, and she elbowed a snickering Naomi in the side—she was enjoying this far too much.

"I see." Jada took a sip of wine, giving her a brief reprieve. "When will we meet her?"

Chloe nearly choked on a mouthful of chicken. "What? It's not... I told you, it's not like that. It's casual."

"You can be casual here, can you not?"

"Yeah, Chloe." Naomi leant back in her chair, sliding one arm over the back of it, shit-eating grin on her face. "When are you bringing her here?"

"Have you met her?" Jada asked, gaze flickering to her daughter.

"Uh-huh."

"What's she like?"

Naomi shrugged. "I met her a couple of times. She seems nice enough. Big on family values. Still lives with hers, in fact." She left out the finer details of Amy and Chloe's history, picking out those her mum would appreciate, and Chloe was thankful.

"All the more reason to meet her. Introduce her to your family."

"She's a busy woman," Chloe said, gaze falling to the tablecloth, tracing the swirls on it with one finger. "Running a farm and all. Not much chance for a holiday."

"What type of farm?"

"Dairy. The, um, ice cream I brought you the other week is from there."

"I still can't believe there was an ice cream parlour nearby and you never took me while I was there," Naomi mumbled under her breath.

"I brought you back a tub, didn't I?"

"Not the same."

"I want ice cream," Zara said, the novelty of the Alleyene Inquisition apparently wearing off. "Can we come visit? You said we could, when the house was further along."

"I...did say that." The idea held less appeal now, with her weekends so numbered. "We'll see."

"That means no," Zara said, bottom lip sticking out.

Kiara reached across the table to poke it. "It means we'll see," she said, and Chloe breathed out a sigh of relief when no more questions came.

She'd survived.

For now.

She was sure Jada would be asking her about Amy at every subsequent family dinner from now until the house was done.

Turning her attention to the girls, Chloe asked, "How's school? Anything changed over summer?"

"We got a new teacher," Zara said. "Ms. Tranter. She's scary."

Chloe chuckled. "Why's she scary?"

"She shouts a lot."

"Because your class is loud," Tessa said, waving a fork toward her sister. "Our class can hear you down the hall."

"At least we're not all quiet and boring like yours."

It sparked another argument—Chloe swore they hadn't been this bad a few months ago.

Leroy passed a hand over his face. "This is the worst age. The pick a fight with everything you say phase."

"We never had that phase," Naomi said, and her dad scoffed.

"Yes, you did. From the ages of eight to twelve, you and Kiara couldn't agree on a thing. What to have for dinner, what you wanted to do at the weekend, what you wanted to watch on the television."

"I have no recollection of this."

"Me neither," Kiara said.

He shook his head. "Well, I do. You see this grey hair? Started the day you started talking back."

"I thought it started when we turned into teenagers?" Kiara asked, brow arched.

"No, that was when it started falling out."

Chloe chuckled, enjoying having the whole lot of them around. It hadn't happened enough lately, and she hoped Kiara's shift change meant the eight of them would be seeing a lot more of each other.

Film nights when the kids were around always ended up with something animated and Disney. True to form, they argued over a selection, until Tristan snatched the remote out of their hands.

"Enough. The adults are picking this one. Anyone have a preference?"

"*Coco* is good," Chloe said, when no one else had a suggestion. She'd barely watched a minute of it last time, too busy focusing on the warmth of Amy's body pressed close to her own.

She'd have no such issue today, though she had even less space, with Tessa curled into one side and Naomi squeezed against her other, couch space growing more and more limited as the girls continued to grow.

"Anyone have a counter offer?"

After chorus of no's, Tristan pressed play, and Chloe vowed to give it her full attention this time.

Then she wouldn't have to scramble for something to say the next time Adam started talking to her about it.

Friday arrived in a rush of breathless anticipation. Amy kept one eye on the clock throughout her morning duties, debating what time Chloe would arrive.

Not that they'd made any plans for when she *did* arrive, but that didn't stop her from checking her phone every five minutes, waiting to see if she had a text, fully aware that her behaviour bordered on obsessive, and if Gabi wasn't at school and had been around to witness it, she would be telling her to calm the fuck down.

Except she couldn't. She had been thinking of Chloe with increasing regularity as the week wore on, the radio silence hard to bear after spending so much of the previous weekend together.

And she knew she could rectify that, could pick up the phone and text her, but…it seemed like such a delicate balance, this line they were walking, not quite friends and not quite lovers, and she didn't want to upset it by doing the wrong thing.

Didn't want to risk pushing too hard, coming on too strong, or God-forbid, too *eager*, and send Chloe skittering away.

The text came as she was tacking up Regina—a ride through the fields exactly what she needed to release some of the nervous energy coursing through her veins—and she nearly dropped her phone in her haste to open it.

Want to come over for dinner tonight? Test out my new kitchen?

Amy let out her breath, all of her worry and anxiety that Chloe might not want to see her that weekend fading away as she read the message.

I thought you couldn't cook?

I can't. But you can…

So you're inviting me over to cook for you?

Maybe? But I can make it worth your while.

A wink accompanied the message, and Amy's mouth went dry at the possibilities, at the prospect of a night uninterrupted. No nephews to come bursting through doors, no farm duties to cut their time together short.

What time do you want me?

They agreed on six, which seemed too many hours away. She filled the time with a trek so long, Regina drank a full bucket of water upon their return, and Amy gave her an extra handful of carrots to make up for it.

Still, she had another hour to kill by the time Regina was back out in the field, munching happily on the grass and warding off Storm with a stamp of her back leg when he dared to venture too close.

Sceptical of Chloe having a single ingredient in her fridge, she was raiding the farmhouse cupboards when Gabi caught her pilfering a bag of pasta.

"What're you doing?"

"I'm going over to Chloe's tonight."

"And you're taking her a bag of pasta? How romantic."

Amy rolled her eyes. "I'm cooking."

"Ooh, that *is* romantic."

"It is not."

"Have you told Mum you're not here for dinner? Are you staying the night? Do I need to make sure no one goes looking for you too early?"

"Jesus, one question at a time." She shoved the rest of her stolen ingredients—eggs, pancetta, cheese, garlic, and butter—into her bag. "No, I don't know, so I don't know."

"Do you want to spend the night?"

Amy thought of Chloe's text, of the warm press of Chloe's fingers beneath her shirt, and felt her cheeks warm.

"Your face says yes," Gabi said, delighted. "About time. How long has it been?"

"None of your business."

"Cranky. You really do need to get lai—hola, chiquito!" She changed track as Sam toddled into the room, empty cup held loosely in one hand. "You want some juice?"

Amy seized the opportunity to escape, slipping into the hall in search of her mum. She found her in the living room, a game of Uno set up between her and Adam.

"I'm heading out," she said, hoisting her bag further up her shoulder. "Won't be back for dinner, so don't wait for me."

Her mum peered at her over the back of the couch. "Going anywhere nice?"

"Chloe's." She kept her voice even, not wanting to betray her true intentions for the night, because that was a level of mortification she couldn't handle.

"Does Chloe not want to come over here?"

"She's just put in her new kitchen," Amy said, grateful Chloe had given her this excuse. "Wants to try it out, but I don't think she trusts herself not to burn it down. You know how she is."

"All right. Have fun."

"See you later, chiquito." She waved goodbye to Adam and retreated back to her barn, a spring in her step as she glanced at her watch. Half an hour—enough time for a shower to wash away the grime of a day of farm labour.

Chapter 19

AMY GREETED HER WITH A kiss when she opened the door, one filled with the enthusiasm of having spent four days apart.

Chloe returned it with equal fervour, her hands settling on Amy's waist, trying not to think about how everything felt right with Amy in her arms.

"Hi," Chloe said when they parted, left breathless and dizzy. "That was quite a welcome." *Miss me?* She didn't ask, but she thought, from the way Amy pulled her down again, that the answer was a resounding yes.

The rumble of Chloe's stomach eventually separated them.

Amy laughed against her mouth as she leaned away. "Hungry?"

For a lot of things. "A little."

"Come on." She took Chloe's hand and tugged her into the kitchen, letting out a low whistle when she stepped inside. "Wow. It looks amazing in here. Exactly like the pictures you showed me. I'm scared to touch anything."

"Why? In case it all falls apart?"

"No." Amy swatted at her shoulder. "Because it looks so pristine. I don't want to mess it up."

"Someone's going to, eventually. May as well be you that christens it."

Amy turned to her, one eyebrow raised.

Chloe cleared her throat. "Not like that. Although..." She paused, tilting her head as she studied the counter. "It is sturdy."

"Not very hygienic, though," Amy said, voice low, eyes dark.

Chloe thought it would be a miracle if they made it through dinner without her dragging Amy upstairs.

"Yeah. Right." She shook her head, trying to clear the haze of desire. "What are we making?"

"Thought I was supposed to be cooking?"

"I can help."

"Can you?"

"I can try," she corrected, and Amy grinned.

She tasked Chloe with chopping pancetta and grating cheese—which should have been simple, but Chloe kept getting distracted, watching Amy move about the kitchen with an easy grace, like she belonged. She nearly sliced through her finger on more than one occasion.

"Okay, enough," Amy said, when Chloe inspected her thumb for blood for the third time, taking the knife from her hand and steering her toward the table. "Sit. Watch. Don't injure yourself. I've patched you up enough times already." She ghosted her fingertips over Chloe's head, where the bruise had faded to a faint green. "That's looking better, at least."

"I heal fast."

"Have to, with the amount of injuries you seem to get. What's this from, anyway?" She smoothed her thumb across the scar through Chloe's eyebrow.

"Caught it on an overhanging nail. Wasn't pretty. And wasn't a mistake I made again." She could say the same for most of her scars, a litany of errors she hadn't ever repeated. "All part of the learning curve."

Amy shook her head and dropped a kiss on Chloe's lips before returning to the hob, where she stirred a bubbling pan of pasta with one hand and a pan of sizzling pancetta with the other.

"There you go," she said, once everything was done, setting a bowl in front of Chloe with a flourish. "Carbonara. Not much, but you didn't exactly give me much time to plan."

"Sorry," Chloe said, though she wasn't sorry in the least, because the pasta tasted great, and she had Amy in her kitchen, her foot sliding along Chloe's calf and making it hard to concentrate on chewing. "Had a good week?"

Amy shrugged. "Same old, same old. Not much exciting happens around here. You?"

"Yeah, it was all right. Took Naomi's nieces to the zoo on Monday. Then just working." The rate she was eating was probably going to give her heartburn, but she didn't know how long Amy could stay for and had things she'd much rather be doing, things she hadn't been able to stop thinking about all week. "What time do you have to get back?"

"I don't," Amy said, and Chloe's fork clattered into her empty bowl.

"You don't?"

"I'm off-duty until morning," she said, eyes burning into Chloe's from across the table. "Doesn't happen often." She stood, grabbed both their bowls, and dropped them into the sink before slinking back over to the table and fisting her hand into Chloe's shirt with purpose. "Got any idea how I could spend my time?"

"I'm sure we can come up with something," Chloe whispered, following when Amy tugged her upright, leaning in to kiss her, open-mouthed and messy, steering Amy backwards with her hands on her hips.

Too lost in the heat of Amy's mouth to concentrate on where they were going, Chloe crashed them into a wall in the hallway. Amy's laugh turned to a moan when Chloe pressed close, hands slipping beneath her shirt and thigh falling between her legs.

When Amy pulled away, Chloe took the opportunity to trail her lips over the sharp angle of her jaw and down, pressing open-mouthed kisses to the skin of Amy's neck.

"Fuck, Chloe." Amy's voice was low, breathy.

Chloe nipped at her pulse point and felt Amy's hands fist into her hair in response, holding her close. She wanted to hear Amy say her name like that a thousand times, and it still would never be enough.

Encouraged, she slid her hand further up Amy's shirt until she was cupping a breast through the padding of her bra. Amy arched into her, hands grasping, urging Chloe into another kiss when her fingers dipped into the bra to circle her nipple until it was a stiff peak straining against Chloe's palm.

Amy's hips rocked against her thigh, and Chloe slid her other hand lower, into the pocket of her jeans, dragging her closer, encouraging the movement. Amy's groan echoed in her mouth, sending a bolt of desire straight to her core. Hands came to rest on her shoulders, Amy pushed slightly, and Chloe stepped back immediately.

"Upstairs," Amy said, in response to her questioning look, eyes dark and stormy, propelling Chloe toward them. "Please."

Chloe was happy to oblige, letting Amy drag her to her bedroom, where hands scrabbled for the hem of Chloe's shirt as soon as the door shut behind them. Amy's fingers fell to her ribs, to the sprawling bouquet of flowers across them, and Chloe shivered when Amy's nails scratched over her skin.

"Told you I had more tattoos," she said, voice raspy, and then lost the ability to speak entirely when Amy yanked her own shirt over her head.

Chloe pressed Amy onto the bed, settling her weight carefully on top of her, a knee on either side of her hips. Amy's hands ran up her sides, and Chloe couldn't help but squirm beneath the touch, breaking away from Amy's mouth with a huff.

"I forgot you were ticklish." Amy's eyes were bright in the darkness, looking at her like she wasn't sure this moment was real, and when she tried to tickle her again, Chloe was quick to grab her wrists and press her hands to the mattress above her head.

She watched Amy's eyes darken, throat working as she swallowed, and kept her hands pinned when she leant to kiss her again, tongue dipping into her mouth. Chloe groaned when Amy arched into her.

Chloe released her soon enough, wanting to feel Amy's hands on her skin, swearing against her neck when Amy ran her nails across Chloe's back before slipping beneath her jeans to squeeze her ass.

Chloe didn't know if she was going to survive the night. She felt aflame wherever they touched, and when Amy divested them both of their jeans so that they were skin on skin, Chloe felt like she was going to combust.

"Take it off," Amy murmured, when Chloe's fingers brushed against her bra, so she reached around and undid the clasp with a flick of her wrist.

Chloe's breath caught when she caught a glimpse of a topless Amy Edwards, chest flushed and heaving, looking at her with wanting eyes.

"You're so beautiful." She couldn't keep the reverence out of her voice and worried that it might be saying too much, might send Amy skittering away, but her response was to slide a hand into Chloe's hair and bring her down for another kiss that left them both breathless.

Hips shifted against her thigh when Chloe brushed her thumb over a nipple, and when she ducked her head to take the other into her mouth, Amy's fingers tightened in her hair as she breathed her name. Chloe wanted to see what other sounds she could drag from her before the night was through.

Amy had a scar on her stomach. Chloe's lips trailed over the raised skin on the path towards her hips, and she paused. "What's this from?"

"What?" Amy was breathless, a frown of confusion on her face as she glanced at Chloe, settled between her thighs, and Chloe traced a finger over the same spot. "Oh. It's nothing exciting. I caught myself on a fencepost, pointy end first, a couple of years ago."

"And you call me clumsy," Chloe said, lips pressed against her hip.

"Shut up." Amy shoved at her shoulder and Chloe grinned, obliging by ducking her head and continuing her path over Amy's stomach, bypassing her underwear in favour of pressing a line of kisses to one of her thighs. When Chloe nipped at her skin, Amy swore, muscle quivering beneath Chloe's lips.

She could smell Amy's arousal, see the damp patch on her underwear, and it made her mouth water because that was because of *her*, and never in her wildest dreams had she ever thought she'd be here in this moment, with Amy's sighs echoing in her ears and the taste of Amy's skin on her tongue.

"Are you sure about this?" Chloe had to ask, thumbs hooked in Amy's underwear, looking at her through her lashes and wishing she could commit the view to memory.

"Yes." Amy's eyes were pleading, and she lifted her hips to help Chloe slide them down her legs. "Please."

Chloe lifted one of Amy's legs over her shoulder before dipping her head, wasting no time in exploring Amy's soaked folds with lips and tongue. Fingers fisted in her hair, hips rocked against her mouth, and Amy bit her bottom lip to keep herself quiet.

"Don't," Chloe said as Amy's thigh shook against her cheek. "I want to hear you."

"Fuck." Amy couldn't hold back a moan when Chloe slipped two fingers into wet heat, tongue circling Amy's clit, and a curl of her fingers was all it took to have Amy clenching all around her.

Chloe tipped her over the edge twice more before Amy tugged her away, and Chloe thought she could do this all night, because the sight of Amy, breathless and spent, splayed across the mattress with her chest heaving and her cheeks flushed, was the most perfect thing she'd ever seen.

"Come here." Amy pulled her up, into a lazy kiss, and Chloe settled beside her, fingers drawing random patterns over Amy's hip.

"You don't have to," she murmured against Amy's lips when she felt a warm hand sliding over her stomach.

"I want to."

Chloe's pulse quickened at that, at the acknowledgement that Amy *wanted* her, in all the ways she'd never dared to before. She let Amy roll her onto her back, mouth going dry at the sight of Amy settling astride her hips, naked and beautiful.

Amy's hair tickled her chest as she leant down, lips trailing along her neck, hands reaching for the clasp of Chloe's bra. The first touch of Amy's thumbs against her nipples had Chloe seeing stars.

A thigh settled between her legs, teeth teasing at her pulse point, fingers pinching at her nipples, and Chloe couldn't help but arch her back into the touch, hips shifting against Amy's thigh.

"Oh, fuck," she breathed when Amy ground against her, pressure perfect against her clit. Her hands fell to Amy's ass, digging into supple skin and encouraging Amy to move against her.

When Amy's lips descended on her chest, Chloe couldn't hold off any longer and clenched her jaw to smother a groan, back arching as ecstasy sparked through her, stealing the breath from her lungs.

"Fuck, that was hot." Amy's voice was husky, and when Chloe blinked her eyes open, she found Amy looking at her like she wanted to devour her. "*You're* hot."

"Yeah?"

"Yeah." Amy didn't give Chloe a chance to catch her breath before a hand was dipping beneath the waistband of her underwear, brushing through damp curls.

Chloe groaned at the first swipe of Amy's fingers through her sex, sensitive to the touch. The fact that it was *Amy* pressed against her was almost enough to make her come again.

"Is this okay?"

"More than okay." Chloe urged Amy away from her breasts so that she could kiss her, a tongue sliding into her mouth as two fingers pressed inside of her, and her eyes rolled, nails dragging down Amy's back.

Her heartbeat was loud in her ears, skin burning wherever they touched, and Chloe wanted this moment to last forever, in case she never got the chance to experience it again.

But she couldn't hold out for long, not when Amy was pressing deep, not when her palm was sliding against her clit, and she had to bite back a cry of Amy's name when she came, glad that her whimper was quietened by Amy's mouth on her own.

When Chloe stopped shaking, Amy rested her forehead against Chloe's, both of them slick with sweat and panting.

She half-expected horror to bloom in Amy's eyes once the haze of lust had faded, for her to quickly make her escape and flee back to the safety of the farm, but instead she shifted so that she was lying on her side beside Chloe and slung one arm over her stomach, fingers tracing the outline of the tattoo on Chloe's ribs.

"Is this one for your mum, too?"

"Her favourite flowers."

"And I'm guessing this one isn't." She tapped the skull sitting high on Chloe's thigh.

"That one's just for me."

Chloe leaned in for another kiss, one that started slow but soon began to build as Amy's hips shifted beneath hers and her hands clutched at the small of Chloe's back like she couldn't get enough, like she needed to be closer. Chloe knew the feeling. Her hands dipped back between Amy's legs until she cried out Chloe's name.

Addictive, this feeling, Amy rocking against her and pulling her in deep, Amy's nails digging into her skin with desperation.

Addictive, and heady, and downright *dangerous*, and there wasn't a thing Chloe could do about it.

Amy rarely slept to her alarm, the years of waking early too ingrained in her circadian rhythm.

Except, apparently, when she spent the night wrapped around another woman, both of them with an itch that never seemed to be satisfied, not submitting to unconsciousness until late into the night, when they were too exhausted to keep their eyes open any longer.

The buzzing sliced through her subconscious, unfamiliar and loud, and it took her a long moment to register the source as the phone discarded on the floor, still in the pocket of her jeans.

"Make it stop," Chloe said from beside her, and Amy leant over the side of the bed for the offending device. "What time is it?"

"Six." Still enough time for Amy to slip back unwitnessed.

"S'early." Chloe rubbed a hand over her face, and Amy thought she could get used to this view: Chloe, hair mussed from Amy's fingers, blinking sleepily up at her. The sheets had pooled to her waist, revealing a tempting expanse of smooth skin, littered with the occasional mark from Amy's mouth or nails. "D'you have to go?"

"I should." She should already be tugging on yesterday's clothes, should already be walking through Chloe's front door, but she hesitated, and Chloe pounced on it, sliding a hand around the back of her neck.

"But you don't have to?"

"Not right away." Saturday mornings were usually lazier than the others, especially with Gabi and Adam not yet used to being back at school.

Was it risky, to linger? To let Chloe tug her close, to let her mouth drift across Chloe's neck?

Certainly, but Amy wasn't complaining, not when Chloe moaned, raspy and beautiful, when Amy's teeth nipped at the junction of her shoulder. Not when fingers tangled in her hair when she took a nipple into her mouth, teeth teasing, tongue swirling, until Chloe's hips jerked beneath her, painting a trail against the bare skin of her thigh.

Risky, but Amy would gladly take the consequences of her lips sucking a mark on Chloe's hip. Would gladly reap the rewards, too. Chloe arched into her mouth at the first swipe of her tongue through wet heat, and Amy's hands slid up the back of her thighs.

She wished she could spend every morning like this, with Chloe's nails scratching over her scalp, Chloe's sighs ringing in her ears, Chloe jolting beneath her lips when Amy curled her tongue over her clit.

Wished she could spend every night like this, too, working Chloe up with broad strokes until she was whimpering, until was begging, until she was saying Amy's name like a prayer.

"Please, Amy." Fingers tugged at her hair, trying to direct Amy to where she needed her most, trying to stop her teasing, and Amy relented, tracing swollen nerves until Chloe cried out, the taste of her thick on Amy's tongue.

She kissed the inside of Chloe's thigh, slinking up her body and trying to memorise the sight of her with one arm thrown over her eyes, chest heaving, sweat shining on her skin.

"I have to go," Amy said, lips pressed to the underside of her jaw, and Chloe whined in protest.

"No." Chloe reached for her, but Amy ducked out of the way easily. "Stay."

"Believe me when I say I wish I could."

It wouldn't take much to tempt her, she knew, when half-lidded eyes met her own. Wouldn't take much at all. Her self-control—already in tatters—would probably shatter completely if Chloe pulled her close.

"Go back to sleep." She traced a hand over the curve of Chloe's cheek, smiling when her eyes fluttered closed. "I'll text you later."

Chloe didn't protest, and Amy suspected she was already half-asleep. She hunted around in the dark for her clothes, giving Bella—who had been admitted into the room at some point in the night after whining outside the door—a pat on the head on her way out.

Thirty-six years old, and it was her first time doing a walk of shame—back to her family's house, no less. She hoped she managed to sneak into the barn before anyone caught a glimpse of her.

Because she smelled like sweat and sex, her hair a mess, and her clothes rumpled from spending an evening on Chloe's bedroom floor.

She spotted movement in the farmhouse kitchen as she edged past, prayed everyone was still inside, and breathed out a sigh of relief when she reached her front door without detection.

"All right, boss."

She'd forgotten all about the farmhand, who was usually up and about before she was.

"Hi, Jack." She turned, found him looking at her with a smirk, and wanted to die.

"Good night?"

"Yes, thank you."

He chuckled, and Amy groaned, cheeks hot, and slipped through her door before anyone else could spot her.

Still.

It had been more than worth it.

Chapter 20

TINA RICHARDSON WAS A DODDERING old lady with a Zimmer frame and an oxygen tank that squeaked along the wooden floor as she led Chloe through to her back garden.

"Thank you for doing this, dear." She had a kindly smile and eyes hidden behind thick-rimmed glasses. "Eleanor said you liked scones, so I made you some."

"Oh, thank you, Mrs. Richardson, but that wasn't necessary." She was going to start getting a reputation.

"Nonsense, it was no trouble."

Chloe couldn't help but glance toward the oxygen tank.

"Don't be fooled," she said, wagging a finger in Chloe's direction. "I'm still capable. Independent. Just not when it comes to climbing ladders." She flashed Chloe a toothy grin, though half of her front teeth were missing. "Can I get you a drink? Some tea, perhaps?"

Chloe lifted the Thermos she'd brought with her. "Already got it covered."

"All right, dear. I'll leave you to it. Let me know if you need anything." She retreated inside, and Chloe took a sip of her coffee, hoping the caffeine would kick in soon.

She could still feel Amy's touch like it was imprinted on her skin, a lingering reminder of what they'd shared.

Which she probably shouldn't be thinking about as she climbed a ladder. It wasn't the time for distractions, not when a lapse in judgement could send her tumbling to the ground.

The gutters were packed full of debris—leaves and twigs, weeds growing in places and blocking the flow. Chloe got to work, scooping out as much as she could and dumping it into a bucket.

It wasn't hard work, but her muscles ached whenever she stretched too far, a souvenir of a night spent tangled up in Amy. When she was done, she washed away the last stubborn bits with a hose, glad to see the water running freely.

She climbed back to solid ground with weariness settled in her bones and no idea how she was going to summon the energy to work on the house later that afternoon.

"All done?" Mrs. Richardson asked, poking her head out of the back door when she heard Chloe taking down her ladder.

"Yep. They should be fine now, but let me know if you have any more problems next time it rains."

"Scone?" She already had one on a plate, and how was Chloe supposed to say no to that?

"Thank you, Mrs. Richardson," she said around a mouthful.

"You're welcome, dear. Here, you can take these away with you." She pressed a nearly overflowing box into Chloe's hands. "Now, how much do I owe you?" She pulled out her purse, brimming with crisp banknotes. "One hundred? Two hundred?"

"Oh, no, that's far too much."

"But I looked it up on the Google." Mrs. Richardson pushed her glasses up her nose, peering up at Chloe from behind the rims. "That was the suggested cost."

"From a professional," Chloe said, shaking her head when Mrs. Richardson tried to press several twenties into her hand. "I'm not a professional."

"Seem professional to me. Got a van with a logo. Got your own set of ladders. Louise said you gave her a business card."

"I—well, yeah, but not for this."

"I'm not letting you go without payment. I may not look quick, but I can move fast when I need to."

Chloe chuckled, trying to imagine Mrs. Richardson chasing her down the lawn. "How about we call it twenty? You did give me these, after all." She waved the scones, and Mrs. Richardson pursed her lips.

"Fifty," she said, waving one toward Chloe. "No less."

"Okay." She felt guilty accepting it, though she knew she'd technically earned it, and that an actual professional would have charged much more.

Was she going soft? Maybe. Jin and Naomi would certainly say so, if they ever found out.

But the feeling of a good deed well done was better than any payment, and a feeling of contentment settled in her chest as she made her way back to her van.

Mrs. Peterson was in her front garden opposite, chatting to her neighbour over the fence, and Chloe crossed the street when the old woman waved her over, leaving her ladders propped against the side of her van.

"Good morning, dear. How are you?"

"Good, Mrs. P. You?"

"Fine, fine. I hope you didn't mind me telling Tina about you. She saw you, is all."

"It's all right. I don't mind lending a helping hand every now and again."

"Don't say that too loud," Mrs. Peterson's neighbour said, hands tucked into the pockets of his coat. "Ears everywhere around here. You'll have all sorts of daft requests coming your way."

"Noted. I'd, uh, better get back to work. Nice to see you again, Mrs. P."

"And you, dear. Don't be a stranger—pop around for a cuppa any time you like."

It was strange, Chloe thought, as she drove back toward the house. Strange how she'd never thought she fit in here, never thought there would be a place for her in Corthwaite, and yet here she was, doing odd jobs, making connections, leaving an imprint of herself that would linger when she left.

She'd expected to get in and get out, as fast as physically possible.

She'd never dreamed it would be a place she'd struggle to leave behind, or that there would be people here she would miss, when all was said and done.

One in particular, she knew, gaze flitting toward the Edwards house as she pulled into her drive, she'd miss more than all the rest combined.

A crash echoed through the house as Amy stepped through Chloe's door.

"Chloe?" She heard the pitter-patter of paws as Bella tore down the stairs to greet her. "You still alive?"

"Uh-huh. Come on up."

Amy let Bella lead the way, following her to one of the upstairs bathrooms. In spite of how often they'd distracted one another, Chloe had gotten a lot of work done over the past two weekends. This was the last big project left.

Chloe stood in the centre of the room, surrounded by bits of broken tile.

"Having fun?"

"Best part of the job, destroying stuff." She was wearing safety glasses and had denim overalls over her clothes. "Want to try?"

"I don't want to break anything."

"Doesn't matter if they break," Chloe said, pressing a chisel and a hammer into her hands and sliding a second pair of safety glasses onto her nose. "They all need to go. Can't exactly mess it up."

Amy wasn't so sure about that, but she set the chisel on the wall above one of the tiles Chloe had already removed and tapped the end with the hammer—pausing when she noticed Chloe watching her with a grin.

"What?"

"Don't be so timid about it. Here, let me show you." She stepped close, front flush to Amy's back, hands curving gently over Amy's own. "You can put some force into it. Like I said—doesn't matter if they break."

Chloe managed to make it seem effortless, the tile peeling easily away when she tapped the chisel. "Now you try." Her voice was close to Amy's ear, her hands on Amy's hips.

Amy huffed out a breath. "I'm going to need you to stop touching me, or I'm going to end up hammering my thumb."

Chloe chuckled but relented, stepping aside and making a noise of approval when Amy copied what she'd done. "Just like that."

It was kind of fun, pulling the tiles away to reveal the wall beneath, ready to be transformed into something new. Chloe worked around her, chipping off any bits Amy left behind, smoothing away grout and adhesive until the surface was smooth.

"I'm starting to think I should be getting compensation for this," Amy said, once the floor around her feet was littered with broken bits of tile and one wall of the bathroom stripped bare. "This is the second room I've helped you with."

The first being the wallpapering they'd done in the dining room last weekend, though Amy's help there had mostly consisted of keeping Chloe company and slathering wallpaper glue on pieces that had already been cut to size.

"The faster I get my jobs for the weekend done, the more time I have for other things," Chloe said, gaze flicking over Amy's body. "But I'll bite. What kind of compensation are we talking?"

"Hmm, I don't know." She let Chloe back her up against one of the untouched walls and press her hands to the cool tile.

"This kind?" A kiss, pressed to the side of her neck, and Amy sighed, tilting her head to allow more access. "Or this?" A nip, this time, teeth closing around her pulse point, sting soothed away by Chloe's tongue.

"Both," she said, breathless and wanting already. Chloe had this maddening effect on her whenever she got too close.

"Both, huh?" Chloe switched to the other side of her neck, teasing with lips and teeth and tongue until Amy's knees were weak.

Her fingers dug into Chloe's, trying to free herself from her grip.

"Ah, ah," she said, nuzzling the underside of Amy's jaw. "Your hands are all dusty."

"You are all dusty," Amy said, turning her head to capture Chloe's lips in a heated kiss. "And there's a shower across the hall."

"There is," Chloe agreed, a glint in her eye that was going to be the death of her. "But we should be getting back to work."

Amy groaned when Chloe released her and retreated back to the other side of the bathroom. "Tease."

"I'll make it worth your while later," she said, and Amy stayed where she was, watching the flex of Chloe's arms as she gathered up some of the rubbish on the floor and dumped it into a heavy-duty bag. An uncomfortable ache settled between her thighs.

"That wasn't compensation. That was the opposite of compensation."

"You'll have to think of something else, then, won't you?" A lazy grin spilled across Chloe's face when her eyes met Amy's, no doubt noticing her burning cheeks, her heaving breaths.

"I will," she said, grumbling as she got back to work, hoping it would dull the desire pulsing through her, the temptation to shove Chloe onto the floor and sit astride her shoulders, dust be damned. "Ow, fuck."

The chisel had slipped, the hammer catching the end of her middle finger—thankfully not hard enough to break it.

"Careful." Chloe was beside her instantly, taking her hand in gentle fingers. "Are you okay? Can you move it?"

"That was your fault," she said, wiggling her finger experimentally.

"Why? Something on your mind?"

"You know exactly what's on my mind."

Chloe grinned and kissed the corner of her mouth.

Amy wondered how she could get her own-back as she returned to the job at hand, watching Chloe work out of the corner of her eye. She lay on her side on the floor, moving along the wall with such self-assuredness, a frown of concentration on her face, tongue sticking out the corner of her mouth as she smoothed away imperfections.

Amy ached for her camera, wanting to capture Chloe in her natural environment, at home with her sleeves rolled up and a hammer in her hand.

"I've thought of something you could do for me," she said, an idea already forming in her head, and something in her voice made Chloe's gaze wary when she glanced up at her. "Pose for me."

"What?" Chloe's wariness transformed to alarm. "Like...naked?"

She laughed. "No. Not that I'd complain about that, but it's not what I had in mind."

"And what do you have in mind?"

"You'll have to wait and see."

Chloe swallowed, and Amy grinned, mind already running through all of the possibilities.

Own-back indeed.

"You're supposed to act natural, Chloe."

"This is me acting natural."

"It is not. I have literally never seen you make that facial expression before."

Chloe huffed, shifting under the weight of Amy's gaze, fingers tugging at the hem of her shirt.

Amy lowered the camera into her lap. "Want me to stop?"

"No." Chloe liked the quiet intensity of Amy's gaze, watching her from the end of the bed, liked the intimacy of lying in Amy's bed, legs tangled up in her sheets. "It's just...this is awkward. I feel awkward."

"You were okay before."

True—Amy had been photographing her all day as she worked on the house, but then it had been easy to ignore the flash, the click of Amy's finger on the button. Here, under the soft lighting of Amy's bedside lamp, half-dressed in a button-down shirt and a pair of boxers, it was a different ballgame entirely.

"Yeah, but that wasn't as...much as this."

Amy hummed and set aside the camera in favour of crawling into Chloe's lap, placing a knee on either side of her hips. "You need to relax," she said, cupping Chloe's face in her hands and kissing her, slow and thorough, until Chloe's heart beat loudly in her ears.

"This is the opposite of relaxing," Chloe said when she pulled away, dazed and breathless.

"So it's not helping?"

"It's...doing something."

Amy chuckled, low and dirty, and reached behind her for the camera, eyes never leaving Chloe's face.

"Okay?" she asked, thumb on hovering on the shutter, and Chloe nodded, gaze fixed squarely on Amy's lips.

She barely registered the flash, too busy reaching for Amy, one hand tangling in her hair, the other settling at the small of Amy's back and pulling her in for another kiss, groaning into Amy's mouth when hips rocked against her stomach.

A click sounded when she set her mouth on Amy's neck, her moan loud when Chloe teased her tongue across delicate skin.

"Have you ever done this before?" Chloe asked, breath ghosting across Amy's collarbone.

Amy's fingers dug hard into her shoulder. "N-never," she said, voice trembling when Chloe's other hand skated up the inside of her thigh to toy with the button of her jeans. "Is it...is it okay?"

"So long as they never see the light of day."

"They won't," Amy promised, whimpering when Chloe slipped a hand beneath her underwear, groaning when Chloe found her slick and ready, hips rocking when Chloe's fingers brushed against her clit.

Amy's forehead thudded against hers and their eyes locked, though Amy's eyelashes fluttered when Chloe pressed two fingers inside, and she panted against Chloe's lips.

"You feel so good," Chloe said.

Amy wrapped her free arm around Chloe's back as she rocked into her, Chloe's palm pressed against her clit.

"Kiss me." Amy dragged her closer, and Chloe obliged, seeing the flash of the camera behind her eyelids as Amy's hips shifted. She rode Chloe's fingers with a steady determination that soon turned frantic. Chloe supported her with a hand pressed to the small of her back.

She came with her cries muffled against Chloe's mouth, thighs trembling on either side of Chloe's wrist, kisses turning messy and uncoordinated as she went boneless in Chloe's arms.

Amy set the camera down and pushed Chloe onto her back with a hand on her sternum, eyes dark as she followed.

Chloe's last thought—as her head hit the pillow, deft fingers plucked open the buttons of her shirt, and Amy's mouth descended on her neck—was that this woman was going to be the death of her.

Chloe's phone buzzed with a text, and she swiped it up from the table, smiling when she saw Amy's name on the screen.

"You'd better not be cheating," Jin said, eyeing her from across the table.

"How could I possibly cheat at Articulate?"

"I don't know." Jin's eyes narrowed, suspicion written on his face. "But you could."

"Well, I'm not."

Naomi was gathering cards for their next go, so Chloe thumbed opened the message as she took a sip of beer—and choked when she got a glimpse of the picture.

Amy.

Topless.

Hand in Chloe's hair, tongue in Chloe's mouth, and Jesus *Christ* she was going to explode.

"You okay, Chlo?" Naomi asked, patting Chloe on the back when she sputtered.

Chloe shoved her phone into her pocket. "Fine," she squeaked.

Naomi eyed her with concern. "You sure? Cause you're a…very interesting shade of red."

She cleared her throat, forcing her voice deeper. "I'm good."

Naomi looked at her like she'd grown a second head. "Okay, well we need four of these to win," she said, waving the cards in her hand. "You ready?"

"Uh-huh."

Except she wasn't, because all she could think about was that photo— the curve of Amy's jaw, the sheer amount of bare skin on display—and decidedly *not* the famous people Naomi was trying to describe to her.

"Chloe!" Naomi smacked her on the arm when she managed only one, and Jin crowed in victory. "What is the matter with you? You couldn't remember the name of the fairy in *Peter Pan*? Seriously?"

"I had a…brain freeze moment," Chloe said, still not able to form proper sentences. She downed the remainder of her beer in one long gulp. "Anyone need a refill?"

She escaped to the safety of the kitchen, phone clutched tight in her hand. When she opened the message and was confronted with the photo again, Chloe's mouth went dry, and she wondered whether sticking her head in the fridge would do anything to calm her burning cheeks.

I lost a very intense game of Articulate thanks to you, she typed, her fingers shaking. *I hope you're happy.*

The reply came seconds later.

How is that my fault?

You can't send me pictures like that without warning. I think my brain short-circuited.

Photos like this one?

Attached was one of Amy on her lap, face visible in profile, Chloe's mouth on her neck. Nothing terribly provocative, but Chloe knew where her hand was, buried between Amy's thighs, knew why her eyes were closed and her lips parted. Her stomach clenched.

Are you trying to kill me?

Maybe.

Another photo, one Chloe hadn't realised she'd taken, of the sharp planes of Amy's stomach and Chloe's hand in her underwear, the outline of Chloe's fingers visible beneath black lace.

She couldn't take any more and lifted the phone to her ear, glancing out the door to check no one else was nearby.

"You are evil," she said when Amy picked up, voice hoarse. "Pure evil."

"I know." The words were low and wrapped around her like silk. "Where are you right now?"

"In my friend's kitchen. I think they think I have a fever. Don't laugh!" she said, when Amy chuckled. "It's not funny."

"It's kinda funny."

"Nothing about me being here and you being there right now is funny."

"There are ways around it," Amy said, and Chloe swallowed, mouth dry, heart pounding.

"I can't do that here."

"No, but..." She heard a rustle and wondered if Amy was already in bed. "You could call. When you get home."

"I...yeah. O-okay."

"Don't keep me waiting too long. I might start without you."

"Jesus Christ."

Another laugh.

Chloe took a deep breath. "I'm going to hang up now."

"Talk to you later," Amy said, with promise.

Chloe slid her phone back into her pocket with shaking fingers.

"Chloe!" Naomi yelled before she'd had a chance to cool down. "Hurry up. We're playing Taboo next, and I refuse to lose two games in a row."

Okay.

Okay, she could do this.

Another hour or so, and then she could leave, she could call Amy, and she could start functioning like a normal human being again.

Her phone kept buzzing.

She didn't dare look at it until she was home.

Chapter 21

"CHLOE. I DIDN'T REALISE YOU were here."

Chloe froze in place, one foot out of Amy's front door and decidedly unprepared to come face-to-face with her mother.

"Uh, yeah. I came over to…" Why had she *said* that? She didn't need an excuse to be over here. She was coming over with increasingly regularity, in fact—not that Leanne needed to know the reason for that. "Talk to Amy," she finished, well aware of how lame that sounded.

Green eyes appraised her carefully. Oh God, had she put her shirt back on the right way?

She should've run a brush through her hair, too. Should've followed Amy into the shower to wash away the scent of her lingering on Chloe's skin. Leanne couldn't tell, could she? That half an hour ago Chloe had been wrapped in her daughter's sheets?

"Are you coming over for dinner?"

"I, uh…" Shouldn't. Should go back to the house, because she'd barely done so much as lift a paintbrush all weekend. Absolutely should *not* sit for dinner with Amy's family when not ten minutes ago, Amy'd had her thighs wrapped around Chloe's head.

"Gabi is making enchiladas. They're delicious."

"Oh, I wouldn't want to intrude—"

"Nonsense. We'd love to have you. I don't know why Amy didn't invite you herself." She peered around Chloe's shoulder. "Where is she?"

Chloe could lie, but the sound of the water running was loud. "Said she wanted to grab a quick shower."

"I see. Well, come along." Leanne hooked an arm through Chloe's and steered her toward the farmhouse. "She can join us later."

The kitchen was a flurry of activity. Gabi stirred a pan on the hob while Danny chopped vegetables beside her. At the table, Adam was chewing on a pencil as he frowned at his homework, and Sam was watching something on his tablet.

"Chloe!" Adam scampered over to hug her. "I didn't know you were coming!"

"I just invited her," Leanne said. "I didn't think anyone would mind."

"Not at all." Gabi welcomed her with a warm smile. "We're making plenty."

"Where's Bella?" Adam asked.

"She's back at the house."

He looked crestfallen. "You didn't bring her?"

"I would've, if I knew I was coming over."

"Why are you here if you didn't know you were coming over?"

She scratched at the back of her neck. "I came to talk to your auntie. Sorry, your tía." Her pronunciation was terrible compared to the rest of the Edwards family, but Adam didn't bat an eye.

"About what?"

"Uh…" She cast around for a reasonable excuse, watching a smirk bloom over Gabi's face. She'd forgotten Gabi knew about them—Chloe wondered what Amy had told her.

Christ, did *Danny* know?

She stared at his back. He didn't look especially mad, but it was hard to tell.

"Adam," Gabi said, taking pity on her. "You need to finish your homework before dinner."

"But—"

"But nothing." Gabi settled a hand on her hip, and Chloe could see her in front of a room full of teenagers, putting them in their place. "Homework. Now."

"Can Chloe help?"

"Depends what it is, kiddo."

"Science." He took her hand and tugged her over to the table. "I'm labelling body parts."

"Don't think you need any help," Chloe said, glancing at his worksheet over his shoulder. "They all look right to me. You like science?"

"Yeah! It's the best. Better than maths." His nose wrinkled. "And English is boring. I like PE, too. We played football today."

"You score?"

He puffed out his chest. "Yeah. Mr. Eccles said I was the best on the team. Tomorrow we're playing rugby, but that's not as fun."

Chloe chuckled, glancing up when a shadow fell across the doorway. Amy blinked when she saw Chloe perched in her usual seat, brows creasing into a puzzled frown as she stepped into the kitchen. Damp hair curled at the back of her neck, and her sweatpants sat low on her hips.

"I took the liberty of inviting Chloe for dinner," Leanne said, without looking up from where she was preparing a salad at the kitchen counter. "Seeing as you didn't extend the courtesy."

"Because I know she's a busy woman." Amy stole a tomato, popping it into her mouth and ducking out of the way when her mum tried to swat her on the side of the head. "Did she strong-arm you into this?" she asked, turning to Chloe like she hadn't just left her bed. "Are you here against your will?"

"She's exactly where she belongs," Leanne said, and Chloe swallowed, trying not to think how right the words sounded.

This was the kind of easy domesticity she'd always loved about coming over to the Edwards house. Those evenings with Amy's mum bustling around the kitchen, her dad sitting and reading the newspaper, enjoying a quiet few minutes to himself, while the three kids did homework or played games, before they all came together for a home-cooked meal.

This was different but the same, somehow, that same content feeling settling in Chloe's stomach.

"Are you here on the second, Chloe?" Adam asked, distracted from his homework once again. "It's a Sunday."

"I should be. Why?"

"It's Día de los Muertos," he said. "You should come celebrate with us."

"Oh, you should, if you're around," Gabi said, touching Chloe's shoulder as she leant over her to put the salad on the table. "There's a big gathering at the church cemetery."

"The whole village gets involved?" Chloe couldn't keep the surprise out of her voice.

"Not the whole village, but it seems to grow every year. I started things, when I moved here, for us, but…more people kept asking about it. Wanting to be a part of it, and now it's a yearly staple. A splash of culture, if you will."

"That's cool." And something she could never have imagined, growing up here. "Yeah, I'd love to join you. Do I need to bring anything?"

Adam bounced in his seat. "You need to make an ofrenda for anyone you want to remember. Favourite foods, photos, and candles, so their souls know where to go."

"I make one for your mother every year," Amy's mum said, voice soft, and Chloe remembered the freshly placed flowers on her grave. "I didn't think you'd mind."

Chloe's throat felt tight. "N-no, not at all. Thank you." She'd need one for her father, too. She didn't believe in the afterlife, in ghosts coming back to haunt the living, but she knew they'd want to be celebrated together. "I'll bring things."

"And we can make tamales and pan de muerto," Adam continued, eyes bright, speaking at break-neck speed. "And Mrs. Peterson and her old lady friends make really good sugar skulls. And you can have your face painted, too, if you want, but you don't have to. Sam doesn't like it. Me and my friends do, though."

"Breathe, chiquito," Amy said, ruffling his hair. "And don't spoil all the surprises for Chloe."

Her eyes met Chloe's, gleaming in the kitchen lights. She was beautiful, never more so than when relaxed and at home, wearing comfy clothes and a warm smile. Chloe's breath hitched; she wanted nothing more than to reach for her, pull her into a kiss, and never let her go.

"Welcome to the madness," Gabi said, when Chloe arrived at the cemetery on the second, Bella's lead in one hand and a bag of offerings in the other.

People milled between gravestones, talking in quiet voices. It was a bigger turnout than Chloe had expected. Some ofrendas were already complete, candles flickering in the November breeze and plastered with photographs and gifts.

Craft tables were set off to one side, similar to the village fair. One was overflowing with bright yellow and orange flowers, another with what looked like pastries. Mrs. Peterson sat behind a table of the sugar skulls Adam had mentioned. Sam was painting one. Leanne had one hand on his shoulder, and Mrs. Peterson was talking her ear off.

"Amy and Danny got held up with a calf emergency," Gabi said, noticing Chloe's eyes scanning for a familiar face. "But they should be here soon. In the meantime, I'm sure Adam would love to help you set up your ofrenda."

He nodded, then took her hand and walked with her to her parents' graves. A headstone for her dad now sat beside her mum's. "Abuela told us some stories about your mum. She said they were friends."

"Best friends." She touched her fingers to a petal of one of the lilies lying on the ground.

"Like you and Amy are best friends?" he asked, and Chloe nearly choked.

"Sure," she said, because she couldn't exactly spell out the differences. "They met when my parents moved in next door to your house. Used to ride horses together. Bred some together, too."

"What was she like?"

"My mum? I...don't know. I was younger than you when she died."

"Oh. Well, it's okay if you don't have any stories to tell. You can just listen. That's what I do, because Abuelo died before I was born. You knew him, didn't you?"

"I did."

"Tía Amy says he was a Tottenham fan like us."

"He was. He'd always make sure he had all his farm jobs done before kick-off. You could always tell if a match was on, because you'd see him running in from the fields."

Adam giggled.

"Wanna tell me what I'm doing here, Adam?" A table was already set up beside the graves, courtesy of Amy's mum, she assumed. She looped Bella's lead around one of the legs, trusting she wouldn't yank the whole thing over.

Adam clapped his hands together, a man on a mission. "Did you bring photos?"

"I did." Dozens of them, taken from the boxes she was storing in the garage, belongings she'd be taking back to London with her once the house was done. "Do I put them on here?"

He nodded.

Chloe placed the largest, a picture from her parents' wedding day in a large, ornate frame, in the centre, ghosting her fingers across their faces.

"You look like your mum," Adam said, and Chloe tilted her head, trying to find the resemblance.

"You think so?"

"Yeah. You have the same eyes. And smile."

Chloe wasn't sure she saw it herself. And that was certainly where the similarities ended. Her mum had been a slight figure, almost frail, and a full eight inches shorter than Chloe.

"What else did you bring?" Adam asked, peering into Chloe's bag.

"Well, Dad always said you couldn't beat a meat and potato pie, so I brought him some of them. My mum had a real sweet tooth, so I picked up some of her favourites. And I know they used to drink whiskey, so I got a bottle of that, too." She laid them all out on the ofrenda, and Adam took her hand.

"Flowers next! The florists grow flor de muerto specially for us every year. They're bright, so they attract the souls of the dead."

The marigolds were beautifully vibrant, their petals soft beneath her fingertips. She bought a few bunches, and Adam helped her to scatter them over the ofrenda. Chloe thought her mum would approve.

"It looks beautiful." Leanne approached with a smile and drew Chloe into a hug. "Sam has something he wants to give you."

"He does?"

Leanne squeezed his shoulder, and he stepped forward, head down but palms held aloft. Two sugar skulls sat balanced in them.

"One for each of your parents," Amy's mum said. "He decorated them himself."

Chloe felt her heart constrict and her throat tighten, more touched by the gesture than she'd ever be able to say. "They're beautiful," she said, kneeling so they were a similar height and taking them gently from his hands. "Thank you, Sam." She refrained from hugging him, knowing he'd hate it. "You wanna hang out with Bella for a while? I think she's missed you."

He glanced at the Labrador sitting beside her, patiently waiting to be set free, her tail wagging in the grass. Sam nodded, a quick, jerky motion, and Chloe smiled.

"I'll give her lead to your Abuela, shall I? And you can take her for the afternoon."

"Careful," Leanne said to Chloe, watching Sam wind his arms around Bella's neck and bury his face in her fur. "You might not get her back."

"She might not want to come back. She loves kids." Loved the fuss, more like. That dog was never happier than when she was the centre of attention.

Chloe sent the three of them off with Bella and a tennis ball. She watched Bella tear over the grass of the field behind the cemetery and the boys trying—and failing—to keep up with her. Their laughter carried back to Chloe on the wind.

An arm wound around her waist and she jumped, turning to find Amy grinning behind her.

"Hi." She looked good, a faint flush on her cheeks and a woolly hat on her head, wisps of blonde hair escaping its confines to curl around her cheeks.

"Hi. Did you fix your calf emergency?"

"Four hours, one vet bill, and a healthy mother and baby later," she said with a nod. "Are you having fun?"

"Not as much fun as Adam." Chloe glanced over to the field, amused to see Bella had gained a following. A few other kids had joined in the fun.

"Oh, he loves this time of year. Halloween, Día de los Muertos, and bonfire night all one after the other, and then before you know it, it's Christmas."

"If he's this hyper today, what's he like on Christmas morning?"

"Dial it up about a thousand, and you get the general idea."

"And I thought Naomi's nieces were bad."

"You spend the holidays with them?"

"Yeah. We all stay over at her parents' on Christmas Eve, watch films until the kids pass out, have a few glasses of wine, and get woken up at the ass crack of dawn because they want their presents."

"Sounds nice."

"It is." She never used to be big on Christmas, after leaving Corthwaite. For a few years, it had been just her and her dad, where once it had been them and Amy's family together, a quiet celebration instead of the riot of noise and chaos they were both used to.

And then Naomi's parents had started inviting them over, inviting them into their traditions, and after Zara and Tessa came along, Chloe loved nothing more than seeing their wide-eyed excitement on Christmas morning.

This year, a part of her was dreading the holidays, because she knew it would mean her time in Corthwaite was over. She couldn't stretch the renovations into next year, much as she might want to try. Already, the drive was getting harder, the nights darker, the weather miserable more often than not, rain sluicing over her windscreen as she manoeuvred her van around country lanes. Frost, ice, and snow would be arriving soon, and with it, the end of the project she was supposed to have finished a week ago.

Amy's arm was still looped around her, fingers splayed at the small of her back, more intimate, perhaps, than the setting called for, but Chloe didn't shift away. She wanted to shift *closer*, and wasn't that the problem? That no matter how close she got, it would never be enough?

"You okay?" Amy asked, brows creasing into a frown as she looked up at Chloe.

She nodded. There would be time to be sad later, time to dread the ticking of the clock, time to mourn this thing between them when it was done, but tonight wasn't it.

Tonight was a night of celebration, of remembrance, of stories shared between friends and family alike, of a village drawing together for a tradition unlike anything Chloe had ever seen before.

There were tears, laughter, drinks, and so much food she didn't know if she'd be able to make it home. And she was surrounded—*accepted*—by people she'd never thought she'd see again.

Chapter 22

HAY SCRATCHED THE BACK OF Amy's neck, the bale she was using as a makeshift chair not comfortable in the slightest.

"The things I do for you," she said, looking over at Regina, whose head rested on top of the stable door. Her eyes were closed, and her bottom lip was drooping.

Amy was bored. The food Gabi had brought out to her was long gone, and from the look of Regina, it would be at least another hour before she could be left unsupervised. She'd exhausted all of the apps on her phone, and her thumb hovered over her recent messages. Chloe's name was at the top of the list.

They'd been talking more and more, sometimes by text, sometimes on the phone, but not a day went by when Amy didn't hear from her in some capacity. It was becoming a problem, the need to speak to her, the impatience with which Amy waited between messages. The co-dependence, the way a single text from Chloe could brighten her whole day.

It was a sign of her burgeoning feelings, the ones Amy still tried to staunchly deny, even to herself.

It's fine, she thought, breath quickening as she glanced at the photo Chloe had sent earlier that day, of her in a hard-hat and a high-vis vest, getting to work on her latest renovation. *It's fine you can't stop thinking about her. It's fine you can't imagine a life without her in it. Totally under control.*

She scoffed, tipping her head back and staring up at the rafters, where a dove stared back at her, taking shelter from the howling wind outside.

Nothing about the situation she found herself in was fine, but she knew only one thing would quell her rioting thoughts.

Which was part of the problem, she thought as she tapped on Chloe's number, because who was she going to go to when Chloe left? Who was she going to call at the end of a bad day, to ease it all away?

"Hi," Chloe said, answering on the third ring. "You okay?"

"Yeah. Just thinking about you." Why did she say that? It was a miracle Chloe hadn't figured out how deep Amy was in already. Would she stop things, if she knew? Would she pull away, let Amy down gently? Would she—?

"Oh yeah?"

Chloe didn't sound wary—she sounded interested, maybe a little touched, and Amy sighed.

Stop overthinking.

"Yeah. What are you doing?"

"Catching up on my neglected Netflix queue."

Amy imagined her stretched out on her couch. "Oh. Should I let you get back to it?"

"No, it's okay. What are you doing?"

"Waiting for my dumb horse to come around from the very expensive anaesthetic the vet gave her." She glanced over, but Regina hadn't moved.

"What happened?"

"Dunno. Had a fight with a fence, by the looks of it. Ended up with wire wrapped around her leg and was very grumpy about getting it removed."

"Hence the anaesthetic?"

"Yup. Cost me two hundred quid."

Chloe whistled. "So you've had a good day?"

"Oh, splendid." But she felt better already. "Looked like yours wasn't so bad."

"You know me. Love a chance to get my hands dirty."

"Oh, I know."

Chloe chuckled, low and warm. "It sounds loud there."

"It's the wind. Some stupid storm. I'm freezing my tits off."

"Would this be a bad time to tell you I'm currently under a blanket with Bella keeping my feet warm?"

"Go away."

"I can, if you want."

"No," Amy said, too quickly, and Chloe laughed again. "Can I...? Can I see your flat?" She'd seen glimpses of it, grainy background in some of the photos Chloe sent her, but she wanted a proper picture, wanted to be able to imagine Chloe in her own space whenever she called.

"What, on video?"

"Yeah."

"One sec. Let me call you back." The line went dead, but Chloe rang her back on video mere seconds later. When Amy answered, Chloe's smiling face filled her screen. "Hi."

"Hi. Give me a tour."

"I don't know how well you'll be able to see, but okay. This is my couch," she said, turning the camera around, and Amy saw Bella stretched out on black leather, one eye open. "And my living room."

Open plan, Amy noted with amusement, the kitchen sleek and grey and familiar. In fact, she spotted a lot of similarities between Chloe's flat and what she was doing with the house. The style, the colour scheme, even a similar pattern on the wallpaper.

"I guess you're right," Chloe said, when Amy pointed it out, sounding like the idea had never occurred to her. "Just my taste, I guess."

Minimalist, Amy would describe it as, a world away from the pile of furniture crammed into her own place. Chloe's bedroom seemed more personal, with memory boards full of photographs on the walls, and Amy wished she could see them properly, could get a glimpse of the life Chloe had lived in-between knowing her.

"And that's it," Chloe said, turning the camera back to herself as she walked through the hall. "Not much, but it's mine."

"No, it's nice. What can you see out your window?" she asked, noticing the glittering lights over Chloe's shoulder.

"Some of the city." She showed Amy the view. "You miss it?"

"Yeah," Amy breathed a wistful sigh. "It's been so long since I've been."

"Would you want to visit?" Chloe asked, and Amy's heart nearly stopped dead in her chest.

"Are you inviting me down there?"

"Why not?" Chloe shrugged, like it was nothing, like she wouldn't be inviting Amy into her space—a space they were yet to share. Into the part of her life she'd so far kept closed. Like it wasn't opening another door, wasn't going to send them tumbling further down the rabbit hole, further away from the line drawn into the sand.

"I...yeah, okay. I'll have to talk to the others, but I think they can spare me. For a few days at least."

Chloe smiled, warm and soft, making Amy's chest tight.

Too deep, she thought, as she hung up the phone. *Too deep, too far gone, and there's no way to stop it now.*

Amy had forgotten how busy London was.

The second she stepped off the train, she was caught in a stream of people hurrying for the exit, dragged along in the undertow as announcements boomed through the Tannoy. Dozens of different languages surrounded her as she headed for the ticket barriers.

Chloe had said she'd be waiting outside WH Smith, but the crowd was so dense Amy couldn't see her. She jumped when she felt gentle fingers on her elbow and turned to find Chloe, smiling crookedly and looking better in black jeans and a leather jacket than anyone had a right to.

"You okay?" she asked, eyes alight with amusement, and Amy let herself be steered out of the rush of the people to the safety of the wall.

"Yeah. Forgot what it was like here. Everyone in a hurry."

"Ah, yes. Bit of an adjustment. It's not so bad in Twickenham, but to get there I'm afraid we're going to have to brave the Tube. Think you can handle it?"

"I'm sure I can manage."

Chloe tangled their fingers together—a first—and Amy held on tight as they weaved through tourists and locals alike to the escalator leading underground.

The platform was rammed, the carriage they were pushed into so full there was barely room to breathe. Although Amy had frequented the rush hour train in another stage of her life, it had been years, and the suddenness of it—that morning she'd been milking cows, and now she was packed into a small space with the equivalent of double Corthwaite's population—was a shock to the system.

"It'll get quieter soon," Chloe said, noticing her discomfort. "In a couple more stops."

She was right. People spilled out, very few came in, and Amy felt better once Chloe had steered her into a seat.

Chloe looked at ease, her head tipped against the back of the seat, seemingly unperturbed by the man beside her spreading his legs so wide he took up half of her seat as well as his own. Amy thought she'd seen Chloe in her natural habitat, but she'd only caught glimpses of it, because Chloe wasn't truly at home in Corthwaite.

Had been once upon a time, maybe, when her dad was still around, when she'd had a place at the Edwardses' dinner table, when there was nothing complicated at all about the relationship between them, no lines blurred.

But this was her home now, among skyscrapers and city slickers, and the life she'd carved out for herself when she felt like she had nowhere else to go.

In another life, this could have been Amy's normal. A photography studio nestled away in Camden, with a tiny flat above where she could lay her head. A dream she'd never get the chance to realise since tragedy and necessity had drawn her three hundred miles away.

And she didn't regret it, loved what she'd done with the farm, loved the animals, loved the success she'd managed to breathe into something close to dying.

But still, being here, seeing Chloe here, in her little corner of the universe, made Amy want with an ache so fierce it stole the breath from her lungs.

If their paths had crossed, years ago, when they'd both lived within London's city limits, would things be different, now? Would Chloe have still forgiven her? Would they have had the chance to be happy, together?

Amy didn't believe in fate, but she couldn't ignore the draw she felt to Chloe. How simply existing in the same space as her was like a balm to Amy's soul. Eighteen years apart, and still they'd fallen back together, chance and circumstance bringing them back into the same orbit with magnetic force.

That had to count for something, didn't it?

"You okay?" Chloe asked, turning to her with her brows creased.

Amy wondered what Chloe saw on her face.

Casual is all I can give, she'd said, and if that had changed, wouldn't Chloe have said?

"Yeah. Strange being back."

"Bringing back memories?"

Bringing up something. "Mm. I was a whole different person back then." She'd been twenty-three when she'd first moved, fresh-faced and naïve, and no idea what road lay ahead. "It'll be fun to see things with wiser eyes."

It took another hour to get to Chloe's flat. The stands of Twickenham stadium were visible in the distance as Chloe swiped a key fob against the door of an apartment block, Amy's hand still held in hers. Bella greeted them with enthusiasm, and Chloe told Amy to make herself at home. She made a beeline for the photographs in Chloe's bedroom, the ones she'd so desperately wanted to see the other night.

"I want the story," Amy said, pointing to one of Chloe sprawled on someone's front lawn, a garden gnome in her arms. "How drunk were you in this one?"

Chloe groaned. "Uh, very. Needless to say, I don't remember that night well."

"So you don't know why you're cuddling a gnome?"

"I mean, it *was* a good-looking gnome."

"And this one?" In it, she had her eyes half closed, a bottle of whiskey held aloft in one hand, a pair of boxers on her head, and a moustache scribbled on her top lip.

"I may have had a drinking problem at uni," Chloe admitted, her smile wry. "That sharpie took days to wash off. I had to do my final exam with it on my face."

"You got wasted the night before your final exam?"

"...Three days before, and it was my roommate's fault. She finished earlier than me and threw a house party, and naturally, I couldn't manage to stay away. But I still passed! Moustache and all."

Amy shook her head, trying to take all the photos in. Chloe, tall and gangly, still not looking comfortable in her own skin, with Naomi's arm wrapped around her. Chloe, lounging backwards on a chair with a rainbow flag draped over her knees, lazy smile spread across her face. Chloe, sitting cross-legged on the floor of a retirement home, eyes shiny, her dad's frail hand on her shoulder. Chloe, holding a bundle of blankets, tiny fingers wrapped around her thumb.

A dozen memories and more, but not a single photograph of her as a teenager, as a child, or any evidence she'd ever lived in Corthwaite at all. Even the pictures of her parents, scattered through those with her friends, couldn't be tied to the village, to the house. Amy wondered if she'd stripped herself bare, stripped away all the memories. Wondered if she'd do it again, once the house was sold.

"Anything in particular you want to do today?" Chloe asked, perching on the end of her bed, not seeming to notice Amy's spiralling thoughts.

Amy reached for a fistful of her shirt and pulled her into a kiss she'd been waiting for since Chloe had grabbed her arm in Euston station.

"I have some ideas," she said, pushing Chloe onto her back, knees sinking into the memory foam mattress as she straddled Chloe's hips.

Amy had lingering little reminders of Chloe back in Corthwaite—the memory of a kiss here, the ghost of Chloe's fingers pressing between her legs there—and thought it was only fair for her to return the favour.

To leave an imprint of herself her in Chloe's bed, for Chloe to hold when Amy was gone.

The smell of bacon wafted through Chloe's open bedroom door, summoning her from the depths of sleep.

The sheets were cold beside her, and she lamented—she'd yet to wake up with Amy by her side in the morning, since she was often deep into her duties by the time Chloe roused. She'd been hoping this weekend would prove to be an exception.

Evidently not.

She rolled out of bed and pulled on some boxers and a shirt before padding down the hall, where she stumbled upon a scene she never wanted to forget.

Amy, with her back to Chloe, watching over a sizzling pan, hair messy and untamed, backlit by the rays of the winter sun.

She was wearing the shirt Chloe had worn yesterday—which barely covered her ass, offering a glimpse of black lace beneath—and humming softly along to the radio. Bella gazed up at her with hopeful eyes, waiting to see if a piece of bacon would get tossed her way.

Amy looked so at home, so like she belonged, that it nearly knocked Chloe on her ass.

She'd known it was a mistake to invite Amy here the second the offer had left her lips.

A mistake, to know what Amy looked like, half-dressed in Chloe's kitchen cooking her breakfast. A mistake, to let her linger in a place so markedly her own, a space where few had ventured, in recent years, to let Amy taint these walls with her presence, with her memory, with a glimpse of a life together Chloe desperately wanted.

A mistake, but she'd deal with the consequence, because it all seemed worth it, when Amy turned and smiled over her shoulder.

"Morning, sleepyhead."

"It is"—Chloe paused, checking her watch—"seven thirty. An unreasonable hour to be awake, for most people. Especially after last night."

Amy grinned, and Chloe rolled her shoulders, a pleasant ache in her muscles that nights with Amy always left behind. "How long have you been awake?"

"About an hour. I was going to wait, but thought I'd prove myself useful instead."

"Very useful," Chloe said, sliding her arms around Amy's waist from behind and kissing the inviting slope of her neck. "You can come every weekend, if you like."

She made sure the words were light, teasing, and hoped Amy couldn't tell she meant them.

"I think my brother would have something to say about that." A gentle reminder of why it could only ever be temporary, of why their lifestyles didn't mesh in all of the ways that mattered.

Chloe distracted herself with her lips on Amy's neck, revelling in her breathy sighs, in the way Amy went boneless in her arms, head lolling back on her shoulder.

"If you keep doing that," Amy said, nails digging into Chloe's bicep, "breakfast is going to burn."

Let it, she thought, want curling in her stomach. How was it possible to still feel like this, her skin alive wherever they touched, slick between her thighs, when only a few hours ago they'd been wrapped around one another?

Weeks of this, of Amy tugging her close, of Amy's mouth on hers, Amy's hands on her skin, and Chloe wasn't sated, didn't know if she ever would be, if she would ever tire of this feeling, of Amy groaning her name.

Chloe kissed the underside of her jaw, letting her lips linger before pulling away. Amy blinked at her through hooded eyes as Chloe reached for a coffee mug.

"Coffee?"

Amy's nose wrinkled. "No, thank you. I already made myself a tea."

She slid into one of the stools at Chloe's counter like she did it every day, and after a delicious breakfast of bacon, scrambled eggs, and toast, she tried to follow Chloe into the shower.

Chloe stopped her with a gentle hand to her sternum, wiping away her pout with a kiss. "If you follow me in there, we aren't making it out of the flat again, and I made plans for today."

Those plans involved venturing back to the city centre. Amy stuck close to her side, their hands intertwined as they wandered through crowded streets. There was a chill in the air, and Amy's nose was cold when she tugged Chloe close and kissed her, pressing her back against the railing lining the banks of the River Thames.

"What's that?" Amy asked when they parted, pointing toward wooden stalls and twinkling fairy lights in the distance.

Chloe pulled her toward them. "Christmas markets. I forgot they'd be here already."

"Christmas? It's November!"

"Yeah, I know. They always start stupidly early, though. Gotta get their money's worth, I guess."

"Sometimes we take the kids to the markets in Keswick, but that's only usually on for a day."

"These are here for weeks."

"And have more of a selection to browse."

Chloe was content to let Amy do that. She bought some treats for the boys and an ornament for their Christmas tree before they paused for lunch at one of the dozens of food stalls.

"Mac and cheese on a sandwich?" Amy raised her eyebrows at Chloe's choice in cuisine. A plate of pizza was cradled in her own hands.

"Hey, don't knock it 'til you've tried it. It's delicious."

"It is good," Amy conceded, after Chloe offered her a bite. "But it's still weird."

"We'll have to agree to disagree about that." They huddled together out of the way of other people to eat, and they shared a gooey cookie dough from another stall for dessert.

"God, that was amazing. I could get used to eating like this."

"Well, you can come and visit whenever you want," Chloe said, licking chocolate sauce off her fingers.

Amy's gaze was heavy on the side of her face. "Really?"

"I mean, yeah, if you want. Why do you look surprised?"

"I guess I didn't know if we'd keep in touch," Amy said, tugging at the sleeves of her coat, a nervous habit she'd apparently never grown out of. Her mum used to tell her off when she was younger because her school jumpers always ended up with holes from her thumbs. "After you go."

Chloe wasn't sure if this was the place for this conversation, pressed close together beneath the London eye, wind whipping through their hair, but...

"I'd like to."

She didn't know what she'd do if she lost Amy from her life again. Would it be difficult? Absolutely. Would it be worth the pain?

She'd like to think so.

"Do you not?" Chloe frowned. If Amy could close the book on this chapter of her life, on Chloe, and turn another page, and be fine, Chloe didn't know if she could survive it.

"No, I do." Amy reached out, hand wrapping around hers and squeezing. She sounded small and looked fragile, curling in on herself, curling away from Chloe. "I didn't know if you'd want to."

"Of course I want to." She opened her fingers, and Amy's slotted through them. Chloe pulled her close. "We're friends, right?"

Friends, like it didn't have a jagged edge, like the word didn't cut through her heart life a knife. *Friends*, like that came close to encapsulating the weight of what she felt, with Amy's eyes on hers. *Friends*, like that could ever be enough.

"Right," Amy said, and if the word sounded hollow, if her lips were downturned, if the light in her eyes dimmed somewhat, Chloe wasn't going to read into it.

Couldn't.

Not if she wanted to survive the next couple of months.

"Come on," Chloe said, tugging her away from the railing. She needed to move, needed to do *something* to stop thinking, to stop herself from doing something stupid, like telling Amy how she felt. "Is there anything you want to do?"

"Show me your favourite places around here."

That, Chloe could do, and she welcomed the distraction, leading Amy away from the river and onto the familiar streets that had always felt like home.

Chapter 23

"I HAVE A SURPRISE FOR YOU," Chloe said on Sunday morning, stretched out naked in her bed, sweat cooling on her skin.

Amy raised her eyebrows, fingers tracing the stems of the flowers on Chloe's ribs, her interest piqued.

"One second." Chloe kissed her on the cheek before rolling out of bed, not bothering with clothes, and Amy turned to take in the view of her backside as she disappeared into the hall.

When she returned, she was holding something behind her back, and Amy's jaw dropped when she was presented with two tickets, 'Arsenal v Tottenham' written across the top.

"How...how the hell did you get derby tickets on such short notice? In an executive box!"

A lazy grin stretched across Chloe's face. Amy probably shouldn't find smugness so attractive, but on Chloe—especially like this, naked and crawling back onto the mattress—it just *worked*.

"Naomi's brother-in-law is a hotshot lawyer with some very high-profile clients. He has connections. Unfortunately for you," she said, grin widening, "those connections are Arsenal fans. He got us a box. Try not to shout too loud if Spurs score."

"I make no promises," Amy said, reaching out for Chloe's shoulder and dragging her into a heated kiss, filled with more gratitude than she knew what to do with. "Thank you."

"S'okay." Chloe blinked at her, expression dazed like it so often was whenever Amy kissed her stupid. "It wasn't any trouble."

Somehow, Amy doubted that. She'd had to think of her, had to go out of her way to organise it, and that made Amy kiss her harder, fingers sliding around the back of Chloe's neck.

"Before you, um, thank me too much," Chloe said, stilling Amy's other hand as it drifted along her hip. "Two things: one, kick-off is at half one and it takes a while to get there, so we can't get too carried away; and two, um, some of Naomi's family will be there."

Amy froze, and Chloe leaned away, ducking her head. "I think they wanted to meet you. And seeing as they're technically Tristan's tickets, I couldn't exactly say no. But if you're not comfortable with it, we don't have to go."

"No, it's okay." It felt a bit too much like meeting the parents, maybe, too *real* for the state of denial Amy was trying to keep herself in when it came to their relationship, but... "I'd like to meet them."

"You would?"

"Yeah." She drew her fingertip over Chloe's skin, marking patterns on her hip. "You know my crazy family. Maybe it's time I met yours."

And Chloe's smile made the trepidation swirling in her stomach worth it, her lips soft and warm as she drew Amy into a kiss. It was another piece of her shared, another part of her life she was letting Amy see into, another part of her for Amy to hang onto, when all was said and done.

"We're not supposed to be getting carried away," Amy said when Chloe tried to roll her onto her back, stopping her with a hand on her shoulder. "We can't be late to meet Naomi's family because we couldn't keep our hands off each other."

"No," Chloe agreed, falling onto her back beside her. "Because Naomi will definitely comment on it."

Amy wondered how much Naomi knew. That they were sleeping together, clearly, but did she know more? Was she Chloe's confidant? Did she know more about Chloe's feelings toward her than even Amy did?

It wasn't the first time she'd felt a spark of jealousy toward Naomi. It was unwarranted, irrational, and she knew it—she didn't have any *right* to it, and yet she couldn't stop it. Naomi had been there to pick up the pieces of Chloe's broken heart the first time around, Naomi would remain constant when Chloe left Corthwaite behind again, and Amy should be happy about that. Should be happy that Chloe had a shoulder to cry on, a friend to keep her busy at the weekend.

She shouldn't be worrying what Naomi might think of her. What Naomi might see written all over her face if they spent an afternoon together.

"What, um, what do they know about me?" she asked, regretting it as soon as the question left her lips.

Chloe turned away, glancing out the window, flush on her cheeks. "More than I'd care for them to know."

Oh.

Wonderful.

"Sorry. Naomi let a stupid comment slip, and her mum has ears like a hawk. But it'll be fine. I've told them all to behave."

"And will they?"

Chloe grimaced. "Potentially not."

Okay, she could do this. She could force down the butterflies in her stomach long enough to hold a conversation with the most important people in Chloe's life.

"So, who's going to be there?" she asked, because she needed something to focus on. "I need names. Occupations. Something I can make awkward small talk about if I'm left alone with them."

She watched Chloe's face relax, some of the lines smoothing out as she ticked the names off on her fingers. Amy listened intently, and tried not to wonder how many other women Chloe had introduced to the Alleyenes.

Tried to quash the determination to make the best impression of them all.

Nervous energy radiated off Amy in waves, and Chloe pressed a hand to the small of her back, trying to get her to relax.

Bad idea, she thought, as the door to their executive box loomed in the distance. *This is a really bad idea.*

But it was too late to back out now.

She'd been tricked. Had approached Tristan alone, knowing how much watching a match like this would mean to Amy, and wanting it to be a private moment.

But Tristan had told Kiara, and the kids had overheard, and somehow Jada was insisting it had been *too long* since they'd last all had a family day out together. Going on about how there were plenty of spare seats, and it would be a shame for them to go to waste.

And now, somehow, Chloe was leading Amy into the lion's den, into a meeting with the whole goddamn family, and it was going to be a disaster. Because one of them would say something, let slip how her face lit up whenever Amy texted, how eagerly she awaited her weekends in Corthwaite, or tease her about how good they looked together, how happy Chloe had been, these last few weeks.

Bad idea, but worth it, for the look in Amy's eyes when she'd seen the tickets. For the look of grim determination that had spread across her face when she'd asked Chloe to quiz her on what she'd learned about the Alleyenes on the Tube ride over.

They reached the door, Chloe's fingers still pressed to Amy's back. Amy played with the fringe of the scarf she'd bought outside, a souvenir to remember the day by when it was done.

The hum of voices cut off upon their arrival, and several heads turned to face them. Naomi lounged on one of the chairs at the table, cards in her hand. Tessa and Zara were playing with her.

"Chloe!" Tessa scrambled to her feet and threw her arms around Chloe's waist. "I won the art competition!"

"You did?" Chloe cupped Tessa's beaming cheeks in her hands. "Well done. I told you it was good." She wrapped an arm around Tessa's back, keeping her close. "Zara, do I not get a hug from you?"

"I saw you, like, three days ago," she said, trying to sound older than she was.

Chloe pressed a hand to her chest. "You wound me."

Zara rolled her eyes, and Chloe grinned.

"You're being rude," Tessa whispered, tugging at Chloe's sleeve. "You haven't introduced your friend."

Her eyes sparkled when she said *friend*, and Chloe poked her in the side. Of all the people she'd expected to tease her about this, Tessa had been last on the list.

The traitor.

"Right. Everyone, this is Amy."

Like they didn't already know exactly who she was. Like Jada hadn't been asking about her at every family dinner.

"And Amy, you already know Naomi. This is her sister, Kiara, her husband, Tristan, and their kids, Zara and Tessa." She listed the names like she hadn't spent an hour describing them to Amy in detail while trying to ignore the fact that not a single one of her exes had expended the same amount of effort when she'd taken them to family dinner. "And Naomi's dad and mum, Leroy and Jada."

Jada was the one who bustled over to meet her first, wrapping Amy in a hug that made her squeak with surprise. "Lovely to finally meet you, dear," she said, shooting Chloe a look over Amy's shoulder.

"It's nice to meet you, too, Mrs. Alleyene. Chloe's told me a lot about you."

"And we've not heard nearly enough about you." She wrapped an arm around Amy's shoulder and guided her toward the table in the centre of the box. "Come, sit. Tell me about yourself."

Amy glanced toward Chloe, eyes wild, but before Chloe could intervene, she was halted by another tug on her sleeve.

"Chloe, your girlfriend is really pretty," Tessa whispered.

"She's not my girlfriend," she whispered back, praying Amy was too busy being grilled to overhear them.

"Over fifty cows?" Jada said, both of her hands clasped over one of Amy's. "How do you keep track?"

"Do they all have names?" Zara asked.

"What breed are they?" Even Leroy was getting involved now, and Chloe wondered if she should go and rescue Amy.

"Why not?" Tessa peered up at her with eyes wiser than her eight years.

"It's...complicated," Chloe said, eyes fixed on Amy's face. Some of the tension began to ease as she talked about the farm.

"Doesn't seem complicated to me. You like her."

"And sometimes that's not enough," she said, not having the heart to deny it.

"That's dumb."

Chloe chuckled and squeezed Tessa's back. "Yeah, I know. D'you think we should go and rescue her?"

"Maybe. Before Gramma scares her off."

Chloe slipped into the seat beside Amy, settling her hand on Amy's thigh beneath the table and squeezing gently. Amy covered it with her own, fingers sliding into the gaps between Chloe's.

Jada zeroed in on the way Amy relaxed into her, eyes glinting as her mouth opened. "Don't you two look—?"

The arrival of canapes and champagne cut her short, and Chloe breathed out a sigh, reaching for a glass and taking a generous gulp.

"I'm going to go video call Adam," Amy said, phone already in her hand. "Show him the pitch. Make him jealous."

Chloe watched her slide open the glass door leading out to their seats and lean back against the railing as she lifted her phone in front of her. She looked happy, carefree, a grin stretching across her face when she started to speak. Yeah, this was worth it.

Worth it to see her looking like that.

"Girl, you are so far gone."

Chloe turned to find Naomi watching her watching Amy, shaking her head.

"You've been telling me that for months now." Chloe had been *denying* it for months now, too.

"I know." She set down her champagne and leant closer, lowering her voice to guard against prying ears. "But this is the first time I've seen you together since Corthwaite. Chloe, you're fucking glowing. You going to keep telling me there's nothing there?"

She glanced back outside. Amy's hands were gesticulating, lips curving as she laughed at something Adam said. Chloe sighed.

"No. But it doesn't matter, because there's not long left on the house, and then I'll be here and she'll be there, and there's nothing either of us can do about it."

"So you're going to keep pretending you're not head over heels in love with her?"

"Yes. And you're going to stop bringing it up."

Naomi's jaw clenched. Clearly she wanted to say more, wanted to press, but they both knew this wasn't the place for it. Especially when the doors slid open and Amy re-joined the fray, smiling when her eyes met Chloe's across the room.

"We're going to have to talk about it eventually," Naomi said, keeping her voice quiet. "You're going to have to *deal* with it eventually."

"I know." She was well aware of it, of the problem it presented, of the pain she'd be in when things came to an end. "But not yet," Chloe whispered back, forcing a smile when Amy sat beside her. "Is Adam losing his mind?"

"Oh yeah. You're in big trouble."

"Me?"

"Uh-huh," she said, grabbing a canapé from the tray on the table. "For not inviting him. You've got a lot of grovelling to do, when you get back home."

Chloe's heart clenched, at the thought of Corthwaite being a home— *their* home, a place to get back to, instead of away from. Naomi caught her eye, her gaze knowing, and Chloe kicked her under the table.

"I'm sure I can bribe him with something," Chloe said, already thinking of ideas. On the pitch, the players were beginning to stream out of the tunnel, and Chloe touched Amy's elbow. "Come on, it's about to start. Time to watch you get your butt kicked."

"In your dreams."

"Don't say that too loud," she said, grinning as she slid open the door. "Or you're gonna get yourself in trouble. Surrounded by Gunners, remember?"

"Don't remind me. It's your biggest flaw."

Chloe laughed, winding an arm around Amy's shoulder when they took their seats. Tessa came to sit on her knee, Naomi on her other side, the rest of the Alleyenes trickling out behind them as the referee's whistle blew.

Surrounded by her family, with Amy tucked into her side, Chloe had never felt more at peace.

"Are you sure about this?" Chloe asked, pausing with Bella by the door of an office building. Roberts Property Development was written beside one of the numbers on the buzzer. "I'm sure there are much more fun ways to spend your last day than in my office."

"No, I want to see it." Amy had been witness to all the other aspects of Chloe's life over the weekend—her usual haunts, her favourite restaurants and coffee shops, and Amy had shown Chloe her old favourites in return, the spots she'd used to frequent when she'd led a different life.

This was the last remaining part of Chloe's life she hadn't seen, and in a way, it felt like the most important. The origin of her career, the evolution of her professional life, the thing she'd built from the ground up with her own two hands.

"All right." Chloe pushed the door open, nodding toward the receptionist sitting behind the desk, and swiped a card to call a lift.

"We're on the third floor, and we have done far too many steps this weekend."

Amy had to agree. A day of labour on the farm was nothing compared to the paths they'd drawn around the capital. Her feet ached at the end of each day, but she wouldn't have changed a second of it for anything.

"I told them I wouldn't be in until after lunch, so this will surprise them," Chloe said, when she stepped out onto the third floor. "If anyone's around."

The office was small but pleasant, a handful of desks scattered around the room. Two of them were occupied, and Chloe smiled at a brunette woman sitting behind the closest one. A Spaniel appeared from beneath it, and Bella's tail wagged as they sniffed one another.

"What are you doing here, boss? We weren't expecting you for a while."

"A tour was requested," Chloe said, glancing back toward Amy.

She felt herself appraised by shrewd brown eyes. Amy hadn't considered that she should be making a good impression on Chloe's colleagues, a family of its own kind.

"This is Maria, our receptionist, and that's Dash. Maria, this is my friend Amy."

"Friend," Maria said, gaze flicking back to Chloe.

It wasn't a question.

"That's what I said."

There was an edge to Chloe's voice, and Amy wondered how often she brought people around here that weren't clients.

"I didn't think you had any," Maria said, lips twitching, and Chloe narrowed her eyes. "Workaholic, this one." She leaned across the desk to shake Amy's hand. "Lovely to meet you. Are you from nearby?"

"Uh, no. I'm from Corthwaite."

"The hometown?" Interest sparked in Maria's eyes.

"Visiting for the weekend," Amy said. "Couldn't go without seeing where Chloe spends all her time."

"Not all my time." Chloe huffed. "I have a life outside these walls."

"Since when? When's the last time you went on a date?" Maria asked, eyebrows raised, and Amy pushed away the wave of horror the thought incited.

"None of your goddamn business." Chloe turned away from Maria's desk, cheeks stained pink. "This is Devon, our accountant. They are much nicer to me than Maria is."

Devon grinned, stretching out a hand toward Amy and shaking a shock of blue hair out of their eyes. "Nice to meet you."

"Where's your husband?" Chloe asked, perching against the edge of the desk opposite Devon's.

Her own desk, Amy surmised when she spied a photograph of Naomi's grinning nieces sitting on it, and Bella went to curl up on the dog bed set beside it. Curiosity drew her closer. Her fingers pressed against the wood, eyes scanning over a dozen more photos, a desk calendar with puppies on it, and a mug that said World's Best Boss in obnoxiously large letters.

"He drank the last of your coffee, so he ran out to get a refill before you got back."

"He did what?" Chloe feigned outrage, and Amy hooked the mug on one of her index fingers. "A gift from Jin," Chloe said, when she noticed Amy's raised eyebrows. "He wasn't coerced into it."

"Much," Devon said amiably, and Chloe groaned.

"I take back what I said—you are as bad as Maria. Why do you think I never bring anyone around here?"

Devon's mouth opened, and Chloe silenced them with a wave of her finger.

"Do not answer that."

They grinned. "Is Amy coming to games night tonight?"

"What's games night?" she asked, setting the mug aside and joining Chloe at the front of her desk.

"Little get together at mine and Jin's place. We play games, get competitive, eat pizza. Always room for one more."

"Sounds fun, but I'm afraid my train home leaves at two."

"Ah, that's a shame. Maybe next time."

Next time, Amy thought, with an ache in her chest. Like this could become a permanent fixture, like Danny and the farm could survive without her every weekend. Like she could ever fit into Chloe's life here, laughing with her co-workers over a round of Articulate.

"Ah, here he is," Chloe said, when the office door opened. "The coffee thief."

Jin, who had been shrugging out of his jacket, stopped dead, eyes widening when he saw Chloe's folded arms. "What are you doing here?"

"You're supposed to be happy to see me."

"I'm always happy to see you, darling. It was just a surprise." Brown eyes flickered to Amy. "Who," he said, looking like Christmas had come early, "is this?"

"Amy, Jin. Jin, Amy," Chloe said, waving between them. "My second-in-command. And constant pain in my ass."

"You love it."

"Do not," Chloe said under her breath. If Naomi was like her older sister, Jin appeared to be like her younger brother.

There was an easy smile on his face when he asked, "Is Amy here for long?"

"Just long enough to see the place. Which," she said, turning toward Amy, "we've done. Ready to go somewhere more exciting yet?"

This is exciting in its own kind of way. Seeing you with these people, completely at ease.

But she didn't know how to say that without sounding like a weirdo, so she nodded. "Sure. I reckon we can fit in another gallery before I have to catch my train."

Chloe groaned. "Another one? Have we not exhausted them all yet?"

"There's like, a thousand galleries in London, Chloe," Amy said, shoulder bumping her. "And we've been to three. But we can do something el—"

"No, it's fine," Chloe said, before she could suggest an alternative. "We can go and take yet more photographs of old paintings." Her voice was teasing, her eyes sparkling, and Amy wished she could stay in this moment forever. "Can I leave Bella here with you?"

"Of course you can," Devon said. "I'll keep Jin from feeding her too many treats."

"You overfeed her one time," Jin mumbled.

"I'll see you later. Be good." Chloe bent to scratch behind Bella's ears.

"We will," Jin said, and Chloe flipped him off.

"It was lovely to meet you all," Amy said, before following Chloe to the door. A chorus of goodbyes rang out behind them as it closed. "They seem nice."

"Yeah, they're a good bunch." Chloe smiled fondly and threaded her arm through Amy's as she steered her out onto the street. "Now, where to? We have"—she checked her watch—"four hours before your train leaves."

"Whistle-stop tour of the Tate?"

"Lead the way."

Chapter 24

CHLOE SPREAD WALLPAPER GLUE OVER the back of some paper before transferring it onto her old bedroom wall.

Gone was the dark, stormy grey of her teenage years, replaced with a light blue that was already making the room look brighter—and certainly less dingy—as she covered the plaster that had been on show for the past few months,

Chloe smoothed the paper carefully, trying to concentrate on pushing out any air bubbles, on making it a perfect finish, and not on the sense of impending doom building in her stomach.

Because after this, she had only the office and the master bedroom to decorate, new carpets to lay, and... the bulk of the work would be done. All that would be left would be small, superficial things—things she didn't necessarily need to do, things that would add little overall value to the house, things that would be nothing more than an excuse for her to linger longer.

Already, she could start inviting estate agents to the house, start getting appraisals and evaluations, and work out how much she could put it on the market for. But she was yet to pick up the phone, fingers feeling like lead whenever she tried, because she knew the jig was almost up, the sand in the timer nearly all gone, and she didn't know how she was ever going to be able to say goodbye.

Not to Amy, who came over whenever she had a break, sometimes helping, sometimes hindering Chloe's progress for the day, her kisses that much harder, her hands gripping Chloe that much tighter, as though she was trying to keep her in place, trying to keep her *here,* like she didn't want her to leave.

Not to this house, which was feeling more and more like home. Amy had been right—she'd decorated it exactly to her tastes, and all without realising it. Naomi would have a field day when she saw pictures of the finished product.

Not to this village, where people waved whenever Chloe drove past, recognising her van. Where the calls had increased, "My roof is leaking, could you come and have a look?" "I'm thinking about adding an extension, could you come and let me know if it's feasible?" "Could you come and do some repairs on the outside of the church?" Calls dragging her all over Corthwaite to lend a helping hand.

She'd never expected to feel so at ease here, never dreamed she'd miss it, once she was finally gone, once her last tie to the place she'd loved and hated with equal measure was in someone else's hands.

She couldn't imagine it, someone else inside these walls. Someone else cooking family dinners in the kitchen where her dad had used to despair, someone else curling up beside the fire in the living room for a television marathon, someone else laying their head in the bedroom where she'd gone through so much.

Her imprint was all over the house, and on the village, too. Her hands had built lasting markers of her time here. Would they hear stories about her? Would they be tinged with good, this time, instead of bad?

Would Amy look over when the lights flickered on in the house and think of her?

She clenched her jaw and moved on to the next piece of wallpaper. *One step at a time,* she thought, laying it over the table. *It's not over yet.*

But it would be soon. Chloe was again reminded of the edge she was careening toward when Amy appeared in the doorway, one shoulder leaning against the freshly painted frame. "Wow. It's coming along, huh?"

Chloe could see the sadness in her eyes and knew she wasn't the only one struggling with the walls closing in.

"Yeah. Not much left."

"How much longer?" It was the one question they'd both been avoiding, neither of them bringing up their impending expiration date.

Chloe turned her back and pressed the next piece onto the wall, hiding her expression. "Couple of weeks. A month, maybe, if I stretch it."

"You shouldn't," Amy said, like Chloe hadn't been doing that all along. Like Chloe wasn't supposed to have put the place up for sale weeks ago. Like she hadn't been finding more and more jobs to keep her busy.

Naomi and Jin were right—she was stalling, had been for a long time, and she was running out of plausible excuses to keep coming back.

"We'll see how it goes," Chloe said, throat tight, thick with emotion she didn't dare name.

"Okay," Amy said, and Chloe was grateful she didn't press. "Anything I can do to help?"

After ensuring the wallpaper was secured, Chloe grasped Amy's hips and manoeuvred her over to the edge of the bed. "You can sit right there and keep me company. Tell me about your day."

Amy shrugged and shuffled until she was against Chloe's headboard, smiling when Bella took that as an invitation and leapt onto the bed beside her to demand a tummy tickle. "Not much to tell. My life's boring, you know."

"Tell me anyway," Chloe said, hoping she didn't sound too pleading.

Tell me anything, anything to stop me thinking about the fact our days are numbered.

Brown eyes appraised Amy from across the couch. "Why are you moping?"

"I'm not moping."

"Uh, yes, you are." Gabi poked her in the side with her foot. "Carlos cheated on his wife and you haven't said a word about it. Where's your outrage?"

Amy blinked, turning toward the TV and realising she hadn't seen a second of the episode of *Married at First Sight* playing on it. "He did? When?"

"About five minutes ago." Gabi shifted, pausing the show and turning her full attention toward Amy. "Are you all right?"

"Sorry. I guess I'm just distracted."

"And mopey," Gabi added as Amy sighed. "Talk to me."

"It's dumb."

"If it's making you feel something, it's not dumb."

"Is that a line you use on the kids?" Amy asked, fingers drawing patterns on the pleated blanket covering her knees in an attempt to ward off the winter chill. "It sounds very teacher-y."

"Amy."

Not as teacher-y as *that* sounded.

Gabi's eyes narrowed, unimpressed by Amy's attempt to change the subject.

"Fine. Chloe's got an estate agent coming around the house tomorrow, okay? She's nearly finished."

"Oh, Amy." Gabi shuffled across the couch and pulled her into a hug. Amy pressed her cheek into Gabi's shoulder. "Have you guys not talked about making it a more permanent thing?"

"We haven't talked about it at all," Amy said, words muffled. "It's not… we're not supposed to be serious. It's supposed to be temporary. Casual."

"Has it ever been?"

Amy closed her eyes, tears threatening to spill free. "No. But she doesn't know that."

"Don't you think you should tell her?" Gabi asked, and Amy was shaking her head before she'd finished.

"It'll make everything worse."

"Why?"

"Because I can't keep asking her to come back up here. She's given up so much of her time, driven so many miles. I can't ask her for more than she's already given me." *Can't ask for more than she offered.* "She has a life there—she deserves to get back to it."

When Amy's resolve began to crack, when the words *please don't go* threatened to escape her—usually late at night, when Chloe was spread out beside her, and her mind was hazy with tiredness—she reminded herself of that fact.

Chloe had a rich, fulfilling life in London, one Amy had seen with her own eyes. Friends, a family, a job she loved more than anything. Amy refused to do anything to jeopardise it.

Cared about Chloe too much to let her give anything up for her.

She thought Chloe might, if she asked. If she wavered. She'd seen it in her eyes, watched her stall the house sale more and more over the past few weeks, seen her reluctance to end things.

Eighteen years ago, Amy would have made the selfish decision. *Had* made the selfish decision, in the end, had put herself before Chloe, what *she* needed before Chloe, and she'd regretted it every day since.

And I'll regret this one, too, but not for the same reasons. This time I'll put her first. This time I'll make the sacrifice, so she doesn't have to.

"Is there anything I can do?" Gabi asked as Amy's tears soaked into her jumper. "Want some ice cream? Or the brownie might be done. I can go get you a slice."

"I'm okay."

"You are very clearly not okay." She lifted Amy's chin with her index finger and swiped her cheeks with a tissue.

"I will be. I just might need my sister when she leaves for good."

"I'll always be here," Gabi said, tugging her into another hug. "Whenever you need me. You know that."

She did, knew she'd lucked out in the family department—even if she and Danny didn't always see eye to eye.

She had a feeling she was going to need all of them to stem the tide of sadness over the coming weeks.

Trusted that they'd help pull her through to the other side.

"You've done a remarkable job with the place." Armed with a clipboard and a pen, the estate agent scrawled copious notes as Chloe led him from room to room, and she tried not to be offended by the surprise in his voice. "You did all of this by yourself?"

"Uh-huh." Property evaluations weren't something she particularly enjoyed, and sometimes she wished she could sell without the help of a third party.

"That's impressive."

"Why?" Chloe asked, folding her arms across her chest as Gareth peered around the upstairs bathroom. "Because I'm a woman?"

"N-no." He looked startled, pen pausing a few inches away from his paper, and Chloe watched panic bloom in his eyes as he desperately tried to think of a way to walk his statement back. "I don't see many people managing to singlehandedly renovate a property, at least in my experience. Certainly not so well."

Chloe decided to let it go. "Unless you want to go into the garage, you've seen it all."

"I don't think that will be necessary." Gareth slipped his pen behind his ear and quickly scanned his notes. "Shall we sit downstairs and go over everything?"

"Sure."

They were halfway down the stairs when she heard a light knock on the front door. Amy's head poked through a moment later, her eyes widening when she realised that Chloe wasn't alone.

"Oh, sorry." She paused, half in and half out of the house. "I thought you'd be finished."

"It's all right. Come in. I don't think we'll be too long." She hoped not, anyway. She'd met with a different agent earlier that morning, and unless Gareth suggested he could sell the place for a much higher amount, Chloe didn't think she'd be choosing him.

He didn't, and his fee was greater, so Chloe was quick to usher him out before going to seek out Amy. She found her in the kitchen, cup of tea held in her hands and gaze focused out the window.

"Hey."

Amy jumped at the sound of her voice, clearly lost in thought, her tea dangerously close to sloshing over the edge of her mug. "Hey. Sorry, I was miles away."

"You okay?"

"Yeah." But it sounded like a lie, and there was a sad look in her eyes that she was quick to blink away. "How did it go?"

"Good. Better than I expected." Which was promising, because it meant that if she did have to lower the asking price to get it to sell, she'd still be making a profit. "Even taking into account all the fees."

"Did you ever consider selling it independently?"

"Briefly, but it'd be a lot of work. I think it's easier to hand it over to somebody else, especially if I'm not going to be around for viewings and things."

"Right, of course." Amy's eyes were still focused on the window, and Chloe ached at the sadness that was heavy in her voice. "So, is this is it, then? You're all finished?"

Chloe poured herself a cup of coffee with shaking hands, this conversation one she'd never been willing to prepare herself for. "I'll be coming back next weekend to do all the final touches, and get the rest of my stuff, but... yeah. It'll be all done."

I'll be back in London, and you'll be here, and nothing about any of that is fine.

It wasn't fair, that they could find their way back to one another, work so well together, only to be forced apart before things between them got started. Chloe didn't believe in soulmates, but sometimes when she was with Amy it felt like they were meant to be.

"Well," Amy said, with forced brightness, voice so brittle it was a wonder it didn't break. "If we've only got a few days left together..." She took a step closer before fisting a hand in the worn cotton of Chloe's T-shirt, and Chloe's mouth went dry as their eyes met. "We'd better make the most of them, hadn't we?"

Chloe didn't have a chance to reply before she was being kissed senseless. Amy slid her tongue into her mouth, using her grip on Chloe's shirt to pull them flush together, until Chloe was backed up against the kitchen counter, her hands wrapped around Amy's hips, feeling the delicate point of her pelvis beneath her palms.

Kissing Amy was addictive, her lips soft and inviting. Today, there was an edge of desperation to the way Amy's mouth moved against hers, in the way she clung to Chloe like she was afraid of her drifting away.

And Chloe understood the feeling, because it was echoed in her own touches. She couldn't help but wonder how many more times she'd get to kiss Amy before this thing between them was done, how many more times she'd hear her breath catch in the back of her throat, hear Amy moan her name, feel her nails digging in when she came, the taste of her strong on Chloe's lips.

It made her throat tight, made her kiss Amy harder, but she was quick to push the thoughts away—because this wasn't the last time, though she knew that was fast approaching. She forced herself to focus on the moment, on the fact that Amy was here with her, now, pressed up against her, hips arching as Chloe's hands explored soft skin.

Amy's hands dropped to Chloe's thighs, urging her to jump up onto the counter, and she was eager to comply, spreading her legs so that Amy could stand between them, her body warm as she pressed close, lips sinful as she settled her mouth at Chloe's neck, every open-mouthed kiss setting her alight.

"Would it decrease your property evaluation if they knew we'd fucked on this kitchen counter?" Amy asked, the words whispered against her skin, deft fingers making quick work of the button of Chloe's jeans. Chloe's laugh was lost to a groan as Amy's teeth nipped at her pulse point, and her hands fisted in Amy's hair as her tongue soothed away the sting.

"I don't know." Chloe's voice was breathless, affected, her heart hammering in her ears despite the fact that Amy had barely gotten started. "But I'm not planning on telling them."

"That's probably wise," Amy agreed, letting Chloe use her grip on her hair to urge her up into a deep kiss.

Chloe's thighs wrapped around Amy's hips, ankles locking at the small of her back. Calloused hands slid under Chloe's shirt and up over her ribs until Amy was palming her breasts, thumbs dipping beneath the cups of her bra to tease her nipples. Chloe's hips arched against the taut muscle of Amy's stomach, and she knew she'd already soaked through her underwear. One kiss from Amy could make her melt, set her aflame, fill her with a thirst that could only be quenched by the deft touch of her fingers and tongue.

"Come over tonight?" Amy suggested, forehead resting against Chloe's, breath hot on her lips. "So I can take my time with you like I want to right now?"

"O-okay." Chloe was never going to refuse an offer like that, not when Amy was looking at her like she wanted to devour her, pupils blown wide and cheeks flushed with colour.

Amy dipped forward to kiss her, open-mouthed and messy, before shifting until she was settled between Chloe's thighs. Gentle hands urged her hips up enough for Amy to ease down her jeans and underwear, and Chloe hissed at the feeling of cool marble against her bare skin. She was soon thoroughly distracted as Amy's tongue flattened against her. Her hips jerked and her hands gripped the edge of the countertop, knuckles flashing white as she desperately tried to keep herself grounded.

Amy was too damn good at this. Chloe bit at her bottom lip as Amy's mouth explored wet heat with hands splayed across her hips, playing her body like it was an instrument and she was performing a one-woman symphony.

Two fingers slipped into her oh-so-easily as Amy's tongue teased at her clit, each stroke pushing her closer and closer to the edge, her heart racing and heat coiling low in her stomach until she couldn't keep it at bay any longer, her orgasm washing over her like a wave and leaving her breathless.

"Come here." Chloe urged Amy upwards once she'd eased her through the aftershocks, kissing the taste of herself from Amy's lips. "Tell me I've got time to return the favour?"

"If you're quick."

"I can be." She hopped off the counter on unsteady legs and backed Amy up against the nearest wall, hands dropping to the buckle of her belt. Already, she was looking forward to that evening, to having Amy spread out beneath her, breathless and wanting, to taking the opportunity to explore every inch of her body with her lips until Amy was begging for more.

But for now, she knew she couldn't linger, knew Amy had jobs to get back to.

Chloe found her hot and slick as she pressed a hand between their bodies. A leg wrapped around her hip, opening Amy up to Chloe's searching fingers, two of which dipped inside and pressed deep. She loved how wet Amy got for her, loved that it was *her* that had done this, loved the way she felt when Amy was clenching all around her.

She used her hips to drive her fingers deeper, palm grinding against Amy's clit, and when Amy's head thudded back, resting on the wall, she used the opportunity to press her mouth to Amy's neck, kissing and nipping at her skin.

Amy's hands were on her back, nails digging in. Chloe always knew when she was close because she gripped her harder, pulled her closer. She leant up to capture Amy's lips in a kiss when she came, stilling her fingers when Amy went slack, leg sliding back to the floor, leaning her weight into Chloe. Her forehead fell onto Chloe's shoulder, breath coming in quick pants against Chloe's skin.

They were pressed so close Chloe could feel the beat of Amy's heart along with her own, their rhythms matching as they both caught their breath. She could stay there forever, as long as Amy was in her arms.

But they couldn't linger, had lives to get back to, and it was with reluctant sighs that they separated. Amy made herself look presentable before Chloe walked her to the front door.

"Call me when you want me to come over later?"

"Of course." Amy kissed her one last time, tongue sliding against her own in a promise of what was to come, and Chloe watched her drive away before heading back inside.

Her back thudded against the door, and she passed a hand across her face. She had an estate agent to ring, boxes to pack, and finishing touches to begin, but she didn't want to do any of it.

All she wanted to do was drive across to the Edwards house and tell Amy she was going to stay.

Chapter 25

"DON'T YOU WANT TO STAY IN?" Chloe asked when she got to Amy's on Saturday afternoon, trying not to think about the fact that she'd done everything in the house she'd set out to do, and how it had brought her more sadness than a sense of accomplishment.

"We can stay in tomorrow," Amy said, not allowing herself to get distracted by the kisses Chloe pressed to her neck. "Come on, let's drop Bella off at the house. I've got plans."

"Why don't those plans involve you, me, and a bed?" she said, but complied, leaving Bella in Sam and Adam's capable hands before Amy tugged her toward her van. "Where are we going?"

"That would ruin the surprise."

"I don't like surprises." She glanced out of the windscreen as Amy drove through the village, burning with curiosity.

"I thought it would be nice for us to spend the day together," Amy said, fingers tapping against the steering wheel. "You showed me some of your favourite places in London, so." She shrugged. "I want to show you one of mine. One that used to be yours, too."

Chloe's eyebrows knitted into a frown, trying to think. She had a moment of realisation when she saw the signs for Keswick cropping up with increasing regularity. Amy steered them into a car park that looked vaguely familiar.

"I haven't been here for years." It was the closest big town, so when they were kids, they'd often come here on the weekends. "Is the pencil museum still here?"

"Of course. Where else would you find the world's first pencil?" Amy asked, voice serious, and Chloe snorted. "The boys love it."

The weather was nice, for late November, the sky clear but the wintery sun doing little to ward off the chill in the air. Chloe dug her hands into the pockets of her coat as they climbed out of the van, breath fogging in the air.

The narrow streets were bustling with others taking advantage of the sunshine, and Amy pressed close to Chloe's side to avoid losing her in the crowd.

"Come on, it should be quieter by the lake." Amy led her out toward it, away from the shops, weaving through groups of giggling children feeding birdseed to flocks of hungry ducks and swans.

The water shone in the sun, the temperature not cold enough for it to freeze, but in the distance, the mountains were topped with snow.

"You don't get views like this at home," Chloe said as she and Amy perched on an old piece of driftwood. It was moments like this where she wished she could draw, so she could commit it to memory.

"No, you don't." The lake's shore was made up of shingle and stones, and Amy grabbed one with smooth edges. "Remember how to skip rocks?"

"I could never do it." Chloe watched as Amy climbed to her feet and walked the few paces to the edge of the lake, flicked back her wrist, and sent the rock skittering across the water's surface four times before it sank.

"Try."

Chloe searched for a decent looking stone before joining her, and Amy laughed when Chloe's attempt plopped straight into the water. "Told you."

"It's all in the wrist."

"Well, my wrists are apparently weak."

"Come here." Amy handed her a stone and went to stand behind her, breath tickling Chloe's neck when she curled a hand around the back of Chloe's and pulled it back. With Amy's assistance, it bounced twice before sinking into the depths of Derwent Water.

"Try again," Amy suggested, moving to stand back at Chloe's side, and shaking her head in exasperation when she once again failed miserably.

"I guess you have the magic touch," Chloe said, and Amy wiggled her eyebrows. "Shall we walk? It's freezing."

"Sure."

Dozens of trails meandered out from the lake, and they chose one at random. Leaves and twigs crunched underfoot, and Amy kept pulling her away from the path, the two of them winding through thickets of trees, disturbing squirrels and birds with their footsteps.

"We got lost in here, once," Amy said, pausing beneath an oak tree and reaching for Chloe's jacket to pull her close. "Do you remember?"

"I remember you insisting you knew the way back to the path, yes."

"I got us back to our parents, didn't I?"

"After about an hour, yeah. I think your mum was about to send out a search party."

Amy's smile pressed against her lips as she drew Chloe into a kiss, her arms sliding to the back of Chloe's neck. Back then, she'd never have dreamed of doing this, of kissing Amy where someone—unlikely though it may be—could stumble upon them.

Now Amy was the one drawing her in, tongue brushing against hers, fingers gripping tight. Now Amy didn't seem to care who saw, who knew what they were to one another. She kept her fingers tangled with Chloe's when she dragged her back toward the path.

They stumbled upon a clearing looking over the water at the top of a small cliff and sat together on the edge. Amy rested her head on Chloe's shoulder as they took in the view and listened to the gentle lapping of the waves and their quiet breathing.

"Thank you," Chloe said, her lips brushing Amy's forehead. "For bringing me out here."

For the last few months. For being my friend. For making Corthwaite feel more like a home than I ever thought it could.

"The day isn't over yet," Amy said, though she made no move to stand up. "What do you say to Chinese food at Golden Hills?"

"It's still open?"

"Uh-huh. Same family still run it and everything."

"Sounds perfect."

The whole *day* had been perfect, and Chloe didn't want it to end.

"Nope," Danny said, when Amy stepped out of her front door on Sunday morning. "Go back to bed."

Amy, still half-asleep and running late because of her reluctance to drag herself away from the warm body currently lying *in* her bed, frowned. "What?"

"Go on." Danny tried to shoo her back through the door. "Go back to Chloe."

Amy froze. "What?"

"Oh, come on." He rolled his eyes. "It's obvious there's something going on between you. I haven't said anything 'cause I figured if you wanted me to know, you'd have told me. I know she's leaving today, so you should go. Spend some time with her."

"I...thank you."

"S'all right. You give me and Gabi a lot of time to ourselves. Time I returned the favour."

He disappeared down the path, and Amy slipped back into her barn, stripped off her clothes, and joined Chloe beneath the sheets.

She stirred, eyes blinking open, a hand curling around Amy's hip. "You're still here," she said, voice rough with sleep, and this was an image Amy didn't ever want to forget—Chloe, hair tousled, eyes bleary, stretched out on her sheets.

"Apparently I've been given the day off. So I'm all yours."

"I like the sound of that." Chloe mumbled the words against Amy's shoulder, already beginning to fall back asleep, and Amy wondered if she was meant to hear them at all.

Amy let her sleep for a while longer, drawing patterns across the bare skin of her back, watching the clouds float past her skylight. Chloe shifted when Amy's fingers traced across her ribs, ticklish even in sleep, and a groggy hand swatted at her shoulder when she did it again.

"Stop it."

"Make me," Amy said, grinning.

Chloe grumbled, then grabbed her wrists, rolled on top of her, and pinned her arms to the bed on either side of her head. "You are far too awake."

"And you are not."

"Getting there," Chloe said, when Amy's hips shifted beneath her.

Amy chuckled. "I was thinking about getting in the shower. Care to join me?"

Chloe nodded, releasing her wrists and following Amy to her bathroom. The two of them brushed their teeth while they waited for the water to warm, stepping under the spray once the mirror had steamed up.

There was an intimacy to sharing a shower that Amy had always loved, the ability to be vulnerable with another person, skin on skin but not necessarily sexual. Chloe's hands were gentle as she soaped up Amy's hair, and Amy returned the favour, then poured shower gel in her hands and ran them over Chloe's body, admiring the marks she'd left on her skin the night before, a lingering reminder of what they'd shared.

Chloe drew her into a lazy kiss. Amy's hands rested on her hips, water poured over their heads, and Amy thought she would stay there with Chloe all day if she could.

But her water bill wouldn't appreciate that, so they separated and towelled off, slipping into their comfiest clothes before going in search of breakfast.

"What do you want?" Amy asked, riffling through her cupboards.

"You don't have to cook for me."

"I know, but I don't mind. Do you want a full English again? Or pancakes? I kind of feel like pancakes."

"Pancakes it is."

Chloe kept her company while she whipped up the batter, sitting on the kitchen counter, and Amy tried not to get distracted by the sight of damp hair curling at the back of her neck, or by the heavy feeling in her stomach.

She wished that she could slow time, but she felt like it was speeding up, the day getting away from them as they ate and walked Bella hand in hand, then curled up on the couch together when they arrived back home.

"What time do you have to go?" Amy asked, though she didn't want to know. She wanted the answer to be never. She wouldn't give up the last few months for anything, but God, they were hurting her now.

"I'd like to be back before it gets too dark, so about half two?"

Amy glanced at the clock, throat tight as she realised that only left them with a couple more hours.

"The boys will want to see you before you go."

"See Bella, more like," Chloe said.

Amy shook her head. "And you. They love you."

"Sam loves me? Really?"

"He likes you a lot better than he likes most people."

"I'll take it."

"And Mum and Gabi will want to say goodbye, too. You're gonna be missed around here." She tried to keep her voice light, tried not to let any tears spring into her eyes. "I'll miss you."

"I'll miss you, too." Chloe curved a hand around her side, fingers slipping beneath her shirt. "But we're gonna keep in touch, right? It's not goodbye forever."

No, but it's goodbye to this. Goodbye to Chloe, warm against her. Goodbye to Chloe, here, in her home, close enough to reach out and touch.

Amy shifted and slid a knee over Chloe's hips, climbing on top of her in one smooth movement and kissing her breathless, tongue slipping into her mouth, fingers grasping the back of her head.

With the knowledge that their time was limited, things heated up quickly. Clothes were shed and kisses turned frantic, hands running greedily over exposed skin, and God, how was Amy supposed to say goodbye to *this*? To the feeling of Chloe's sex against her thigh, the sound of her moans quiet in her ears, sparks erupting over Amy's skin wherever Chloe's fingers touched.

She slid a hand slid down Chloe's stomach, dipping between her thighs, drawing teasing circles around her clit before slipping two fingers inside. Chloe echoed Amy's movements, found her wet and wanting, and Amy rocked her hips into Chloe's hand, pressing her palm against her clit.

They worked one another up in tandem, their kisses turning messy and uncoordinated until they were panting against each other's mouths.

Knowing she wouldn't hold on much longer, Amy curled her fingers and felt Chloe clenching around her and fingers rake her back as she toppled over the edge herself, eyes slamming closed as she surrendered to the feeling.

They collapsed against one another, breathing hard, Amy's mouth pressed to Chloe's neck.

"Should've waited for that shower," Chloe said, and Amy chuckled.

"You can get in again. I won't charge you."

"How kind."

She didn't, in the end, though they both spent some time making themselves presentable before going to face the rest of her family.

Not that it mattered—they'd all probably guessed what they were up to, anyway.

"Come on. We should be just in time for lunch."

They were, as it turned out. Bowls of soup were already set out on the table for them both. It wasn't fair, how seamlessly Chloe fit, sliding into a seat beside Adam and nodding along as he chattered about school and football.

It wasn't fair, how it felt like she belonged, laughing along with Gabi and Danny like she'd been doing it for years.

It wasn't fair, how time slipped through their fingers like water, for the clock to strike two, for Chloe to start making moves to leave.

"I, uh, I brought you guys a present," she said to Adam and Sam, unzipping her bag. Amy craned her neck to see what she pulled out, because Chloe hadn't told her a thing about it. "Here you are, Adam." She handed him a Tottenham shirt, carefully folded, Edwards written across the back of it in large black letters. Amy was going to cry. "I know it doesn't make up for not taking you to a match, but I hope you like it anyway."

"Thank you!" He wrapped his arms around her neck and tugged it over his head the minute he'd leant away.

"I got a big size, so you can grow into it," she said, grinning when the shirt nearly touched his knees. "Figured it'd last longer, that way."

"I'm never going to take it off."

"Yes, you are," Gabi said, shaking her head. "Thank you, Chloe."

"And for you, Sam, I got this." She handed him a set of *Paw Patrol* toys and some colouring pens. "I, uh, noticed you were running low on some of these last time I was here." She tapped the pens. "So I got you some more. I made sure to get the same brand."

He responded with a hug, quick as lightning, and Amy watched Chloe's throat bob as she swallowed.

"I got you guys some stuff, too. Wine, and a bottle of whiskey." She set them on the kitchen table. "To thank you for, uh, everything you've done for me these past few months. And for making me feel so at home here."

"Oh, Chloe." Amy's mum pulled Chloe into a fierce hug, tears brimming in her eyes. "Don't be a stranger, okay? You're welcome here whenever you want."

"Yeah, we'd love to see you again." Gabi was next, squeezing her tight. "It's been lovely getting to know you."

Her brother opted for a handshake, and Amy wondered if Chloe had ever thought she and Danny would reach this level of civility. "Get back home safe, all right?"

"I will."

"I'll drive you back to the house," Amy said, unwilling to say goodbye, not yet, not in front of her family.

"Thanks."

Leanne wrapped Chloe in one last hug, and then Chloe followed Amy to the door. The drive was filled with an uneasy silence.

"I guess this is it, then, isn't it?" Amy said, when she pulled up in Chloe's drive, every breath she took feeling like a knife in her chest.

"Yeah." Chloe turned to look at her, tears glinting in her eyes. "I guess it is."

And Amy didn't know what to say, how to close this chapter, how anything could possibly come close to explaining how much Chloe meant to her, how much she'd miss her, how much she wished things could be different.

She settled for a kiss, instead. One last kiss, one she'd make sure they both remembered. Her fingers tangled in Chloe's hair, Chloe's mouth a hot slide against her own.

"If you keep that up," Chloe said when they parted, breathless and wide-eyed, "I'm never going to leave."

Good. Stay.

Sacrifice, she reminded herself sternly. *You can't keep her here. You have to let her go.*

"I, uh, I got you something, too." Chloe looked nervous, fingers playing with the zip of her bag, and when she produced a box, Amy's breath caught in her throat. "You don't have to wear it, or anything. It's dumb, but I... I saw it, and well." She passed it over. "I thought you might like it."

She opened the lid and stared at the bracelet. It was dainty and silver, with a tiny horseshoe hung in the middle of it.

"I love it. Thank you. I…I didn't get you anything."

"That's okay. You've given me…you've given me a lot over the past few months."

And what about what you've given me? Forgiveness? A second chance? Love?

"I should let you go," Amy said, her throat tight. If Chloe didn't leave soon, she was going to fall apart, and Chloe was going to *see* how hard this was, how much she cared. "You'll let me know when you get back?"

"Of course." Chloe reached over, curled her hand around Amy's knee, and squeezed. "I'll talk to you soon." She leant over, ghosting her lips over Amy's, and Amy felt tears on her cheek and knew they weren't her own, knew she wasn't the only one struggling. "Goodbye, Amy."

Chloe climbed out of the van with Bella in tow, and Amy didn't linger to watch her disappear into the house.

Couldn't. She needed to get out of there, needed to get home, needed somewhere safe to fall apart.

Tears dripped off Chloe's chin as she stepped inside the house, knowing it was for the last time. The imprint of Amy's face, stricken and pained as she'd driven away, burned onto her eyelids whenever she blinked.

It wasn't supposed to be this hard. Her chest wasn't supposed to burn with every breath. She wasn't supposed to be filled with the urge to get into her van and go back over to the farm and say she wasn't leaving, after all.

It was never supposed to be like this. She was *supposed* to be happy to leave, to close this part of her life for good, to cut her final tie to this tiny village that had managed to wind its way around her heart, squeezing tight.

Instead, she felt closer to it than ever before, was finding it difficult to summon the strength to leave, even though all her belongings were already packed into her van, ready to go.

She wiped her sleeve over her cheeks, knowing this was all her own doing. She'd made her bed—when she'd been standing in this very kitchen, when she'd pulled Amy close and kissed her for the first time—and now she had to lie in it.

Naomi told you it was a bad idea, and you didn't listen, she thought, running a hand through her hair. *You didn't listen, and now you have to deal with it.*

Would she take it all back, if she could?

No, she decided. She wouldn't trade the last few months for anything. The pain would lessen, she told herself, swiping at yet more tears, and it would leave behind the sweetest of memories.

She forced herself to move, to wander through the house one last time, to take in everything she'd managed to do. The transformation was a good one, she knew. She was proud of what she'd manage to achieve, and she liked to think her dad would be too.

She paused in the doorway of his office, and if she closed her eyes, she could imagine him being there. Chloe didn't believe in ghosts, but it felt like his presence was in the room with her, reaching out to her, begging her not to go.

"I hope you like what I've done with the place," she said, her voice quiet in the empty room, and she hoped that he'd come to terms with her decision to leave, though neither of them would have ever guessed what it would cost her.

Letting out a heavy breath, Chloe opened her eyes and left the room, closing the door behind her. She didn't think she'd ever be back, and she allowed herself one final moment to reminisce, remembering all the happy and the sad times that she'd had within these four walls, before she called out to Bella and led her to the van.

"Take one last look, girl," she urged, once she was safely tucked onto the foot well. "I hope you don't miss the open fields too much."

Bella merely blinked at her in reply, and Chloe turned the key in the ignition and pulled out of the drive, watching the house in her rear-view mirror until it was out of sight, a tightness in her throat, more tears slipping down her cheeks.

She wiped them away and cranked her music up loud, singing at the top of her lungs, anything to drown out the thoughts swirling around in her head, to ignore the voice inside it urging her to turn the van around.

When she got home, she fired off a text to Amy as she trudged up the stairs, not allowing herself the luxury of reading through their old messages. She didn't expect Naomi to be sitting on her couch.

"Oh, Chlo," Naomi said after taking one look at her, voice heavy with sympathy. "Come here."

Chloe sat beside her, and Naomi pulled her in for a hug. She buried her face in Naomi's shoulder and let more tears fall.

"What do you need me to do?"

"Being here is enough."

"Let me crack open a bottle." She pressed a kiss to Chloe's temple, leaving her side to pour them each a glass of wine. "I brought comfort food, too. Chocolate, popcorn, and I splashed out on your favourite Ben and Jerry's."

"Even though you think it's overpriced?"

"It is overpriced, but I got it anyway because I thought it might cheer you up. Here, take a spoon."

"I'm not hung—"

"Tough, I bought it so we're eating it." Naomi plonked a tub of cookie dough ice cream into her lap, the sides of it damp with condensation. "It'll make you feel better."

Chloe wasn't sure about that, but she wisely chose not to argue and instead dug in, spoon in one hand and glass of red wine in the other.

"You gonna be okay?" Naomi asked, after a few moments of silence, ice cream smeared across her mouth and somehow on her chin.

Chloe didn't know if Naomi was trying to be funny, but it made her chuckle and eased some of the ache that had settled in her chest.

"Why are you laughing at me?"

"Because you look like you've dived face-first into the tub. It's everywhere."

"You think you're much better?"

"Yeah, because I'm not an animal."

"Oh, we'll see about that."

Naomi swiped a finger first through the ice cream and then across Chloe's nose.

Chloe's mouth opened in shock. "What did you just do?"

"Nothing." Naomi blinked at her innocently, and Chloe huffed, getting some ice cream on her own hand and painting Naomi's cheeks as she tried to squirm away. "Stop it! This is a waste of valuable resources! Do you know how much that cost?"

"You started it!"

"Okay, you've got a point there," Naomi admitted, long arms trying to keep Chloe at bay. "Truce?"

"Only because if we get any on the couch it'll be a nightmare to clean." Chloe stopped her assault and leant back against the cushions. Her hands and nose felt sticky, so she couldn't imagine how Naomi felt with half of her face covered. "You still look ridiculous."

"Yeah, but so do you."

They finished off the tub—a decision that Chloe would probably regret later—before cleaning themselves up. Chloe glanced in the mirror when she was done. Her eyes were red-rimmed and lost, haunted by a sadness that she'd never seen there before, but her cheeks were flushed from laughter. Naomi always knew exactly what to say or do to get her out of her head.

"You never answered me before," Naomi said when Chloe returned to the kitchen, her cheeks damp and a towel wrapped around her shoulders. "You okay?"

"Not right now," she said, because she'd be lying if she tried to pretend that her heart wasn't broken, that she didn't wish she was back in Corthwaite right now, curled around Amy's body, "but I will be."

Chapter 26

"Hey, boss." Jin and Devon greeted her with matching smiles on Monday morning, and Chloe hoped her answering one didn't look as much of a grimace as it felt. "You're here early."

"Wanted to get back into the swing of things," she lied. In reality, she'd barely slept last night after Naomi left, had tossed and turned for hours, trying to forget the way Amy had looked, curled up in her bed.

"So, you're back for good now?" Jin settled into his chair and booted up his computer, bending to say hello to Bella when she trotted over.

"I am. Luckily for you."

"You got pictures of the house? I want to see if it's up to standard."

Chloe laughed and opened up the listing. Jin and Devon crowded around her desk.

"Oh, I love that kitchen," Devon said, as Chloe flicked through the pictures. "And the bathroom. And those views! It's gorgeous. It'll sell in no time."

Devon patted Chloe's shoulder, and she wished the words were reassuring, wished the thought didn't make her stomach swoop, every cell in her body rejecting the thought of someone else setting foot in her house.

"Boss," Jin said, drawing out his words. "Are you aware that this is startlingly similar to your flat?"

"Why does everyone keep pointing that out?" She closed the page. "I choose kitchens like that in all the houses we flip."

"Do you, though?" Jin was looking at her with knowing eyes, and Chloe glared. "That exact style? Those bathroom tiles?"

"I like them, okay? Is that a crime?"

Jin's eyebrows raised, and Chloe knew she needed to calm down—protesting so much was going to do the opposite of help her situation. "All right, all right. It's a coincidence."

Chloe ground her teeth. Coming to work was supposed to *help*, not make her feel worse. Not make her dwell on the place she'd left behind.

Her phone rang, and she half-hoped it was some kind of emergency requiring her immediate attention, a distraction for her mind to cling to. She hesitated when she saw Amelia: Estate Agent flashing on the screen.

"Hello?"

"Hi, Chloe. I have some good news."

"Already?" she asked, a note of panic in her voice, because she hadn't prepared herself for this. She'd been expecting the house to remain on the market for a few weeks at least. A few weeks for her regret to lessen, for her to come to terms with never setting foot in the house again.

"I told you—you've done a wonderful job and it's in a nice area. The offer is below asking, but—"

Chloe clung on to that titbit of information for dear life. "How much below?"

"Ten thousand, but there's no chain, and for the sake of an easy sale I think—"

"I'd like to wait," she said. "It's only been on the market for what, a few days?" Two pairs of eyes turned her way, and Chloe wheeled her chair around. "I think we can hold out. Get a better offer."

"Are you sure? This is a good offer, Chloe. You should at least think about it."

"I have. I'd like to wait."

"Okay." Amelia didn't sound impressed. "I'll go back to them, but I don't think they'll raise it. I'll let you know if anything changes."

"Thank you."

She hung up, and the look on her face must have been stormy, because neither Jin nor Devon uttered a word. Even Maria, when she strolled into the office at nine, seemed to sense the mood, and offered Chloe a mere hello in place of her usual chatter.

It wasn't fair on any of them, to subject them to her foul mood, especially when they didn't know what was wrong.

Trying to concentrate on budget reports for her latest project wasn't working. There was an itch under her skin, a need to keep busy, a need to do something with her hands that wasn't stare at numbers on her computer screen.

"I'm going to go and see how Chris and his guys are getting on at York Street," she decided, because the place they'd bought at auction last week was a mess, run-down and derelict, a squatter's paradise before they'd managed to snatch it up. There would be no shortage of jobs to do, of ways to get her hands dirty, which was exactly what she needed. "You all right here without me?"

"'Course." Jin's gaze lingered on her as she picked up her keys. "Are you, uh, all right, boss?"

"Yeah. Yeah, I just..." She trailed off, searching for an excuse. "Need to get out for a bit. Missing having a renovation to tinker with."

Jin didn't look convinced but didn't press, letting her go with the promise to give Bella her lunch.

York Street wasn't too far from the office, so she drove, not feeling like being crammed together with fifty other people on a train carriage. Scaffolding ringed the outside of the property, roofers hard at work to sort out the leak that had decimated most of the upstairs ceilings.

A true fixer-upper, as Chris would say. The kind of project both he and Chloe relished.

"What are you doing here?" he said when he noticed her in the doorway.

"Felt like getting my hands dirty. That all right?"

He gestured to the half-demolished wall in front of him. "Grab a sledgehammer."

Chris wasn't much for conversation, and Chloe had never been more grateful. It was easy to push away all other thoughts when she could concentrate on lifting a sledgehammer, absorbing the vibrations as it repeatedly thudded into the wall.

This was what she needed, tearing into plaster and concrete, muscles burning with exertion, sweat beading on her brow.

This is where you're supposed to be, she thought, and tried not to think about the fact it felt like a lie.

Amy walked into a scene of chaos.

Open boxes were scattered throughout the farmhouse living room, and a Christmas tree took up half the room, so large its top brushed the ceiling. Danny was precariously balanced on a ladder, a pair of shears in hand, trying to trim and straighten the tree at the same time. Adam and Sam sat riffling through the boxes of decorations. Her mum was curled up in a chair, knitting furiously, trying to get her blanket finished before the holidays. Gabi stood at the foot of Danny's ladder, shouting up instructions in rapid-fire Spanish and sipping from a mug of eggnog.

"Tía Amy! Have you come to help?"

"Of course. Wouldn't miss this for the world."

Gabi was worried about her and kept appearing with one task or another—new cakes to bake, or recipes to trial, or a new TV show for them to watch. She knew Gabi meant well, but it was driving her crazy.

She needed time to herself, time to mourn, time to put the shattered pieces of her heart back together again.

"It's still wonky," Amy said when Danny stepped off the ladder, leaning one shoulder against the wall and taking a bite out of the gingerbread man she'd stolen from the kitchen table. "Needs to go further left."

Danny crossed the room to stand beside her. "It's not. It's straight."

"It's wonky!"

"Your eyesight is wonky, because it's straight." He stole her gingerbread man, snapping off one of his legs before handing it back. "And if it's not," he said, cheeks full, "you're going to have to deal with it, because I ain't moving it again."

He settled himself in his usual armchair, leaving her and the boys to tackle the monstrosity with the decorations they'd accumulated over the years. Some of them, Amy noted, as she riffled through boxes, looking for the Christmas lights, were as old as she and Danny were.

There were decorations they'd made in primary school, garish and awfully painted, but her mum insisted they have pride of place on the tree, alongside ones Sam and Adam had made.

Her fingers paused on a felt snowman. His head lolled to one side, his eyes stitched on by clumsy hands. Chloe's, she knew without thinking, remembering the day the two of them had sat at the kitchen table, thirteen and pretending to be bored, their heads bowed as they'd both tried to make the best family of felt decorations.

Not many had survived the test of time, but this one remained. She swallowed, the reminder unexpected, unwelcome, when she'd been thus far having a good day.

She wondered what Chloe was doing, if a tree sat in her flat, or if she was one of those people who waited until the last minute to put it up. Her dad had been. He'd always driven out to pick up a tree a few days before Christmas, and Amy had helped the pair of them decorate it, all of them wearing matching Christmas pyjamas.

She snapped a quick photo of the snowman and fired off a text to Chloe—*Remember this?*—before she could change her mind. They'd agreed to stay in touch, but conversation had been sparse since she'd gone.

For Amy, it was because she didn't know what to say. *I miss you* seemed too heavy. *I wish you were here* even more so. *What are you doing?* felt too impersonal. Every time she picked up her phone, she'd second-guess herself, type out a text, delete it, type out another text, delete it. Scroll back through conversations they'd had before, when it had been easy. When the distance between them hadn't felt so insurmountable.

She shoved her phone back in her pocket so she didn't sit staring at it, waiting for a reply. Adam and Gabi helped her drape the lights over the tree, and then it was time for the baubles. Amy put Sam on her shoulders so he could reach the highest branches while Adam did the lowest.

When they were done, Amy stepped back to admire their handiwork and chuckled. It was a mess, a mishmash of clashing colours, red and green and blue and gold and silver scattered over the branches, their homemade decorations mixed in at random. Some were too close together, some too far apart, but Amy loved it all the same.

"Well, we won't be entering a tree decorating competition any time soon," Amy said, carefully setting Sam back on the floor. "But the most important thing is we had fun."

"So much fun! Can we make the gingerbread house now, Mami?"

"Sure. Come on, let's go get the moulds."

Adam trotted off after Gabi, Sam following in their wake, and Amy reached for her phone, heart thudding when she saw a notification from Chloe.

I do. I can't believe he's still standing.

He looks drunk, but he's still going strong, Amy typed back, lips threatening to twitch into a smile.

Let me see your tree.

It's a mess.

But she took a picture anyway, standing in the doorway to get in the whole room. It was a fusion of English and Mexican culture, poinsettias spilling over the mantelpiece by the fire, a nativity scene tucked into the corner, and Gabi's decorations on the tree, too.

Looks nice. Bit big, though. Mine is pathetic in comparison.

The accompanying picture showed a much smaller tree tucked into the corner of Chloe's flat, and Bella stretched out in front of it. Based on the decorations, Amy suspected Naomi's nieces had been the ones to help her put it up.

At least yours is proportional.

She lingered over the photo, imagining Chloe curled up on her couch to take it, blanket over her legs. A familiar ache settled in her chest. She wanted to *be* there with her.

When was it going to stop hurting? When was it going to pass? When would she be able to think of Chloe without wanting to cry?

True. Are you excited for the holidays?

"Amy!" Gabi's voice sounded from the kitchen. "Get your butt in here. I need your baking skills. Do you have any idea how much biscuit you have to make for an entire house? No wonder we've never done this before."

She chuckled as she typed out a reply to Chloe, a small spring in her step. Her smile grew when she felt her phone buzz in her pocket.

Chloe's front door thumped open dramatically a couple of hours after she'd gotten home, and she was thoroughly unsurprised when Naomi strolled into view a moment later.

She did, however, do a double take when she saw what Naomi was wearing, the dress a deep blue, tight to her hips before flaring out and stopping shy of her knees. Chloe's eyebrows rose as she came to a stop in front of the TV.

"We're going out."

"We're going where?"

"Out. Come on, get dressed."

A hand reached out to wrap around her wrist and haul her upright, a determination in Naomi's eyes that told Chloe wriggling her way out of this one wasn't going to be an easy task.

"I don't want to go out. I'm happy here, thank you." Chloe resisted, heels digging into the carpet as Naomi tugged. She swore when she managed to wrangle Chloe to her feet. "Jesus Christ, have you been going to the gym?"

"Yes, thanks for noticing."

Naomi didn't let go of her wrist until they were in Chloe's bedroom, where Chloe settled herself on the edge of her bed as Naomi riffled through her wardrobe.

"You're not moping around here for another weekend."

"I am not moping."

"Oh, please," Naomi scoffed, pursing her lips thoughtfully before tossing a pair of dress pants and a white shirt toward her head. "Put this on."

"Naomi…"

"Come on, Chlo. You can't sit around here forever."

"I'm fine—"

"You are clearly not fine. And you deserve to get out and have some fun, and more importantly, I deserve to go out and have some fun, so suck it up and put this on."

"If fun is what you want, why don't you call Melissa? How many dates have you been on now the library's done? Four?"

"Five," Naomi said, smile playing around the edges of her lips.

Chloe was glad she was happy, glad Naomi had someone to spend time with who wasn't as miserable as she was.

"And I don't want to be with her tonight. I want to be with you."

"But—"

"No buts." Naomi shoved a jacket toward her. "It's happening. Accept it."

Chloe sighed, but did as she was told, shrugging into the clothes and making at least some effort with her make-up so that she didn't look like a zombie.

"No clubs," Chloe warned as she slipped into a pair of boots. "Bars only."

"Yes, ma'am. I know clubs hurt your delicate head with their loud music."

"You make me sound elderly."

"Because you sound elderly."

Chloe shoved Naomi out the front door, promising Bella that she wouldn't be out too late before following after her.

"God, it's cold," Chloe said, shivering in the night air as they walked toward the station.

"Calm down, Grandma, we'll be inside soon."

"Not wanting to freeze to death doesn't make me a grandma."

"You are so dramatic."

Chloe rolled her eyes, refusing to rise to the argument. The trains were busy, full of other people heading for a night out. Chloe eyed a group of girls sitting opposite them—their dresses barely covering their asses and not a coat in sight—and shook her head.

"We're getting too old for this," she said to Naomi, who grinned.

"Weren't those the days? Going out clubbing until four in the morning and not waking up with a killer hangover the next day?"

"I don't miss them." Even back then, Chloe was happier curled up on her couch with a good book than out getting drunk and grinding on a dance floor.

The girls got off at the same stop as them, and Chloe and Naomi followed them out onto Old Compton Street. It was bustling with activity, queues forming outside some of the clubs, and bouncers ready at the doors of the more popular bars. Pride flags hung in the windows around them. Chloe would always have a soft spot for this place, for giving her a safe space to be herself when she'd been a wide-eyed eighteen-year-old, still terrified of what it meant to be a lesbian.

Their preferred bar was one of the quieter ones, tucked away at the end of the street. The prices were too expensive for those on a students' budget, and they easily claimed a table by the window, close to the bar.

"I'll buy the first two rounds seeing as I'm the reason you're here. I assume you want a porn star martini?"

"Naturally."

"Be right back."

Naomi disappeared off to the bar, and Chloe's eyes skittered around the space. If she was going to open a bar, it would probably look like this, monochrome throughout, tables nestled between comfortable black booths, and exposed wooden beams on the ceiling.

A woman locked eyes with her from across the room, a gorgeous redhead sipping from a glass of champagne, her lips curved into a smile. Usually, Chloe would smile back, might take it as an invitation to approach, but not tonight. Her heart wouldn't be in it, still lay three hundred miles away with a pair of haunting blue eyes, and Chloe didn't think that was going to change any time soon.

"Sorry, the queue was longer than I expected." Naomi dropped into the seat opposite her and pushed Chloe's drink across the table, a Manhattan in her other hand. "The DJ starts at eleven."

"So we're leaving at half ten?"

"Yes, Grandma, we can leave at half ten."

"Long week?" Chloe asked, eyebrows climbing as Naomi drank half her drink in a couple of gulps.

"Long day. Why do I keep accepting clients who seem lovely when I first meet them but turn into a nightmare when it comes to working with them? I spent two hours looking over patches of paint today. Two. Hours. And guess what? She still couldn't find a shade she liked."

"Can you not palm her off on an intern?"

"I can't put the poor little suckers through that. They'd never come back."

"You like these ones, then?" They'd both had several interns over the years, good and bad, and had frequently shared horror stories over cocktails on nights like this.

"Yeah, they're all right. Becky has real potential, but she's not with me for much longer. I hope she's still interested when she graduates next year."

"I think most kids would jump at the chance of a guaranteed job right out of uni. I did."

"Well, here's hoping. How's your work been, anyway? I've dropped in a couple of times, but you weren't there. Not avoiding me, are you?"

"Like you'd let me get away with that," Chloe scoffed. "I've been out on jobs a lot, lately."

"So, you've come back to the office...to not be in the office?"

"I've still been in some days." Chloe felt defensive, though she knew she had no need to be. "It's not like I've never gone out on jobs before."

"No, but it's usually the more important ones, and I know you don't have many of those on the go at the moment. What are you avoiding, Chlo?"

"I'm not avoiding anything."

"Sure you are." Naomi leant back in her chair, shrewd eyes fixed on Chloe's face. "I know you as well as I know myself, remember? So, let me guess. Being back doesn't feel as good as you thought it would?"

Chloe clenched her jaw, hating that she was so easy to read. "I'm not used to it yet."

"Oh, please. You and I both know there's only one reason you're not enjoying being back here, and her name starts with Amy and ends with Edwards."

"It'll get easier," Chloe said, with little certainty in her voice, and she knew Naomi would notice. "With more time."

"Counter argument—maybe it doesn't."

"What do you mean?"

"You're miserable, Chloe."

"Gee, thanks."

"And don't get me started on the house."

Chloe frowned, chasing the halved passionfruit at the bottom of her glass with her straw. "What about the house?"

"You're stalling on it. Again."

"I am not."

"You are. How many offers have you refused, now? Six, seven?"

Nine, but Naomi didn't need to know that. Much to Amelia's frustration. Chloe was surprised she hadn't been palmed off on another agent. "They've all been below asking."

"Is that still the excuse you're going with?"

"It's not an excuse. They have been. I know what it's worth, what I can get for it. And I'm holding out for that."

"Sure you're not holding out for something else?"

"Like what?" Chloe asked, annoyance colouring her tone. "It's on the market, and it's going to sell, when I get the right offer."

Naomi didn't look convinced.

"And what about your Amy problem?"

"There is no Amy problem. Not one I can solve, anyway."

"Chloe…"

"I don't want to talk about this anymore," she said, draining the last of her drink. "Let's talk about you. And Melissa. Tell me how it's going."

Naomi hesitated, and Chloe sighed.

"I don't want you to feel guilty because things are going well for you. I know you haven't been talking about it much because you feel bad. It's okay."

"It's… going really well. Too well, almost? I keep waiting for the other shoe to drop."

"What, and find out she's secretly a serial killer?"

"Judging from some of my exes," Naomi said, grimacing, "it wouldn't surprise me."

"Wouldn't surprise me, either. So, when do I get to officially meet her?"

Naomi shook her head. "Uh-uh. Not happening."

"Why?"

"Because you're going to embarrass me, and things are going too well." Naomi, sensing a chance to escape, scooped up their empty glasses. "New rule: when I get back from the bar, we don't talk about Melissa or Amy for the rest of the night. Deal?"

Chloe supposed she could get on board with that.

Chapter 27

WHEN AMY WALKED INTO THE kitchen, she didn't expect to find an inquisition waiting for her. Gabi, Danny, and her mum sat at the kitchen table with their arms folded.

"Sit," said Gabi.

"We need to talk," said Danny.

"About you and Chloe," said her mum, and Amy fell into to nearest chair, not sure where this conversation was going.

She tugged at the sleeves of her jumper, anxiety twisting in her stomach. "What about me and Chloe?"

"Amy, you're not happy." Gabi's voice was gentle, and Amy knew she couldn't argue. "Ever since she left, you've been…not yourself. A ghost, almost. Like you're here, but not really."

"I know." She twisted a strand of her hair around her finger. "But I just need time, and—"

"No," her mum said, shaking her head. "What you need is to be with her."

"But I can't." Amy ground her teeth, because if she thought they could make it work, she would've said something, would've *done* something. But she'd made the decision to let Chloe go, because she could never ask Chloe to give anything up for her, and she knew Chloe would never ask her either.

"What if you could?"

Amy eyed her brother with suspicion.

"Look, we all know you never wanted to come back here. It was never on the cards for you, never the plan, but everything changed. And we know you love it here, that you've poured everything you have into this place for the last ten years, but Amy... It's time for you to go after what you want. You let Chloe go once before and we—none of us—like seeing you this upset. She makes you happy. And we can figure out things here. Give you guys some time together. Gabi and I have been looking over the finances—"

"You've willingly looked at the finances?" Amy interrupted, eyebrows raising, because he *must* be serious.

"Yeah, and I think we can afford to take on someone else. Someone to ease the load on the rest of us, if you want to start spending more time in London."

"But what about the accounts? The deliveries? The—"

"We can figure it out." Danny reached over the table to cover her hand with his. "You came back here for me, and for Mum, when we needed you, to stop this place from going under. It's time for me to do something for you. Think about it, okay? And we can talk. You can decide if you trust me enough to run this place without you always here, breathing down my neck."

His grin was lopsided, and she felt tears spring into her eyes. She didn't know who was more surprised—her or him—when she rounded the table to pull him into a hug, filled with more gratitude than she knew what to do with.

"You'd do that for me?"

"Of course I would."

"You always wanted to live in London," her mum said, reaching for her hand. "You were so sad when you had to give it up. And so happy after you got back from visiting Chloe."

Because I got to pretend for a weekend it could work. Because I got to see all of the things she loves about it, and fall in love with them too.

"I wouldn't...I wouldn't move there permanently." Couldn't leave behind her family. Not now she and Danny got on, not now Gabi was there, not while the boys were growing, changing every day, not while the lines on her mum's face grew steadily deeper.

"You don't have to. Don't have to go there at all, if you don't want to," Danny said, keeping one arm looped around her back. "But it's an option. It's a way for you two to be together, if you want to be."

If you want to be.

Amy had never wanted something more in her life.

Eighteen years ago, she'd pushed Chloe away; five weeks ago, she'd let her go. She knew the onus was on her to get her back, knew she was the one that needed to reach out, needed to be honest, needed to lay her feelings out bare, needed to show Chloe how much she meant to her, so there was no shred of doubt in her mind that Amy was all in.

"I've got an early Christmas present for you. An offer. Above asking price, this time." Excitement quivered in Amelia's voice at the prospect of a deal nearing completion, and dread curled in the pit of Chloe's stomach. "A family. Mum, Dad, and two kids. Coming from the city, looking for somewhere small to settle. They're lovely, Chloe. They'd fit into the village perfectly."

Chloe hummed, feeling like she was spiralling, short of breath, edges of her vision going fuzzy. "I…can I call you back?"

"Chloe." Amelia sighed heavily. "This is an incredible offer. I don't think you're going to get better—"

"I need some time," she said, aware she sounded hysterical and unable to do a thing about it. "I call you back later."

She hung up on Amelia's protests and shoved her phone back on her desk, then retreated into the safety of the kitchen, feeling several pairs of alarmed eyes watching her go.

Jin was the one sent to comfort her, and he approached with the same wariness one would use with a skittish animal "Boss? You okay?"

"I'm fine."

"Okay, but you don't look fine." He grabbed the biscuit tin from the table and shoved it into her hand. "Was it…was it about the house?"

"How did you know?" Chloe asked around a mouthful of chocolate digestive.

"Because you get this look on your face whenever you get a call about it. Like you're having your teeth extracted."

Chloe sighed and moved toward the window, where she leaned her head against the frame and gazed out at the city beyond. It didn't bring her the same sense of comfort, not anymore.

"I got an offer. Above asking."

"Which should be great news, but you look like someone died."

"I know I should be happy, but I... I'm not."

Jin came to stand beside her, resting a hand on her shoulder. "Because you never wanted it to sell," he said, words gentle. "Because it's your last link to that place, and without it, you'll never have an excuse to go back there again."

She closed her eyes and let out her breath, knowing he was right. Knowing she'd been sinking into a pit of denial these past few weeks, insisting she was holding out for the right price.

"You know, you've not been the same since you came back. Haven't had that fire in your eyes. We've all noticed it. And I don't know for sure, but I suspect it has something to do with the gorgeous blonde you brought in here a few weeks ago."

Chloe huffed out a laugh. "Am I that obvious?"

"When you're heartbroken, yeah." He nudged her shoulder with his own. "And come on. A friend coming all the way here for the weekend who you just had to introduce to us all?"

"She was the one that wanted to meet you."

"Then she must be head over heels for you, too," he said, tossing the words out carelessly, like they didn't make Chloe's heart grind to a halt. "Because no woman in her right mind would want to spend a morning here when there's the whole capital to explore, would they?"

The thought had never occurred to her, in all honesty. She'd thought it was weird, but Amy had kept saying Chloe knew everything about her work, so it was only fair for her to return the favour.

But had she just wanted to get to know her better?

If she went back to Corthwaite, if she told Amy how she felt, would Amy say she felt the same?

Would Amy want her, in all the ways she never had before?

Chloe didn't know, and a part of her was terrified to find out, because what if she *didn't*?

"Look, boss," Jin said, as Chloe's mind spun out of control. "I want you to know that if you want to go back there, if you ever wanted to make it a more permanent thing... We could figure something out. I like to think I've done a good job of running the place the days you've been gone, and I've learned a lot from you over the years. I could take on a bigger role if you wanted me to. Something to think about, okay? You're not tied to here. And you deserve to be happy."

He patted her on the shoulder before retreating to his desk, leaving her to wipe away the tears gathered in the corners of her eyes.

She thought about the house, about signing the deeds away, about someone else living there, and... She couldn't imagine it. Didn't *want* to imagine it, her stomach roiling at the thought. She considered Jin's words, knowing it wasn't a decision she was going to be able to make on her own.

It wouldn't be right to, either. Not when the city wasn't the only thing she'd be leaving behind.

"I'm nipping out," she said, grabbing her keys from her desk. "Jin, can you handle things while I'm gone?"

"Absolutely."

"I don't want to sell the house," Chloe said, bursting into Naomi's office like a woman possessed.

"Of course, Mr. Stephenson," Naomi said into her headset in her best customer service voice, and Chloe felt her cheeks grow warm.

"Shit. Sorry." She grabbed a chair from the next desk over and spun in slow circles, her eyes fixed on the ceiling, waiting anxiously for Naomi to finish her call.

"Uh-huh. Uh-huh. I'll have the new plan drawn up by the end of the week. How does that sound? All right. I'll speak to you soon." Naomi hung up the phone before spinning to face Chloe, eyebrows raised. "Conference room, perhaps?"

She ushered Chloe into it, away from prying eyes.

"Now, what's this about the house?" she asked, settling into her usual chair, leaning back and resting her elbow on the table, chin propped on her hand.

"I don't want to sell it." Chloe couldn't sit still, chose to pace around the table instead.

Naomi watched her every step. "Well, no shit. I could have told you that weeks ago. Did, in fact, though you still denied it. What inspired the change?"

"I got a perfect offer." She paused and ran a hand through her hair. "But I don't want to accept it. I can't accept it. I think I want to keep it. I can't believe I'm saying this, but I miss Corthwaite. And not just because Amy's there."

"It's your home, Chloe. Of course you miss it."

"I know. I know, but it never felt that way before, you know? Hell, I didn't want to go back in the first place, and now... I can't imagine leaving it."

"So keep the house," Naomi said, like it was easy, like Chloe should have realised this was where the story ended a long time ago. "It's not like you can't afford it. And you've spent so much time on it. Got so many memories of it. Take it off the market."

"R-right."

"And you can go and stay in that big old house when you drive up there to tell Amy you're in love with her."

"What?"

"Come on, Chloe. It's been weeks, and you're not remotely over her. You flinch every time I say her name. And don't think I haven't been able to tell when she messages you. Your whole fucking face lights up. It's sickening."

Chloe couldn't deny it. The texts were becoming more and more frequent, never anything meaningful or deep, not the *I miss yous* brimming beneath the surface whenever she saw Amy's name, but enough to brighten her days.

"You're in love with her, and that's okay. But for the love of God, tell her. None of this skirting around your feelings bullshit. Be honest with her, or you're never going to get what you want."

"But what if she doesn't feel the same way?"

"Chloe, I've seen the way she looks at you. She does. And if I'm wrong and she doesn't...we'll deal with it. Together, like we always do. Won't be the first time I've patched up your broken heart, will it? And wouldn't it be better, to know? To really know how she feels?"

Logically, Chloe knew the answer was yes. It would at least give her closure, make it easier to move on, if she wasn't left wondering what could have been if she'd have been braver.

But the thought of *getting* closure? Of going to Amy and laying it all out on the line, baring her heart and soul?

Terrifying.

"Even if she does," Chloe said, refusing to think about what it might be like to hear Amy say *I love you, too*. "It's still not... I can't leave the business. She can't leave the farm."

"You've managed all right going back and forth the past few months," Naomi said. "It's not a million miles away. You could figure something out, if you wanted to. You could find a way to make it work, if you wanted to. So, the question is, Chloe, do you?"

She didn't have to think about it.

Which, in the end, could only mean it was the right decision.

"Yes."

"Then go. Pack a bag. Drive up there and talk things over with her. Find out what you both want, and the rest of the finer details can come later."

"What? I can't. It's Christmas Eve tomorrow. Your mum would kill me if I missed it."

"My mother will understand. In fact, she'd be shoving you into the van herself."

Chloe shook her head. "No, I don't want to intrude on them at Christmas, either."

"Because a part of you still believes she's going to shoot you down, and you don't want to be sad at the holidays?"

Chloe's jaw clenched. Naomi knew her too well. "Look, I'll go on Boxing Day, okay? I've waited eighteen years for this. Two more days won't kill me."

Chapter 28

"THIS IS CRAZY," AMY SAID, as Danny pulled into a parking space at Lancaster train station. He'd driven her over an hour from the farm to catch a train to London on Christmas Eve. "This is crazy, we should go bac—"

"The only thing you should be doing," Danny said, voice patient as he turned off the engine, "is getting on that train, and going to find Chloe."

"But it's Christmas." Her leg bounced against the seat. "I don't remember the last time I wasn't at the farm for it."

"There will be other Christmases."

"But what if you need help on the—?"

"We can manage without you for a few days. We did when you last went to London, didn't we? And we've got some extra hands now. You know Gabi's papi will be happy to help me out."

"But—"

"But nothing." He reached across to pat her on the shoulder. "Stop freaking out."

"Sorry." Her fingers played with the bracelet around her wrist, the one she'd rarely taken off since the day Chloe had given it to her. "I can't believe I'm doing this."

Especially without telling Chloe she was coming. Which could either be a nice surprise, or end in disaster.

Amy wasn't sure what she'd do if it was the latter, and she ended up stranded in the capital on her favourite holiday.

"Honestly? Me either." Danny slung an arm over the back of Amy's seat. "Hey, who would've thought, all those years ago, that one day I'd be helping you go get the girl?"

"Not me. That's for sure." She looked at him now, older, wiser, and more grown-up than she'd ever thought it possible for him to be, not a single trace of the teenager filled with vitriol she'd used to know.

"I really am sorry," he said, eyes turning dark. "For everything. I was a shit brother."

She leant over to pull him into a hug, trying not to cry. "You're more than making up for it now."

He squeezed her back hard. "Let me know when you get there," he said, cheeky grin spreading across his face. "If you can tear yourselves away from one another long enough to pick up the phone."

She shoved him away, flipping him off for good measure before she grabbed her suitcase from the boot and forced herself to step into the station. It was quiet, most people having already travelled home for the holidays, and that suited Amy.

It meant she could get a ticket, even if the price of it did make her wince.

Worth it, she thought, paying the hundred-pound fare. *Worth it, if we can find a way to be together.*

Four hours, two trains, and a Tube stretched ahead of her, and Amy was glad for a window seat where she could rest her forehead against the glass and watch the countryside flash by. She lived in a beautiful part of the world, she knew, looking at snow-topped hills dotted with sheep, evergreen trees stretching over canals, a fox darting past the railway line.

But there was something alluring about the city, a beauty to the towering buildings, the ability to lose yourself in a crowd of people, being somewhere where not everyone knew your name.

A hybrid life, she thought, stepping out of Twickenham station and pulling her jacket tighter around herself to ward off the chill in the air as a few snowflakes began to fall, would suit her perfectly.

A life where she could split her time between her two loves: Corthwaite and London, perhaps picking up the photography she'd so recently gotten back into. Two halves of her, coming together as one, in a way she'd never believed possible.

The one thing missing was Chloe, and Amy hoped, as she rounded a corner and saw Chloe's building looming in the distance, she'd want a place in her new life, too.

"You're supposed to be helping me pack," Chloe said, shoving a few clothes into the overnight bag open beside Naomi on her bed.

"I said I'd come over so we could walk to the station together," Naomi said, scratching Bella behind the ears. "I said nothing about packing."

Chloe rolled her eyes and tossed her charger in Naomi's general direction, earning herself a glare.

"You know, there's still time to change your mind," Naomi said, watching Chloe grab her one Christmas jumper—to match the rest of the Alleyenes in their family Christmas photo. "You could be in Corthwaite by midnight. Give Amy a nice present."

"Boxing Day," Chloe said, so her resolve didn't crumble, so she didn't take off recklessly into the night. "I want to—"

A knock sounded at the door.

"What if it's carol singers? Could you imagine?" Naomi hurried off to answer it, and Chloe kept an ear out as she scanned the room for anything else she might need for her two-night stop with the Alleyenes.

Her hairbrush was probably a good call, and she was reaching for it when the front door clicked open and an "Oh, shit!" made her pause.

"Chloe?" Naomi called, her voice wavering. "You might want to come out here."

Frowning, Chloe dropped the brush into her bag and headed for the living room. When she spotted Amy over Naomi's shoulder, suitcase in hand, she forgot how to breathe.

"I'm, uh, I'm gonna go," Naomi said, reaching for her jacket and inching her way past Amy. "Give you two some time to talk. I'll tell Mum you'll be late. Or... not coming at all. You can do whatever. Bye."

The door closed behind her, and Chloe crossed the scant few metres between them, feeling like she was in a dream.

"Are you...are you really here?"

"I'm really here." Amy dropped her suitcase to the floor so she could reach for Chloe, hands cupping her cheeks. "I've missed you so much."

"I've missed you, too." She closed her eyes, tilting her forehead against Amy's, and breathed her in. "What are you doing here?"

"I couldn't go another day without seeing you. I know we said it we'd keep things casual, that it could only last for a few months, but I... I can't stop thinking about you. All the past few weeks have taught me is that life without you in it is miserable."

Chloe's heart pounded in her ears, making it hard to hear. She could barely *believe* what was happening, that Amy was here, in her arms, saying the words she'd always wanted to hear.

"I want to be with you. I want to make it work. If it's something you want, too."

Chloe answered with her with a kiss. Amy's nose was cold as it bumped against hers, her lips chapped but her mouth warm, and Chloe felt the stress of the last few months melt away. Tears slipped from her eyes—happy, where all the others had been sad—and when she pulled back, she found Amy crying, too.

"Want to hear something funny?" she asked, gently brushing Amy's tears away with the pads of her thumbs. "I was going to drive up to see you. Tell you how I felt. Tell you I wanted to make it work, too."

Amy laughed, and her fingers slid around the back of Chloe's neck, tugging her into another kiss. Chloe felt like she could do this forever.

"I took the house off the market," she said when they next paused for breath, her hands splayed across the small of Amy's back. "I couldn't sell it."

"Does that mean... Are you moving back?"

"Not right away. Maybe someday." A quiet life in the country wasn't for her, but she had some ideas brewing. Property development wasn't exclusive to London—maybe it was time for her to think about extending the business. And there were the phone calls that kept trickling in, people from Corthwaite asking if she could do work for them. "But I'd like to start spending some more time up there. With you."

"And I... I wouldn't mind spending time here, too. I'd forgotten how much I loved living here, but those few days with you... I'd like to be here more often. Maybe start picking my camera back up."

"We can figure it out," Chloe said, pulling Amy closer. "I'll be happy anywhere as long as I'm with you."

Words she would have never dared utter aloud eighteen years ago. But here, now, with Amy's arms wrapped around her, Amy's lips moving against her own, it was easy.

The ringing of Chloe's phone had Amy pulling away, and when she saw Naomi's name on the screen, she was tempted to press ignore.

"Hello?"

"I'm sorry, but Mum would like to know whether or not you're coming. Apparently how many plates she needs to set out is a matter of life or death."

Chloe heard Jada's voice in the background and chuckled. "Uh, I don't know." She glanced at Amy. "We haven't talked about it."

Naomi snorted. "I bet you haven't."

Chloe rolled her eyes. "I think we'll probably stay here."

"Don't," Amy said, shaking her head. "I don't want to get in the way of your usual plans."

But Chloe didn't want to leave Amy's side. Unless… "Will you come with me?"

"To Christmas? At Naomi's?"

"Yeah. Let's… let's spend this Christmas with my family, and we can spend the next one with yours."

Amy's smile was so bright it rivalled the lights Chloe could see out of her window. The prospect of a next Christmas, of a future, for them, together, made Chloe's heart thud in her chest.

"Tell her we'll both be there," Chloe said to Naomi, listening as the information was relayed, as squeals could be heard in the background.

"Don't get too distracted," Naomi warned. "You're already late."

Naomi hung up, and Chloe pulled Amy to her, kissing her soft and slow, figuring a little distraction never hurt anyone.

And they still had a lot to talk about—how, exactly, things would work, what sacrifices they'd each be willing to make in order to be together. But there would time for that later, time tomorrow, and the next day, and the next, to figure it all out, but for now, there was only this: Amy's hands in her hair, Amy's mouth on her skin, Amy whispering "I love you." against the shell of her ear, and that…

That was all Chloe had ever wanted.

Other Books from Ylva Publishing

www.ylva-publishing.com

Never Say Never

Rachael Sommers

ISBN: 978-3-96324-429-2
Length: 220 pages (75,000 words)

Ambitious Camila might have lost her marriage but she doesn't need love to build a TV empire and raise her young son. What she does need is a nanny.

Enter Emily—bright, naive, and new to New York City. Emily is everything Camila is not and that's not all that's unsettling.

Surely she can't be falling for the nanny?

An age-gap, opposites-attract lesbian romance with a puddle of melted ice queen.

A Roll in the Hay

Lola Keeley

ISBN: 978-3-96324-355-4
Length: 185 pages (66,000 words)

Veterinarian Tess has quit the city and her cheating girlfriend for a new life in a Scottish village. On day one, she has a run-in with stuck-up Lady Karlson who tries to boss Tess around as if she owns the whole town… which she sort of does. But could there be something more to the constant, rising tension between the warring pair?

An enemies-to-lovers lesbian romance about making your own path.

Write Your Own Script

A.L. Brooks

ISBN: 978-3-96324-156-7
Length: 248 pages (87,000 words)

Beloved famous British actress Tamsyn Harris works hard to keep her career alive, which means hiding that she's a lesbian from the world. The last thing she expects at a retreat is to meet Maggie Cooper, an alluring author and fan who makes her question whether it might be worth risking everything for love.

A sizzling lesbian romance about finding out what's important in life.

Hooked on You

Jenn Matthews

ISBN: 978-3-96324-133-8
Length: 281 pages (98,000 words)

Anna has it all — great kids, boyfriend, good teaching job. Except she's so bored. Perhaps a new hobby's in order? Something…crafty?

Divorced mother and veteran Ollie has been through the wars. To relax, she runs a quirky crochet class in her English craft shop. Enter one attractive, feisty new student. A shame she's straight.

A quirky lesbian romance about love never being quite where you expect.

About Rachael Sommers

Rachael Sommers was born and raised in the North-West of England, where she began writing at the age of thirteen, and has been unable to stop since. A biology graduate, she currently works in education and constantly dreams of travelling the world. In her spare time, she enjoys horse riding, board games, escape rooms and, of, course, reading.

CONNECT WITH RACHAEL SOMMERS
Website: www.rachaelsommers.com

Fool for Love
© 2021 by Rachael Sommers

ISBN: 978-3-96324-575-6

Available in e-book and paperback formats.

Published by Ylva Publishing, legal entity of Ylva Verlag, e.Kfr.

Ylva Verlag, e.Kfr.
Owner: Astrid Ohletz
Am Kirschgarten 2
65830 Kriftel
Germany

www.ylva-publishing.com

First edition: 2021

Credits
Edited by Alissa McGown and Sheena Billet
Cover Design and Print Layout by Streetlight Graphics